S.L. CHOI

Bad Girls
BITE

BLOOD FAE DRUID | BOOK TWO

S.L. CHOI

Bad Girls BITE

BLOOD FAE DRUID | BOOK TWO

BAD GIRLS BITE
Blood Fae Druid, Book 2

CITY OWL PRESS
www.cityowlpress.com

Cover Design by MiblArt. All stock photos licensed appropriately.

Edited by Heather McCorkle.

For information on subsidiary rights, please contact the publisher at info@cityowlpress.com.

Print Edition ISBN: 978-1-64898-275-0

Digital Edition ISBN: 978-1-64898-276-7

Printed in the United States of America

PRAISE FOR S.L. CHOI

"FANTASTIC SERIES! EACH BOOK IS A MUST READ!" — *Faith Hunter, New York Times and USA Today bestselling author*

"With tantalizing hints of a wolfy blood tryst, a heavy dose of sisterly love, and plot twists to make the ride a surprise, S.L. Choi's, *Bad Girls Drink Blood* is too much fun. This brand-new world and mythos are a pleasure to explore. Solid world building, easy to grasp politics, hints of future romance and plenty of snark are the perfect scaffold to a story about finding that your scars are only the signposts of your hidden abilities, and that the part of you that brings you the most pain, can also be the wellspring of your deepest satisfaction. If you like the Hollows, you will love this." — *Kim Harrison, #1 New York Times bestselling author of the Hollows series*

"Choi loads her debut and *Blood Fae Druid* urban fantasy series launch with snark, action, and characters who will steal readers' hearts. Lane Callaghan is a hybrid blood fae, which makes her an outcast in the fae world. She and her sisters, Mae and Y'sindra, operate a struggling private investigation firm on the edge of Las Vegas and the mystical Interlands... Choi delivers plenty of fast-paced action, but it's the individual characters who steal the show. This promising series premier will leave readers wanting more." —*Publishers Weekly*

"Welcome to a sexy, *new* spin on the fae. Deliciously gritty and full of snark, you'll find your new hero in Lane Callaghan." – *International and award-winning author of the Weird Girls UF romance series, Cecy Robson*

"*Bad Girls Drink Blood* is an action-packed good time that delivers wit, grit, and an unforgettable heroine." – *Kat Turner, author the Coven Daughters series*

"*Bad Girls Drink Blood* has everything I love: a heroine that can put bad guys in the dirt, side-splitting humor, and characters you're invested in from page one. In a debut that is both heart-wrenching and wildly hilarious from start to finish, Choi carves out her place in a crowded genre with what I hope to be a long series." — *Gabrielle Ash, author of The Family Cross and For the Murder*

"Magic, modernity, and multiple dimensions collide in the richly imagined world of S.L. Choi's page-turning debut *Bad Girls Drink Blood*, where a snarky, badass heroine with a monster complex and a sexy spark of friends-to-lovers romance will delight fans of urban fantasy and fae intrigue." – *Erin Fulmer, author of Cambion's Law*

"This urban fantasy debut will have readers on the edge of their seats as they follow Lane's action-packed adventure! Choi's voice and style pulled me in right away and I instantly loved Lane, who is a total badass. I also adored her sisters and Teddy and loved the found family theme—it's one of my favorites! I hated to put this book down and I found myself wondering what would happen next for Lane and company. I am thrilled to read the next installment in this series and can't wait for more adventures with one of my favorite characters to date. Fans of urban fantasy will want to sink their teeth into this brilliant debut!" – *Ashley R. King, author of Forever After, Painting Lines, The Wilde Card*

"Want a fast-paced urban fantasy with a badass fae heroine, a hunky love interest, and a snarky cast of mythical beings? How about found family, sisterly love, and multi-layered world building? Then sink your teeth into *Bad Girls Drink Blood*. Craving satisfied." – *Sarina Dahlan, author of Reset*

"I was thrilled for the chance to read an advanced copy of *Bad Girls Drink Blood* by S.L. Choi and let me tell you, it did not disappoint. This story hits the ground running and sprints full-tilt to the end until I was turning pages faster than my kindle could keep up! The writing is crisp, the characters delightful, and the worldbuilding is absolutely phenomenal. Faes, shifters, druids, and a hot bartender who's not what he seems. Yes please! I loved Lane and her sisters so much, and I can't wait for more stories about them and their detective agency. *Bad Girls Drink Blood* is a sparkling urban fantasy gem with a gooey romance center. Highly recommend." – *Jess K Hardy, author of Love in the Time of Wormholes and I, Bionic*

For Loki and Freya, the new kitties on the block with big paws to fill, whose kitten zoomies and antics kept me out of the office and in the coffeeshops writing.

AUTHOR'S NOTE

Dear reader, my sincere thanks for giving Blood Fae Druid series a shot! This is a slowburn to spicy truemate urban fantasy romance set amidst plenty of action and laughs. Expect the language to be salty, the violence stabby, and the romance to get hot!

1

EIGHTY PERCENT PRIDE

I'D NEVER SEEN ANYTHING AS PERFECT AS TEDDY BARBOUT'S ASS IN DENIM. Hard to believe I'd staked a claim on that ass. He refused to let me brand him. Weird, but I'd wear him down. I pursed my lips and let loose a catcall. The sharp notes echoed back from the trees lining the grassy lane where, almost six months ago, my body lay shattered.

My man patted those criminally firm cheeks. "Come and get it."

I jogged toward him and vaulted onto his back. He hooked his arms under my thighs as I wrapped my legs around his lean torso and looped my arms loose over his shoulders. The warmth from the sun on his flannel and his own body heat soaked into me. "Looks clear to me. Time to show me around your old bar like you promised." I leaned in to nip his earlobe. I had a plan. It was a good plan.

Three hours of patrolling this ghost town was more than enough. The corrupted moon fae, along with the two stolen sun stones still in their possession, were long gone.

Teddy shook his head, his shoulder-length, bourbon-brown hair tickling my cheek. "This place doesn't feel right. I say we do one more lap."

I groaned and made myself dead weight on his back—arms hanging loose down his chest, head drooped over his shoulder. He tightened his hold, which was a good thing because it was a long way to the ground. Teddy was tall, and thanks to my refusal to sip from his vein, I was still a little broken. Falling would hurt.

"Lane..."

I groaned louder.

"Didn't know my girl was a toddler."

"If you're trying to motivate me by wounding my pride, you've forgotten I have no pride to wound." Not true, but come on, he'd called me his girl. I was all rainbows and butterflies in the general vicinity of my hearts.

"Who do you think you're kidding?" Teddy jiggled me higher on his back, the bounce interrupting his smooth gait and causing the persistent ache in my legs to intensify.

I gritted my teeth and smothered the reaction before Teddy noticed and I got another lecture.

"Sweet fangs, you're at least eighty percent pride." His words danced with laughter.

Teddy was being generous. Eighty percent was way too low. I watched the ground pass beneath his sure steps as we moved between buildings, following the same path we'd taken over six months ago in pursuit of my sister Mae's kidnappers, but in reverse. "What's the other twenty percent?"

"At least ten percent are those awful artificial cheese snacks you choke down on a daily basis."

I gasped with righteous indignation. "How dare you malign the exalted cheesy poofs?"

He ignored me. "You're about eight percent stubborn."

"You might want to revisit your ratio. I'm much more stubborn."

He reached behind him to pat my butt as we stepped into the shadowy alley between two buildings. "Two percent sweet ass."

"Ouch, just two percent?" I laughed and squeezed my thighs against his ribs. We had mutual respect for posteriors—particularly, each other's.

"Evidence of that pride I was talking about."

"Ha!" I smacked his shoulder and slid down from Teddy's back. The impact when I hit the ground sent a dull ache arrowing from my shins to my femurs.

Unable to steady myself fast enough, Teddy turned in time to get an eyeful of my wobble. He scowled, and I bared my fangs. We were not having this argument again. He shook his head and held out his hand. I melted at his gesture and threaded my fingers through his. Me showing PDA, who knew?

I'd gone all in with this male less than a year ago. Sure, I was unconscious for two months of our dating lives after I'd almost fallen to my death thanks to his delightful brother, but it still counted. I'd learned for such a big, strong, sometimes scary guy, he was nothing but a gooey marshmallow on the inside—the correct state for marshmallow perfection. I set those babies on fire. My sisters, Y'sindra and Maerwen, were as much in love with him as me.

Not that I was in love. Figure of speech.

With my five feet zero inches to Teddy's six-foot-four, I had a magnificent view of his strong-cut jaw. My latest obsession, his lips, tipped up at their corners.

I pulled him close to my side as we walked, bumping his arm with my shoulder. "Come on, you promised to show me your life before me."

"Not sure we have that kind of time. We're talking a lot of years to cover."

I rolled my eyes as he steered us onto the main road cutting through Outerlands. "Stop sidestepping. You agreed you'd take me on a tour once I was well enough to join you on the patrols."

He grunted, and I narrowed my eyes at the dubious sound. "You might be okay limping around with me, but you're not prepared for an attack."

I shook my hand free of his. "Can we not? This place is dead. Let's just go home. I need to finish packing, anyhow."

Today was the big move to Las Vegas. With new real estate on the market we could afford—free—I'd said farewell to Interlands and made the move Y'sindra, Mae, and I had always dreamed of. Vaughn, the Blackthorne Casino and Resort's vampire head of security, was less than happy, but the official letter of my legitimate claim to the luxury penthouse provided by the sun fae keepers, Iola and Torneh, was something he could not dispute.

When I'd reminded him my sisters and I were a package deal—which included my mega-hot sun fae sister, Mae—Vaughn had perked right up. His kind might be moody prima donnas, but I was on team vampire. Anything and anyone to keep her away from Cirron. The piece of shit who, less than a year ago, had carried her into the enemy's cage and forced me to go on a rescue mission. Sure, he'd done it for his sister, but fuck that guy.

Teddy folded his large hand over mine pulling me to a stop, and he brought my fingers to his lips. "You win. Let's go have a look."

Despite this being my idea, I dragged my feet as we angled toward his old bar. The closer we got, the faster my heart rate pulsed in my throat. My first and only look at the place had come as I'd disemboweled soldiers and decapitated one of the most notorious spymasters in the fae's very long history. None of which came close to affecting me as much as being forced to cut off my snow fairy sister's wing.

Why did I want to revisit this place?

My gut churned, as it always did, when I flashed back to the moment I'd severed Y'sindra's wing.

"Hey, it's all right. We don't have to do this today." Teddy stopped us on the threshold to the bar. The tendons stood out over the ridge of my knuckles from the force of my grip, and my talons pricked the back of his hand, drawing blood. I licked my lips and tore my gaze away.

"No, it's okay. I want to see this part of you." A very specific part of him that wasn't in his past, but in his pants. I had a plan. Not the most elaborate plan. Step one: rip off his clothes. I was great at ripping things, and it had better work. There was no step two.

With my slow healing and refusal to drink his blood, he'd wiggled his way out of consummating this relationship again and again, month after month. This celibacy bullshit ended today.

If I got past the ghosts inside this building.

Teddy took his time looking me over from head to toe in an asexual, clinical appraisal of my well-being. I released his hand to cross my arms and tapped my toes on the white wood porch planks. This mother-hen nursemaid nonsense needed to stop.

His lips flattened into a hard line, but he pushed open the front door and motioned me inside.

I had two purposes in coming here, and the first was to confront the evidence of what happened only a few months ago.

Blood rushing in my ears, I stepped past him and blinked. This wasn't what I'd expected. No broken furniture and not a trace of blood remained. The grapefruit-scented cleaner I was so familiar with from Teddy's Interlands bar told me who'd done the cleaning.

Locked in tense expectations of what I'd find and the memory riding beneath, my muscles spasmed in surprise at the soft thump of the door hitting the frame behind me. It swung back open, a slice of sunlight cutting across the room. I curled my fingers into tight fists. I flexed my hands, releasing the unspent adrenaline. This constriction of my lungs, this heightened level of anxiety I hadn't expected. I was tougher than this, a certified badass. I'd brought down a wyvern, after all.

With a mediocre shot of confidence, I lifted my chin and waded deeper through the heavy silence I felt down to my bones. My talons raked a line into the polished bar top as I trudged toward the back corner of the big, square bar in the center of a room the size of a small grocery store.

Badass I might be, but I couldn't drop my gaze to the floor. Couldn't risk seeing the bloody stain where I'd maimed my sister. Instead, I looked from repaired tables to gouge-free walls, down the long hall to the new back door. Teddy and his best bud, Lo—my sister Y'sindra's new main squeeze—had been busy on their Outerlands patrols. Though they no longer lived here, why waste their time? I supposed it could be nostalgia, or maybe they were bored walking up and down empty streets.

At last, I stopped and drank down a fortifying breath. My hearts tapped my rib cage faster, harder with each millimeter my gaze fell until it landed... on an evidence-free floor. "What the hell? The floor's clean." More accurately, spotless and gleaming. We'd painted this place in blood, and there wasn't a spot in sight.

"Have you seen the fights at my bar?" Teddy eased up behind me as if I were a feral beast, which wasn't completely inaccurate. He drew a circle around my waist with his arms and pulled me against him. The delicious heat he always seemed to exude seeped into my back. He whispered in my ear, "I can clean anything."

The tension stretching every tendon in my body to the breaking point popped, and I laughed. A little maniacal, but I'd cut myself some slack. This was an emotional roller coaster I wasn't certain would stay on the tracks.

"There was so much blood. It had to be soaked into the wood. Did you replace the floor?" A spike of suspicion stabbed me. I spun inside his arms to face him. "Why would you do this? Are you leaving me? Moving back here? To Outerlands?"

Great job, Lane. Why not add a page to your new, fancy YML Investigations website and bare your insecurities to the world?

Teddy slid his hands down to grip my ass. "Your sister and Lo asked." He shrugged, the movement lending a slight jiggle to my butt cheeks.

Weird Y'sindra would be interested in getting this joint cleaned up, but then it hit me. How had I not seen it? She didn't want to be reminded of what I'd done to her, either. I still marveled she hadn't gone into a rage and frosted me in my sleep. Instead, she swore she didn't hold it against me. She was grateful. And what the hell was that about? *Thank you for severing a vital part of my body, sis.*

It wouldn't surprise me if she was playing the long game. Girl could plot and scheme like no other. I squeezed my eyes shut and pressed my forehead into Teddy's chest, the familiar ache of guilt pinching somewhere beneath my ribs.

Teddy slid his large, capable hands up my back again. He tunneled his fingers under my waist-length hair to support my neck while he tipped my face toward his with his thumbs, forcing me to meet his gaze. Unless I closed my eyes, and why not? He didn't need to see the depths of my self-loathing.

His dark eyes, the color of fertile soil, searched mine. "I know what you're thinking."

"That I'm hungry?" Avoidance was key to emotional conversations.

"That you cut your sister's wing off. You ruined her."

"Whoa, why slap me in the face when you can hit me with a wrecking ball?" I tried to pull away, but Teddy moved his hands to the small of my back and held me tight.

"You gotta get out of your head." Teddy bent to press his forehead to mine. My eyes crossed, trying to stab him with my death glare, but I gave up and instead focused on his lips. He had the sexiest mouth. "Y'sindra is alive because of you."

I continued to stare at those mobile, kissable, perfect lips and shrugged.

He sighed. Breath, spicy from the cinnamon gum he'd been chewing, caressed my cheeks. "All right, let's approach this in a different way. The alternative would have been living with the knowledge you could have cut off your sister's wing and saved her, but you didn't. You let her die."

Like a lightning strike, I straightened and stared dumbfounded at Teddy's crooked, knowing smile. Gods damn him, he knew he had me. He'd said the same thing as everyone else, but different, and forced me to view the trauma through a new lens. Enough people berated my self-flagellation over the event, even Y'sindra. They'd pointed out she was alive because of me, but this slight shift in perspective made all the difference.

What if I'd let her die?

I brought my hands up to frame his face. "Thank you." Tunneling my fingers into his thick, soft hair, I pulled his face toward me.

Time for the second reason I'd brought Teddy to this little oasis of privacy.

"Don't mention it. You—"

Our lips collided, and I opened my mouth, devoured whatever his next words might be. Heat blazed from my core through my chest. This was more than a tepid flame. This was a sun-blessed bonfire, and I wanted him. I had to have him this instant. I would not accept one more excuse from this male. "I'm no porcelain doll," I growled and shoved Teddy against the bar.

"Lane, you're not healed." Even as he spoke, tried for escape, his hold tightened, and he coasted his hands down my back and slipped them beneath my shirt. Goose bumps rose on my skin as the cotton climbed with his caress.

Oh, I had him. Sucking his bottom lip between mine, I nipped just enough to sting, but not to break the skin. Even if his blood did taste like mana delivered directly from the universe, I was serious about not drinking anymore. I would not be an anchor around Teddy's neck. My emotional hearts already depended on him. I would not add my strength, my life, to that list.

Teddy pulled away. He was reluctant as hell, first taking a small step and then following with his hips, putting less than an inch of space between us. He wasn't getting away, not today, not now. I needed to get laid, and I needed Teddy to do the laying.

With my back against the bar, I fisted my hands in the front of his flannel and held tight. He wasn't going anywhere except between my legs. I hopped atop the gleaming counter and pulled him precisely where I intended. He didn't quite touch me, but he was in the right vicinity, and he fit better than anything else that had ever been between my legs. Even better than Thumper—my little pocket rocket bringing me body-rocking orgasms since I first discovered their existence.

He pushed his arms forward, and his palms smacked the bar top on either side of my hips. Teddy bowed his head into the crook of my neck, his heavy breathing tickling my throat. "You know what I am."

"Horny, I hope?"

"I'm not willing to risk hurting you. There are consequences you don't understand, and you mean too damn much to me." His arms strained. Veins popped on his bulging muscles for want to touch me. He wanted it. Our water bill was through the roof, thanks to all the cold showers he'd been taking.

Poor guy was still trying to resist. I hooked my feet together behind his hips and pulled him closer until the evidence rising to life in his denim pressed against the sweet, sensitive spot he explored so well with his tongue. My eyes nearly rolled back in my head. Today, I would have more than his tongue.

"This…" I moved my hips, and he hissed. My inner bad girl waved her pompoms. "Says you don't want to go anywhere. Come on, I'm tired of waiting."

Teddy groaned and fisted his hands at my side, still not touching me. "Lane, you—"

Nope, not hearing "I'm not healed" again.

I pulled his head up and face to mine. There was nothing gentle in my kiss. I licked the seam of his lips, applied pressure, coaxing his mouth open, and invaded with my tongue, making my intentions pretty damn clear.

While I had him distracted, I moved my right hand to the button fly of his jeans. After a few fumbled attempts, the first button came free and then the second. The third button was a different story. It caught on the fabric and refused to let go. Who the hell thought this sort of fly was a good idea? Impatient, I curved a talon under the remaining buttons, popping them off one by one.

True to his nature, Teddy didn't have a stitch on beneath his jeans. Would he never learn? I sure hoped not.

I dug my heels into his ass and forced him to me. My gaze dropped, and my breath stuttered. The smooth head of his rock-hard, thick, and delicious length flattened his flannel against his belly. Saliva pooled in my mouth. I licked my lips, staving off an embarrassing moment of uncontrolled drool, and reached for my prize.

Teddy locked his fingers around my wrists and pressed my hands against the bar top. "Don't you like what I do to you?" He leaned in and demonstrated what he meant with a slow drag of his tongue along my throat.

My stomach went weightless, and I whimpered. "You know I love it, but Teddy, I want all of you. Right here, right now. Stop playing with me." I pressed my heels into the delicious divot where his lower back met his butt, relishing the heat of him between my thighs. My clit ached where his thick, hard length rubbed against me. Teddy did indeed do wicked things with his tongue, but it was time for more.

"Fuck," Teddy ground out between clenched teeth.

"I'm trying to." I put more oomph into my pull. He and his misguided white knight attitude made a last-ditch effort to escape my octopus grip, but I wasn't letting him go. He could break my hold, but he wouldn't. This not wanting to hurt me thing benefited me, not him right now.

"Come on, Teddy." I gyrated against him, which didn't do wonders for my tailbone, but if it got the job done, I'd take the bruise. "You want this as much as I do. Stop pussyfooting around."

He choked and blinked at me. I should stick with sexy talk. Threats and insults killed the mood.

"I won't break." I strained to press my chest to his, to suck at the sensitive spot just below his ear. He was softening—his body, not his dick. He tilted his head, giving me access to his throat.

My lips curved against his flesh, and then I did the thing guaranteed to drive him over the edge. I licked from his collar to his ear. I sucked his earlobe into my mouth and then dragged a fang down the path I'd painted with my tongue.

"Damn you." Teddy cursed, and I laughed, deep and throaty, triumphant.

He wedged a hand between us and pressed against the juncture of my thighs. I gasped, bucked against his hand, and threw back my head. The cotton and leather of panties and pants was almost painful.

"Damn you," he said again, voice hoarse against my ear as he popped my button with much more agility than I'd shown. The descending zipper was a whisper beneath our ragged breaths. When my pants sagged open, he straightened from me and tried to step away.

Oh, hell no. I glared and tightened my legs, pulling him closer than I thought possible. Bless Mae and her insistence on squats.

Teddy caught himself and chuckled. "If you want those pants off, you need to get your ass off the bar."

"Oh, yeah." I dragged my kiss-swollen lip between my teeth. "Good point."

I eased my hold but didn't unhook my feet. I'd waited too long. This was so close to happening, there was no way I'd take any chances.

Teddy rolled my pants from my hips, his eyes locked on the bare flesh it revealed. When he reached my hips, I lifted my butt and let him tug my pants from beneath me.

He licked his lips, breath shaking and rough. "I can't pull them off unless you let go."

I shook my head. Sure, I was stubborn, but he could figure something out.

And he did, shoving a finger inside me. Surprised, I clamped down on a scream at the instant, intense onslaught of carnal sensation.

"You're so wet. I give up. I want inside you." He worked his finger in and out, slow, hard. "I need to be inside you."

Reclined on my palms watching his hand work magic, I couldn't speak.

Teddy added a second finger, plunging deep. His thumb grazed close—so close. "I can't make love to you unless you let go."

Shit. I thought I won, but maybe he did too? Whatever, I had to have this. My legs loosened and dropped. My feet dangled and heels thumped the bar from the sway his pumping hand created. He paused for a heartbeat to peel my pants and panties from my legs.

Without me holding him to me, his delicious cock leaned forward, heavy and thick.

"Are you sure?" Teddy asked, never slowing his rhythm.

"Are you kidding me?" I curved my spine into a C to pull him closer, watching the part of his body I craved bob toward me. Stars, this was torture. "Teddy," I warned, and drilled him with the most intimidating look in my arsenal.

Chest heaving from his restraint, he withdrew his hand to slip his fingers into his mouth and moved closer.

Oh, gods. Was he trying to kill me? Body flushed, chest tight with anticipation, I once again slung my legs around his hips. This time when I pulled him to me, it was heat to heat, flesh to flesh. I slipped my hand between us, but he wrapped his fingers around my wrist and maneuvered my hand away.

"Lie back. Let me." His chest rumbled with his growled words. He moved my hips forward until I hung off the edge of the bar. A breeze kissed my bared flesh as he reached between us and took hold of himself. I almost came undone at the sight.

I licked my lips, watching his cock fill his palm. "Anytime now."

"Patience." He laughed and guided himself to me. His laugh dropped to a moan as he pushed inside in one smooth, swift surge.

A scream erupted from me, and he froze. I pounded the back of his thighs with my heels. "What the fuck are you doing? Move."

He chuckled and groaned all at once. "You're going to kill me."

"Yeah, if you don't do this." I did a little circle with my hips. He hissed. I grinned and rotated again.

He withdrew slowly. The delicious friction sent my talons into the bar top. It was too polished anyhow. He eased back inside me with the same deliberate torture. The smooth glide, the friction, set me on fire. Filled me again and left me empty. I wanted more, needed more.

I'd had him in my hands, in my mouth, but this...

My thighs shook against his sides. A tiny flame nestled in my core. It sputtered, begging to be stoked. "Faster."

Sweat beaded on his brow. His teeth gritted from holding back. He pumped into me, faster, but not fast enough.

"Harder."

"I won't last."

"I don't care. Make me scream." My demand was a breathless plea as he tilted his hips, angling up inside me. So close. My inner muscles contracted, released. Something built and built. "Oh gods, so close."

His restraint broke, and he hooked my legs over his straining arms, angling my hips to thrust deep. He drove in hard and pulled out fast.

That demanding thing inside me quickened and went taut. The heat, the friction, the pleasure spiraled from my hot chest to my pulsing core, all blended and tightened low in my belly, skating the delicate line between pleasure and pain.

I was on the edge of something, something huge. My body was so tight. All sensation focused on one spot. Part of me wanted to escape the unbearable pleasure, but I also wanted to ride him hard. Only one thought —*more, more, more!*

Teddy shifted his hips a final time and hit that mysterious, mythical spot. Surprised by the sudden, intense climax, I came apart. A lung-searing scream ripped out of me. Starbursts popped behind my eyelids, but Teddy kept going, seeking his own satisfaction.

"Cum with me." His voice was deep, hoarse, his own command.

I was a puddle of pure satisfaction, unable to draw in enough air or energy to answer.

"Cum with me, Lane." His voice was so tight I could barely make out his words, which was hot as hell.

A flush of renewed lust flooded into me. My core tingled, tightened, but I was boneless. "Can't."

"You can." The wicked grin in his voice was all the warning I had. When his thumb brushed my well satisfied lady parts, I almost launched off the bar.

I whimpered and writhed. He held my hip tight with one hand, pushing my leg higher. It allowed him deeper than I'd thought possible. His other wicked hand continued to draw torturous circles on my sensitive clit. It hurt so good.

The hot, liquid, intangible sensation in my belly coiled, and then everything inside me shattered for a second time. I screamed again, and this time, I did as Teddy commanded as he sank himself to the hilt and roared. I came so hard I swore I passed out.

He released my legs, and his big, sweaty body draped over mine, becoming the best weighted blanket of all time.

My mind had become as dirty as Y'sindra's mouth. I'd need to scrub it with soap after I finished floating in this bubble bath of pure pleasure. My body hummed from the tip of my toenails to the ends of my hair. If I thought Teddy was a keeper before, he didn't have a gambling addict's chance in Vegas of getting away now.

The bright lights flashing behind my eyelids faded to the pleasant shadows of day. I smiled and ran my fingers through Teddy's silky hair falling over my chest, making me wish I wasn't still half clothed. We were so getting naked next time.

Wait, why not now? He was virile. He'd be good to go again in like, what, five minutes? Maybe ten. Yeah, I might need ten judging by the tremble in my thighs.

Teddy hummed against my chest. Pleasant chills teased my neck, and I shivered. "Sweet fangs, I never would have guessed how filthy you are. Like, decorate your body in mud, face in bloody war-paint, and break out the whips and chains kind of filthy."

A laugh exploded from me, so loud, so hard, tears wet my lashes. "Silly boy, I distinctly remember warning you I was a bad girl." And I did own a couple of whips.

"So you did." Warmth infused Teddy's voice. He stood and stepped back, slowly sliding out of me, wet and still semirigid.

My breath stuttered, and the sting of cold air that replaced his heat made me feel his absence all the more. Did this mean we weren't going for round two? Bummer, but there was always tonight.

He looked down at his pants. I sat up on my elbows and grinned, unashamed at his predicament.

"You're going to cost me a fortune in pants if you don't curb your impatience."

"Invest in Velcro?" It was a solid suggestion, but the scandalized look Teddy gave me said he didn't agree.

I shrugged, scooted toward the edge of the bar conveniently hip height to Teddy, and hopped off. A sharp burst of pain twisted from my ankles to my hip bones, and I wobbled against the bar for support.

Teddy was there, gripping my hips to support me, his palms branding my still-bare flesh. Stupid, sweet male. I pushed at his hands. "I'm fine."

"You aren't fine." There was more anger in Teddy's voice than concern.

Warning bells went off in my brain. I recognized the signs, knew where this was headed, and frowned up at him as I pulled on my pants. My frown turned to a grimace at the touch of the cold-damp of my underwear.

"You almost fell down, Lane. Why do we keep arguing about this? You need my blood."

Need him? Wrong thing to say. My molars ground together, fangs clacked. I took my time fastening my pants and smoothing my clothes. Difficult to do when I still needed the support of the bar, but I wasn't about to step away and risk falling again. My legs needed a minute to recover.

"I'm using my father's portal to go home and finish packing." I jerked away from the bar and headed for the front door we'd left open. If any other patrols came by, they got a show.

Thank the stars I didn't fall over on my way to the exit, because I'd never hear the end of it. When I looked back, Teddy remained where I'd left him, legs wide, arms crossed over his chest. The leg stance was probably to keep his jeans above his hips. "Why don't you think about dropping this topic forever while you walk home? Oh, and have fun running back with those pants."

An itty-bitty kernel of guilt lodged in my sternum for forcing him to run what would take a normal being days to walk, but Teddy was not normal. I wasn't sure what he was. I'd never seen his true form. All I knew was that the black wolf was not a wolf. It also wasn't a wyvern like the rest of his family.

If nothing else, the run would give him time to reconsider his gods damned insistence that I drink his delicious blood.

2

I STILL WANTED TO PUNCH HIM IN THE FACE

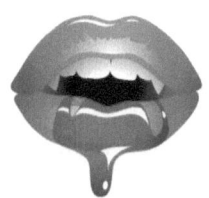

THE CRUSH OF VIVID EMERALD BROADLEAF GRASS SURROUNDING THE STONE slab beneath my feet was not my Interlands front yard. A quick scan confirmed my suspicion. I'd landed in Eodrom, in my parent's house where my father had removed the ward that prohibited portals—specifically, his hybrid magic version of portals.

"Shit."

I turned and yanked the chain looped around my hand, and my father's portal device hopped through the gate, leaving me with both halves of a full disk of sun shards, some spent, some not. With my father's invention, he didn't lose his precious shards. Before this fancy new creation, when the portal closed, it sliced the device in half, and half the disk—sun shards and all —got left behind. It still got sliced in half, but now I could pull the severed piece to me across space and time and save any sun shards still holding power. My father's version of recycling.

I traced a finger over a brilliant amber shard. It felt smooth and warm beneath my fingertips. The spent, muddy-yellow shards next to it had lost their natural heat. My father had been hard at work upgrading his magic in the months since my sisters and I helped recover one of the sun fae's sacred sun stones, stolen by the exiled and still on the warpath magic-corrupted moon fae.

He'd even been training Mae. She spent full days and sometimes nights under our father's tutelage. Seemed overkill to me, but she soaked up every ounce of wisdom he chose to drop.

Remembering my sister was training today, I headed toward the single building in the distance. As I drew closer, faint voices carried from the open windows of the home I'd lived in until I reached the ripe age of fifteen. None of those voices had the honeyed tones, sultry and bright, of my sister.

I paused to brush the dirt from my father's device, turning it over in my hands and finding the heart drawn in permanent marker.

Why had I agreed to let Y'sindra label the devices? Oh yeah, guilt. She'd insisted she had a foolproof strategy for keeping my personal supply organized. I knew better, but I'd still let her. In permanent marker she'd drawn a heart for Interlands, a smiling face for Eodrom—which I vehemently disagreed with, but whatever—and a frowning face for Outerlands.

Would my sister intentionally turn my personal stash of disks into a game of roulette? Abso-fucking-lutely. With a growl of frustration, I stomped off the portal pad and down the short, cobbled path bordered by my mom's wildflowers and healing herbs, toward the exit.

Through the garden gate, I crossed the gravel drive and headed for the house. Debris crusted the disk halves, and I rubbed the device pieces on my pants, counting the unspent shards—two of ten, a terrible ratio. These new portal devices my father designed were a game changer, but they used an ogre-sized amount of power. Instead of my father having to activate his own device, he created disks with preset coordinates anyone could use. Which reminded me, we still needed disks linked to the penthouse. Since Mae visited almost daily, he had the coordinates. I knew he didn't want to waste his precious sun stones, but if he wanted us to continue our Outerlands patrols, I needed an easy way home. And the penthouse was home.

As I neared the open door to my parents' home, a voice I recognized but was not in the mood for rose above the low tones of my father. I spun and dove for the closest bush, but I was too slow. Duskmere called my name.

I pressed my forehead against the grass and sighed. Pasting on an obvious fake smile, I stood and waved the disk in the air. At least I tried to look polite. "Found it."

The Royal Fae Guard captain, Duskmere, arched a skeptical brow. He'd come close to dying in my front yard six months ago, and I'd felt terrible. I'd sworn to be nicer, but he made it so hard. The shine of his survival had already worn thin. Still, I'd take him over his partner, Cirron, who turned being a pompous ass into an art form. Oh, and there was that whole traitor business. How the RFG had welcomed him back boggled my brain.

I made a show of dusting off the disk I'd already cleaned and tucked it in my pocket as I walked toward the moon fae. "So nice weather, right? Great seeing you, but I gotta be going." With a wave, I tried to skirt past Duskmere, despite him rudely taking up the entire cobbled walk.

"Malaney Callaghan, we must speak."

Y'sindra swore I growled when I was pissed, and yep, there it was, scraping over my vocal cords. This guy had an incredible talent for bringing out the worst in me, especially when he couldn't remember my name. Lane— was that so difficult?

His air of superiority had, if anything, worsened since his close call with death. One would think he'd lighten up after that.

A breath puffed over my lips, and I slouched, waiting for him to approach. So much for escaping the tedium of a conversation. "I'm in the middle of something. Maybe I can pencil you in for..." I pretended to think about it. "Never."

Duskmere's keen gaze roamed from my head to my toes.

Irritation shoved my brows together. Suddenly self-conscious, I smoothed a hand over my clothes. So what if he could tell what Teddy and I got up to?

"What do you want, Duskmere? I am actually in a hurry." To get away from him. Though, the new tenants for the Interlands house would stop by soon for the keys. They could wait, but who knew what sort of damage those little Smurf farts might do if I'm not there to impress upon them the consequences of breaking agreed upon rules?

"I have a job for you." Duskmere stopped in front of me, arms crossed over his chest, a chest corded with scars no medicine could repair.

The reminder plucked the anger from my breast and threw it back in my face with a heaping dose of guilt. I scowled at my toes and mimicked his posture, folding my arms over my chest. "You mean you have a job for YML Investigations, and we already have a job."

"This is more important."

"Uh, more important than the sun stones?" The corrupted moon fae—a large contingent of fae banished after the Great Fae Divide, a war waged over a hundred years ago—stole the stones, which were the source of the sun fae power. A real dick move, and one I would have approved of if not for the fact that Mae and my father were also sun fae.

Duskmere shook his fingers through his silver waves, sending them into a riot of short, loose curls. Since recovering from the whole poison daggers to the chest ordeal, he hadn't returned his hair to its former close-cropped length and had yet to understand the art of styling. Who knew the boy had curls? "For the moment, we are able to sustain a surplus of shards for those that require them with the stone you returned."

When three of the five stones were broken in half and stolen away, the remaining stone's roots fell into a slow death. However, the first time I'd met the keeper, Iola, she'd assured me that once we returned the stones, she could bind the halves and heal the stones. Based on Duskmere's lack of concern, it seemed she'd been right.

I uncrossed my arms and turned my hand over to study my talons. Six months ago, as I lay dying in the Outerlands street, I'd spotted the stone in the distance, but it wasn't me that brought it back. A team of RFG did that and rescued me while they were at it, much to my everlasting shame.

Sighing in his face, I asked, "Fine. What's the job?"

"Follow me." Without waiting to see if I'd follow—because of course I fucking would—Duskmere set off down a gravel path, heading in the opposite direction of my parent's home.

"Sure, no problem. I've got nothing better to do." I waved my hands theatrically at his rigid back. With a sigh and petulant kick of grass, I followed.

Duskmere traveled full steam ahead, never breaking stride to strike up conversation. We wound our way through meadows of tall grass and multicolored wildflowers. Forest grew in rolling waves, diving in and out of the field like a leafy ocean, nearly choking the path on some stretches and leaving a wide-open swath of green in others.

Too soon, the forest retreated, allowing an unobstructed view of the palace to rise in the distance. My gaze traveled over the wall's slopes and peaks. The creamy-white stone covered in climbing vines and embedded amber shards was wide enough to encompass a small city. That's really what Eodrom was—a small city.

The closer we drew, the heavier my steps and more unbearable the anxiety itch between my shoulder blades became.

Despite the beautiful veneer shellacked over its rotten core, I would never happily enter this place. I'd never let go of the catalyst that sent me running from Ta'Vale. Who could blame me? Anyone lured to the apex of the impossibly tall sun bridge and shoved over the side would hold a grudge. I still didn't know who did the deed, and I shouldn't care. Ancient history. What doesn't kill you makes you stronger. Made me who I am now. Blah, blah, blah.

I'd almost died then, too. I seemed to have a thing for falling to my near death, as I'd already accomplished the feat three times in my brief existence. Then there was that time when I fell out of a tree, but that only injured my pride.

As cool air from Eodrom's shadows replaced the pleasant burn of the afternoon sun, I caught up with Duskmere. "Want to give me a hint what we're doing here?"

"No."

Typical. Why did I feel bad when this guy was bleeding out in my front yard? I glared daggers at Duskmere's rigid back. Unfortunately, the actual power had yet to manifest, and he disappeared unscathed beneath the arch leading to the palace interior.

"Sure, fine, whatever. I'll give you five minutes." I rubbed my suddenly sweaty palms on my thighs and entered the empty hallway. Duskmere was already disappearing around a corner in the distance. Would it kill him to slow down? My legs were achy from more than my accident. The long overdue romp with Teddy had them throbbing in the best way. Too bad he'd gone and ruined the afterglow, pressuring me about his blood.

I followed Duskmere through the winding halls of the palace, up stairwells, and around hidden corners, deeper and deeper into the sun fae residences. Many sun fae roamed the area. News of their queen's trust in me and their misconception that I had returned one of the stolen stones meant they at least hid their animosity. I could feel it, though. A heavy heartbeat of disgust pulsing in the air. Chin raised, I marched through the halls, not giving any the satisfaction of acknowledgment.

Mae swore the lingering undercurrents of animosity were in my imagination, but she was wrong. No matter what I did for these fae, they would never accept me. Truthfully, I didn't care. It wasn't so long ago that I'd almost lost everyone that meant anything to me. It was a hard and fast wake-up call that I already had everything I needed, and the acceptance of anyone else meant nothing.

At the end of a suspiciously empty hallway, Duskmere waited by an open door. I slowed and looked around. The halls we'd passed through to reach this one had been quiet, but there had been activity. None had been completely empty, not like this residence area. Not just empty, but silent.

I stopped in front of Duskmere and tucked my hands into my back pockets. At five foot nothing, my nose was even with his chest, reminding me once again of his recently emaciated form. I ground the rising guilt beneath a mental boot heel and lifted my bicolored irises—one black, one violet—to meet his gray gaze. "Where is everybody? You have a bomb scare? Maybe another escaped kelpie?"

His lips thinned, his left eye twitched, but he didn't answer. He put his back to the open door and gestured me into the room with a wide sweep of his arm.

Directly off the foyer was a surprisingly cozy living area. I walked to the center and turned in a slow circle, taking everything in. Nothing was out of place, nothing broken. I neither saw nor scented any blood, without which there was little I could do. Eyebrows raised in question, I faced Duskmere. He watched me expectantly. I'd had it with the silent treatment.

"Tell me what I'm doing here, or we're done. It's been a long day, what with it being my first day fit to patrol." Not to mention the bone-melting pleasure I got up to with Teddy, but I had no qualms about playing the poor little me card. Sure, Duskmere almost died, but so had I, and it didn't hurt to remind him. "I still have plenty on my to-do list for today."

That little worry-wrinkle between his brows that always appeared when he didn't quite believe what I was saying formed. "You detect nothing?"

"What? Motherfu..." I dropped my head forward and bit my lip, reining in my runaway temper. "Can we please move past the guessing game, and you tell me—explicitly—what it is I am doing here?"

He turned away to take in the room, dragging his hands up and down his face in an exhausted reaction. The feeling was mutual. Though this time, I got the impression it had nothing to do with me.

"I apologize for keeping you in the dark," he said at last.

My head spun three times in surprise, or it would have if it could. Duskmere, apologizing? Something hot just froze over. Perhaps that was just my temper turning down a notch.

"This fae has gone missing."

Okay, he had my full attention. I scanned the room once again, seeing it from a new perspective. One I might have had if he'd informed me why I was here in the first place. "You should have told me that to begin with."

Those cute little curls of his bobbed as he shook his head. "I assessed the situation and decided it would be best if you entered blind, with no preconceived opinions."

Gripping my hips to prevent me from strangling him, I narrowed my gaze. "What opinions? All these theatrics only wasted time I could have spent investigating. You know, the thing you apparently want to hire me to do?"

"You make no secret of your feelings toward the sun fae. I did not want you going into this assuming the missing are leaving of their own accord."

Well, he had me there. That would have been—and still was—my first thought. "You might not be entirely wrong." I went back to studying my talons and found a piece of Teddy's bar top beneath a nail. I really needed to let Y'sindra do her thing and polish my talons. They were a mess.

"We do not wish to foment fear within our walls. Rather than spread rumors that would likely lead to those results, we would like to keep this private. We first wish to understand what is going on." He couldn't quite meet my eyes, something that told me he either wasn't being entirely truthful, or he wasn't telling me everything. "This is also why I chose not to share this information where we might be overheard. It is why we emptied this wing today."

"This sounds dangerously close to how, not so long ago, you used an *internal investigation* as an excuse to keep vital news to yourself while my sisters and I were risking our necks to find your stolen sun stones." I wagged a finger, messy talon and all, in Duskmere's face. "I told you then that I would only work with you if you divulged any and all information with me, and that still applies."

A muscle ticked in Duskmere's sharp-angled jaw, but he gave a tight nod. "Agreed."

I crossed my arms over my chest and tilted my head. "To be crystal clear, this applies to escaped prisoners who want my head on a pike. Like say, the crazy-ass spymaster I sent into your dungeon and then had to decapitate after you forgot to tell me he was on the loose."

He swept a hand in front of him, the same way he tried to sweep everything under the rug. "Yes, of course."

Duskmere didn't like being reminded of the great Royal Fae Guard's failings, so I enjoyed reminding him—loudly and often. A grin curled my lips as he actively avoided looking in my direction, because yes, I was that petty.

In my defense, I had every right to bring up the whole dungeon escape thing. They did still have two prisoners who I had a part in putting there. At least I hoped they did. One was my great—many times great—grandfather, Blackthorne. I couldn't say if that old druid wanted me dead or wanted an invitation to holiday dinners. And Dacian, Teddy's brother, who definitely wanted me in the dirt.

Time to get down to business so I could get home. I rolled my shoulders and turned a slow circle to take in the room. My first opinion of cozy wasn't quite right. The room was small but elegant.

A sofa with butter-yellow upholstery and delicate copper filigree sat artfully arranged at an angle on a large square, a handwoven rug in the center of the space. Overstuffed, pale-green and blue throw pillows tucked into the corners of the sofa were the room's only nod to comfort. An equally delicate square coffee table with rounded corners and curlicue legs sat in front of the sofa with two matching chairs on either side. Books, a large collection of tea sets, and small figurines no bigger than my index finger filled the shelves of several storage units.

I walked to a shelf and ran my fingers over the glossy green leaf of a houseplant. Its dry brown tip and edges flaked beneath my touch. The room was littered with plants. The hints of brown showing on their leaves meant whoever went missing had probably been gone at least two weeks. No more than a month, unless this fae invested in a longevity spell for these plants.

Nothing was out of place in the nauseatingly spotless room. My version of both a laundry hamper and a closet—my bedroom floor—would horrify whoever lived here. Whatever, the lived-in look was more comfortable.

I strolled to another bookshelf and dragged a finger along the surface. A little dust, but not much. This room was too arranged, too perfect, for the owner to allow a speck of dust to dare accumulate. The small amount backed up the timeline in my head. But why not see how forthcoming Duskmere planned to be?

"How long has this fae been missing?" I strolled down a short hall to the bedroom and found it as tidy as the living space.

Everything was in its place, meaning whoever lived here had not been forcibly removed. The small pile of dirty clothes lay in a wicker basket and feminine beauty products of the fae variety on the dresser implied this fae had planned to return.

I took a slow stroll around the room. Clothes hung neatly in the wardrobe. The portrait of an attractive but somber-looking sun fae hung on the wall. There were no pictures of family, or couples, just the female, who I assumed was the missing sun fae.

On closer inspection, I finally found something out of place. Among the scattered cosmetics on the dresser lay a small orange crystal aimed at the bed. I snorted. Judging by the angle of that communication crystal, which projected the connected speakers as holograms on either end, this female had a freaky side. Then again, that wasn't unusual among the fae.

A chill chased away my brief spurt of amusement. *Well, crap.* The fact that the crystal was still here didn't bode well for whoever it belonged to. Communication crystals were to the fae what cell phones were to humans. No one left home without them.

Except me. I spent most of my time in the human or between worlds and kept forgetting to grab mine since I rarely needed to use it.

I checked two more rooms, plus the water closet, and passed through the living area, heading to the kitchen. "You still haven't answered my question."

"Because we do not know."

My foot froze midstep, and I swiveled toward Duskmere, who still hadn't moved from his position by the door. "I thought we agreed no secrets?"

He shook his head. "I am telling you what we know, and that is nothing."

Projecting all the skepticism I could muster into one look, I glared. "You expect me to believe that the mighty Royal Fae Guard knows nothing?"

Unlike my tattletale complexion, Duskmere's charcoal tones hid his discomfort, but it was there in his jerky movements. His stiff posture didn't mean a thing. He always looked like he had a stick up his ass. My gaze fell to his fidgeting fingers—a sign that he didn't want to talk about this.

Of course, we were going to have this conversation.

I hooked my thumbs into my belt loop, all casual-like, and leaned against the wall. "So this fae went missing under the great RFG's noses. If you don't know when, how did you find out?"

"The sun fae who resided in these apartments had missed three apprentice lessons at the stables where she was training. The stable master notified the placement committee that they needed a new apprentice. They require someone reliable. The committee contacted us to track her down when she did not answer her door."

"Wow, okay." That was a lot of hoops to jump through to find out someone was missing. A tiny part of me felt bad for this missing female, who appeared to have no one in her life to check up on her. I'd clearly misread the placement of the crystal. That was just coincidence. Here I'd made it a habit of loathing all sun fae, but maybe it was unfair to lump them all into the same shit pile.

I glanced around the room, reevaluating my opinion of why this sun fae needed to be so meticulous. She'd probably been looking for purpose, value, worth. "Is there any reason you don't believe she is off visiting family or took a vacation?"

Again, his gaze fell away. "She is not the first to go missing."

"Once again leaving out the information you should have led with." I ran a hand over my braided hair and tugged on the length. If this wasn't an isolated incident, who knew how long they'd been keeping this on the down-low. "How many, then?"

"We are uncertain of the number."

I blinked and dropped my braid.

Duskmere shrugged and then threw his hands wide in a helpless gesture completely out of character for him. "We believe it has been a slow trickle over many years. If they, like this sun fae, had few to no ties within the community, no one would know. No one would report their absence. Had she not been an apprentice at the stable, we might never have known she was gone."

Wow, the RFG, Duskmere in particular, had to be desperate to bring in outsiders. This glimpse beneath the idyllic and obviously artificial surface of sun fae life astounded me. The callous attitude of the nobility and the RFG desire to save face over lives churned acid in my gut. Gods, I hated this place.

I dragged a hand over my mouth and looked around at the everything-in-its-place. "All right, we'll help, but the only thing I can do here is tell you this fae has been gone no less than two weeks and no more than a month. None of her belongings are missing that I can tell. Her closet is still full, and her communication crystal is on the bedroom dresser."

Duskmere jerked at that. A minor detail, but one he'd missed. He really was rattled to miss something so obvious.

"That suggests she was taken, or she chose to return to the stardust," I said. "If someone took her, it didn't happen here. Judging by what you've told me and the state of her home, I don't believe she would have ventured outside the walls of Eodrom."

I stared hard into Duskmere's glinting silver eyes. Harsh as I could be, I didn't know this fae, and it felt disrespectful for me to speak the words aloud. Of course, Duskmere only stared back, so I had to say it. "I don't think anyone took her."

Returning to stardust was cause for celebration. Unlike the tragic parody I'd witnessed living on Earth, or Earth adjacent, it was an honor for the ancients to return their essences to the stars, knowing a part of that essence would breathe life into new fae lives.

This did not feel like a celebration. It reeked of sadness, of a lonely life, and I suddenly wanted out of this room.

"You know the practice." Even as I said it, I knew it didn't fit. This fae had been too tidy to leave clothes in the laundry basket and the single dirty dish in the sink.

There was another option—something or someone was taking these fae from inside the palace. If I told Duskmere, he would insist I investigate. It would send me down a rabbit hole I didn't want to visit. Besides, the communication crystal left on the dresser poked holes in that theory, too.

"There's nothing else I can tell you here. If someone else turns up missing, call Mae." I headed for the door Duskmere blocked.

Duskmere didn't move. Were we about to throw down? Right here? I rolled my shoulders, loosening up—just in case.

At last, he put his hand on the door and turned the knob, but stopped. "Is your hate for the sun fae such that you will not help?"

I snorted a laugh. "A job's a job, but if the other missing fae's places were anything like this, there's nothing I can do. I read clues, track scents left by blood, neither of which is here. Mae, on the other hand, can trace auras if they're fresh enough. She's your best shot at finding out what happened. I'll give her a heads-up about the job."

"This is a reasonable arrangement." Duskmere nodded at the ground. I didn't think his inability to look at me had anything to do with subterfuge. This was shame.

Then again, it was dangerous to assume with these cagey pricks. "Hey, so

Blackthorne and Dacian are still behind bars, right? There's nothing else you need to tell me?"

No time like the present to check in on the two most wanted criminals I'd had a hand in slapping behind fae bars.

His head shot up, and he scowled. "Why would you continue to ask such a thing?"

My brows rose. "Hey, it's a valid question with the revolving door of traitors you've got going on here."

Duskmere jerked open the door. "There will be no more surprises. With the help of Cirron, we have rooted out any who would betray us."

I grunted and walked past Duskmere, through the door he held open, waiting for me to precede him into the empty hallway. "Just let me know if anyone turns up missing, will you?"

"You directed me to contact Maerwen should another fae go missing." Duskmere pulled the door shut behind him and turned a key in the lock.

"Yes, that, but I meant missing from the dungeon." I flashed a grin, all teeth and fang, in his affronted face and swaggered away, down the hall. Now I just had to track down my father and hitch a ride home.

3

PUT THE HO HOS ON THE PORCH AND STEP AWAY

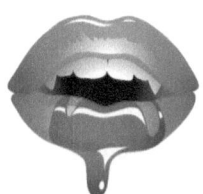

TEDDY HADN'T BEATEN ME TO THE INTERLANDS HOUSE. NEITHER HAD THE new tenants. Those little hamster nuggets better not back out of the deal. I didn't like them, but I liked their money, and we would need it after the big payday I'd received from the local bookie, Rip, ran out.

The penthouse we planned to squat in might be free, but the lifestyle that came with living in a high-profile casino and resort on the Las Vegas Strip was not.

I sat on the porch swing with the last case of my carefully packed weapons—long daggers, short daggers, push daggers, and the tri-blade daggers I never gave back to the blood fae I'd *borrowed* them from. I might disrespect my wardrobe, throwing it wherever it landed and shoving it in boxes, but never my weapons.

That wasn't entirely true. My dragon skin leathers, the rarest and most prized possession I owned, had been packed with equal care and were already waiting for me in my new walk-in penthouse closet.

I pushed against the old wooden porch slats with my dangling toes and closed my eyes, enjoying the gentle sway of the swing and cool caress of the forest breeze. The property was beautiful. My safe place—if you didn't count the time an assassin killed someone in our backyard. It hurt a little to give it up, but Mae and Y'sindra were certain we'd pick up more business in Vegas. Since the perfect living arrangement had become available, we couldn't pass up the opportunity. To get my hands on the real estate, I'd relocated my very old, and very evil, grandaddy to the Eodrom dungeons.

Worth it.

The deep rumble of an engine growled in the distance. I recognized that engine. Teddy was making good time over the ruts and divots. A smile slid over my lips, and I opened my eyes, watching the driveway for his Jeep. I'd forgiven him almost as soon as I left this morning. He didn't need to know that. I planned to make him work for it. Inexplicably, he would, too. Being a former prince of Shadwe aside, with some mysterious beast caged inside him, I got myself a good one.

The Jeep's rumbling voice carried high and wide out here, surrounded by forest. The house was on the quiet outskirts of Interlands—a bubble of space the universe inserted between Earth and Ta'Vale to protect the worlds from colliding, or merging, or any other world-ending disaster after the veil was opened between realms. Interlands didn't have an ecosystem all its own. Instead, it drew from the worlds it bordered.

Downtown Interlands, near Las Vegas, looked and felt more like the old wild west with its dirt streets and dirtier wood buildings. Tourists loved it, though. They could mingle with an odd assortment of creatures, some human, most not, and try not to be eaten. Weird way to get your thrills, if you asked me, but no one asked.

Out here, farther from the Earth border, leaned more toward Ta'Vale flora and climate. The creatures that popped up in Interlands, like the new tenants, were something unique to the universe. A freakish mix of both worlds.

The nose of Teddy's black Jeep rolled into view between the tall trees that bordered the long driveway. A far cry from his atomic orange Trans Am I'd borrowed and subsequently trashed earlier this year. The Jeep was much more utilitarian and great for getting around the bumpy, unpaved roads of Interlands. I knew Teddy had a stable of cars, but I'd yet to see more than the Jeep, a pickup, and the Trans Am. Maybe he'd bust out something fancy when we got our permanent parking spot at the Blackthorne.

The Jeep slowly rolled to a stop behind my Bronco, and the engine cut off with a few angry pings and hisses. I dragged my toe across the porch to stop the swing's motion so I could admire Teddy and his magnificent ass as they both stepped out of the Jeep. He paused by the driver's side to tuck his hands into the front pocket of his jeans and watch me.

Unease painted the perfect architecture of his bone structure. Unsure if I was still angry, he approached with caution. Smart boy. I fought a grin as we watched one another.

Afternoon sun speared through the dense forest skirt, drawing a gold line between us.

"Is it safe?" Teddy called and held up a box of Ho Hos.

Score! He knew the way to my hearts.

I jerked my chin at him. "Put the Ho Hos on the porch and step away."

His low growl reached my keen ears, and I brushed my chin against my shoulder to disguise the smile that wouldn't stay hidden. This was such a fun game.

He placed the box on the porch, just past the top step, and moved back, brows rising in question—*had he done enough?*

Not yet. "Open the box and toss me a packet."

"Lane..."

"Teddy..." I could keep this game going forever. Maybe not forever, but at least another ten minutes.

Blowing out a breath, he jerked the box off the porch, tore it open, and tossed a cellophane-wrapped package of chocolate-covered delight into my lap.

"Listen, I'm sorry I brought up the whole blood thing again," Teddy said.

"I know." I punctured the plastic with a fang and tore it open like the wild animal I was when it came to snack cakes. A piece of cellophane stuck to my tongue. *Pfft, pfft, pfft.* I tried spitting it free, but the stupid thing wasn't going anywhere. I scraped a talon on my tongue and dragged it from my mouth.

Teddy's hiking boot landed on the porch. My gaze flicked to his, and he stopped. I hadn't given permission to enter my domain. Not yet.

He held his hands out in supplication. "May I?"

I rolled my eyes and laughed. "Duh." I was done with the game, and I didn't even last two minutes. Time for chocolaty goodness.

The ridiculous pink porch swing rocked as Teddy dropped onto it and draped an arm over my shoulders, pulling me into his side. With his long legs stretched in front of him and heels braced on the ground, the bench swing barely swayed.

I devoured the cake in two big bites.

From the corner of my eye, I saw Teddy's wide-eyed astonishment.

"Whuf? Mmm hunry."

He shook his head. "With those table manners they won't let you inside any of the fancy restaurants on the Strip."

I flashed a grin, complete with chocolate-covered fang, and he leaned forward, kissing me full on the mouth.

Sitting back, Teddy licked his lips and grinned. "I need to get back for my shift at the bar. I'm already late since someone made me do my cardio"—he winked—"but I had to make sure we're good first."

"Yeah, of course we're good. You can't get rid of me that easily." My mouth twitched to the side, and I sagged against the back rest. It sucked admitting I was wrong. "I could have behaved better."

"Hey," Teddy said. "Look at me."

I gave him side-eye.

"Things are always so difficult with you." He laughed and cupped my jaw, his fingers on one side, thumb caressing the other, and pulled my face around toward him. Still holding me steady, he leaned in and kissed me, slow and deep. No chaste kiss, but a reminder of our morning escapades. The same bone-deep lust reignited inside, low in my belly, and I pressed into him.

He smiled against my lips and eased away.

"Tease." I slapped his shoulder.

Teddy stood, sending the bench into a twisty motion that forced me to keep turning my head if I wanted to maintain my glare. Of course I wanted to keep glaring. I did not appreciate getting hot and bothered and then shocked with an ice bath of denial.

Though, it was probably best for my still-broken body that I tried to disguise from everyone. I needed lectures less than I needed forced abstinence. If push came to shove, I knew how to satisfy my own needs. I should remind Teddy of that next time he told me no because he was *"worried about me."*

Teddy leaned down and put a hand on either side of my hips, halting the swing. His brow had those ripples it got when we were about to have a serious conversation.

"Ugh." I folded my arms across my chest. *Here we go again.*

"I told you I'm sorry, sweet fangs, and I am. It doesn't mean I'm going to stop worrying about you, but I won't pressure again. Unless—"

"Good." Full stop. He didn't need to ruin the moment with an ultimatum.

He smiled and tilted his forehead to mine. "Unless there is a time when you truly need my blood."

"Your definition of need, or mine?"

Teddy kissed my forehead and stood. "If you want to be weaker than you need to be, to live with persistent pain, so be it. I hate seeing you diminish yourself, but it's your choice."

"Yep." At last, he got it.

"But," Teddy added, and I groaned—again. There had to be a but. "If your life is on the line, I'm going to force the issue. "

"Sure, why not? Deal." I fluttered my eyelashes up at him. He rolled his eyes in response and headed for the drive, taking the three steps down in one long stride.

It wouldn't come to that again. I didn't plan to tango with another wyvern like Dacian anytime soon—or ever again. Blackthorne was behind bars. He was the only druid I knew of, so I didn't have to dodge that freakishly potent magic. The corrupted moon fae were long gone, disappeared over the border to Shadwe with the remaining two sun stones in tow. They'd be idiots to come out of hiding now.

Another low grumble grew in the distance. This wasn't the mechanical sound of Teddy's truck, but an organic vibration resonating through the ground. It knocked against my eardrums, like a slow-building thunderclap.

Only the thunder was blue, about three feet tall, and rolled onto my driveway like a tidal wave of fur, pointy teeth, and sharp claws. About time they got here.

Teddy's laughter pulled my focus from the approaching swell of grounders. He laughed so hard his hand dug into his side, and he bent at the waist.

My lip peeled up and brow drew down, giving him my notorious death glare.

He laughed harder.

My repertoire of looks needed work.

"I thought you were kidding." Teddy dragged his fingers beneath his eyes.

Maybe I should consider a new profession. I heard stand-up comics killed on the Strip. Might be nice not getting into knife fights and beating up derelicts for unpaid debts for a change.

Who was I kidding? I loved that shit.

"Why would I joke about this?" I asked, because seriously, I didn't see the joke here. Another reason I wouldn't make it as a comedian.

Teddy gestured from me to the grounders. "Last I remember, you shaved half the pack without their permission."

"Hey, they had it coming." The holes in my favorite leather jacket proved it. "And it wasn't half the pack, more like half a dozen."

"Hope you have a blade handy." Teddy hopped into his Jeep, started the engine, rolled down the window, and backed into the start of a three-point turn, until he was almost parallel with the porch. "If it were me, I'd want payback over something like that." He winked. "I'll see you at the penthouse after my shift. I'm on until midnight."

I grunted, not at all amused by the laughter that trailed after his Jeep.

The herd of grounders parted around Teddy's Jeep and didn't stop rolling until they reached the edge of the porch. One after another, they popped out of the furry balls they'd tucked themselves into for travel. A mixture of dust from downtown and loamy dirt from the damp, hard-packed soil leading to my house blended with their blue coats. A scent cloud of everything they'd rolled through blew past me. Thank the stars my super sniffer keyed in on the unique scent in an individual's blood, but not much else.

Despite their grayish-blue button noses, fat cheeks, and adorably tiny round ears atop their heads, they were vicious little lushes that loved to gamble. They weren't great about paying back their debts. Not because they weren't good for it, but because they were as greedy as they were small. They'd pay me, though. I'd seen to that with the shaving incident.

The de facto leader of the grounder pack waddled to the front of the group and puffed up. Puffed was a strong description of what he managed to do with the uneven, short tufts of blue fur sprouting over the surprisingly rotund body I'd discovered when I gave him a haircut.

Along with evidence that "it" was a "he." *Awkward.*

"You have keys?" he asked.

"Rude. How about a hello? How are you doing today?"

"Keys?"

Couldn't teach an overgrown hamster manners. I pulled the key chain from my pocket and tossed it off the porch. The big guy in the center—about three-foot-five—plucked it from the grass and studied the shiny metal emblem nearly the same size as his palm.

"Had it made just for you, a parting gift." I braced a shoulder against one column bracketing the porch steps and slid my hands into my back pockets. "Something to remind you of me."

The round, red frame containing a giant coin with lips and fangs on one side and crossed daggers on the other, spun in his grip, the sun hitting its surface and shooting rays in all directions.

The creature's round eyes narrowed up at me.

I smiled. "Expect someone the first of every month to collect rent. I'm keeping a key, so if you won't be here, leave the payment on the kitchen counter."

"Tunnels," the grounder said, opening a fanny pack nearly hidden beneath his pelt of ragged blue fur and dropped the key inside. Thankfully, the pack shielded my eyes from the masculine evidence.

Mae had a great coat made from the fur I'd collected. I should have worn that today. "What about them?"

"We dig."

"Good for you." Giving the grounders my back, I returned to the swing and picked up the last case of weapons. I jogged down the steps and waded into the fifty-something grounders gathered on my lawn. Which might not have been the smartest move. The sudden thought that I didn't have an easily accessible weapon, as Teddy suggested I should, and I might die by furry piranha attack scratched between my shoulder blades as I strode for my Bronco.

The sun rolled toward the horizon. I wanted to make it to the penthouse before dark. I'd yet to have any time alone in the new place. I planned to get a good look at the druid circle on the penthouse's roof with no one else around to distract me. I was going to fix that damn thing if it killed me. Maybe that was a tad dramatic. I only had to figure out how to reattach the crown to the pillar Blackthorne broke, but it was going to happen. Even if I had to visit the druid in the dungeon and beat the information out of him. Better plan, less dramatic.

I opened the Bronco's rear door, slid the case onto the back seat, and—

"We dig here."

"The hell you will." I rounded on the furballs, my hand cracking against the door. Hot pain throbbed in the wrist I cradled to my chest.

"We travel by tunnel. We need tunnels."

Now that the mangy rodent mentioned it, I'd never seen grounders traveling around Interlands. I'd experienced their rolling attack when they'd chased me after I stole from them. Well, I didn't steal. A job's a job, and at the time, they owed an outstanding debt to Rip. I might have skimmed a little extra for myself. They were probably still a tad miffed about that. Tunnels made sense. Did that mean there was a honeycomb network beneath Interlands? This was the stuff of every B rated horror movie Y'sindra ever forced me to watch.

That girl had a thing for trashy reality TV and bad horror flicks.

"We dig good." The leader of the grounders waddled through his pack toward me.

"So you've said before." I flexed my wrist and winced. My healing had slowed. I'd have to ice this thing and hope the swelling went down before anyone—Teddy—noticed. "No digging on the property. I told you that was a stipulation, and you agreed."

"Your kind hired us for tunnels. We dig good tunnel."

I stilled, its words tickling my latent anxiety. "My kind?"

"Fae. Not like you. Dirty moon fae."

My breath tangled in my throat. I'd bet my last Ho Ho the furball meant a magic-corrupted moon fae, and I knew who he was talking about. I couldn't just decapitate a guy and move on. He had to come back to haunt me.

How had I forgotten the grounders told me a moon fae hired them for a job? Probably because I was in the middle of pocketing the stolen sun shards they'd been paid with. "You dug tunnels, where?"

"Big green place. Over the border."

Ta'Vale, it was telling me they dug tunnels in Ta'Vale. My hearts accelerated. "Where in Ta'Vale?"

The deranged gerbil knew he had me. His small half-moon ears twitched, and he rubbed a furry paw on his chin. Yeah, that didn't look like the picture of evil.

"You let us dig, we tell you."

Shit. This was information I couldn't unhear. I had to know where these tunnels led. Would there be an assassination attempt on the keepers, Iola and Torneh, the sun fae version of ruling royalty? That would cause an unfuckable clusterfuck. How big were the tunnels? Could an army of corrupt moon fae march inside undetected?

Cold sweat blistered the back of my neck. I pulled my braid over my shoulder and stroked a hand from neck to tip over and over in a nervous gesture. "One tunnel."

"More. Five tunnel."

I shook my head. I needed the information, and I would bargain for it. If push came to shove, I could also hold down as many of these little creeps as I could catch and shave them. "One."

"Four tunnel."

Turning away, I opened the Bronco's driver's door and leaned in to grab a dagger holster from the passenger seat. I slid the dagger free, tossed the sheath back into the seat, and faced the grounders. "One." I dragged the single syllable into the length of three.

The grounder's yellow eyes flicked from the blade to my face. A small pink tongue darted out to wet his lips. He jerked a nod. "One."

I smiled wide and pulled my ever-present notepad from the inside chest pocket of my jacket. You never knew when you had to take notes. I hopped into the driver's seat, letting my legs dangle outside and waited, pen poised over pad. "Excellent. So where are these tunnels?"

4

STUPID QUESTION

A QUICK SHOWER AND NAP DID LITTLE TO EASE MY PERSISTENT ACHES AND pains. At least I'd earned some of these aches in the best possible way. I made my way down the stairs and crossed the living room to the balcony, a flush climbing my neck at the memory.

The new sliding glass door I'd once pushed Blackthorne through was a little tight on its track. I made a mental note to add WD-40 to the already long list of items we needed for the new place. On our walkthrough of the property we did last week, Vaughn, the head of security for Blackthorne Casino and Resort, informed us the old druid had ordered repairs not long after my sisters and I made our escape.

Vaughn still resented us—or more specifically, me—forcing his involvement in our original investigation that had brought us here several months ago. Not my fault he owed the notorious Interlands bookie money. A debt that I, Rip's go-to debt collector, had leveraged for the access we needed to his penthouse.

I made my way to the side of the balcony and forced myself to face the over seven-hundred-foot drop. My hearts skipped into overdrive, and I closed my eyes, focusing on tamping down the instant, primal reaction. I figured that inelegant leap I'd made over the side while fleeing from my homicidal grandpa entitled me to a little anxiety.

Blackthorne swore he hadn't been trying to kill me, but using magic to incapacitate strangers was a weird way to say hello. My sisters and I had been trapped on the penthouse balcony. It wasn't like we were going anywhere when he found us. At least we weren't going anywhere until we had to, and I'd grabbed my sister and jumped.

The resulting gouges in the building's face stood out like an angry scar. I'd asked Vaughn why those weren't being repaired, and he'd informed me, with no small amount of disgust, that the board of directors had voted to leave the damage. Apparently, it drew more tourists, and Vegas valued profit above all else.

I squinted for a better look in the late day glare of desert sun. That vampire, Vaughn, hadn't lied. The hydraulic lift hanging halfway down the side of the building wasn't repairing anything or washing windows. In Blackthorne's absence, the board had done more than left the damage. They hired a team to paint the grooves my talons had left so they would be easier to spot from the street.

Maybe I could con the board into paying me to scale the building once a week. It'd be good practice in case Gramps ever got out and my sisters and I needed to make another quick escape. With thoughts of what I could charge for hazard pay in my head, I pushed away from the rail and headed for the spiral staircase leading to the roof garden.

Something drew me in that direction, and it wasn't just the mind-boggling assortment of fruit growing on a rooftop in the desert. I gripped the sleek wooden railing and mounted the stairs.

Emerging onto the roof, I paused to take in the rolling green of the garden in the sky. Trees, limbs heavy with fruit and fragrant with blossoms, marched in neat rows along the roof. They left a wide corridor down the center with a clear view of the opposite side of the garden and the circle of rough-cut gray stones. Though no wider than a few feet, each pillar varied in width and height.

That crazy old druid really created something special.

"I was beginning to wonder if you'd ever get here." That crazy old druid's sardonic voice preceded him as he stepped from beneath a fig tree, sipping from a dainty white teacup embossed with a cherry tree I recognized from his cupboard.

I screamed embarrassingly high and loud before pushing backward, away from the stairs, and dropping the twenty-something feet to the balcony, landing in a crouch. Pain rocketed from my soles, riding my nerve endings all the way to my scalp.

I pressed my hand to the thunder crashing against my breastbone. "What the actual fuck?" I shouted, the concrete floor still vibrating beneath my feet. Blackthorne should be rotting in the bowels of Eodrom. How was he here?

Stupid question. That place was so full of traitors wanting to throw their lot in with the corrupt moon fae and topple the ruling sun fae, it would be more difficult to escape a paper bag than that dungeon.

"Are you coming back up, granddaughter, or shall I join you?"

"Not your granddaughter," I snapped, glaring up at the smiling, literal bane of my existence. He was the reason for my twisted DNA, both by blood and by magic.

Instinct told me to attack, but for once, I listened to my brain. He was too powerful and too much of an unknown for me to take that chance. "Blackthorne." His name grated past my clenched teeth, and I stood, getting myself under control.

Solid, sure, I radiated confidence as I climbed the stairs and brushed past Blackthorne. *See, not afraid of you, old man.* My neck itched, the skin pulling taut. I wasn't comfortable having him at my back, either.

I slid my hands into my pockets all casual-like and faced my— unfortunately for me—relative. There wasn't a speck of dirt on him. His long braid was smooth and filth free. He wore a blue Hawaiian shirt, denim cutoffs, and flip-flops. His deep-purple eyes watched me from over the cup's rim as he took another sip.

Did the old druid make a detour to the Bahamas after his escape? Duskmere was going to lose his mind when he realized he'd lost another prisoner. Only one prisoner, I hoped.

Unbidden, my gaze rose to the sky.

Blackthorne followed my gaze and chuckled. "You won't find what you're looking for up there. That wyvern is still a guest of the sun fae dungeon. Good girl, bringing him down."

I returned my focus to Blackthorne's face, which, despite his salt-and-pepper brown hair and ancient age, was light on the wrinkles.

It's easy to have smooth skin when you didn't have a care in the worlds, I thought with a heavy dose of bitterness. So long as he was outside the Ta'Vale borders, there was no way the RFG would risk pursuit. Trickery on my part landed Blackthorne in that dungeon—brutal force would not return him.

"Only I excused myself from the sun fae accommodations." He smiled wide, the barest touch of crow's-feet pulling at the corners of his eyes. "I have you to thank for that."

"You what?" My spine went rigid, and I began stalking a half circle around him, checking him out from all angles. Where had he gotten the clothes? They didn't look like a Vegas Strip gift shop find. Where had he found a shower?

Oh, of course. This was *his* house. How long had he been here? He better not have touched my cheesy poofs.

"During our previous tête-à-tête, you shook my staff hard enough to send a seedpod into my cell." Blackthorne saluted me with his cup, and suddenly my precious snacks weren't so important.

My eyes widened, and I froze. The memory of my dungeon visit and the questionable lesson Blackthorne gave me to control my newly unearthed druidic powers played back.

"No," I whispered, tugging the hem of my shirt.

It wasn't a traitor in Eodrom's midst. It was me. Blackthorne taught me how to tear the veil between worlds after those corrupt bastards stole my sister. I'd done it, and I got her back, but I remembered the seedpod I shook loose from the staff during our lesson. It rolled into the druid's cell, and I thought nothing of it.

Blackthorne was an egomaniac. I glared, but I would not give him the satisfaction of asking how he used a seed to break out of a magic-proof dungeon he himself helped to create.

I groaned. Of course. "They trapped you in your own magic."

"Brilliant. You once again prove you are my blood." He beamed, and I gnashed my teeth at his prideful declaration.

Sure, I considered myself a bad girl, or at least morally gray—very dark gray—but I wasn't Blackthorne's level of evil. I didn't eat the life of my followers or alter the genetic makeup of an entire race.

Hooking his elbow on the waist-high wall surrounding the garden, Blackthorne set his cup on the ledge and began peeling an orange I hadn't noticed him holding. "I would have worked my way from that abysmal excuse for a dungeon, but when you gifted me the piece of my focus, it sped things along."

He beamed.

I felt nauseous.

Moving away from the staircase and deeper into the garden, I dragged my talons across the rippled bark of a persimmon tree. With my back to Blackthorne, I asked, "How'd you do it?" Me and my inconvenient curiosity.

"My staff is ancient and powerful. But a mere splinter can be manipulated into a lethal weapon." Blackthorne had slipped into his more archaic measure of speech, an annoying habit. Grass swished beneath his feet, alerting me to his approach. I heard the smile in his voice, pleased I was interested before he came into view. "Where might my staff be? I did a quick perusal of my home, and it didn't appear to be here. It didn't call to me."

"Sorry, I broke it." I didn't break it. Got it a little bloody maybe, but it was in one piece. It was also here now, but I only had so many hands. I'd been forced to leave it in the car. It wasn't that I wanted to keep the staff. It was that I didn't want Blackthorne to have it. I hooked a talon into the rough bark and drew a curl of wood from the trunk. It fell into my palm, and I flicked it at him.

He caught it and closed his fingers over the sliver of wood. Brilliant jade-green light leaked from between his fingers. The light grew steadily brighter, with traces of gold sparking in the thin green beams. A stick emerged from both ends of his fist, growing thicker the longer it stretched. Small branches adorned with tufts of leaves sprouted along the...staff? Holy shit, Blackthorne created a staff from a piece of persimmon tree bark.

"For you." He held the staff out.

After a short hesitation, I took the length of wood but dropped it immediately. That thing wasn't just warm—it was scorching hot. The pale flesh of my palm now sported a bright-red line. Great, I wouldn't heal fast enough to beat the blisters. Teddy would see this, and he would lecture. I scowled at Blackthorne and shook my throbbing hand.

"Sorry," he said and smiled, not looking the least bit sorry.

"Do me a favor. Don't go through our things. This is our place now. You lost it when you got caught." When I caught him. I grinned, not the least bit sorry myself.

"Yes, it is. I confirmed with Vaughn that for the time being, this is your home."

I pushed the staff with my toe. "You didn't have to. I'd already handled it."

"Hmm." He made that annoying, noncommittal sound, like he would agree with me, but he didn't actually agree with me.

I crossed my arms over my chest and gave him one of my lethal looks, this one about a six on a scale of one to *prepare to die*. "I don't think you came here to make sticks. What are you doing here, old man?"

The sooner he left, the better. As much as it killed my pride to admit, I was no match for this guy's magic. Probably not on my best of days, which the constant ache in my bones said this was not. The party trick he'd just displayed proved that.

With nothing to channel his potent magic through, how did he make a magic stick? I toed the staff toward Blackthorne and went still. The center of the staff where it had grown from his fist was a different, chalky shade of gray, as if he'd leeched from the wood. As if it had petrified. It was the only section without a small sprout or leaf. He'd channeled even as he created. Okay, I was impressed. I schooled my features, so he'd never know. He was full enough of himself.

Blackthorne pulled the orange halves apart and offered me half. I took it and threw it. He shrugged and popped a segment into his mouth.

What was going on here? Afternoon tea and chat with an escaped abomination? Never mind the fact I'd been called an abomination all my life. Blackthorne was the real deal. It was like I'd detached from reality.

"Did they survive?" Blackthorne waved his half of the orange in my general direction. "Whoever's blood you wore when we last met."

Oh, right. I'd been wearing Duskmere's jacket to gain access to the dungeon, to the druid. It had been drenched in Duskmere's blood after he'd taken two daggers to the chest by the very corrupt moon fae his partner had helped escape. The same corrupt moon fae I'd later helped separate from his head.

"I don't think it was the Shadwe prince's blood." Blackthorne popped the last segment into his mouth and licked his fingers. "You said he goes by Teddy now, not Aventheo?"

"Listen, Blackthorne. You and me? We aren't friends. We might be related, but that doesn't mean I'm going to gossip in the garden with you." The frayed edges of my temper barely held on. If he stuck around much longer, I would do something stupid. Maybe end up over the side of the building again, and this time not by my choice. "I'll ask one more time. What do you want?"

Unfazed by the threat in my voice, he set his cup in the grass and beamed at me. "This is the good china, expensive stuff. Can't have that falling to the balcony below." He brushed a hand down the front of his untucked floral shirt. "Now, I'm here for your training."

"What? No, I don't need your help." I laughed and waved a finger at him. "And if I ever need help, I promise I won't need *yours*."

Blackthorne dug in his chest pocket and fished out a small card, extending it to me between two fingers. "When you change your mind, let me know."

When I didn't take the card, he shrugged and crouched to tuck it under the cup. Without another word, he strode for the druid circle. The *broken* druid circle.

My mouth dropped open and hung there. I might have eaten a bug. After all the begging I did to get this circle fixed—okay, more like threatening—he planned to use the thing now? Frustration and fury bubbled up inside me. I stalked after him. "Hey, that doesn't work, remember?"

I was right on his heels, but the moment he crossed the perimeter, I felt it. Electricity charged my blood, fizzled in my chest, and I jumped back. A thin, brilliant green thread of magic traced the edges of the circle. I'd not seen this the two times I'd stumbled through, but I'd been on the inside.

When had Blackthorne had time to fix this? How had he fixed it? My gaze flew to the stone he'd deliberately broken, and sure enough, it was whole.

"I'll be waiting for your call." He smiled and waved.

A roadmap of razor-thin green lines of magic created a dome over the circle, and then they were gone along with Blackthorne.

Should I have let him get away? I wrung my hands together in front of me. Could I have stopped him? Indecision knocked around inside my brain.

The stone cracked anew, and the crown hit the soft ground with a muted thump. Well, I wouldn't be following him now.

"That asshole." I stomped across the garden, picked up his precious teacup, and launched it over the balcony.

5

A CHARGING BULL

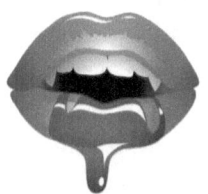

Y'SINDRA MIGHT BE DEVIOUS, BUT SHE WAS ALSO PREDICTABLY CONSISTENT. Another of my father's portal disks labeled with a heart returned me to the place I'd fled only a few hours ago. I'd visited Eodrom more times this past year than I had in the previous eight years combined.

Acting quickly, I yanked the chain, pulling the severed section of the device to me.

Not much larger than a mint tin while whole, both halves easily fit into the back pocket of my jeans. Wiping my hands on the front of my pants, I glanced around, listening for voices. I didn't want to deal with Duskmere again, but he was the fae I needed to see about a certain druid-at-large.

I'd also decided to let him know about the tunnels. While the grounders knew where they began digging, they didn't know where the tunnels led. For secrecy, they were hired to dig a certain distance and stop. I'd coerced the grumpy grounder into giving up the starting location for the two tunnels they dug. One entrance, two tunnels, he'd said. I could hand that juicy bit of information over to the RFG as well, one less thing for me to do, and I was all about less work.

Despite the tangerine rays of late afternoon sun, fae lights and fire blazed inside my parents' home. My nostrils flared as Mom's home cooking hit me right in the face, sending my salivary glands into overdrive—grilled meats, cinnamon, clove, wild onion.

If I had to come to Eodrom, I'd picked the right night. She'd made a roast.

More voices than I'd heard earlier floated from the open window of my parents' home, and my steps slowed. The voices were loud. Instinctively, I glanced up and down the long, gravel driveway, but it was empty. My folks wouldn't be concerned about being overheard. There was no one else for miles, and they certainly wouldn't have expected to see me again today. *Surprise!*

Sunlight captured inside beads of water dotting the grass shone gold. It must have rained between my earlier visit and now. I leaned against the fence lining my parent's drive and brushed away the water droplets gathered on my shins. I once got freaky with Teddy against this fence. Good memories. I smiled and turned my gaze upward. At least there were no clouds left in the sky. I wouldn't get stuck in a downpour.

"Her training is coming along well." My father's voice rose, a thread of anxiety winding through it.

Well, that was unusual. The great Finnlay Callaghan was so stoic, I was pretty certain he was at least ten percent granite. Yes, he was erudite, but to be the chief royal wizard, the magical terror of battlefields, he had to have a rock-solid core, and he did.

I pushed from the fencepost and strode toward the front porch.

"But will she be able to face Hielmal?" I froze, hearing keeper Iola's melodic tones, and then her words registered. Hielmal? The most notorious sun fae in history? A distant relative of Iola had decided the best way to rule the sun fae was to assassinate the keepers. She'd failed, but barely, and she left a lot of bodies in her wake. It happened shortly before my time, but I knew the story. Every fae knew the story. Hielmal would have succeeded if my father hadn't brought the magic hammer down on her head.

"The question is, will she want to?" Keeper Torneh, Iola's partner, asked.

What kind of gathering had I stumbled into?

Hoarfrost froze my blood and scorched my flesh with a wave of blistering heat. My hearts leaped into my throat, and I swallowed, twice, as the threads of conversation came together. Why would Mae have to face Hielmal? How would she face Hielmal? That rotten-to-the-core female hadn't been seen since my father thwarted her attack. If I were a betting girl, which it turned out I was, I'd bet she'd long ago been returned to the stars.

I curled my hands into fists, talons piercing my palms. I gasped a small breath as the bite of pain brought focus, clarity. Instead of barging inside and demanding answers, I held myself still and listened. A huge accomplishment on my part. Mae would be so proud.

The pause between the keeper's questions and my father's answer was heavy, long, and telling. My father was a very decisive man. If he wasn't answering, it was because he didn't want to.

"I do not know." His heavy words came at last. "On either account, I do not know."

Fabric rustled. Footsteps, someone moving inside.

"Finn." Mom's sympathetic voice, followed by more rustling fabric.

I closed my eyes, easily picturing her rubbing hands back and forth across my father's shoulders, something she did often while I grew up in this household. My hearts compressed at the memory. I didn't miss this place, but I missed my family.

"This is our girl." Mom had a smile in her voice. She always smiled when she spoke of my sisters. They might be adopted, but they were fiercely hers. "Maerwen would not fall prey to such a creature as Hielmal."

"But—"

"But nothing." Mom cut my father's objections off at the knees. She was ruthless like that. "Our girl is brilliant, and she has the famous Finnlay Callaghan as her mentor. If the time comes and they meet, she will be ready, with her heart and with her power."

Damn right. I had no idea how Mae and Hielmal would ever meet or why. I knew my sister, though, and she would be ready for whatever came her way.

"Are you certain?" From the sound of Torneh's question, he sure wasn't. "Blood calls to blood."

My eyes flashed wide, and a dizzying array of lights exploded in my vision. By all the forsaken gods, was I going to pass out?

I leaned into the wall.

Shit.

Torneh's question couldn't possibly mean what I thought.

What else could it mean?

My breath came in shallow pants, and I lowered myself into a squat before I stopped wondering if I would pass out and actually did. Placing one hand on the ground for balance, I covered my face with the other, focused on slowing my hearts and getting my breath under control. The voices inside droned on, but I tuned them out. I'd heard enough.

No way was my sweet book-and-boy-ho sister related to that monster.

I laughed under my breath. The irony of me calling Hielmal a monster. Something I'd only recently embraced about myself was now the worst moniker I could think of for someone else, but we were two different beasts.

How could she be related to Mae? An aunt? A cousin? Of course, that put Mae in Iola's family tree. Did Mae know? Had they told her, and she kept the news to herself? She had been distant recently, but... No. No way. That girl would have told Y'sindra and me news like that faster than I could make a cheeseburger disappear.

My brain finally stopped circling my skull. I stood and rubbed my sweating palms on my thighs. The desire to curl into the arms of Teddy and shut out the world took hold. What a foreign thought. One I would never have believed I'd have. The idea of leaning on anyone, let alone someone who was not one of my sisters, was so surprising, so strange, yet felt so right.

Flexing my back, I stretched and then stood straight, pulling in a long breath. Crisp evening air invaded my lungs, just cool enough to tickle. When I released the breath, I let go of the anxious jitters.

I walked slowly toward the porch, trying to decide how best to approach this situation. The big question was, how long had my parents known about this, and did they plan to tell Mae? This was the sort of thing I expected from Duskmere, but from my family? Never.

"It is decided," Torneh said, voice louder as I neared the open window. They were probably gathered at the dining table, just inside.

Stupid panic attack. Who knew how much of the conversation I'd missed?

"Yes," my father agreed. "It is best Mae does not know who her mother is."

Shock ricocheted across my nerves, and I stumbled. "No." I slapped a hand over my mouth and retreated around the corner. My eyes ached. Involuntary tears clouded my vision.

"She has a mother." Mom spit the words, and my hearts twisted in my chest. "We knew what it meant when we learned who took her, but she's safe now, and Finn will ensure she is prepared."

I pressed a trembling hand to my mouth. Hot tears rolled over my knuckles.

"Of course, love." My father used the soft tone he reserved solely for my mom. "She doesn't need to know. We will tell her only if a meeting between the two looks imminent."

"Hopefully, we can prevent that," Duskmere said, speaking up for the first time.

I gnashed my teeth together.

"Between your daughters' and Prince Aventheo's patrol along the border, and our assassins searching for Miro and Hielmal's new base inside the Shadwe border, the odds are in our favor."

My circle of distrust just grew exponentially from this asshole, to the keepers, to my *parents*. Betrayal settled like a poisonous snake in my gut. How could they doubt Mae? Not her magic abilities against that...that... Oh gods. They were talking about the corrupt sun fae who almost killed us when we ran into her in Outerlands. The one who had Mae kidnapped.

The entire conversation I'd overhead hit me with the emotional impact of a charging bull. I shot a hand out to catch myself on the wall but missed. Blindly, I fell forward, my knees hitting the ground, folding me over my thighs as the churning nausea was replaced by bile rising in my throat.

I threaded my hands beneath the heavy sheet of my unbraided hair and interlocked my fingers behind my arched neck. With tight, shaky gasps, I breathed through the pain racking my hearts, through the anger.

Unlike this monumental information about my sister, the tunnels had no impact on me or mine. Yet telling Duskmere, or any member of the RFG, about the grounders' work wasn't happening. At this point, I didn't believe a word Duskmere told me, and that included his word that they still had Dacian locked away in the dungeon. As the L in YML Investigations, I could confidently say we'd be performing our own internal investigation because I planned to check out those tunnels.

Maybe I would talk to my parents in private. I played the conversation back in my mind, looked at it from all angles. Despite the betrayal of hiding this information for who knew how long, they didn't doubt Mae. Maybe her power, but not her loyalty to family—our family. I recognized Mom's question for what it was: fear that she wasn't enough.

Ready to deliver the news about Blackthorne and get out of here, I pushed to my feet. Part of me wanted to hug my mom and tell her Mae could not have stumbled into a better family, but my anger was still too raw. Someday, probably after I ripped the heart of that bitch Hielmal straight from her chest.

Shoulders back, chin up, fangs out, I stalked to the porch and stopped below the first step, fighting the desire to stomp up the steps and kick down the door. This wouldn't work. For Mae's sake, I needed to play this smart. First thing was first, I would pretend I hadn't heard a thing, and to do that, I needed to back up and let them hear me coming.

Rolling onto the balls of my feet—why, I wasn't sure, since they hadn't heard me yet—I tiptoed in reverse, down the path I'd taken to arrive here. Playing dumb would be hard, and not because I wasn't sometimes dumb, a thought Mae would slap me upside the head for having. Maybe not dumb, but not smart. For once, though, it wouldn't be because I acted first and damn the consequences.

When I judged myself far enough away, I stopped and smoothed a hand over my hair. I separated it into three chunks at my nape and began to twist it into a fat plait. The monotony would help me shed some of the angry jitters that continued to poke my nerves, making me twitchy.

Sure enough, by the time I reached the ends hanging by my waist, a calmness had settled over me. I cracked my neck and took off at a sprint toward the house, aiming for every obstacle in my path to make as much noise as possible. A pile of freshly raked leaves, small branches that snapped beneath my feet, a kick to a rock that flew into the outer wall of the house. The sound ricocheted through the quiet countryside night like a gunshot.

There was no doubt they heard me now.

I took the two steps to the porch in one long stride, gripped Mom's delicate bronze door handle shaped like a bouquet of wildflowers, and shoved the door open.

Torneh stood fast. His chair tilted over, hitting the throw rug beneath the table with a muted thump. Mom had dropped back from my father, fangs elongated, ready to defend. My father followed Torneh's example and stood. I didn't miss the gold sparkles of his sun magic dripping from his fingers. Duskmere had drawn the short sword he wore strapped to his hip these days. Only Iola remained calm. Although, maybe not calm. Meeting her eyes, I saw the tempest alive behind her sunset gaze.

Breathing heavy, though I didn't really need to, I put on my best acting face and looked wildly around the room. "Blackthorne! Blackthorne escaped."

Notably, my parents remained shocked, while Duskmere, Torneh, and Iola showed zero surprise at my words. Son of a swamp troll, they knew.

Duskmere knew, even after his declaration of full disclosure this morning. Even after all his secrets that got us into a world of hurt before, I'd believed him. I'd wanted to because I still didn't want him to be *that* asshole.

But he was. And he lied—again.

Through narrowed eyes, I cast him a look that promised pain. His chin inched up, and I knew right then that he *was* that asshole. He believed he was right not to tell me.

"Fuck you," I said, before he could even try to justify himself. It didn't matter Torneh and Iola were here. They might be able to smite me into stardust, and Iola might be one of the kindest fae I'd ever met, but screw them, too. I stabbed a finger at Duskmere. "You knew, and you didn't warn me. I was just here, and I asked you, and you swore you'd tell me. Do you even still have Dacian, or is he going to show up at my house, too?"

Scandalized, my mom gasped. "Blackthorne visited your home?"

I rolled my eyes. Suddenly exhausted, I pulled out one of the few chairs left at the table and dropped into it. "It's his house. I'm a squatter there." Only Mom would get the squatter reference. She loved Earth and visited often. She wasn't dependent on a stationary power source like the sun fae and their sun stones. She only needed blood for power, and unlike me, any blood would do.

"Where is the druid? Is he still there? How did you escape?" Torneh asked in a tornado of questions.

I pulled my glare from Duskmere and put it squarely on Torneh. Huge mistake. It'd be easier to stare into the sun.

"I didn't put a tracker on the guy." Slumping in my seat, I closed my eyes and rubbed my temples. "He was already there. I don't know if he came through the portal circle, but he left through it. Had I known, I could have been prepared."

Prepared for what? I had no idea, but at least I would have been on the lookout. We might have even been able to capture him again. Doubtful, but we could have tried.

"You escaped?" Torneh asked again.

I scowled at the smooth knots and whorls on the hand-carved dining table. No way would I try to get into another stare-off with that guy. "Escaped what? He offered me tea, wanted to train me in his druid ways. I refused, and he left." I shrugged and fell back in the chair.

"You must take us through the circle," Duskmere demanded, because that's what he did. Demanded, but offered nothing in return. He wasn't just all business—he was a selfish ass that put duty above all. It might work for my parents, but not me.

"I don't have to do anything," I snarled.

"Lane," Mom warned. She came up next to me and rested a hand on my shoulder—the better to dig her talons in. She didn't fool me. She could be a ruthless bitch, and I was proud to say that's where I got it from.

"Listen, I can't." I held up my hands. "The stone broke again. It fell over as soon as he was gone."

Mom patted my shoulder, and I turned to look up into her face. I didn't have to look that far. At four-foot-ten, she was even shorter than me. Barely, but I was proud of those two inches I had on her. "You aren't bothered that they knew? That Y'sindra, Mae, and I were in danger?"

"Well, I…" she stuttered, a hot-pink flush lighting her pale, rose-kissed cheeks.

"We trust the Royal Fae Guard knows what they are doing." My father moved to my mom's side, a united front. "I am certain if they believe you were in danger, we, and you, would have been made aware."

"Ha! You trust the same fae that put your daughter's life at risk, who almost killed one of their own?" I flung my arm toward Duskmere and pointed a finger. "His own partner, the one that is inexplicably back in the RFG instead of turned to stardust, kidnapped Mae and let Duskmere get stabbed *in the chest*."

My voice rose with my agitation. I pushed from my seat and stalked up to Duskmere. No one moved. "How dare you?" I demanded.

"We would have informed you once our internal investigation was complete. We needed to keep everything quiet. Surely you understand?"

"Whoa." I stepped back and barked a humorless laugh. No, I absolutely did not understand. "You had an investigation going? Exactly how long has he been gone? More than a day?"

Duskmere's jaw flexed, muscles pinging at the corners from tension, but he didn't answer, wouldn't even meet my eyes.

"More than a week?" Still nothing. I shook my head and backed away, not just from Duskmere, but from all of them. "I should have known better."

"Laney…" This time, Mom's tone was gentle.

I shook my head again, feeling behind me for the doorknob, and realizing the door was still open, retreated over the threshold. I'd give him, all of them, one more chance. I took a deep breath and looked around the room, meeting each of their gazes one by one. "Is there anything else I should know?"

Predictably, no one spoke up.

"Lane, trust the Royal Fae Guard. They are more than capable of handling this situation. They will see to the fae's best interest."

"Right, okay. Time for me to get back. I'll be needing a portal home." Crap, my Bronco was at the casino. "My new place."

My father only nodded. Duskmere had already dismissed me and joined Torneh, heads bent close together in hushed conversation. Iola offered a soft smile while Mom beamed. If they thought I was over this, they didn't know me at all.

I turned and stalked through the door and to my father's permanent portal pad in the back garden. The pad wasn't necessary, but it did make the journey more precise. Thank the gods, at some point over the last week, Mae and Duskmere had accompanied my father to the penthouse so he could gather the coordinates. Otherwise, I'd be taking the long way home.

I'd done the right thing keeping the information about the tunnels to myself. I didn't trust the RFG any further than I could throw Rip, and with the state of my health, I'd be lucky to lift that ogre off the ground.

Unlike the portal pad we were installing at the penthouse, the solid stone surface here had always existed among the grass paths, swaying fields, and endless green, green, green. My father, the chief royal wizard and old-school fae to the core, had converted a piece of nature to his purpose.

I pulled the two halves of the broken, used portal disk from my back pocket and tossed it into the grass, then stepped onto the pad to wait for my father. Toe tapping, I watched the front door. My impatience bellowed and thrashed inside me, but he finally emerged.

Focused on my father's approach, neither of us spoke. I ached inside with something far worse than my poorly mended bones. I needed my sisters. I needed Teddy. I needed to go home.

6

I LIKE THAT GUY'S STYLE

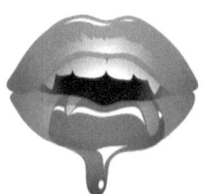

"WHILE I APPRECIATE THE VIEW, WHAT ARE YOU DOING IN THE GARBAGE, sweet fangs?"

At Teddy's amused drawl, I whipped a glare over my shoulder at my honey bunches o' hotness. He leaned against the archway into the kitchen, making lazy look sexy. Fresh from a shower, damp hair brushed his collar. Glistening beads of water dripped from his hair and rolled down the corded column of his throat, and I almost forgot I was elbow deep in the trash.

I shook my head, scattering my lusty thoughts, and focused on the task at hand. "Blackthorne gave me a card, but I threw it away. I need it."

Taking that news poorly, Teddy strode across the kitchen to hover over me. "The druid? How? He's locked in the Eodrom dungeon."

Poor guy was in denial. I knew that feeling well.

"Apparently not." I rummaged beneath a paper towel and gagged when my fingers dipped into last night's take out. We'd been moving from Interlands to the penthouse for the past two weeks, crashing wherever we ended our day. This place was a mess. None of us took out the trash, not even Mae. Shocking, and it showed how distracted with her training she'd been.

"That place isn't a dungeon. It's the Airbnb everyone tries, but no one stays," Y'sindra said from her perch on the pass-through between the kitchen and open concept dining room-slash-living area. She'd been sipping on a blueberry lemonade undoubtedly spiked with vodka while she watched me dig through the garbage. She toasted Teddy with her drink. "Zero stars for that place, am I right?"

Teddy squinted at her, mouth slightly ajar in a look of befuddlement. Y'sindra had that effect. My sis was an EF5 tornado condensed into a three-foot package, topped with a cloud of white curls and snow-shedding wings.

Correction. Wing.

My hand convulsed in reflex and turned a rotten banana peel to slippery mush in my palm. Ugh, gross. I yanked my attention from the glitter-bombed sleeve she wore over her wing nub and scrubbed my hand on a towel lying on the counter.

"You're gonna wash that, right?" Y'sindra drawled.

The state of her wing didn't seem to bother her. Small blessings, and all that.

"Blackthorne." Teddy came back to himself, remembering the conversation. "Tell me."

I pushed to my feet with a grunt and strode to the stainless-steel farmhouse apron sink and lathered my hands with some fancy French lemon-scented soap. If nothing else, Blackthorne had good taste. Except for food. There hadn't been a potato chip or pint of ice cream when we moved in.

The towel landed in the sink as I rinsed my hands.

"There, washed it for you." Y'sindra walked across the counter and plopped back on her favorite spot.

I pulled a dry hand towel from a hook next to the pass-through, purposefully dragging it over Y'sindra's head, and answered Teddy. "Blackthorne was here when I showed up this afternoon. In the garden, sipping tea."

"Classic." Y'sindra cackled. "I like that guy's style."

"You would." I tossed the towel next to the sink and put my back against the unusual green marble countertop. Designed for tall people, the stupid thing hit in that uncomfortable spot just above my lumbar. I crossed my arms over my chest and faced down Teddy's ire. Ire, not directed at me, but *for* me. I knew that, but it still rankled. I hated being coddled, treated like I couldn't handle myself.

Deep in my obstinate soul, I knew if Blackthorne came to take me out, I'd be dead. Even at my full strength, I might not have brought down the druid. That was a confession I'd take to my grave, hopefully not one dug by my great-grandpappy. I'd feel like such an idiot.

So much agitated energy rolled off Teddy, it almost hummed against my skin. "How?" he asked.

"How does anyone get out of Eodrom?" I shrugged and threw my hands out, palms up, in a *who knows?* gesture. "I assume they just walk out. That's how it seems."

"Dacian?"

"Still on a dungeon vacay, if we believe Blackthorne. Though he'd have no reason to lie about your brother."

Lips pursed with the question I knew he wanted to ask—*was I all right?*—Teddy gave me a critical head-to-toe appraisal.

He didn't ask, though. My man was learning.

"Well, you don't look dead." My sister pointed out the obvious. "So what'd he want?"

"To train me." I turned my attention to my talons. "And to flex the fact that he could fix and break the druid circle at will."

Y'sindra jumped to her dirty little feet on the counter.

I grabbed the towel and threw it at my sister. "Keep your gross feet off the counter, would ya? Clean that up. And no, the circle is still broken, or broken again. Whatever, I'm going to figure out how to fix that thing. I tore open the veil between worlds. How hard can it be to glue a rock back together?"

Y'sindra put a toe on the towel and dragged it around the counter. "Mae is going to freak when you tell her the druid was here."

Oh shit, Mae. I had to tell her what I'd learned. Should I tell Y'sindra, now? No, Mae should know first. But now that I was away from Duskmere, the keepers, and our folks, all that righteous anger boiling inside me had fizzled. My stomach soured at the thought of telling Mae. I didn't want to be the one to shatter my sister. Yeah, I was a dirty hypocrite.

"You in there?" Y'sindra snapped her fingers in my face.

I blinked. "Yeah, sorry. Thinking about how I'd fix the circle."

"Mmm hmm." Y'sindra climbed off the other side of the counter, onto a stool, and hopped to the floor. Between her soft slippers and pint size, she barely made any noise when she hit the ground. "Well, I gave Lo a twenty, and he hasn't come up yet. Time to go see what kind of jackpot I scored."

"If he won—"

"With my money. I called halvsies on anything he won."

"You would." I looked at Teddy and hooked a thumb over my shoulder. "See what I live with? Are you sure you want to sign up for this?"

Teddy chuckled, but it was forced, no humor. He was still wound up about Blackthorne's visit. I couldn't blame him. Incalculably powerful druid on the loose aside, what did this mean for his brother? The dungeon seemed too easy to escape. The last thing we needed was a wyvern wrecking our penthouse, or worse, burning it to the ground. Did wyverns breathe fire? I had so many unanswered and, frankly, unasked questions about wyverns. About whatever the hell Teddy was. I still didn't have a clear answer on that one, which was a problem.

"Don't wait up. Lo and I have some stuff to do," Y'sindra said. From the other side of the pass-through, only the fluff of her white hair was visible as she bounced away. Moments later, she appeared in the hallway to the foyer leading directly to the elevator. We lived in style now.

"What are you two up to? You're always doing *stuff*." I used air quotes, because I had no idea what that pair was up to these days. She could sniff out trouble faster than a bloodhound could find a dropped hotdog.

Y'sindra shrugged and hit the elevator call button—three times. Girl loved her buttons. "A little of this, a little of that. No biggie. Deuces." She flashed the peace sign, hopped into the elevator that opened smooth and quiet, and disappeared behind the typical silver doors. Moments later, a carved wood panel slid closed over the reflective doors.

Unlike a nearly identical panel I'd first seen at the hotel in Treasure Island, Florida, where Great-Gramps now lived, this elevator led to the casino floor, not another world. Though, that would make Outerlands patrols infinitely easier, since that was where the Treasure Island elevator led. Damn, I had to fix that druid circle.

Teddy wrapped his arms around me, pulling me away from the counter and into his chest. I let my head fall against his typical flannel. He'd showered and changed, smelling of soap and the pure Teddy scent of woods and earth and vanilla. The weirdest and best olfactory combination.

With over a foot between us in height, my forehead rested against his chest, and I breathed deep, inhaling his intoxicating aroma that never failed to relax me. And turn me on. I slid my arms around his waist and cupped his butt.

His soft laugh vibrated against me. "You just can't help yourself, can you?"

"I mean, it's right there."

"You sure you're okay?"

"Yes." I stepped back, but not out of his arms. Keeping a hold on the sides of his shirt, I tilted my head to meet his gaze. A brown so deep and rich it appeared black sent heat spiraling down to my marrow.

He brushed my hair from my shoulders and feathered his hands down my arms. "What is it, then? Are you..." His lips pressed into a tight, troubled line. "We haven't talked about this morning. That's not how I wanted our first time to happen. Are you...disappointed?" His brows pushed together, and his voice turned rough. "Do you regret it?"

Satisfaction swept over me. He'd wanted this morning as much as I had, and he'd thought about it long enough to have plans for something special. It didn't feel good seeing him worry how I felt about what happened between us.

"Did you already forget how things went down? You do realize I had the whole thing planned, right? Maybe not *on* the bar, but it was definitely happening *in* the bar. Today. It's been too gods damned long." I backed out of his arms but held his hands, remaining connected. "You've slept in the same bed with me for six months, and the skill with your tongue aside, I needed all of you."

Teddy expelled a breath, and the rigid line of his shoulders relaxed. That fool actually believed I might have been disappointed.

"I do regret one thing," I said.

He tensed.

"We never got to round two." The smile I gave him was pure sex.

His laugh cut off when he caught sight of my expression. "Did you eat bad sushi again?"

"What? No." I really needed to work on my seduction skills.

"Good, because that's what I'm craving for dinner. Blue Fin makes the best sushi I've ever had."

"All right, dinner it is." Fortunately, the aforementioned bad sushi hadn't come from Blue Fin, an award-winning James Beard sushi restaurant conveniently located one elevator ride away. As hungry as I was, I nearly suggested going down now, but the whole Mae thing was still screwing with my head. I hadn't decided what to do. I didn't think I could actually eat until I got this sorted out, and Teddy knew a thing or two about dysfunctional families. "Hey, can I talk to you about something first?"

"Should I be sitting down for this?" His thinly veiled joke fell flat. He tilted his head and gave me a sort of sideways look, as if waiting for the shoe to drop.

I waved away his concern. "Don't worry, it's not me. It's a family thing. I need someone to talk to, is all."

He reached out to rest a hand on my hip. "You can talk to me about anything."

"It's about Mae."

"Not what I was expecting."

"And Duskmere."

He crossed his arms over his chest and nodded. "That, I did expect."

I laughed, couldn't help myself. The two had a wary truce, but there was still a lot of bad blood under that bridge.

"And the keepers. And my parents." I traced a talon back and forth across my lip. "It's a really messed-up situation."

"I'm listening." Teddy reclined against the counter and waited.

Facing Teddy, I put my hands behind me, against the island's countertop. I drummed my talons against the cabinet door and raised my gaze to Teddy. "I'm not sure where to begin."

"We've got all the time you need, sweet fangs." He leaned toward me and tucked an errant chunk of hair behind my slightly pointed ear. "What happened first?"

"Blackthorne happened."

He snorted. "Figures."

"Damn druid was on the roof when I got back from...polishing the bar." I winked.

Teddy choked, coughing with laughter.

I grinned and told him what happened, right up to the moment I headed to Ta'Vale to let the RFG know Blackthorne escaped. "Spoiler, they already knew."

"Can't say I'm surprised." He reached for me, curling a finger through my belt loop, and pulled me toward him.

I pressed my hands to his chest and laid my cheek on them. "That's when I heard the news."

Electric guitar stopped me from spilling the story. The ringtone Teddy specifically programmed for calls from his bar.

He sighed, and I stepped back to give him access to his front jeans pocket.

"It's okay." I waited to see what this was about. Calls rarely came in from the bar unless it was an emergency.

Teddy dug the phone from his pocket. He looked at me, finger poised over the dismiss call button. "I can call them back."

"They wouldn't call if they didn't need to." I jutted my chin toward the phone.

"Yes?" Teddy answered. He listened, eyes slid shut, and pinched the bridge of his nose.

With my better-than-average hearing, Zee's urgent tones hit my ears loud and clear. She was Teddy's best bartender, one of my few friends, and also a werewolf. If she was calling for help, the bar was getting wrecked.

Sounds of furniture clattering and glass breaking played as a soundtrack to the conversation. That's what happened when you owned the most popular bar in a town full of the biggest baddest degenerates around. On any given day, at least five different species that starred in the most knee-trembling nightmares anyone could conceive stopped in for a drink.

Somehow, my cuddle bug, Teddy, was a bigger, badder nightmare who no one dared cause a ruckus around. I still didn't see it.

He hung up and shoved the phone into the front pocket of his jeans.

I walked into Teddy's arms and gave my man a squeeze. "Bar-room brawl, I heard. My news can wait. Go save Zee before she goes furry and eats someone. That'd be bad for business."

Teddy's grunt closely resembled a growl. "Make my life a lot easier. Rain check for that dinner date?"

"Always." I rested my chin against his chest and smiled up at him. "You don't ever have to ask."

The hard lines and rigid muscles of irritation in Teddy's arms relaxed. He tucked his thumbs under my chin and held my face tipped to his as he bent, lips descending to mine. This wasn't the hard, rushed kiss I'd planted on him moments ago. His lips were soft as they danced against mine.

I stuttered a breath, inhaling the cinnamon flavor of his favorite gum. The warm, spicy taste tingled down my throat and into my lungs.

Teddy pulled away, took something from his back pocket, and put it on the counter behind me. "This was on the floor. Call the druid if you need to."

"What..." My eyes rounded at the sight of Blackthorne's card. "You had that all along, but still let me dig through the trash?"

"Now, now." Laughing, he danced away when I tried to smack him again. "So violent. No, I did not know the whole time. You were already rummaging through the trash when I got here, remember?"

"Hrmph." I snatched the card and ran a thumb over the surface. "I need to call. You'll understand when we talk."

"Yeah, that." He grimaced and pulled the phone back out of his pocket. "I can tell Zee to call Mick. You're more important."

"No, go. It's not urgent, just confusing."

It was kind of urgent, but only to my sanity, since I had no idea what I was going to do.

His thumb hovered over the phone's screen.

"I promise. Go. Nothing needs to be resolved between now and tomorrow." I pushed his nearly immovable mass toward the hall. He took a single step. "It's fine, I promise. *Go*."

"All right. I'll call as soon as I get things settled at the bar." Teddy pressed the elevator call button. "If I'm not back too late, we can still grab dinner."

"It's a date. That reminds me, can you grab some duct tape while you're out?"

The elevator doors slid open, and Teddy stepped inside but kept his hand against the track to prevent the doors from closing. "Sure, we have some at the bar, but for what?"

"I'm going to fix that stupid circle."

The door closed on Teddy's roar of laughter.

"Duct tape fixes everything!" I shouted at the closed elevator. The wood panel slid silently into place.

An involuntary rub of my thumb over the glossy business card pulled my attention back to the small rectangle in my hand. The sappy smile bled from my lips as I looked at the name and number glaring up at me, daring me to use it.

"All right, you old asshole. You win." I slapped the card onto the counter and strode for my phone I'd left on the floor by the garbage can. Muttering my irritation, I dropped the bin back into the slide-out cabinet and kicked it closed beneath the counter.

Shit, now I needed to wash my hands again.

After another hot lather and rinse, I picked up the phone and punched out the number on the screen before I could change my mind. I hit the speaker button and left the phone on the counter. Head down, hands on my hips, I gripped so tightly, my talons pierced my denim as I paced the square perimeter of the kitchen.

Blackthorne answered on the second ring. "The Shadwe, we have rooms with an ocean view and an elevator to another world."

I twisted toward the phone and sputtered. He couldn't...

He laughed. "Hello, granddaughter."

"Ugh, stop calling me that." I bared my fangs at the inanimate hunk of metal, circuit boards, and lithium. "How did you know it was me?"

"Caller ID."

I rolled my eyes and resumed pacing. Blackthorne was way too familiar with modern-day trappings for such an ancient guy.

"Whatever. It doesn't matter. I'm calling." I waved my hands in the air for sarcastic emphasis. He couldn't see, but it made me feel better. "I need my strength, and I definitely need to heal. Tell me how to fix whatever is wrong with me."

On the other end of the line, Blackthorne made a tsking sound. "That isn't what's wrong."

My eyes went wide and then narrowed. "Then why don't you tell me what's wrong?"

"Granddaughter, I already did."

I grabbed the phone off the counter, tapped the green speaker button to turn it off, and pressed it to my ear. "What's your problem? I called you. Isn't that what you wanted? Either teach me how to use these druid powers or make them go away."

"No."

I pulled the phone from my face and stared, blinked, and put the phone back to my ear. "No?"

"No. You keep trying to control what is uncontrollable. I will not help you self-destruct. You may call again once you are ready to let your power do what it wants to do."

He hung up.

My phone joined the teacup.

7

I WAS SUCH A COWARD

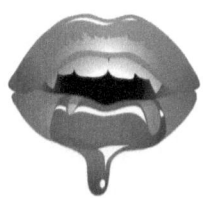

"WHAT?" VAUGHN, THE HEAD OF HOTEL SECURITY, BIT OFF THE WORD. HE was a major grump, at least with me.

"Just calling to check in, make sure you got your evening sip of blood—only the good stuff. Since this was Blackthorne's place and it's mine now, I figured I should make sure they're looking after you." I leaned a hip against the kitchen counter, absently twirling a strand of hair round and round a finger.

Irritation had a sound. Silence, punctuated by growly breaths, and it stretched on the other end of the phone.

"Fine, starve. See if I care." I folded beneath the barrage of silence. Hopefully, I was never tortured for information. I'd break like a stale cracker.

"Mr. Black is still the owner, but he confirmed you are his relation."

"Yeah, well, *Grandpa* is an asshole, and I threw my phone over the balcony. Scoot on out there and see if you can find it."

The vampire's laughter came through the earpiece like a speeding train, rumbling and roaring. I held the house phone—the *corded* type—away from my ear and glared at the hunk of plastic in my hand.

"Time for a new phone. That thing is in a million pieces," he said, still laughing.

I clenched my fists so tight, my knuckles threatened to turn to dust.

"Just go look or send one of your underlings to do it. It has a specially designed case to protect against damage, all right?" Y'sindra used to fly with it, so we took all precautions. Then again, we never put it to the test. This trip over the balcony probably destroyed it, but I was still making Vaughn check. "It's in a thick, rubberized, black case with a bright-red fangy mouth biting its bottom lip. Pretty distinct."

Vaughn snorted. "Fine." The phone clicked.

He did not? I pulled the receiver away from my ear to stare. After a moment of dead air, an angry hornet buzz issued from the phone.

He did.

I banged the corded phone on the counter. I banged it three more times for good measure and slammed the earpiece into the cradle set on the counter.

The phone rang. That was fast. My cell phone couldn't have shattered if they already found it. An inordinate amount of smugness drew a smirk onto my face.

"You found it, and I was right." I twirled the twisted phone cord like a mini-lasso. "It was in one piece, wasn't it?"

"Want to tell me why I had to call the hotel to get through to you, Laney?" Mae drawled.

I stopped midtwirl, and the cord drooped onto the counter. "Uh, not really."

Mae's headshake of exasperation was audible enough to visualize.

Then, it hit me. Mae was on the other end of the line, and I had colossal news I needed to share. Did I spill it now, or did I wait until I talked to...someone else? No, this was face-to-face type news. I'd wait. Decision made, I already felt lighter. I wasn't being a hypocrite. This wasn't a Duskmere need-to-know situation. When I saw her, I would tell her.

Unless something more important came up. It could happen.

Gods, I was such a coward.

"I need you to meet me at Dad's portal," Mae said, interrupting my mostly failed attempt to convince myself I was doing the right thing by waiting to drop a metric ton of awful news on her.

"Ugh, why? I've already... Wait. How are you calling me?" Phones didn't work in Ta'Vale. But communication crystals did. My gaze slid to the empty basket I was supposed to fill with the crystals we kept in a kitchen drawer at the Interlands house. Oops. I couldn't be expected to remember everything.

"I'm at our Interlands place. You forgot the communication crystals, and I needed to get in touch."

I winced. At least it didn't sound like an emergency.

"It's an emergency."

Oh, for fuck's sake.

"Are you okay?" I clutched the phone with both hands, one on the receiver, one on the cord beneath the mouthpiece.

"I'm fine. Duskmere found me for the job he hired us on. Thanks for the heads-up."

I winced. "Sorry about that. Been a long day."

"It doesn't matter." She sounded pretty annoyed about something that didn't matter. "A fae was just discovered missing. The aura trail is faint, but viable enough to trace. I need you to join me to check for a scent trail."

If I hadn't smelled the fae's blood, any scent they gave off would be no more apparent to me than any other fae, including Mae, but we were in this business together, so I'd go. Besides, I could tell Mae everything I knew and convince her to explore the tunnels with me.

"All right, I need to wrap up a couple things. I'll be there in thirty."

Mae was quiet for several heartbeats. "You agreed awfully easily." She was full of suspicion—and rightly so. I loathed Eodrom trips, and I *did* have ulterior motives.

"What? Pfft, no. I need to pull my YML Investigations weight, that's all." Sounded reasonable.

"Mmm hmm. See you soon." In a rush she added, "Oh, wait."

I pulled the phone back from the cradle I'd been about to drop it in. "Yeah?"

"Did you tell the grounders it was okay to dig on the property? There's a huge hole next to the house."

Two packages of apology Ho Hos, five mozzarella cheese sticks, and a shower later, I was back to kicking grass in my parent's front yard. It was childish, and I didn't care. Despite the literal bang that started my day off, it had been on a steep decline ever since.

Speaking of bangs, Teddy would be worried when he couldn't get a hold of me. I was learning how to do this relationship thing, though, and I'd left a note explaining I'd lost my phone. Close enough to the truth. Since I planned to make the most of this trip and explore the grounder's tunnels, I'd also jotted down the location the blue bundles of terror had given me in case he got home early enough to join me in my expedition. This could have waited until tomorrow, or next month, but Mae called, so here I was. Again.

Playing into my tantrum, I tossed the broken halves of the portal disk to the ground. My father would find them.

I wiped my hands on my thighs and looked around for Mae. She said she'd be expecting me, and I hadn't taken longer than the thirty minutes I'd told her I'd be. I even thought ahead, bringing two differently labeled disks and one of Duskmere's portal stones, just in case I got stranded in Outerlands. Knowing Y'sindra's aptitude for chaos, it was a real possibility.

"Oh, thank the stars," Mae shouted.

She sprinted toward me not from the direction of our parent's house, but from the palace. It was a long run, but of course, she wasn't out of breath. A health food and exercise junkie, she could run laps around me all night. I knew this because she had once done it to prove a point.

"Hurry." Mae grabbed my arm and started hauling me in the direction she came from. "The trail is almost gone. I've been following it, and the aura led to some weird places."

Shit, she was going to make me run. My joints protested with a deep ache as I picked up my pace to keep up with her. It wasn't long before my stomach heaved in complaint. Those Ho Hos might have been a mistake. I put a hand to my belly, trying to press the rising nausea into submission. My sister's abilities to follow auras was unparalleled. If she was onto something, I had to trust it. So running it was.

"Like where?" Nope, wasn't working. I breathed through my mouth. This was not looking good.

"A couple of strange spots." She glanced over her shoulder, her brows bunching in a frown. "You okay? Bad sushi again?"

"M'fine." I waved a hand. I was *not* fine. I would also never live down that sushi. "Where?"

"This is new." Mae slowed her pace and gestured to the periwinkle-blue maxi dress she wore like a supermodel. "Just aim the other way if you get sick."

I snorted. "Thanks for the concern."

She shifted gears to a fast walk. "Okay, the weird thing is, the trail only led to two places."

"You said the trail went strange places."

"It did," she insisted. "Two places, and both were puzzling destinations."

The palace rose in front of us. A multitude of windows, backlit by pastel-shaded fae lights, turned the lawns into a kaleidoscope of soft colors. We'd covered the distance quickly. I was grateful my stomach had stopped trying to eject itself in protest of all the running. Apparently, it was okay with speed-walking.

My sister moved with grace, but also with determination. She was so alive, so vibrant with energy, energy that had dimmed since her kidnapping. The case had done that, given her purpose. My stomach soured once again. It had nothing to do with Ho Hos. I couldn't tell my sister, not now. Not until I knew more. Was this why Duskmere hadn't told Mae?

I licked my lips, trying to pull moisture into my dry mouth, trying not to give away my inner turmoil. "Okay, why the drama? What's so weird?"

Mae stopped me a few hundred feet from the archway leading inside. She looked over her shoulder toward the palace and then back to me, as if she didn't want to be overheard.

The first hint of worry ratcheted up my spine. "Mae?"

"The trail ended at the forest."

I squinted at my sister and looked around. "That's not what I'd call weird. We're surrounded by forests. Which one?"

"*The* forest," she said, glancing around the lawn and then turning to the windows. "In the courtyard."

"Runach," I asked, and Mae nodded. My rusty brain wheels churned, trying to process that bit of news. A forest so ancient and full of unknowns, the fae rarely uttered the name. "Are you sure?"

"I am." Despite there not being a soul in sight, she inched closer. "But that isn't the biggest mystery. It's where the trail was strongest, where they lingered longest, that has me confused."

"Confused is a mild word for this behavior." I wrinkled my nose and leaned away. "I love you, but I don't want to smell what you had for dinner."

"This is serious," Mae hissed. "Something's going on in Eodrom."

"Duh." I rolled my eyes. Such histrionics for a couple missing fae. I picked at imaginary fluff on my jacket sleeve. "It's not weird for a fae to walk into the forest. Dryads are the main vehicle that long-lived fae can use to return to the stars."

The method of returning a fae's essence to stardust was a secret once held by both druids and dryads. By all accounts, it was a peaceful, joyful moment of surrender and rebirth. I knew a druid. Maybe one day I'd get curious and ask Blackthorne.

"No. I mean yes," Mae said, her blue eyes blazing with fae light reflection. "It could have happened, but it's highly unlikely no one would have known."

I opened my mouth to agree, but she held up a finger.

"But seven sun fae have gone missing since the RFG first took notice."

"Seven isn't that many."

"Seven this year."

"Whoa." My head bent forward, and I stared unseeing at the ground. I slid my hands into my jacket pockets and paced away from my sister, thoughts circling in a wild churn. This one fae walking into the forest could be coincidence, but with seven already missing in less than a year, it was suspect. They could also have gone in on a dare. It happened, but generally with the young fae, an adolescent test of courage.

"How old is this sun fae?" I asked as I continued to pace, trying to fit the jigsaw mystery together.

"Two hundred and seventy-six."

I paused and scuffed my booted foot across the grass. They weren't young. So not a dare. They also weren't ancient, so the dryads would never have agreed to send them to stardust.

That put me back to the theory that these fae were being taken while away from their homes, out in the open. What in the stale cheesy poofs was going on in Eodrom?

"Forget the forest, Lane." Mae crowded in front of me.

Raising my gaze, I withered under her intense stare, struck by the memory of Hielmal's intense blue eyes. Eyes very similar to my sister's, minus the blood vessels in Hielmal's brought on by the corruption.

Something else teased through the fog in my head. I'd seen those eyes before, Hielmal's, their exact duplicates, but where?

"Malaney Callaghan, I am trying to tell you the trail led to the hall. The place where I traced your aura after you fell."

My nerve endings caught fire. The emerging memory tumbled away, and I snapped to attention. Mae followed my aura to the sun garden, but couldn't find me, and for good reason. The garden was behind a wall that only admitted those that the sun stones growing within allowed.

She nodded, seeing my understanding of the importance. Mae only recently learned what was behind that wall. Our investigation searching for the stolen sun stones brought me there. For an unknown reason, I was one of the chosen, granted access by the sentient stones. I'd told her what was behind the wall, and she was rightfully concerned.

"What would they be doing there?" I rested my fingertips against my mouth, my index finger tapping. A potential explanation bullied its way into my thoughts, and my hand dropped to my side. "That hallway leads to two other locations."

Her mouth twitched, and she nodded. "I thought of that. I'd worried that they were trying to sneak into Dad's lab or the keepers' private quarters, but they never went beyond the garden. They couldn't without being seen by the guards, which they weren't, because yes, I checked."

"Well, shit," I mumbled.

Mae cleared her throat.

I stared at the fae-lit windows and paced toward the palace. What could they have been doing hovering outside the sun garden?

Mae cleared her throat again, trying for my attention, but I needed to think.

Did it actually matter? According to Mae, this fae never made it inside.

My head jerked up, and I spun toward my sister. "The grounders."

"What about them?" Mae asked.

I clicked a talon against my teeth, looking from the palace into the distance and back. It was time to check out those tunnels. I pivoted in the direction the grounders said the closest tunnel to this spot would be. Neither tunnel entrance was anywhere nearby, but it couldn't be for it to remain undetected. What if that was what the sun fae had been looking for? A way to disappear from the palace where no one would see them leave.

"The grounders dug tunnels," I said at last.

"I hear music in this hallway," Mae blurted at the same time.

My stomach dropped to somewhere around my toes. Everything inside me quivered with nerves. *I hear music* was such an innocuous statement, but I knew what it meant.

The sun stones chose my sister.

8

WE GO TO THE GARDEN

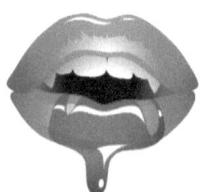

"Tunnels?" Mae's brow furrowed and then smoothed. "Oh, you mean at the Interlands house?"

"What? Yes, no. Doesn't matter. You heard music?" My hearts sang with elation and screamed in fear. This would be everything to my sister, but if the stones claimed her, marked her as a keeper, they could bind her, take her from me.

"Oh, yes. Yes, I did. In that hallway, but I couldn't locate the source. I would swear it was behind the wall covered with plants, but that's impossible." She wrung her hands at her waist. "It is impossible, isn't it?"

"Well…" I nibbled a talon, unsure how to proceed with this conversation.

Mae watched me warily, as if afraid of the answer she already suspected. "You told Y'sindra and me about the stones when you visited the garden during the investigation. How they sing."

I nodded, letting her put things together for herself. Mae was a sharp cookie. This wouldn't take long. For my logical sister, it would be easier for her to absorb if she figured this out on her own. A pain, deeper than blood and bone, throbbed in my chest. I didn't know what any of this would ultimately mean.

"I'd remember hearing that music when I tracked your aura." Mae crossed one arm over her middle and gripped her elbow.

When I'd been pushed from the sun bridge, she hadn't actually followed an aura trail to find me. According to Mae, she'd seen the remnants of my aura in the sky. After scouring Eodrom, she found my aura blanketing an area, faded at first, but it grew darker, deeper, until she found it filling the hall outside the sun garden like a heavy fog. The trail ended there. She never found the sun garden because the stones had not allowed her inside.

They seemed to have changed their mind.

Mae's pensive gaze went distant. I could see the wheels turning so fast inside that big brain of hers, I expected smoke to puff out her ears any minute.

The sun stones were alive, but were they truly sentient? Did they have a sense of humor, a vindictive one, granting Mae the one thing her patricidal, matricidal, homicidal mother desired above all, but could not have? That would be some funny shit.

"There's no other explanation," Mae said.

I inched my eyebrows up in question, waiting for her to admit the truth to herself. "Which is?"

She threw her hands wide and then let them fall, to slap against her outer thighs. "I heard the stones, didn't I?"

"I think so, yes." I ran a toe through the grass, the accumulating dew painting a shine on my black boots.

"All right then, the trail's cold. There's nothing more we can discover about this missing fae."

"I agree." I'd suspected she hadn't called me here to pick up a scent trail. It had all been about the hallway and what it meant. I didn't blame her.

Mae nodded, as if she'd come to some sort of agreement with herself. "I'm ready. How do we find out?"

I pulled a deep breath through my nostrils, scrubbing my lungs with the crisp Ta'Vale night air. *Puh*. The breath popped past my lips, and I shook my head. There was no helping with what needed to be done.

"We go to the garden."

Mae gasped and knotted her hands together in front of her chest. She looked terrified and hopeful—a burrito of emotions.

Shit. I was hungry.

Untangling her hands, I pulled them into mine. Despite a near foot difference in our heights, Mae felt small, vulnerable. I held her hands and shook her arms. "Hey."

Her gaze rose to mine. One cheek ticked with the imitation of a smile.

"Don't worry."

She snorted, but the tension in her arms loosened, and she straightened.

Without another word, I threaded my fingers with my sister's, and together we walked toward the archway leading into the Eodrom palace.

Once we passed beneath the arch and entered the interior, we navigated the halls and turns to the courtyard quickly. From there, it was a short walk to a long hallway manned day and night by guards.

The burly guards saw Mae and nodded, recognizing her, but averted their eyes when their gazes landed on me. It was a step up from the escort out I would have received less than a year ago, before they labeled me a heroine for returning their precious sun stone, rather than monster for my hybrid state—the only hybrid fae in existence.

The cavernous hall lay empty. Our footsteps bounced off the walls. The silence gave way for the implications of the stone's acceptance of Mae to expand. My skin was too tight, my lungs too small, hearts too big for my chest. Would this make her a bigger target for Hielmal? The sun fae, now riddled with the same corruption as the banished moon fae, clearly still wanted the power she saw as hers by right. She'd been behind the theft of the sun stones, but Mae could be her conduit into the garden.

I fanned my hands over my arms. Goose bumps broke over my flesh despite my jacket. Despite the warm air produced by the multitude of sun shards embedded in the architecture of Eodrom.

Mae kept to her thoughts as we passed the reason for the guards—the keepers' private quarters, and then my father's labs. Though I suspected my father was still back home, I glanced inside the archway large enough to drive my Bronco through and open to the hall.

This was no small sterile cubbyhole, but a massive space filled with magic and books. So much magic emanated from there it clung like a second skin as soon as you entered. Growing up, I'd felt it on my father every day he returned from the labs. I felt it still, on Mae, when she came home from a day of spelling with our father.

Inside the room, numerous heavy wood desks hunkered at irregular intervals, each cluttered with papers, rocks, herbs, and tomes, some lying open, some stacked two, three, five high. Books climbed three stories of bookshelves built into all four walls, so high that much was only accessible by rolling ladders. The most forbidden works were kept under magicked lock and key at the very tops of the shelves.

My gaze rose to the cloud shaded with the colors of the universe—flashes of blue, white, yellow, pink, and everything in between—nestled in a fog of black that covered the forbidden books. Those books hadn't always been hidden. Hielmal taught my father a deadly lesson using spells in those tomes to kill many royals while almost accomplishing her goal of taking out the keepers.

I watched the intricate weave of the hall runner beneath my feet as we passed beyond my father's realm of magic, and we continued down the hall.

Somehow, Hielmal got three books out of my father's library. He never enlightened my sisters or me on what those books contained, but I knew they came from the forbidden collection.

My steps faltered, and I slapped a hand against the wall to steady myself. Understanding blasted me with physical force. Hielmal stole books of forbidden magic. Hielmal had the corruption. Bad things happened when fae attempted to blend magic that could not coexist. The Great Fae Divide, a war that ultimately led to the exile of the corrupt moon fae, was a direct result of moon fae playing with darker arts.

The one time we'd seen Hielmal, the dark, telltale veins scrolling across her face were proof of the corruption.

Mae put a hand on my arm, concern in her bright-blue eyes.

I shook my head and forced a smile. "Long day. I'm tired is all. Don't worry."

"Mmm." Mae's noncommittal hum told me she wasn't buying it.

We resumed our silent walk. Only the clomp of my booted feet on the narrow floor runner and soft slap of Mae's sandals on the creamy marble floors accompanied our journey.

Thank the stars she had enough on her mind to occupy her thoughts, because if I was right, those tomes were where that new deadly magic my sisters and I experienced firsthand when we came up against Hielmal and her cronies came from.

If she took that magic to the exiled moon fae...

How had this not occurred to anyone before? Then again, they probably had the thought but hadn't felt it necessary to inform my sisters and me during our investigation. Why should they? We were only the ones facing down the magic. I pushed a breath through my nostrils and rolled my eyes. As far as I'd known, they had buried Hielmal in the dungeon. Had she been locked up? Had she escaped? Who fucking knew? I sure didn't.

Midway down the hall, a second pair of station guards watched our approach. Their location marked the length where the sun garden began. As we neared the arch, I nudged Mae with my elbow. "This will be difficult to believe, but don't panic."

"That's a sure way to make me panic."

I laughed. "Sorry, I just meant this is going to be weird, but don't worry."

We passed the second pair of guards with the same nod to my sister and side-eye to me.

I stopped and strode back to the stone-faced guards—one sun fae, one wood fae.

"Have you seen any other fae while you've been on duty?"

The wood fae, barely taller than me, managed to look down her nose. Her pale-green eyes met mine, and despite her haughty look, she wasn't hostile. Perplexed, maybe. "This is a restricted hallway. Only the keepers and direct descendants permitted."

I glanced at Mae and back at the guard. "And Mae?"

"The Callaghans are permitted, by relation to the royal wizard," the golden-haired sun fae answered.

He offered me a smile and a cheeky wink, which completely freaked me out. I hustled away so fast, the breeze left by my wake lifted Mae's hair. Disdain and I were old friends. Acceptance, even camaraderie, not so much. It made me suspicious, and I kept shooting looks over my shoulder to make sure that fae wasn't tiptoeing up behind me to stab me in the back.

Mae caught up and slipped her arm through mine. Her airy laughter buoyed me. If it took my paranoia to pull my sister back from the edge, that was fine. I'd take my discomfort over hers any day.

Beyond the arch lay the stretch of hall adjoining the sun garden. The wall on our left changed from a creamy blond-and-gray marble to the faded white of old, bleached bone. Honeycomb pockets filled the strange rough stone, overcome with spearmint-shaded lichen and climbing vines. Flashes of color from iridescent birds diving in and out of pink, trumpet-shaped flowers hanging in heavy clusters on the vines.

"Did you have something you wanted to tell me?" Mae asked.

"What?" I pulled my arm from Mae's and smoothed the front of my jacket, my pants. "Why would you ask such a thing?"

She frowned. "Because you mentioned the tunnel the grounders were digging."

"Oh, right. That." I laughed a little hysterically and jammed my fidgeting hands into my jacket pockets. "I was, um, going to tell you about the tunnel I negotiated with them, but you already saw it."

Mae narrowed her eyes, but her steps stopped abruptly the same moment I heard the faint music.

I pressed my knuckles together in front of my chest and bowed my head, readying myself to explain to Mae what we were about to do. How could I explain the impossible? It'd probably be easiest to just show her.

Moonlight splashed into the hallway, and Iola stepped through the wall. My sister's breath hitched. I'd seen this before. Stars, I'd passed through the wall myself, but it was still astonishing to witness.

Iola glanced up and came to a stop, the skirts of her sky-blue robe swirling at her ankles. She looked first to me and then to my sister, the most flustered I'd ever seen from this supremely powerful woman.

Was it finding the two of us here unexpectedly or the secrets she kept throwing Iola off her game?

Iola recovered her mantle of serenity and smiled, wide and inviting. "Maerwen Callaghan, Malaney Callaghan, what a pleasant surprise."

No point in delaying this any longer. I hooked my thumbs in my belt loops and lifted my chin. "The sun stones are singing to Mae."

Iola went still and silent as a deep-water lake. And like deep water, something swam beneath the surface. A golden glow rose to her skin, getting brighter and brighter.

I shaded my eyes and turned away, facing Mae, who stared with unabashed awe at the woman considered queen of the fae. Not just sun fae—all fae. The light emanating from Iola reflected on Mae's flesh, her own glow that I'd only heard about but never seen, bloomed in response.

Good thing I hadn't had time to remove my protective contact lenses. Still, the twin living lamps were outpacing any protection my eye gear could provide.

A long exhalation eased from Iola. Her glow faded with her breath. I turned back as she took Mae's hands and drew my sister forward. Tears shone on her lashes. She laughed, a joyful musical note.

"Come, both of you." She sent a gentle smile in my direction, but when Iola looked at Mae, it was as if undiluted sunshine radiated from her expression. She was a vision of pure joy. "Maerwen, you must meet the stones. I believe they have something special planned for you."

I couldn't find it in me to move as I watched my sister walk away.

9

DROPPING NAMES AND FAKE OFFICIAL BUSINESS

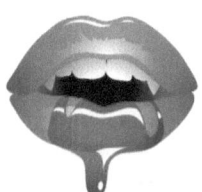

IOLA, TALL AND REGAL, LED MY SISTER THROUGH THE WALL. AS SHE WAS about to disappear, Mae turned a half-terrified, half-awestruck look back on me.

My hearts were crumbling into a million jagged pieces, but I poured all the love I had for her into a reassuring smile. Though she was my sister, my father's brilliant girl, my mom's ray of sunshine, she had first been an orphan. It labeled her abandoned in the eyes of the fae, which wasn't as bad as my impure hybrid DNA that resulted in muddled magic, but it still set her apart. Now that the sun stones chose her, she would belong.

I knew my studious sister. She'd be spending even more time at Eodrom, for her magic, and now also for the stones. This would mean so much to Mae, and even though the thought of potentially losing my sister nearly brought me to my knees, it also filled me with joy.

The warring emotions produced a thrumming ache deep inside my chest, beneath muscle, beneath bone. Down in my soul.

The garden swallowed my sister whole. With the wall once again solid and moonlight cut off, the hallway returned to shadows. Pale-blue light from the faint fae lanterns mounted on the wall opposite the garden lit the way, but just barely.

I tugged absently on my braid as I peered over my shoulder, down the length of hallway we'd traveled to get here. It was the shorter path to my way home, but it also took me back by those guards—the creepily friendly one. No, thank you.

Instead, I continued down the hall to the door Duskmere brought me through on my first trip to the gardens. I paused on the threshold to the courtyard. In the distance was the shadowy folds of the grove where the most recent fae disappeared.

The mass of trees bristled through a two-acre wide arch cut into the opposite side of the castle from where I stood. Though it stretched from the Drifta Mountains, through the Grian Valley, to the moon fae's Lann Ridge and beyond, there was never a question about an invasion coming from that direction. No army would dare march through that forest. That was dryad territory.

Most dryads were old, wild, and feral, able to whisper from one end of Ta'Vale to the other through their trees. Once upon a time, all fae communicated over long distances through dryads. Not anymore. Moon fae blew up that relationship when they undid the natural balance and corrupted their magic. They also torched a lot of trees. If they couldn't march through the forest, they could burn their way through.

Not all dryads were ancient and scary. A few had settled in Interlands and frequented Teddy's bar. I'd met them. They could hold their liquor and a grudge like it was their job. More than a hundred years later, and all it took was a few drinks before the Great Fae Divide always came up.

Scratching a talon over the pad of my thumb, I considered the state of Eodrom. Though I'd tossed out the idea of sun fae using Runach Forest as a way of returning to the stars, that theory didn't sit right with me. Beyond the dirty laundry and dish left behind in the sun fae's home Duskmere recruited me to investigate, dryads didn't kill trespassers unless they were the corrupted kind—that whole grudge thing. They might have the power to return a fae, body and essence, to stardust, but there was a whole petition thing that wouldn't—or shouldn't—have gone unnoticed.

It was more than just the forest situation. Between learning about the tunnels beneath Eodrom, the number of traitors among the sun fae ranks, the monstrous secret of Mae's mother, and the accelerated number of fae going missing, it felt like the building quiet before a storm. The type of storm that leveled the land.

I turned away from the grove to eye the arch cut into the wall on my left. My nemesis. With the state of my legs, that was a pretty accurate description. Unfortunately, if Great-Grandpa Blackthorne was to be believed, Dacian was still in the dungeon, where the spiral stairs beyond the arch led.

With the growing mountain of weird things going on in Eodrom, I had to see for myself if that was true. Which meant I needed a different jacket.

A group of fae passed by, whispering and staring. One dipped her head in acknowledgement. Ugh, no. I would never get used to this. The lack of animosity, the friendliness. I rubbed a hand across my neck. It was too much.

I'd thought I'd wanted acceptance from the beings who rejected me, nearly killed me, drove me from my childhood home, but it just creeped me out.

My shoulders jumped and shook with a shiver as I made a sharp right and headed for a staircase in the distance. It rose twenty floors, but fortunately, my destination was on the fifth.

I mounted the stairs, gripping the polished stone rail every few feet. There was no way around it. If I wanted access to the dungeons, I needed a very particular type of jacket. I'd used Duskmere's not that long ago, but I didn't know where his rooms were. However, I knew where one member of the Royal Fae Guard lived. I laughed under my breath. Boy, would she be excited to see me.

"Shit. Why all the stairs?" I complained after the third flight and stopped to massage my knuckles into my aching thighs. This was a blip in the climb I faced to reach my next destination—the dungeons. Good times.

After ascending two more flights, I exited the exterior staircase and entered the hallway. Most of the doors here had some sort of decoration: an etching, bundle of herbs, fresh flower wreath, but not the dark door that was my destination. It was plain and severe, just like the female who lived inside. Though she had a killer set of red fighting leathers. Or rather, I had a set of red fighting leathers. I never got around to giving them back. Some might call it stealing, I called it... Well, it probably was stealing, but they were mine now, and they made my ass look spectacular.

I banged my fist on the door, checking my talons while I waited. It had been months since they'd been filed, and they were a mess. I backed away from the door to stare down the hall at the balcony open to the night. She could be on duty, or she might be out on the town. What did fae do around here for fun?

It would be a lot easier if she wasn't home.

I raised my fist to knock again, but the door swung wide. A blood fae in a loose-fitting maroon tunic and pants set opened the door. Her black eyes landed on me. She hissed and slammed the door. Or tried to. I slapped my hand on the door to stop it midswing. A loud crack echoed into the hall, and my palm stung from the impact.

I resisted shaking the hundred sharp nips of pain from my hand and smiled. She bared her fangs, looking ferocious as fuck. I could respect that. Under different circumstances, we could have been friends.

"Hey, girl, how are you? It's been a minute. I was in a coma after the whole saving the sun stone thing." I gave a flippant wave of my hand and let my smile slide into a full-fledged grin. Good idea to remind her why it was in her best interest to play nice.

She kept her hand on the door, blocking my entry, and glared. If I didn't know better, I'd say she wanted to rip out my throat. Wait, I did know better, and she definitely wanted to do just that.

I tilted my head and twirled a loose piece of hair framing my face. "You and Duskmere an item yet?"

Her eye twitched.

The blood fae had a thing for that uptight prick, which he refused to acknowledge on account of being her superior. She was better off.

"Speaking of Duskmere, he's down at my parent's place and wanted me to swing by and ask if you would join him."

"Has there been an incident?" Her hand fell away from the door, and she stood at attention. "Why did he not notify me through the crystal?"

Why hadn't he notified her through the crystal? I could hear Mae's voice in my head. *This is what happens when you don't have a plan.*

"You know, I don't think I ever got your name?"

I waited.

She propped her hands on her hips.

I raised my brows in question.

"Prunettia."

"Prunettia?" I asked, unsure if I heard her correctly.

"Yes."

"Lovely name." Not at all. It was awful. Did her parents hate her? "Well, Pru, can I call you Pru?"

"No."

"Well, Pru, Duskmere forgot his communication crystal. Can you believe that?"

"No," she repeated, voice oozing her lack of belief. She drummed her well-manicured talons on her hips.

"Well, it happened. Silly male went over for dinner and probably didn't think he'd need it so close to the palace." I might have taken that a tad too far. Duskmere was a lot of things, but he wasn't silly, and he was always prepared. "Anyhow, he said my father had some sort of job and he wanted you to get right on it. Since I was heading in this direction, I offered to relay the message."

The unfortunately named Prunettia looked down at her attire and plucked at her billowing tunic.

"You look great. It's casual." I almost had her, but I needed to get her out before she took the piece of clothing I'd come for. "Listen, I owe you for helping me out with those clothes."

"Where is my sword?"

Whoops, forgot I still had her hardware, too. "This is better than all that. My mom baked her famous soffleberry pie. If you hurry, you can still snag a slice."

Pru licked her lips. I couldn't blame her. Mom's baking was a gift from the gods. My salivary glands were in overdrive just thinking about that pie.

"All right then, I'm off to meet Iola. Sun garden business." Dropping names and fake official business should snip any remaining threads of doubt. I gave her a finger wave and trotted toward the stairwell.

"Next time, bring my stuff," she shouted after me.

"Sure thing." Not gonna happen.

I hurried down the stairs, taking the steps two at a time until I reached the next floor down. I ran into the hall and ducked around the corner, close enough that I could hear when Pru left.

My only other option was to knock her out and take the jacket. A task that would have been difficult before my strength went on the fritz, what with her being a blood fae, and not the watered-down version like me. In other words, *she had to go*.

I breathed through my mouth, allowing the most oxygen I could pull in and out of my lungs to slow my stampeding pulse.

A young sun fae male walked by and slowed. Panic crawled over me as I watched him change his trajectory and head toward me.

"What?" I hissed. "Keep moving."

The sun fae visibly jerked away and hurried past me into the stairwell. Hopefully, if he ran into Pru, they wouldn't talk. At least, not about me. Maybe I should have handled that better? Maybe I should follow Mae's advice and be nicer.

Gross, no. I wasn't physically capable.

Soft, swift footsteps, light like a dancer's, or a fighter's, hurried down the stairwell. When I could no longer hear the swish of her loose, silky clothing, I peeked around the corner. The hallway was empty and so was the stairwell as I jogged up to Pru's floor.

Breaking into the home of a member of the RFG would probably land me in the dungeon if I got caught. I was trying to visit the dungeon, not move in. I had to get in, get the jacket, and be halfway to the dungeon before Pru realized I'd tricked her. With any luck, I'd be realms away, spending that luck at the roulette table before she figured out why.

Gaining access was a simple matter of utilizing my ragged talons. A quick insert in the lock, wiggle, and twist, and I was inside. I'd been here once before and knew where the closet was since I'd raided it. Legally, that time.

I hurried across the generously sized entrance with its intricate tile pattern. The dark-gray tiles merged seamlessly with the pale wood floors. A work den, formal dining room, kitchen with an informal eating area, and living space made up the center of the apartment. It struck me how much larger this home was to the missing fae's place I visited this afternoon. Paid to have that RFG prestige.

Two hallways split off from the main living area, one opposite the den, one farther in, next to the living area. That would take me to the master bedroom. I jogged toward the hall, glancing at the comfortably decorated living space with surprisingly feminine touches. Sofa, two chairs, oodles of throw pillows, jacket, two blankets—

I came to a sudden stop, slapping my hand against the wall to catch my balance, and whirled back toward the room. A dark-brown leather jacket lay over the arm of the sofa. It couldn't be that easy.

My gaze snagged on the crest stamped on the front of the jacket. A silver moon intersecting a gold sun with a tree rising in front of both—the RFG insignia. Huh, it was just that easy.

I shrugged out of my jacket, turned Pru's jacket inside out, and slid it on.

No one would look close enough to notice the strange fashion choice, but they would notice me wearing the RFG Insignia.

On my way out the door, I stopped to help myself to the fae version of a protein bar—a soft, round cake made of molded oats, berries, seeds, and honey. I considered leaving sweet Prunettia a note, thanking her for her generosity. Fun as that would be, there was a chance she wouldn't immediately notice the missing jacket. She might write off me sending her after Duskmere as a twisted joke, but if she knew I broke into her apartment, she would look.

A fae had to be pretty sharp to be a member of the RFG. I wasn't sure how long I had before Pru realized what I'd done.

Adrenaline hummed through my system and buzzed in my ears. I thundered down the stairs, retraced my steps back across the courtyard, through the arch, and was over halfway down the spiral stairs to the dungeon before the adrenaline fled and all my aches and pains kicked in.

"Ow, ow, ow." I dug my fingers into my cramping sides and bent over. "Son of a toe-stomping troll, I need to have a talk with whoever doesn't believe in elevators around here."

Mechanical elevators wouldn't work, same as most of Earth technology, but that didn't mean the palace engineers couldn't whip up some magical woo-woo system. Maybe I'd drop a note in the suggestion box on my way out. If there wasn't a suggestion box, I'd drop that off too.

I descended what amounted to at least one thousand stone steps on this spiral stairwell to the Eodrom dungeons. Legs burning and wobbling like overstretched elastic bands, I rounded the last curve. With a faint musical hum, a row of marble-sized globes of pale fae lights blinked on in response to what I assumed was the magical identification sewn into the shoulders of the RFG jacket.

My feet finally met the dungeon floor with a soft hiss of sifting black grains of sand and gravel. Not far away, the arch leading into the dungeon glowed red. The light meant anyone without the magic RFG shoulder pads could not pass. *Thank you, Prunettia.*

I took a step closer, gripped the front of the jacket to pull the sides together, but stopped mere feet from the arch. I'd seen Pru enter the dungeon once. That was how we met, but she was on the job. What if she didn't have the authority to come and go as she pleased? I had no idea what could happen. Would it simply stop me, or would it guillotine me in half?

That was what Duskmere warned his portals would do if I didn't get through fast enough.

Still clutching the zippered front of my jacket, I pulled my hands close to my chest and inched forward. The scent of hot metal and something sharp and clean, like chlorine, grew stronger the closer I got to the arch. A bit of tension eased from my neck. Druids, specifically Blackthorne, provided the magic used to coat each cell with an invisible barrier. Elastic-like, but impenetrable. If this was the same magic keeping prisoners behind the bars, I'd be safe.

Pulling my lip beneath a fang, I stretched out my arm and let my finger hover a mere hairsbreadth from where the barrier should be.

Screw it. Either I lost a fingertip, or I got inside. I rocked forward but stopped before I took a step.

"Nope." I curled my index finger and extended my pinkie. I could afford to lose a pinkie. Losing an index finger could prove difficult in my line of work, what with all the stabbing and punching.

I sucked in a fortifying breath, stepped up to the arch, and...a soft click sounded, and the light over the arch turned green.

"Huh." I took a step back, and the light went red, wiggled one shoulder closer, and it switched to green. Shoulder away, red. Shoulder closer, green. "Proximity, cool."

Ninety-five percent certain I wasn't about to be crispy-fried or cut in half, I marched beneath the arch and started searching cell to cell. For all the space, there were no occupants. This place must have been built to house the war criminals before their banishment to Shadwe. Not only was it a waste of space, it was about as secure as Swiss cheese.

Cirron claimed not to have been responsible for all the released prisoners, but he had freed Nyle—the absolute worst of the prisoners. That meant there were still traitors. I wasn't buying Duskmere's claim to have weeded them all out. I believed he thought that was true, which was why I needed to confirm Dacian's continued dungeon residency for myself.

Another row of fae lights running down the central corridor came to life with another soft chime of music, bathing the hall in an eerie blue glow. I passed cell after empty cell, my steps slowing as I approached the cell Duskmere tossed me into less than a year ago. Oh, how times had changed.

I tugged the collar of Pru's jacket. Maybe things weren't that different. If I didn't get out of here and back to Vegas soon, I might find myself behind bars once again. The RFG sort of frowned on my solo visits to prisoners. Weird, considering I was the only one putting them away these days, and I didn't even work for these assholes.

Come to think of it, I should have my own insignia. I'd bring that up next time I saw Duskmere. He was going to love the idea.

I stopped in front of the cell Duskmere had once pushed me into through a portal. It was the only location in Ta'Vale, aside from my father's garden, where a portal could exist. The small square room was empty, with no clue how Blackthorne had escaped.

The cell next to it was a different story. I lost the ability to close my mouth as I stared into the adjacent cell. The RFG must have moved Blackthorne a whole cell over, and it was obvious how he escaped.

A massive tree had sprouted in the center of the cell. The back wall and a portion of the roof were gone. Twisting tree limbs reached up and out. How had no one noticed the top of a tree poking out of the ground? Shock ran hot and cold through my veins.

This was my fault.

Shame ran hard on the heels of shock. The tips of my ears blistered with heat. The seedpod. Blackthorne did this, and it was my fault.

I backed away, dragged my hands over my head, and threaded my fingers behind my neck. My talons pricked my flesh, bringing swift clarity. No, I would not take on this guilt. Blackthorne escaped, but he had given me the information I needed to save my sister. The same information that brought one of the sun stones home and landed Dacian in a cell.

A shrill whistle grated against my eardrums.

My muscles pulled taut in response while my hearts tripped into a gallop. I dropped into a crouch and surveyed my surroundings.

Inside the cell across the hall, Dacian emerged from the shadows.

10

TUG-OF-WAR GAME OF TAUNTS

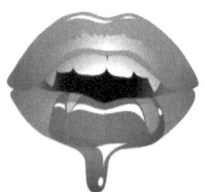

I PUSHED DOWN THE INSTINCTUAL PANIC THAT SPRANG TO THE SURFACE and stood, hoping Dacian couldn't hear my thundering hearts. Rolling my tight shoulders, I let my lips slip into the crooked, taunting smile I'd practiced in front of the mirror a thousand times. Wasn't my best look, but at least top ten.

Dacian chuckled, and I clenched my fists against my thighs. Not the response I'd been going for.

"If it isn't my brother's little female." Dacian's torn clothes hung off his tall, narrow frame. He was filthy and reeked, but none of that dimmed the red-light danger sirens firing off in my head. His gaze scraped from my toes to my face as he approached the bars.

"Enjoying your accommodations?" I propped my hands on my hips and winked.

Dacian rested a hand against the invisible barrier woven between the bars. It bulged beyond the bars, giving slightly beneath his weight like magic memory foam. "I see you didn't die, but I wouldn't expect the black wolf's choice to be a weak thing."

"You've got that backward." I pressed a talon against Dacian's palm, pricking his flesh, and the heady aroma of lemon and lavender trickled my nostrils. Thanks to my borrowed—*stolen*—insignia, I could reach into the cell, but he couldn't reach through the barrier. This was fun. "I chose Teddy.

I need someone who can at least give me a run for my money at arm wrestling."

Right now Teddy would take all my money. My hybrid nature watered my blended abilities down, but strength was one blood fae power I'd always had in spades. These days, not so much, and I had no idea what was up with that.

"Care to test me?" Dacian leered.

"Homicidal megalomaniacs aren't really my thing. Besides, I'd win. Remember when I pulled you out of the sky and you ended up here? I kept the scale." I pressed a hand to the armor-like evidence mounted on a chain beneath my shirt. A gift my sisters had made for me while I'd lain in a coma. They were so thoughtful. My focus shifted to Dacian's abdomen, where I'd ripped the scale from. "How does that work? Do you have a bald spot? A scar?"

He bared his teeth. Oh, I made the big bad wyvern angry.

"I nearly killed Aventheo, or did you forget that?" he snapped.

A surge of fury and fear, all tangled together, ripped through me at the memory. I shifted on my feet, the reaction catching me by surprise.

Pulling a deep breath through my nose, I fought to disguise the fact that his words hit the mark. I tugged my waist-length braid over my shoulder and waved the tufted end at him. "I'm pretty certain Teddy would have torn you to pieces if you hadn't shot him in the back."

I'd thought I'd moved past this, and I had. While I was awake, anyway. Teddy survived with only a scar, but vivid nightmares forced me to continue to relive his near death. At least once a week, I'd watch him fall to his knees. The blood would spread across his chest like a malignant stain, but the endings changed. In some versions, Teddy would shift into some dark beast and attack me. In others, Dacian, in wyvern form, would eat him whole. My brain was twisted.

"I am not stupid." Dacian laughed and moved away from the bars, just out of easy reach—proving he was, in fact, not stupid—and crossed his arms over his chest. "I know what the black wolf is. Do you?"

"Duh." I rolled my eyes.

In an animalistic gesture, he leaned forward, bending at the waist, and *smelled* me from groin level to throat. One long inhale.

Shock sent my spine straight as a steel rod. What. Was. That?

"I smell him. You're mated." His voice was guttural.

If he could smell this morning's sex, I needed stronger soap.

"We live together. Of course you smell him." I rolled my shoulders and forced my posture to relax. My jacket, the one I'd replaced with Pru's all-access jacket, slid from the crook of my elbow and landed in the gravel. I nudged it out of the way with my toe.

He turned his head to the side. "You still don't know what he is."

"Everyone knows what Teddy is. *Who* Teddy is."

"No, I really do not think you do." His low laughter slithered over my skin. He held his arms wide and stepped back from the bars, once again out of reach. "You know where to find me when you figure it out."

His retreat had a magnetic force, pulling me forward until my chest pressed against metal and my fingers circled the bars. I swallowed the sour taste in my mouth. "What is that supposed to mean?"

"The black wolf is not a thing to be tamed. Oh, it wants to be, but it can't. It will eventually chafe and kill you, unless my brother does the noble thing and lets you go first."

"Spoken out of jealousy." I leaned in until the druid magic that created the invisible barrier bit my cheeks with tiny electric teeth. "I know you want what Teddy threw away. Too bad your mommy and daddy don't see you fit to succeed them. Or do they just not like you?"

This tug-of-war game of taunts drew Dacian a step closer. I didn't retreat. From the shadows still holding onto him, his eyes flashed orange, reflecting the dim fae lights. Tapetum lucidum made sense. Improved night vision for hunting from the skies. One thing we had in common—the improved night vision. Though, I suspected his was much better, especially these days.

Dacian's nostrils quivered, and his teeth flashed in a failed attempt at a smile. That last remark really pissed him off. Point for me.

Pleased with those parting words, and satisfied at finding Dacian still locked up, I slid my hands from the bars and gave him my back as I walked away.

"I would not wish the black wolf on anyone, even my brother. I would put him down and have our world ruled without that threat pressing a boot heel to their necks."

Ghostly fingers tickled my scalp, pulling goose bumps onto my flesh. I stopped walking and angled my head to the side, giving Dacian my profile, but didn't speak. He meant to get my attention, and damn it, he had. I knew Teddy was this black wolf. I knew it was something to be feared, and I knew only one was born every few generations to rule, and Teddy had walked away. But that was all I knew.

"The black wolf is an apex predator. Once it shifts and consumes the entire identity, it will kill indiscriminately. So it chooses a mate, driven by instinct to find its other half, who can tame the beast, as they say." His teeth flashed in the darkness. "It hasn't worked yet, but it will never stop trying."

It? Was he saying it wasn't Teddy that wanted me, but whatever he was? *No!* I gasped a stuttering breath, coming back to my senses. Teddy, with his exquisite kisses and annoying worry about breaking me, wanted me. Maybe this black wolf did too, and that was okay. I smirked. If it meant losing the choke hold Teddy had on his control, like this morning, I might even like it.

"I'll be sure they don't let you rot down here," I said. "Dying is too good for you. A nice, century-long death is what you deserve."

"See you soon," Dacian said, all weird and happy.

Six short months in this hole, and he'd already lost his mind.

A noise from the end of the hall snapped my attention away from Teddy's brother. My muscles tightened on my bones like shrink-wrap. A light bobbed in the distance. Someone who couldn't see in the dark was making the rounds. That meant it wasn't Pru, but it didn't mean she hadn't figured out what I'd done and tattled.

Please let it be there. I shoved a hand in my jacket and felt around in the right pocket. Nothing. I checked the left. Nothing. Shit!

My shoulders hitched, remembering *I wasn't wearing my fucking jacket.*

I'd brought it with me, but... Gravel sprayed, and my feet slipped as I spun and raced for Dacian's cell. I grabbed my jacket from the ground and glanced down the hall to the right. The bobbing lantern was closer and rapidly moving this way. My hearts tried to eject themselves through my ribs. Whoever that was, they weren't wasting any time. Another few minutes and they'd be on top of me. Would I get better accommodations than Dacian?

I scrambled across to the cell Blackthorne ruined. My feet slid awkwardly on the shifting gravel. Arms flailing for balance, I almost dropped the jacket.

Yanking the door open, I dug through my jacket pockets and hurried toward the center of the cell. With my heightened sense of danger, the outline of the tree breaking through the back wall stood out stark and bright.

No portal stone. *Hurry, hurry, hurry.* I shoved my hand into the other pocket and searched for the small cold marble. It wasn't there either.

Fuck!

It looked like I'd be spending a lot of time here. I might as well get comfortable. Maybe they'd let me pick my cell? I walked to the back wall and patted the rough bark of the tree. Yep, real. I slumped against the trunk to await my fate.

Dusky pink light from the approaching fae lantern leaked across the dark floor outside the cell, still faint, but growing steadily. A few more minutes.

In the bobbing light of the lantern, something small and solid flashed from a divot in the bed of gravel no bigger than grains of sand. The portal stone. It must have fallen out when I'd flailed for balance.

I shoved away from the tree and sprinted for the stone. Duskmere and his unhealthy belief in the infallibility of the RFG, along with his dogged determination to keep me on a need-to-know basis, even when I needed to fucking know, got me into this situation. It was only fair his portal stone got me out.

Pulse throbbing against my eardrums, all sound but my breath muffled, I ran into the hall and grabbed the stone. Light from the lantern swung in my direction, and someone shouted.

Gotta go.

Moon fae portal stones were finicky. They were one time use, so I had to be careful. If it hit the ground too hard when it fell out of my pocket, it would have counted as a failed attempt. I rolled the small orb between my fingers, feeling its surface for the telltale crack that would determine my fate.

I rolled it round and round and nothing. Smooth as glass. For once, Fate hadn't tried to screw me over.

My knees wobbled beneath a wave of relief as I stumbled the last few steps to the center of the cell. The shouting grew louder. Though I remained calm, my hand shook as I squeezed my fist to activate the stone.

Heat bloomed against my palm. It worked.

Gravel hissed very close by. It pinged the cell bars.

I threw the stone at the back wall so hard, muscles spasmed and pinched in my neck. My right shoulder lifted in reaction to the pain.

The portal stone bounced to the floor on the far side of the cell. Time held its breath and then ripped apart as a disk darker than the shadows opened above where the stone fell. The black film melted away to reveal Blackthorne's rooftop garden—*my* rooftop garden.

"Stop!" a rich female voice demanded.

I wouldn't be doing that.

Heavy breathing sounded behind me. Lantern light rocked wildly on the walls.

They were right there, closer to me than I was to the portal. I threw myself at my means of escape as fingers grazed my back.

But they didn't grab me.

They pushed.

11

YOU SAY ALL THE RIGHT THINGS

Grass went up my nose, aromatic, sweet, and scratchy as a flea-bitten cu-sithe. I pushed to my hands and knees, spitting green bits as I crawled forward, away from the portal and potential amputation at the ankles. With a loud clap, the tear in space slammed closed behind me.

Feet firmly on this side of the portal, I flipped over and lay in the quiet garden. It was that precious time of day when there was no traffic, no tourists, no anything. Pastel-painted pink, yellow, and orange fingers reached from the horizon into the Las Vegas sky. I rubbed a hand on my chest and took my first easy breath since deciding to pay the dungeon a visit.

Good news: Chances were, if I hadn't seen whoever forcefully helped me through the portal, they didn't get a good look at me, either. It was dark as the Marrowghan Swamps in that dungeon, and they only got an eyeful of my best side—my backside.

The more I thought about it, maybe I'd been mistaken. Maybe they'd tried to grab me and in the dark, and they'd miscalculated. Any other alternative made no sense. As the saying went, *the obvious answer is usually the correct answer*.

Even better news, Dacian remained locked up. Unlikely as it seemed, Duskmere could have been right, and they had eradicated all the traitors. Unless I counted myself—which I didn't—since Blackthorne walked out thanks to me. The old druid would have eventually broken out on his own. There was solace knowing I'd only made the process easier.

Footsteps reverberated on the spiral stairs. A steady pace my hearts recognized, slowed, and synced with. My lids slid shut. I smiled, eyelashes tickling my cheeks. A light, effervescent feeling infused me, but a shadow hung in the proverbial distance.

Dacian. Fuck that guy.

He'd infected me with his words, his warnings. I curled my fingers into the grass, its blades bending against my palm.

Teddy's footsteps whooshed across the lawn to my side. He lowered himself to lie next to me. His hip touched mine, and his warmth melted into my side. We lay there together, comfortable in the quiet.

He took my hand in his and pressed it to his lips.

I opened my eyes and watched clouds pull across the sky like cotton stretched thin.

"Whatcha doing up here?" he asked, easy, light, as if not wanting to scare me away.

"How'd you find me?" I avoided the question, not yet ready to talk about the things Dacian said.

"Security camera." He lifted my hand and pointed at a small black object hidden in a tree.

I sat up and narrowed my eyes on the camera. "Where'd that come from?"

"It's been there," Teddy said. "By the way, Vaughn caught me in the lobby and asked me to deliver a bag to you containing what looks to be pieces of a cell phone."

"So much for that shatterproof case. I want a refund."

Teddy's laughter wrapped itself around me like a security blanket. "I could be wrong, but I'm fairly certain throwing the phone off a high-rise is not covered."

Scandalized, I gasped. "What makes you think I threw the phone?"

Teddy rolled onto his side, propping himself up on his elbow. "Security camera."

Heat prickled my scalp, raced down my neck, and blossomed across my chest. Stupid tattletale complexion. "They can watch us downstairs?"

"Only outdoors. Apparently," Teddy drawled, with way more humor than the situation called for, "Blackthorne had the cameras installed after you hijacked his druid circle."

I groaned. Of course, it would be my fault.

"There is a channel on the television, and you can monitor the feed from inside. That's how I saw you appear." His hand whispered over my cheek, tucking hair behind my ear. "You used a moon fae portal, not your father's device. I assume that means you visited the dungeon?"

Humor evaporated from his tone. What he was really asking was, did I see his brother? Teddy knew as well as I did where the only place in Ta'Vale it was possible to generate a moon fae portal was.

Moisture gathered between our hands. Stupid sweaty palms. I slid my hand free and wiped it on my stomach. "The RFG are still keeping secrets. They knew Blackthorne escaped and didn't warn me. They know—" I bit down on the words, stopping short of telling him about Mae. She deserved to know first. Next time I saw her, I'd pull on my big girl panties and tell her the truth. "They know a lot more than they are sharing, even though Duskmere agreed to my demand for transparency."

"The Royal Fae Guard, or any entity that stands between their people and chaos, is not designed for transparency."

I peeled my focus from the clouds to Teddy's face and scowled. "It's almost like you're taking their side."

He held up a hand, palm out. "I agree they should have told you about Blackthorne, but unless it relates directly to you, I understand them keeping their cards close to their chest."

"Someone's been spending too much time at the poker table." He wasn't wrong, but even if they didn't share the news about Hielmal with me, they damn sure should have told Mae.

A smile slipped across Teddy's perfectly proportioned lips. Not too thick, not too thin, and the right size dip in the center. "I've only been there to retrieve Y'sindra after security called to complain. She froze a deck of cards after losing too many blackjack hands."

I bolted upright. "Come again? How did I not know about this?"

"Happened last week when you asked me to bring over that load of boxes. Vaughn called up to the penthouse, more than a little frantic." Teddy plucked a piece of grass and spun it between his fingers. "Your sister is scary."

"Yeah, she is." Y'sindra was a bomb blizzard condensed into a three-foot-tall package, and I loved her with all my hard little hearts. "Hopefully, she didn't hurt anyone. We're not getting fined, are we?"

"I'll cover it if you do." Teddy drew up a knee and hung an elbow over his leg. "I know when you are avoiding a subject, Lane. What happened with Dacian? What aren't you telling me?"

This conversation made me so uncomfortable, I didn't even have the energy to argue about his high-handed offer to cover our fines. I licked my lips and turned away from his penetrating gaze. Why did my chest hurt? Maybe it was a heart attack. I had two hearts. I'd survive.

"Lane..." Teddy prompted.

I shook my head. "Nothing."

Teddy remained silent, and that was louder than anything he could say.

"He told me about your black wolf." I flipped my braid over my shoulder and absently ran a hand down the length, reached the end, and started over. "His version. I know it's a lie."

"Tell me anyhow."

"Do I have to?"

"Please."

That sneaky bastard had to say please. I let loose an aggrieved sigh. "Fine. He said we had sex so you could keep yourself from shifting. Ridiculous, right?"

I hoped.

Teddy's brows drew together. "Those were his words?"

"Yes. Well, no. He said something about us being mated." I laughed, a forced, brittle sound. "Said you claimed me. How could he smell that? Does he have a super sniffer, or do we need better soap?"

"Neither." Teddy pushed to his feet and ran a hand through his hair.

Even as I sat beneath the rising desert sun, I felt the absence of Teddy's body heat. Pressure crushed my lungs. Oh gods, I couldn't breathe. I stood and backpedaled from Teddy, arms crossed over my chest—protective, futile. This wasn't the sort of pain I had any hope of shielding myself from. "He said you would kill me if you didn't do the right thing and leave me first," I whispered, but he heard me.

Teddy's gaze slammed into me. His features warred with emotion: anger, hurt, fear.

I wanted to hold him, soothe him, but I couldn't move. "Tell me he was lying."

He didn't say anything. Not a gods damned word.

My toes curled inside my boots and fists clenched as an inferno of anger swept through me. Even my fangs elongated, slow and steady. With a little coaching from Vaughn, I'd been practicing control. I hadn't punctured anything in over two months. My pride hurt, but my lip did not.

"You won't hurt me, Teddy." I splayed my fingers wide, forcing my hands to relax. "If you're leaving, do it now. Just go."

Teddy shook his head and stalked toward me.

Chin up, I held my ground. This might very well break me, but he would never know.

He stopped close enough his woodsy, vanilla scent caressed my senses, but he kept his hands to himself. Probably didn't want to lose them. That would be an inconvenient handicap for a bartender.

"Lane." Teddy breathed my name like it was life. "Dacian wasn't lying, but he wasn't telling the truth."

"I didn't realize there was a third option."

Teddy dragged a rough hand through his hair once again, ducking his head. "I thought I had time to explain everything, but then things happened so fast in Outerlands."

I stilled. "Are you blaming me?"

"Absolutely." He laughed. "Did you really believe I didn't want you?"

"Sure felt that way."

He groaned and closed the distance between us, folding me in his arms. I didn't break away, but I didn't melt into him.

"I want you every minute of the day." His voice went guttural, low and rough. The sound oozed pure sex across my nervous system. He leaned back, putting space between us, but gripped my arms as he looked down at me with such intensity, my knees almost buckled. "The feel of you, your scent, the taste of you on my tongue—it's all I can think about when you aren't near."

Pressure popped inside my chest. I went liquid and molten in my core, and I squeezed my thighs together. "You say all the right things."

"And I mean every word." Teddy's pupils dilated, and I thought I caught a flash of red. His nostrils flared. Could he smell my arousal?

I licked my lips, and his gaze followed my tongue. He bent and took my earlobe into his mouth, sucked and nipped. His hot breath fanned my neck, making all the fine hairs stand on end. My skin tightened and squirmed in the most delicious way. Holy stars, the things this male did to me.

"We're as good as mated, Lane. You're mine. I wanted you, but so did the black wolf." He rested his chin on my head, and my blood cooled just a fraction. "I wanted you to have a full appreciation of what you were getting yourself into. To give you the choice, but I was a coward. I never found the right time to explain, and once we had sex, there was no going back, not for me. The black wolf claimed you. That's what Dacian could scent."

"Not lying, but not telling the truth," I murmured. Any lusty thoughts still circling my brain were flushed.

Teddy nodded. His chin pulled hair loose from my braid with the motion. "My brother told the truth, but he didn't fill in the blanks. Dacian let you believe the worst, but he might honestly believe those same things. He grew up on stories, tales of former black wolves."

"All right, I'll bite." I gripped the belt loops at his hips. "What stories?"

His chest ballooned against me, forcing me tighter against him until he released the breath. "You know how Y'sindra became an orphan?"

This conversation just took a hard left.

Frowning, I stepped back to meet his gaze. "Of course. Barbaric, but common practice. Young snow fairies are tested. If they can't generate winter magic, their tribe leaders send them on a pilgrimage." I rolled my eyes. "Everyone knows they're being sent out to die. No snow fairy could survive off the mountain without winter magic. Y'sindra would be dead if my father hadn't found her and coached her."

Teddy nodded. "A late bloomer and look how powerful she is now."

"Right?"

"Still, fairies are as long-lived as any fae, yet they reach childbearing age young and can produce multiple offspring." Teddy searched my eyes.

"Okay, I'm with you." Where was this going? He had to know that none of this information was new to me. I'd lived with Y'sindra and her pent-up but rightful resentment all my life.

"Other fae—sun, moon, blood—they are not fertile until at least the age of one hundred. Even then, the gestation is long, and the ability for more than one offspring in a century is impossible, except in the rare case of twins."

My brows climbed my forehead. "You, sir, know an uncomfortable amount about fae reproduction."

Teddy snorted. "I know a lot about population control."

"That's...strange, but okay." I tilted my head, still unsure what any of this had to do with the black wolf.

"That is what the black wolf is, the Shadwenian mechanism of population control." His jaw flexed.

I opened my mouth, but all that came out was some sort of breathy squeak as the implications of his words sank in. "You can't mean..."

He nodded slowly. His throat worked as he swallowed, but he didn't break eye contact. "It's exactly what I mean. The black wolf is born to cull the population. Indiscriminate and brutal. If he or she has not taken a mate, it is up to the royal family to hunt and kill the beast once the job is done."

A chill crept over me, and I fanned my hands down my arms. "And if they have taken a mate?"

His pupils flared. A thin ring of red pulsed around his irises. This felt like a challenge. He was testing the wrong girl. I curled my talons into my palms but didn't back down, didn't run. I leaned in.

And the implication of his words flattened me.

The black wolf's mate ended the rampage.

Oh no. Nuh-uh. Absolutely not. "Don't look at me. I'd let you bleed Shadwe dry before I hurt you." Even if I was physically capable, he was nuts if he thought I would try to end him.

Teddy's pupils returned to normal, and any trace of red disappeared. He smiled and pulled me into his arms. I resisted nuzzling his shirt.

"Honestly, I'm not even certain what would have happened had I remained."

"What does that mean?" I brushed what looked to be flour from Teddy's chest. When he began staying longer and longer at my house, until he officially moved in, I was delighted to learn my sugar muffin loved to bake.

Oh, good nickname. I'd been trying new ones out but had yet to find one that fit.

"Molasses cookies." A crooked smile curved his lips as he pinched the hem of his shirt and shook off the remaining flour. "To answer your question, the length of time from one black wolf to another was growing greater and greater. Before me, there had not been a black wolf for many generations. Everyone was certain the beast was no more. Nature had taken control, and it was no longer necessary."

My legs were aching from all this standing around and this morning's activities. I shifted my weight, low-key stretching. "Why would they think that?"

Teddy shrugged. "Evolution."

"What does that have to do with anything?"

"Races of Shadwe evolved." He trailed the rough pads of his fingers across my cheek to push windblown strands of hair from my face. "Fertility has gone down, and the years before conception can be reached has gone up. Nature has balanced, and the black wolf is no longer needed."

"More offspring, but a long wait." It made sense. "Maybe you were born for a different purpose?"

"All that matters is that I can control the black wolf. You make things easier. You calm him." Laughter worked its way into his voice. "He is especially happy after the bar."

I smiled, but then Teddy's phrasing scratched at the back of my brain, and I squeezed my eyes shut. "You say *he,* as if your black wolf is a separate entity." My previous fear that his beast chose me and Teddy had no say swooped in to swallow me down its dark gullet. I tensed inside Teddy's embrace.

"Yes and no."

"That clears everything up." Needing to see those eyes that could not lie, I put a hand on his chest and pushed him back, searching his warm gaze.

"The black wolf's instincts push me, but it's still all me, sweet fangs."

I looked at my talons, running one over the pad of my thumb and then another. "So you aren't with me because you have to be?"

Teddy barked a laugh and shoved his hands through his hair. He clasped his fingers behind his neck and tilted his face toward the sky. "Is that what this is all about?"

"I resent that." A blush burned onto my cheeks, and I gave him a light push. He stumbled back, grinning like a fool. "Don't laugh at me. It's a legitimate fear."

"No." Teddy drew me into his arms. He crouched and ran his hands down my back, over my butt, until he gripped my thighs and lifted. "It is not."

Even as I glared, I hooked my ankles behind his back. Only because I didn't want to fall, of course. Same reason I looped my arms around his neck.

"I won't lie to you and say part of my attraction is not driven by the black wolf, because it is." His dark gaze drilled into mine.

The raw truth locked an industrial vise around my rib cage and applied pressure. "But...?" Please, for the love of all the forsaken gods, let there be a but.

"But I would have walked away, left Interlands and you behind, if my heart wasn't in agreement." Easing me to the ground, he drew my arm from his neck and pressed my palm to his chest. I felt the unmistakable thud. "On you, the black wolf and I are in harmony."

This was the closest either of us had come to defining whatever this was between us as love, and somehow, these words meant more. I fell toward him. Trapped in his orbit. The sun to my Earth.

"From now until the end, I am yours." Teddy trailed his hands down my arms to rest at my waist. The cloyingly sweet, earthy, malty scent of molasses rose from his shirt, from his skin, and brushed against my senses.

For what could be the very first time in my life, consuming cookies wasn't my priority.

Teddy leaned in. Anticipation locked a breath in my throat as our mouths met. My chest shook. I exhaled and then drew in his sugary essence. He filled my lungs. Teddy worked my lips, savoring them with slow, exquisite torture.

He broke our kiss.

This was bullshit. "I might kill you here and now."

Smiling ten shades of seductive, he stroked his thumbs down my jaw and tunneled his fingers into my hair. Those nimble fingers pulled the tie from the end and shook loose my braid until my hair fell heavy down my back.

"Last chance, Lane." He gripped my hip with one hand and held me at literally arm's length.

"What chance?" Was this some sort of weird kink, because whatever it was, I did not like it. Patience and me? We were not friends.

"If you ever want to get rid of me, this is your chance. I won't offer again."

"Would you shut up and kiss me already, you big idiot?"

Teddy laughed and pulled me to him, his slow kiss growing hard. I gripped the hem of his shirt and pushed up before he could change his mind, but I was too short and couldn't reach over his head.

As impatient as me—thank the gods—he yanked the shirt from my grip and drew it over his head.

I shook off my borrowed jacket and took hold of my shirt, but froze at the sight of his gloriously naked torso. His abs tightened and flexed with his ragged breaths. The breadth of his wide chest expanded and contracted. I licked my lips, and he groaned. Behind his denim, he thickened, and I nearly drooled.

"Is that a whisk in your pocket, or are you just—"

"Lane..." Teddy's warning growl was strangled. He didn't take off my shirt. He ripped it. Right down the center.

Mouth hanging open, I blinked up at him. He wagged his brows, still laughing, even as he branded me with another mind-shattering kiss.

I sank into him, molding my body to his. The thickness of him pressed against my stomach. I reached between us, fumbling with the button of his jeans. This time, the button came loose. I pulled down the zipper, eager to hold his solid, silky length in my palm, to work him until he shouted my name for every tourist on the Strip to hear.

Cotton brushed the backs of my fingers, and my gaze fell. "What the hell? Boxers?"

"I realized I needed to be better prepared for you after this morning." Teddy's grin was full of wicked intentions as he lowered me onto the grass.

I grabbed for his boxers, but he slapped my hands. "Patience."

"You've got to be..." My words broke off on a strangled squeak.

Teddy knelt between my legs and nuzzled my throat, biting lightly, and kissed his way to my chest. His fingers trailed an electric sensation over my ribs and around to my back, where he unhooked my bra with more mastery than I liked. He could have fumbled once or twice.

Sitting back on his heels, he filled his hands with my breasts. "You're so beautiful." His words ached, and he descended to draw circles around my nipple with his tongue before taking the tight peak into his hot mouth.

I arched, my palms going back to support my weight, talons tunneling into the soil. Moisture flooded my panties, and I squeezed his hovering hips with my knees. If I could just pull him a little closer.

He didn't linger long but drew a path with his tongue to my belly button, where he took hold of my jeans and underwear. Crawling backward, he slid them down my legs, pulled off my boots, and the clothes followed.

Teddy's gaze traveled up my body, a near physical touch. He paused at my throbbing center. I squirmed and tried to squeeze my legs together, his look so incredibly, uncomfortably erotic. At this rate, I'd come apart before he touched me.

"No, you don't." Teddy bent forward and grasped my thighs, spreading my legs wider.

Red flared in his eyes as he gazed at the spot I desperately wanted him to bury himself. Holy stars, if that didn't make me hornier.

"Teddy..." I warned.

He lowered his face until his warm breath brushed over my sensitive lady parts. "My fierce little monster is so impatient."

There it was again—the growl. I fucking growled.

His chest rumbled with laughter against my thighs. "Shh. Just lie back and let me worship you."

"But..." My brain seized as the rough stubble on Teddy's cheek brushed the uppermost section of my inner thigh. Warmth from his natural body heat loosened my muscles, and my knees dipped toward the ground on either side of him.

He lingered over my inner thigh, his breath hot on my skin, and then he kissed me.

"Teddy," I warned again, because at the pace he was moving, I could go nuclear.

Laughter tickled my flesh before he bit me. A light nip that sent my back arching and head driving into the grass.

"Oh, gods."

"No gods here," Teddy crooned as he slowly pushed a finger inside me. "You're already wet."

I raised my head to meet his dark eyes staring up at me from between my legs. Liquid heat unfurled in my belly. "Can we skip this and get to the main event?" The breathy, husky quality of my voice undercut the demand in my words.

"Now?" He drew his finger out and then plunged back inside, brushing his thumb over my clit. "Are you sure?"

My back arched. My chest felt tight and hot and light all at once. "Yes," I panted. "You, I want you."

Body rigid, I thought he might refuse. Then, like a wild animal released from a cage, he surged to his feet. Those cursed button-fly jeans came off with only slightly more care than I would have taken.

The thought slipped into the void when his boxer briefs followed his pants and his length sprang free. I licked my lips, remembering the feel of his cock, like velvet on steel. He lowered himself to sit cross-legged between my legs.

"So beautiful," he said as he bent forward and slid his calloused palms up my legs, trailing his thumbs along the insides.

Teddy stopped at my thighs and squeezed.

"I thought we were done with the foreplay," I said.

Gripping my legs, he pulled until my hips rested on his lap and the smooth head of his cock brushed against me. His breathing quickened, and he reached down to guide himself to my entrance.

"You're so perfect," Teddy said, and the deep melty quality of his voice made my insides quiver.

Or maybe it was the broad head of him filling my entrance. All of me focused on that single sensation. I wanted more, could already feel an orgasm building, and he wasn't even inside me.

Teddy bent over me, pushing inside another inch, and tunneled his hands beneath my back. Pulling me up, chest to chest, he slid fully inside me. We'd only come together once, and he still stretched me, filled me. I'd never known anything to feel so right.

Face pressed against me, he nuzzled my breasts and traced a tongue around my nipple. The combination of heat from his tongue and cold of wet bared flesh left behind was maddening. He sucked my nipple into his mouth, and I moved on his lap.

"Fuck," he said, voice strangled.

My inner muscles clenched in response, and he groaned.

"If you aren't still, I won't last." He rested his hands on my hips, holding me to him.

"I don't want you to." I moved my legs until my feet touched behind him. The friction against my clit arrowed a wild sensation to my core. The feeling pulsed, wanting, elusive. It was something right there, just out of my grasp. I needed it, chased it, pressed my heels into him, driving him deeper.

Breath hissing, he cupped my ass and slid me up his length. I whimpered at the sudden emptiness, but he lowered me onto his cock. Up, down, he pulled me up and lowered me again and again with excruciating slowness.

This wasn't our frenzied first union, but something deeper. I couldn't tell where my essence ended and Teddy's began. It was more than just sex. *Mate*, I thought. Not yet, but he could be. I could see it.

The labored cadence of our breaths mingled. I took over the rhythm.

Pulled the spiral building, building, building inside me tighter. It was *right there*.

My head fell back. I gripped his shoulder, moving faster. The heat from the friction grew, the burn ecstasy. My pace grew. "Teddy," I pleaded, unsure what I was pleading for.

Teddy knew and slipped a hand between us. He found the spot sure to make me come undone, pressed, and rotated his thumb. I bucked into his hand and came down hard on top of him. He rubbed his thumb once more, and I exploded with a shout.

Light flashed beneath my lids as Teddy squeezed me tight to his chest. He slammed himself into me until he crashed over the edge seconds later.

He fell onto his back, pulling me down on top of him. I felt my inner muscles pulsing against his still semirigid cock, and damn if I wasn't ready to go again.

A snore rumbled from Teddy.

12

TICK. TICK. TICK. BOOM!

PREPARED FOR WAR, STANDING IN FRONT OF THE DRUID CIRCLE, I SHOOK out my damp hair and braided the thick mass. Even after a shower, the smell of molasses and gingerbread billowed from the strands, and I smiled at the delicious memories of how those scents got there.

Following our romp on the rooftop—for which I was certain the security got a good show—Teddy woke from his sex-induced nap and remembered his cookies. They were bricks by the time we got to the kitchen and rescued them from the oven, but together, we mixed a new batch of gingerbread.

Turned out, baking could be erotic. All that mixing and tasting. Who knew?

We threw a batch in the oven, and then Teddy bent me over the counter. We went for round two. I dragged my sugar muffins to the sofa and rode him hard for round three. With Teddy lying behind me on the sofa, he'd pulled my leg over his, and there was eventually a groggy, sort of disgustingly sweet round four before we finally fell into sleep. I wouldn't walk right for weeks.

A sappy smile tugged at my lips, and ooey-gooey satisfaction pooled low in my belly. I scuffed a toe against the druid stone in front of me, laughing beneath my breath as I thought about the fire alarm that woke us when the gingerbread burned so hard it went up in flames. We had no cookies, but I wasn't complaining. Teddy spent the day finally giving me what I'd craved for months.

Glaring at the druid circle, I cracked my neck and rolled my shoulders. Time to show this stupid hunk of rock who was boss.

Two rolls of duct tape, and an entire bottle of Gorilla Glue later, I slunk back into the penthouse. Fucking Blackthorne.

This time, the intoxicating scent of chocolate wrapped itself around me the moment I stepped inside. Teddy's back was to me as he slid a cake pan into the oven. His shoulder muscles flexed beneath the thin white T-shirt he wore as he positioned the pan on the rack and closed the door. When he turned in my direction and caught me watching, the corner of his mouth hitched in a smile.

Silly male didn't have a clue how much his domestic habit drove up the barometer on his already sky-high sexy factor. Slowly, I savored every inch of him. My gaze traveled from his oven mitts to his *Don't Bite The Cook* apron with the bright-red X crossed through the word *Don't*. Not very subtle, my Teddy.

He tossed the mitts onto the counter. The apron followed. He grabbed a bowl and left the kitchen.

We met in the middle of the great room. Teddy ran a finger through the glossy white icing in the bowl and held the offering for me. I took his finger in my mouth, circling it with my tongue, and dragged back.

Watching me, his eyes fell to half-mast, while inside his pants, he rose. The rapidly thickening evidence pressing against my belly clued me into his condition. For once, my attempt at sexy didn't go the way of pain, gas, constipation, humor... I didn't do sexy well.

Teddy's focus dipped to his pants and then back to me. "This shouldn't be possible."

I rubbed against him, enjoying the tortured groan the friction elicited from him. "You shouldn't have held out for so long."

"Twenty minutes on the cookies. This time, I set the timer."

"We only need three. Five at most." I dropped the empty rolls of duct tape and bottle of glue, unsnapped my pants, and made the most of the next twenty minutes. It turned out round five took a while.

Cocooned inside my fuzzy blanket, I nestled on the sofa, half asleep, sore as hell—worth it—relishing the sounds and smells of Teddy in the kitchen. A soft ding came from the foyer. The elevator. Shit, someone was home. I was completely naked, and the whole place smelled of burned baked goods and sex.

I threw off the blanket and rushed to open the sliding glass door, picking up shed articles of clothing as I went. Where the hell was my bra? The elevator doors slid on their tracks as I wiggled into my shirt. I'd find the bra later.

"Ted-D!" Lo said with so much excitement, you'd think they didn't see each other every single day. He still couldn't pronounce Teddy without turning the latter half into a surname, but at least he'd broken the habit of using the term master.

Lo was roughly the same size as my sister, and the top of his head barely reached past the counters. His mop of brown curls bounced toward Teddy, who bent to give Lo a fist bump. Something Lo only learned how to do this year, thanks to my sister, and he was now obsessed with the gesture.

Coming in behind Lo, Y'sindra hopped onto the sofa, climbed onto the back, and slung her legs over to face me and the kitchen. "It stinks of sex and sugar in here. You two making up for the last six months? Frigg knows you've had some serious lady blue balls."

I scowled, but also discreetly turned away to sniff. The open door hadn't helped air anything out. "I don't know what you're talking about."

"I'm talking about the show you gave the security department downstairs." She stood on the back of the sofa and humped the air.

My cheeks burst into flames, burning a path across my pale complexion all the way to the tips of my petite, pointy ears. "I'm destroying that camera."

"Nah." She waved a hand, teetered, losing her balance, and plopped down on her butt. "Let 'em have their fun. Maybe it'll get that uptight vampire to lighten up. Aren't they supposed to be all blood and sex?"

I shrugged and sat on the arm of the sofa next to my sister. In the kitchen, Lo and Teddy were engaged in animated conversation. Watching the pair, I smiled and then turned to catch the naked expression of adoration on Y'sindra's face. She had it hard, but I wasn't one to judge. I cleared my throat. "How was patrol?"

"How was the sex?" She gave me the slow wink. "Is it true what they say? Once you go mate, you conjugate?"

"What does that even..." My thoughts came to a screeching halt. "Mate? What? How'd you know?"

Y'sindra beamed. "Didn't he tell you?"

"Just today. How did *you* know?"

"Duh, Lo." She pursed her lips. "I'm not sure we're talking about the same thing. What'd he say?"

"What do you think he said?"

She swung her legs back around to stand on the seat cushion, facing me. "Lane, do you know how shifters know they've found their mate?"

"Shifters? I thought this was about the black wolf."

"Huh," was all my sister said, and then she hopped off the sofa and trotted toward the kitchen.

Coward. She knew I couldn't just let this go. "Wait up." I caught up just as Y'sindra pulled herself onto a stool at the big island.

She swiveled to face me. "Remind me, Lane. When did Mom switch your medicine? You know, to Teddy's blood?"

Because my hybrid state had also made me allergic to blood—the one thing a blood fae needed to enhance their abilities—my mom had been mixing a medicine concoction of mystery herbs and blood for much of my life. I'd only recently learned the mixture that finally did the trick was made from Teddy's blood.

"Whoa, what?" I narrowed my eyes. "A little over three years ago, I guess. Right after that piece of trash I was there to warn off abusing his wife pulled a gun on me, and the universe decided it was my day to take a bullet. Two bullets. I'm afraid to ask, but why?"

Y'sindra gave Teddy a pointed look, who did an impressive good job of ignoring my sister.

"Shifters exchange blood when they want to mate, Miss Lane." Lo beamed, completely missing the moment every ounce of said blood in my body drained to my toes. "They wound themselves and exchange blood. If it heals the injury, they are a match. To complete the mating bond..."

Lo kept talking, but I didn't hear another word. My gaze flew to Teddy, who calmly continued to smooth buttercream along the sides of his cake. The only hint of his stress was the inch-too-thick frosting. He just kept slapping it on and avoiding the conversation.

"Teddy..." I left his name hanging in the chocolate-scented air.

"Hmm?" He slapped on another scoop of buttercream and got to smoothing.

Snippets of past conversations, which meant nothing at the time, now landed like a concrete block. When Teddy declared himself after I'd refused to be another lovestruck bar groupie. He'd told me then he'd wanted me, only me, and he hadn't been with another woman in over three years. When his bartender, Zee, thought we'd hooked up and was disappointed when she found out we hadn't. She'd told me then Teddy had nothing to do with the ladies, and she'd been hoping I broke his dry spell. My own mother's reaction—or lack thereof—when I told her who I was interested in. Son of a bitch, *she'd known.*

Aside from the smooth strokes of Teddy's spatula and a low buzz and crackle in my ears, the kitchen had gone quiet.

"Teddy," I said again. This time I didn't so much as let his name hang as slam it down on the counter.

His hand stilled, and his gaze rose to mine.

"When, Teddy?" I could barely unclench my teeth to form a full sentence. "When did you know about us?"

He sighed and leaned his weight onto his knuckles. A glob of icing dropped onto the counter from the spatula curled in his grip. "When your mother came to me for more blood."

The microwave dinged. I jumped, only then smelling the popcorn. Y'sindra used a step stool to reach the microwave and pull out the bag. She opened it, and a plume of steam emitted as she returned to her stool and climbed up.

"Seriously?" I shook my head at her.

She shrugged and dug a half-popped kernel out of the bag. "Ouch." Y'sindra tossed it from hand to hand. "Hot, hot, hot."

"Serves you right." I shot her a smug look. She deserved every buttery burn.

I peeled my gaze from my unrepentant sister. Teddy hadn't resumed his stress-icing, but watched me warily, as if I might explode. I tapped my talons on the granite countertop. Tick, tick, tick.

Boom.

A question did, in fact, explode in my brain. "But you haven't had my blood. How do you know if we're...you know?"

"Lane, I swear when your mother asked for my blood, I didn't think anything of it. She explained she was testing a medical blood replacement for you. What were the odds? But she came back for more. You'd had my blood, and it worked." He shook his head and huffed an unamused laugh through his nose. "Imagine my surprise when I realized the quick-to-temper, foul-mouthed female always taking up a seat at my bar and running her shady business could be my mate."

"You forgot to mention my ass. The female with the out-of-this-world ass."

"How could I forget?" Chuckling, the tension coiling in Teddy's muscles eased.

"No idea. I mean, it's right here." I gave him my profile and wiggled said ass. Slowly I eased around to face him and stared into his ridiculously handsome face. "So we're...mated?"

"No, I told you before. I wanted you to have a choice, and I meant it. I would never take your blood without your consent." Teddy pleaded with his big puppy-dog eyes for me to understand, and stars take me, I did.

Well, that was that. The ball—or bond—was in my court. I nodded and turned away, dropping the subject. Standing on my toes, I leaned onto the counter, snatched the popcorn bag from Y'sindra, and shoveled a handful into my mouth. I didn't realize how hungry I was. Then again, when was I not hungry?

"Hey!" Y'sindra objected, but grumbling, hopped down from her stool, grabbed another bag from the cabinet, and threw it into the microwave.

As I chewed, I glanced across the counter at Teddy, who still watched me.

"We're good?" he asked, slow and tentative, as if testing a minefield.

"We're good." Honestly, I could be an asshole, but what kind of asshole would I be to not appreciate the lengths my honey cheeks went to in order to ensure Fate did not trap me? I'd always thought that bitch hated me, but being bound to Teddy felt like she'd done me a favor. I should send a fruit basket. Maybe chocolates.

"And Dacian?" he pressed.

"I get it. He was trying to drive a wedge. Or he just didn't know better." The aching pit in the general vicinity of my hearts Dacian's words had left me with was gone. I shrugged and tossed another kernel into my mouth. Missed, and tried again. Damn it, missed again. Third time was the charm. "You didn't sugarcoat anything—except the cake. I believe you."

The microwave dinged, and Y'sindra took out her second bag. She waved it at the cake as she passed, returning to her seat. "Seriously, big guy. I love my sugar, but that thing is at least fifty percent frosting."

Teddy looked down and laughed. "So it is."

"Now that we got your new sex tape and the mate stuff out of the way, you want to know why we're really here?" Y'sindra offered the popcorn to Lo, who took a single piece and nibbled while Y'sindra shoved a handful into her mouth.

"Because you live here?" I ventured a guess.

"No. Because of what we found on patrol." Y'sindra pointed at me. "But I still live here. Don't you throw out my stuff."

"Hard to tell these days. You're gone more often than you're home."

She huffed, her poof of white hair quivering.

"Okay, fine." I rolled my eyes with great enthusiasm. "What did you find?"

"We found..." She paused, going for drama. "The sun stones."

Drama, achieved.

13

NOTHING LOOKED BACK

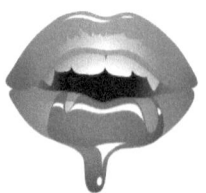

In less than an hour, the cake had disappeared, and we'd hatched a plan to sneak into Shadwe the next night. Teddy assured me it would be okay, but worry had turned the pounds of sugar I'd consumed into simmering battery acid in my gut. There was a chance it was just indigestion.

Y'sindra and Lo took off for another reconnaissance trip while I left to collect Mae with Teddy in tow for moral support. Not to mention physical support. Gods, did my body ache. I was fairly certain the couch and cowboy style were the moment my legs decided they were done.

The ponderous lump of sugar playing chicken with my gag reflex cranked up the heat when I crossed through yet another of my father's portals and stepped into my parents' yard. I was really burning through those babies today. The devices, not the sugar, but that too. Who knew I had a sugar limit?

As Teddy followed and walked past me, I yanked the second half of the portal device to me. My grip tightened on the disk, and I turned it over in my hand. Mae was probably inside telling our parents the news about her new relationship with the sun stones. Trepidation clawed at my chest. It was time for her to learn the truth all of them were keeping from her.

I wasn't ready to do this. I should have practiced on Teddy. It wasn't like he would have treated my sister differently. Chances were, he'd never even heard of Hielmal. Why would he? She was from an entirely different world.

"Did you let them know we were coming?" Teddy walked toward me.

Reminded of where we were and the ultimate purpose of collecting Mae and getting out, I shook my head. "No, I didn't think I needed to."

Teddy returned from the house and stopped in front of me. He rubbed his hands on my arms. "Well, they aren't here. The house is dark."

"What?" I peered in the direction of the house. "Maybe they're just sleeping." Except they always left the hearth burning during the cooler weather if they were home.

"I knocked." Teddy shrugged, the flannel lifting and falling with the rise of his wide shoulders. "Nobody answered. It's your home, too. We can wait inside."

That sugar lump treated my stomach like a trampoline, rejecting the idea that any piece of Ta'Vale might be mine. I glanced into the distance and remembered a loose end I still needed to tie up. Teddy wasn't Mae, but I didn't really need her for this, just a second body.

Sliding my arms around Teddy, I rested my chin against his chest and looked up at him. "Game to lend me a hand?"

"Can't do that, sweet fangs. I'm going to need a month to recover from today."

"That's not what I meant." I gave him a saucy grin. But yeah, a month sounded right. "I have something I need to check out, and it's a two-person job. You willing to help?"

"If the clothes are staying on, count me in." He leaned down for a quick kiss, but I wrapped my arms around his neck and turned it long and slow, sugar bomb forgotten.

The kiss eased to a breathy stop. I asked, "But you enjoyed the clothes off, right?"

"Immensely." He nipped my lower lip, tugging it as he straightened away from me. "So what are we doing?"

I looked at the ground, dragging my toe back and forth in the grass. "Remember the grounders?"

"I do, but I'm worried for your memory, considering you leased your home to them." The corner of Teddy's mouth tilted in a smirk. "Unless you hate that house, because then I understand."

"Why would you say that? They paid a hefty deposit and are well aware of the consequences... You know what? Never mind, that isn't the point."

"Mmm hmm." Teddy's smirk grew into a full-fledged grin.

I stomped my foot. Yes, I was an adult having a tantrum. "Well, laugh at this. Those psychotic gerbils dug tunnels—here." I stabbed a finger in the vague direction of Eodrom. "Etta'wy hired them. The moon fae whose head I collected paid them. Do you think those tunnels might be worth checking out?"

He pinched my chin, and I bared my fangs. "You're adorable when you're angry, but yeah, we should check these tunnels out."

"Humph." Annoyed but mollified, I glanced in the direction of my folk's house as I tugged at the hem of my jacket. "All right, let's do it. Maybe everyone will be home by the time we finish. It's a long walk."

With a warm, caramel-coated chuckle, Teddy turned and gave me his back. "I can take the hint. Hop on."

I wasted no time climbing up, wincing at the raw soreness that hurt-so-good between my thighs, and pointed in the general direction we needed to go. "Once we reach the Neamchloite River, we'll follow it until we reach a particular landmark they gave me."

With his arms hooked beneath my legs, I played jockey and gave his hips a little kick. "Giddyup."

And he did. My hair blew back, tearing from the braid. The wind dried the tears it pulled from my eyes. Some sort of bug went down my throat. I forgot how fast he was. I buried my face in Teddy's neck and held on for dear life.

"Two times tree." I snorted and slowly retraced my steps back to the river to start all over again. According to the grounder I'd negotiated with for this information, the entrance to the tunnels was somewhere between the river bend and the "two times tree."

What in the name of all the Flaming Cheetos was a two times tree?

Three trips back and forth, and still nothing. The tapetum lucidum reflected visible light through my retinas and granted me better-than-average night vision, which allowed me to see each fallen leaf on the ground, but not a tunnel, and nothing resembling the obscure landmark reference.

"I swear if that little Smurf turd was lying, I will go back and shave—" I yelped as my foot pushed through a thin layer of grass and kept going.

Scrambling for something to grab on to, I threw myself forward and dug my talons into the soil.

Teddy raced from the tree he'd been holding up, watching me make a fool of myself, and caught me before I dropped below my hips into the gaping hole that opened beneath my feet.

"Shit, that was close." I caught sight of the tree Teddy had been leaning against as he set me down. Lightning had clearly struck the thing. Its thick, scarred trunk was blackened and split about six feet from the ground to grow into two separate crooked trunks. "I think I found it."

"You almost found a broken leg," Teddy said.

"I wouldn't have broken a leg."

"Do you know how deep the hole is?"

"Touché." I hated when I was wrong. "You could have told me you found the tree."

"But you were getting so angry. It was adorable," Teddy said, completely unrepentant.

For once, I took the high road and let it go, instead focusing on the task at hand. I knelt in the grass and crawled toward the hole, grass stains gathering on my denim. Since the sun fae came back into my life, my limited wardrobe was considerably less. I peered inside the hole I'd made, plunging through the web of overgrown grass. As far as I could tell, nothing looked back, so that was a good start.

A scent hit my nostrils. Not very strong, but pungent—sharp, sour, and rotten. Of course I'd smell *him* here. Nyle, the corrupted moon fae I'd decapitated. Once I smelled blood, I never forgot the scent, and I smelled it now. Faded, old, but there was no doubt this was the path he'd taken on his exit from Eodrom.

"This is it, but I can't see a thing. Too bad I dropped my phone from the balcony. I might not be able to make calls here, but maybe the flashlight feature would still function." Batteries worked in Ta'Vale, but did lithium batteries?

"I thought you threw the phone?"

"Details."

Shaking his head, Teddy took his phone from his back pocket and tried the flashlight feature. "Doesn't work."

"Figures." Wishful and regretful thinking wouldn't get me safely into this hole. I sat back on my heels and began peeling aside the overgrown patch of grass. Relatively new growth, it pulled apart like a spiderweb.

Once cleared, the entrance wasn't as claustrophobically tight as it first appeared. It was wide enough to fit someone Teddy's size, but an ogre like Rip wouldn't be getting out this way. At least, not easily.

I narrowed my eyes at the dark hole. Grounders were little more than hamsters on radioactive steroids. How tall could these tunnels be? I was so not down with crawling all the way back to Eodrom. Filth aside, my knees would for sure quit before I made it halfway there.

"Well, you ran us all the way here. Guess we need to find out where this goes. Lower me down?"

"You think it's smart for you to go first?"

I got close enough to ensure Teddy could see the massive eye roll I gave him for maximum appreciation. My eye rolls were some of the best. "Do you think the big bad dirt monster is down there waiting for me? According to you, you're the biggest threat around here."

"Touché." Teddy echoed my earlier concession and gestured toward the hole. "After you."

Gripping me under my shoulders, he knelt and lowered me into the darkness. My legs dangled. There was nothing beneath my toes. Worry crept along my spine. Had the grounders dug straight down? It would make sense to prevent anyone—like me—from going inside. A ladder left on the tunnel floor could easily be kicked away when someone climbed out.

If I dropped and hurt myself, or worse, actually broke a leg, I'd never hear the end of it.

"Anything yet?" Teddy asked.

I gritted my teeth and flailed my feet, searching for any purchase. Even the wall would do. "Not yet. You need to get me lower. Bring me up, and then lower me by my hands."

"Maybe I should—"

"Of the two of us, who can see better in the dark?" I angled my face upward, arched a brow. "Just get me lower. I got this."

Teddy growled his displeasure but did as I suggested—though I suppose it was less suggestion and more of an order. My sugar buns had the patience of a saint dealing with me.

"By the way, I probably have better night vision than you," Teddy informed me as he dangled me in front of him.

"You've got to be—"

"Down you go," Teddy said with entirely too much satisfaction.

We locked gazes, and he laughed while I attempted to shoot daggers with my glare. Nope, still didn't have that ability. Nor was he intimidated, judging by the air kiss he blew me as I disappeared into the tunnel entrance—at least what I hoped was an entrance and not just a sinkhole or the aforementioned dirt monster's lair. You never knew in the land of the fae. It could be a thing.

The ride down was bumpy as Teddy bent and then knelt to get me even lower. He leaned over the entrance, blotting out what little moonlight leaked through the hole above my head.

"Anything?" he asked, not sounding like suspending me inside an open hole for an extended period was putting any stress on his muscles.

I couldn't say the same for my shoulder joints. "Not yet. Come on, put your back into it. I know you're good at that. Get me lower." If I didn't feel the ground soon, we'd have to try the stone tossing method of determining—

My toes brushed something solid, and I nearly whooped with triumph. Considering I hung suspended in darkness, I decided now might not be the best time for that. While I didn't actually believe there was anything down here with me, no need to ring the dinner bell.

"Hang on, I feel something. Just another inch or so." I pointed my toes, barely touching what I was now certain to be solid ground.

Teddy lowered me at an excruciating snail-like pace.

My toes touched down, and then my feet flattened at an angle. "Okay, stop. Give me a sec to get out of the way."

I extended my arm, feeling for the wall as my eyes adjusted to the full dark, and started down what turned out to be a smooth dirt ramp.

"Clear, come on down. Just be ready to land on a ramp."

While I waited, I studied my surroundings. The ramp led to a wide and tall open space. Teddy could stand in here with room to spare. The roof sloped toward two tunnels across the way, branching off in different directions. Teddy could probably manage the tunnel's height without hitting his head, but it would be close.

Teddy walked up behind me, resting his warm, broad hands on my shoulders.

"There's two tunnels." I took Teddy's hand and led him to flat ground. "Rock, paper, scissors for who takes which?"

"How about you go right, I go left?" he offered.

"What if I want left?"

Even in the pale moonlight, I could see his teeth when he grinned. "By all means, you go left."

"I'll go right." I was nothing if not difficult. I rose up on my toes as Teddy leaned down for a quick kiss. "Meet back here when we're done?"

"See you then. If we hurry, we can be done and back at your parent's place before sunrise." With that, he jogged into the left tunnel, his retreating figure rapidly swallowed by the darkness.

He had to be a show-off. I'd be lucky to speed-limp wherever this led and be back before lunch. As I headed into the tunnel, I had a late realization. If this led into Eodrom, as I suspected, we could have just met at my parents' house instead of walking the length of the tunnel and meeting at the entrance. I sighed. *Woulda, shoulda, coulda.*

Then again, I was certain one of these tunnels led to the dungeon. I might have rolled craps with this decision, and then where would I be? Facing a ten-mile climb to the courtyard. Maybe not ten miles, but right now, a climb was a challenge I dared not face.

Lemon and lavender hit me full in the face less than a second before a battering ram collided with my midsection and slammed me against the tunnel wall.

I shouted and tried to dig my talons into the dirt wall as I my head bounced backward. A momentary image of Dacian's twisted face swam across my pulsing vision. My hearts hammered against my breastbone, the thumping beat of my pulse filling my ears.

How could he be out? I'd just seen him—taunted him.

See you soon. He knew someone was on their way to let him out.

Teddy would hear. He'd... He wouldn't do a thing. Teddy was long gone.

I was in big fucking trouble.

Teddy's brother backed out of reach. I dropped to my knees, boneless, and fell forward. My face met more hard-packed dirt. It filled my nostrils, scraped my cheek. The second bouncing impact of my head sent my vision into vertigo. Squiggly lines and bursts of white light were crystal clear.

I had one advantage—we were underground. Dacian was tall, taller than Teddy. He wouldn't be able to maneuver easily. For once, my height could work in my favor. Give me an even playing field. Taking advantage of the brief lull in Dacian's attack and my semiclear head, I pulled my knees to my chest, leveraged the ground beneath my back, and kicked forward.

"Oof!" He grunted and stumbled from my kick, delivered with more power than I'd expected. Adrenaline was a beautiful thing. I launched myself at Dacian with a banshee's scream.

He recovered, caught his balance, and knocked me to the side. But not before my talons met flesh. I hit the wall again but landed in a crouch. Warm wetness coated my fingers.

Lemon and lavender doused my senses, vibrant and bright. His blood dripped from my talons. A flush of satisfaction burned through me, even as my brain performed the cha-cha from that third blow. I breathed through my mouth and fought for focus. The side-to-side rocking steadied in my head, and I pushed upright. I had to play this smart, wait for my opening.

Dacian had backed out of reach, spitting curses and wiping at his face and neck. His gaze shot in my direction.

I tensed, ready to meet his attack, and... He laughed?

Of all the reactions, this was the last thing I expected. Who did he think he was? Who did he think *I* was? I'd show him.

Growling, my shoulders bunched, quads tightened, as I prepared to leap.

"I told you we'd meet again." In a retina-searing flash of light, scales covered Dacian's skin. He didn't shift into a wyvern, but somewhere in between.

My stomach bottomed out. Son of a rotten cheese curd. Of course this was when I'd learn about this shifter ability. Teddy could have clued me in. I had no blades on me. I knew better than to leave the house without hardware. Heat raced up my neck, tingled across my scalp. A chill clutched my spine.

I panted, panic tearing through me. I'd barely escaped our last encounter alive.

But we were underground.

He couldn't shift, not completely.

I'd ripped one scale off with my talons. I could take a few more.

Almost as quickly as the panic played havoc with my system, I quashed the reaction, rolled the tension from my shoulders. "Round two?"

Without waiting for an answer, because that would be stupid, I launched myself at Dacian. My shoulder slammed into his chest, and he hit the wall. Another puff of dirt dusted the air from the impact. He grunted. We twisted, fighting for the upper hand, and went down.

I landed on top. Using the weapons attached to my fingers, I went for his throat and wedged a claw beneath the overlapping scales. The edge came away from his flesh. I would end this guy. No one would miss him. Teddy would thank me. Maybe I'd get a medal.

Blood turned my fingers slick. The scale made a terrible Velcro ripping sound. He roared and clamped his hands down on my wrist before I could drive my talons into the exposed flesh.

He tore me away from his throat and held me aloft against the tunnel wall. More dirt fogged the hall and filled my esophagus. Coughing, lungs burning, I kicked and twisted. I might as well have been throwing pillows for all the difference my kicks made.

Dacian held both of my wrists in one large hand and unfolded to his full height. His head brushed against the roof, knocking loose dirt into my eyes.

I dangled, helpless. I couldn't break his hold. My knuckles scraped the tunnel's ceiling as he lifted his arm above his head. Furious tears pressed against the back of my eyeballs. I'd noticed my decreased strength, but I hadn't known it was this bad. Or had, and I'd ignored it. Gods, if I'd only listened to Teddy, if I'd drank his blood.

Dacian's strength, on the other hand, hadn't suffered from his incarceration. He tightened his fingers. My wrist bones ground beneath his sure grip. I gritted my teeth against the pain pulsing down my arm.

He lowered me until we were face-to-face and leaned close, his rancid breath rolling across my skin. My stomach heaved. If I vomited on him, he might lose his grip, but I'd lose my pride.

Fangs punching down, they caught my lip. I snapped at his smug face. He got out of the way before I could remove a piece of him.

The slap that cracked against my cheek sent an explosion of white lights cartwheeling across my vision. Before I could gather my wits, he leaned in until his nose brushed my flesh, rustled my hair, and *smelled* me. It was the same animalistic gesture as he'd done in the dungeon, only this was much closer, much more intimate. He drew in one long inhale up my side, along my neck, to the crown of my matted hair. My stomach rolled.

"I knew I smelled him in the dungeon. You are mated." His voice was guttural. He lowered his head, and with the moonlight coming from behind me, I could easily see into the shine of his pale eyes. "Did he tell you before he took your blood?"

"Shows how much you know." I shook off the creepy discomfort and sneered, blood dribbling down my chin from the fang puncture in my lip. I lashed out with a kick, but he rolled his hips, easily dodging my foot. "He didn't take my blood."

"He let the black wolf claim you, but didn't complete the binding?" Dacian chuckled, low and insidious. "Dangerous for you, more dangerous for him. I could taste your blood right now, see if you could be mine, take you from my brother."

Dragging a finger over my blood-wet chin, he sucked it into his mouth.

The gesture shocked me to stillness. Feet dangling, I hung limp from his grip and met his laughing gaze.

He pulled me close. "Shall we feed you mine and find out?"

Idiot. I rocked forward and smashed my forehead into his nose.

Dacian howled and dropped me. He staggered, hand covering his busted nose.

Not giving him a chance to recover, I leapt. Fingers curled into hooks, ready to remove his larynx.

His arm arced to counter my assault. The thunder from the back of his hand meeting my cheek was deafening. Pain shot through me, blinding.

My trajectory shifted midflight. I spun in the air and hit the wall. Breath whooshed out of me. Limp, I dropped to the ground.

I panted. What little vision I had grew fuzzy.

Crouching in front of me, Dacian's form wavered in my narrow line of sight. He stroked my cheek, his touch gentle.

Nothing would satisfy me more in this life than to work up the energy to bite off his fingers, but I couldn't. Too damn weak. Tears of frustration came at last. They burned a path across the bridge of my nose, over my temple, to gather in the hair spread beneath my cheek.

He dragged his fingers across his still bleeding throat. Before I could register his intent, Dacian swiped his bloodied hand over my mouth. I pressed my lips together, resisting the instinct to lick them clean, but the sharp taste of lemon still hit my tongue.

"This is a kindness I am doing for you. My brother will probably leave you when he smells what I have done." Dacian bent close to whisper in my ear. "If he doesn't kill you first."

I strained, willing my arms to move, wanting to sink my fangs into his throat, tear, slurp, *kill.*

No! Not slurp. He took my blood, wanted to bind us. There was some already on my tongue, but I didn't feel any different.

Darkness unfolded over my eyes, and as my vision narrowed to pinpoints, Dacian stood. Absurdly, I noticed his bare feet as they sped him toward freedom.

14

KIND OF KINKY

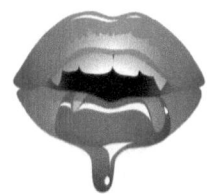

"Come on, Lane. Wake up!"

The vibrating timbre of Teddy's worried voice came to me through a tunnel. Oh, right, a tunnel. My sugar muffin's brother knocked me the fuck out in a literal tunnel.

I groaned and fought the grit trying to glue my eyes together.

Peeling my lids apart, I tried to focus on Teddy.

"How—" My throat seized, and I licked my dry lips with a sandpaper tongue. Unsurprisingly, the gesture imparted zero moisture, but the faint remnants of lemon and lavender hit my tongue. I rolled my head to the side and spat the little moisture I could scrape together from my mouth. I hadn't swallowed it, mostly because I hadn't been able to absorb much of anything from my lips.

What was it about getting knocked out that made me feel as if I'd been sucking on cotton? Raw, scratchy, moisture-wicking cotton.

"Take it easy, sweetheart." Teddy sat on the ground, my shoulders in his lap, head cradled to his chest. He gently brushed the hair from my face.

"Like sweet fangs better." I chuckled. Big mistake. A coughing fit took possession of my body that hurt worse than a direct blast of sun to my raw throat.

"Does anything feel broken?" Teddy asked.

I shook my head, wincing at the pull in my neck. The next time I got ahold of Dacian, I'd remove more than just a scale.

"Let's get you out of here. We'll find Meghan and let her check you out."

As Teddy eased me away from him and stood me up, I angled a look at the tunnel entrance that seemed both too close for the ambush I fell into, and impossibly far away.

"How long has it been?"

"Long enough that you got knocked out." Teddy's jaw flexed as he bent and picked me up, holding me to his chest. "Damn it, Lane, I'm sorry. This is my fault. If I hadn't been trying to beat you back to the entrance, I might have been close enough to hear something."

"I doubt you would have, and if you hadn't been trying to win, I'd be lying here helpless, waiting for you to come back," I argued. Could he smell his brother? Dacian claimed to smell Teddy.

Without another word, Teddy swept me into his arms and carried me from the tunnel. For once, I didn't argue. Every joint in my body protested each step he took. The shadows had been beaten back by light leaking in from the entrance not that far ahead.

Watery sunlight leaked through the small hole, lighting the interior of the tunnel. Hard-packed walls full of sheared-off roots and bits of rock lined a tunnel that went on and on into darkness. No dungeon cells in sight, which meant Dacian had been about to make his escape when I'd arrived. Terrible timing seemed to be my thing.

The ramp I'd only felt the night before was clearly visible. With me in his arms, Teddy mounted the long slope toward daylight, but stopped when his head nearly brushed the dirt and root ceiling. "We can't both fit through here. Do you think you can pull yourself through if I boost you?"

"Yes, I'm feeling better now. Just a little off kilter after being tossed around like a rag doll." I held myself stiff, not quite leaning into Teddy. Dacian's words wormed through my mind, a low insidious burn demanding more and more attention as my scrambled brain cleared.

My blood touched Dacian's tongue. He painted my lips with his.

Teddy didn't move to lift me from the tunnel. His nostrils flared, and he looked away, hiding his expression. "He could have killed you. We need to talk about this. You know that, right?"

Well, I had my answer. He could smell his brother, but no comment on the blood?

"We don't have to." *When in doubt, avoid and hope it goes away.* A motto to live by. If we talked about what happened, I'd have to ask questions, face the things Dacian said. I knew this powerful but gentle male in front of me, yet I knew very little about his black wolf.

He grunted and set me on my feet. "But we will. This can't keep happening."

"Twice. This happened twice, and I think I call the first time a win for me." Though the blood exchange only happened once. Did we even exchange blood? I didn't feel any different. I wrapped my arms over my middle and stepped away until the ground leveled out beneath my feet and my back bumped the wall. Dislodged dirt tumbled into my hair, onto my shoulder.

"He dropped you from the sky." Teddy rested his hands on my shoulders, his fingertips pressing hard through the leather. "You almost died."

"Yeah, but so did he, and I'm the reason. I win."

"Your brain works in mysterious ways." Teddy shook his head.

"Keep talking about my brain, and you'll turn me on." I gave him a slow wink.

"What did my brother say to you?"

"He said fae are pussies for not using guns, and then he tried to shoot me," I answered, intentionally misunderstanding him. "Idiot didn't realize guns rarely work on or for us."

Teddy's brows smooshed together. "What are you talking about?"

I waved a hand in a gesture to indicate the lack of importance. "Something about the combustion, which always made me wonder why cars don't stall and cell phones don't explode. Mystery of the universe, I guess."

"You know that's not what I'm asking." Patience wearing thin, Teddy followed me down the ramp. He pressed a hand against the wall and leaned down until my eyes almost crossed to hold his gaze. "When he tried to kill you this time, what did he say?"

Teddy clearly would not let me avoid this subject forever. I should get this over with. What was the worst that could happen? Killing me would suck. Leaving me would be worse.

"He smeared his blood on my lips and said you'd either leave me or kill me when you smelled it." My eyes tightened and nose wrinkled. "After he put my blood in his mouth."

Teddy pulled away and nodded slowly. "Is that all?"

"Isn't that enough?" The exaggerated throb of my hearts hurt. I rubbed my palm over my sternum to stave off the pain. There, I'd done it. I told Teddy his brother might have stolen me against my will.

I started to run my tongue over my lips but stopped myself and scrubbed any remnants of Dacian's blood from my mouth. Frustration scorched my eye sockets. It would be best if I left now. I looked up at my exit. So close, yet so damn far. Too far without Teddy's blood powering my system.

"Do you feel any different?" Teddy pulled my hand from my hearts and pressed my palm flat over his. I didn't have it in me to fight the hold. He patted my hand where it rested on his chest. "Toward him? Toward me?"

Blinking to clear the sun-dappled specks from my eyes, I focused on Teddy and considered his question. Nothing changed. I still wanted to stab Dacian in the face—repeatedly. I still wanted to kiss the male in front of me senseless.

Still afraid I was wrong, that I'd somehow screwed things up, but hopeful, I shook my head. "I don't think so."

"What about my brother?"

"How would I know how he felt?" I frowned. "I'm not psychic."

The corner of Teddy's mouth hitched. "Since I know you, I assume he didn't take you down without a fight?"

I snorted. "Of course not."

"And did he bleed?"

"Of course," I said again while my addled brain tried to fit together the jagged edges of his question.

"Was this before he tasted your blood?"

Blinking like a dumbass caught in the headlights, I nodded. "He didn't heal."

Teddy rubbed his thumb over my lips. "He didn't heal. And sweetheart, I hate to be the one to break it to you, but neither did you. You're a fucking mess."

"That's not very nice." I tried to scowl, but it hurt my face. I *was* a fucking mess.

"This was just my brother trying to scare you, and he did a good job. Smearing blood on your face wouldn't do a thing." He brushed blood from my lips. "But because you're part blood fae, and healing from the ingestion of blood is a blood fae trait, you could heal a little from drinking it."

I perked up. "How much is a little?"

His lips tilted in that heart-melting, crooked smile. "A paper cut."

"Paper cuts do suck. Guess it doesn't suck enough to always be worried about...about the bond."

"If it makes you feel any better, it takes much more than smearing blood on your face to forge a connection. You'll know when the bond forms."

"Know how?" I rubbed my fingers across my mouth in an involuntary gesture.

"We'll talk about it when you are ready."

"You never took my blood." I gave him a dubious look. "How exactly do you know we"—I gestured between us—"you know?"

"I felt it," he whispered. Teddy's lips melted into a smile that reminded me of ice cream on a hundred-degree day. *Pure joy*. He stroked a finger over my palm and up one finger until it scraped beneath my talon. "I felt it. The first time you ingested my blood and healed. It must have been a terrible wound."

"It was. Sometimes bullets do actually hit the fae mark." I shrugged. "My sisters rushed me to Mom, and she had new medicine to try. You said you knew..." The words were awkward on my tongue. "You knew we could be mates because my mom returned for more blood."

"I did. That was confirmation of what I'd felt." His strong, broad hands stroked a heated path down my back, kneading muscles as they went. His chest expanded with a sigh. "We'll talk more another time. Let's get you to your mom so she can fix you up."

When he tried to step away, I tightened my arms around his waist. The terror that had ripped through me was gone, and he'd done that. I didn't want to go anywhere right now. I just wanted him.

Teddy searched my face. As if reading my thoughts, the dark depths of his gaze turned molten. He put his hands beneath my butt and lifted me until I wrapped my legs around his waist.

"Lane," he groaned and fisted a hand in the back of my hair as his mouth covered mine, hot and hard.

There was no gentle coaxing as he pushed his tongue inside and it danced with mine. My head spun from more than just my knock against the wall. Passion burned a path through my blood, and I panted against his salty, swollen lips.

He backed me up to the wall. I cried out, and not from desire. My bruised back sent a splash of pain to drown out the lust.

Space opened between us. Teddy stood a few feet away, running a rough hand through his hair and adjusting what had to be uncomfortably tight jeans. "I'm sorry. This isn't the time."

"Felt like the perfect time to me." I eased away from the earthen wall and tugged the twisted hem of my shirt into place. "A little pain won't kill me. I'm not fragile."

He snorted. "Wait 'til you get a load of yourself, and then tell me that story."

I scowled, but at least saliva finally gathered in my mouth. Nothing like a shot of lust to get all the juices flowing.

Teddy guided me up the ramp until I once again stood directly beneath the tunnel entrance. He crouched in front of me to wrap his arms around my knees.

"Right here? Kind of kinky." I reached for the button on my jeans. "I like it."

"Sorry, sweet fangs, you missed that train," Teddy said, the deep rumble from his chest vibrating against my thighs. "I'm going to lift you, but you'll need to pull yourself out."

"You really are no fun, you know that?" I let my hands fall away and shook out my arms, ready to lever myself out of this hole. "Lift away."

Surprising me, Teddy nuzzled up my shirt and licked my stomach.

My body went straight as a broomstick, and I squeaked—like a small rodent.

"Gotta keep you on your toes." He chuckled and stood, lifting me up and through the circle that resembled a sewer grate missing its cover.

"Tease." I swatted the top of his head while looking side to side, ensuring we were alone before flopping forward on solid ground. I kicked and wiggled, grabbing handfuls of grass to haul my aching body out of the hole. By the feel, I'd have bruises for days. It might be best to keep my clothes on around Teddy after all.

I rolled over and climbed to my feet, getting my first glimpse of the tunnel entrance in the pink light of dawn. Leaves carpeting the tall grass served as the perfect camouflage to disguise the hole. If I hadn't known exactly where to look, I'd never have noticed it. Come to think about it, I hadn't noticed. I'd nearly fallen through.

Those blue furbags hadn't lied. They dug good holes.

Teddy's hands emerged from the tunnel, and he was up and out before I pushed to my feet.

Just as I had, he looked around and then came toward me. He gripped my chin and tilted my head one way and then the other.

"Hey." I slapped at his hand. "Stop that."

He scowled at me. Rude. He was the one manhandling my face.

"Your face is puffy and bruised." He folded his arms across his wide chest, a single brow arching in silent judgment.

I knew exactly what he wanted to say, but to his credit, he didn't. Who knew how long he could go without trying to ply me with his blood? Not long, I expected.

Oh, holy Ho Hos. A horrifying thought shook me to my horny core. Now that all his black wolf cards were on the table, Teddy might withhold sex if I refused to drink his blood. Nah, he wouldn't.

Would he?

"What am I going to do with you, Lane?" He sighed and stepped forward, folding me into his arms.

"Feed me chocolate?" I tugged the hem of his shirt, rubbing my cheek against the soft cotton covering his chest. Inexplicably, pressure built behind my eyes—again. Relief had a funny effect on the system.

"At least tell me Dacian looks worse."

Ripped from my musings, I barked a laugh and stepped back to show him my talons still crusted with his brother's blood. "I doubt it, but I took a piece of him."

"Good." He nodded and took my hand, leading me toward Eodrom.

"Can't we just go home? I have medicine in the freezer," I whined. I'd had enough of Eodrom to last me at least ten years.

"You mean you have my blood in the freezer?"

"That's different, and you know it."

"I actually don't," he grumbled and waved his hands at the trees surrounding us. "We're in the middle of nowhere—in Ta'Vale. Do you plan to walk all the way to Las Vegas?"

I turned beseeching eyes on him. "You could carry me to Interlands, and we could use one of my father's portal devices."

His sensual mouth went crooked with amusement. "I thought you took all of them with you to the penthouse."

"Right." I kicked grass, but the wobbly state of my legs demanded that was as much of a tantrum as I could afford. My ego could not withstand it if I tripped and ate more dirt. "Fine, but in and out. No hanging around for dinner, or breakfast, or whatever bribe my folks try to get you to hang around for."

It would happen. They'd been dying to get to know him better. Or at least my mom had. I wasn't sure my father even registered that I had a partner in my life in a serious sort of way. Having the excuse to heal me, she could draw this visit out for days.

"You probably need to report Dacian's escape."

At Teddy's suggestion, a hot wash of emotion sat uncomfortably on my neck, itchy and tight. The tie that had bound the end of my braid had come loose in the tunnel scuffle. I hung my head upside down while I twisted my hair to tie it into a bun atop my head.

"Yes," I said. "There are a few other things I need to talk about."

As we made our way back, I told Teddy about the missing fae, the tunnels, and the big secret I planned to force my family to spill.

15

POCKETS WERE IMPORTANT

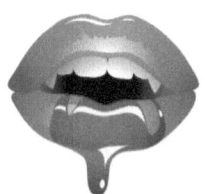

"Do you think this might be a case of the lights are on but no one's home?" In the distance, orange-gold flame flickered behind the open windows of my parent's home. My ferocious need to pull back the curtain and reveal all the sun fae's dirty little secrets had dipped to a mild urge. Right now, food, shower, and sleep sounded much better than family confrontation.

"I don't think you understand the meaning behind that saying," Teddy said.

"Why can't it have a literal meaning?" I slid Teddy some side-eye while I pulled and weaved my waist-length braid into submission. It wasn't as smooth and even as Y'sindra's work, but it was sort of contained. I secured the end with the band of elastic I'd discovered in a jacket pocket. My pockets knew no bounds, except maybe the length of my jacket. Maybe I should start wearing a duster—more pockets.

"Lane," Teddy said.

As we stepped onto the path leading to my parent's front door, I looked up at him. "Hmm?"

Taking my hand, he stopped walking, forcing me to follow suit. "You didn't hear a thing I said, did you?"

Though I wasn't actually sorry, I gave him an apologetic shrug to soothe his wounded pride and what not. "I was thinking about pockets."

Teddy pinched the bridge of his nose. He was definitely annoyed. I couldn't imagine why. Pockets were important. I couldn't count the number of times I'd found something forgotten, buried deep with the lint, that saved my ass.

"I asked if you are ready for this? That is some heavy news you are about to deliver. It could cause an irreparable rift in your family."

Falling into the bottomless depths of Teddy's gaze, pressure ballooned beneath my ribs, pressing against the bones, begging for a release. "No," I answered at last. "No, I'm not really ready. Also, no, I do not believe that'll happen."

The words spoken aloud worked like a release valve on my anxiety, and the bubble of pressure popped. Bonds between fae were difficult to sunder. It was hard to hold a grudge for hundreds of years. Under the right circumstances, I had no doubt I could manage, but not Mae. My sister was the embodiment of sunshine and forgiveness. I still couldn't believe she'd fallen into Cirron's arms. The male whose act of kidnapping her almost led to her death. Their romance had been brief, but a friendship remained.

I would have stabbed the ogre humper.

Glancing toward my parent's house, the fae in question stepped into clear view through the front window. "Fuck."

"What's wrong?" Teddy asked, and I felt his body tense at my side.

"That guy." I spat the words and waved a dismissive hand toward the copper-headed fae on the other side of the window. The one good thing about seeing Cirron was that I'd find everyone I needed to confront under one clay-tiled roof. I blew out a breath. "Let's get this over with. You owe me a sushi dinner."

"Lane..."

"Fine, Mexican? I've been dying to try that cute little cantina they just opened in the hotel."

"Get your sweet ass in there, and then we'll see if you feel like eating when this is done." Teddy led the way to the front door and gripped the handle.

"Am I ever not in the mood to eat?"

"It might happen."

I snorted. "Not bloody likely."

Teddy's brows bunched as he turned the doorknob. "Bloody?"

"Yeah, I heard it on some TV show. Fits, right? And I like the sound of it." I shrugged as I strode past Teddy and over the threshold.

As one, the group gathered inside my parents' home turned at my entrance. Keepers Torneh and Iola looked wary, which was weird since they had no idea I'd overheard them earlier that day. Or did they? I still didn't know the extent of their powers. On the other hand, my father was his usual stoic self, while my mother was red-faced with... I didn't know what was going on with her.

My gaze traveled to a scowling Cirron, and I narrowed my eyes, throwing heaps of disdain his way before looking to Duskmere, whose face held a similar scowl. Figured.

The only one to react to my appearance, Mae broke through the group and raced for me, engulfing me in a hug. Tears smudged mascara beneath her lashes, but she didn't appear upset, so I didn't comment.

"There you are, Laney! I've been trying to reach you on the crystal, but you didn't pick up." Keeping a hold on my hands, she stepped back and looked me over, her mouth slowly rounding in shock.

I looked down at myself and winced. "Yeah, I know. I'm not looking my best. I'll be needing some medicine, Mom."

"You have all the medicine your system needs standing right behind you." Stuffing her hands on her generous hips, my mom's flushed complexion began to fade to the same pale porcelain as mine. A lovely hint of pink continued to color her cheeks while judgmental lines bracketed her mouth.

Sighing, I leaned my head against Mae's arm and let her shuffle us toward the sofa.

Admitting defeat, my mom harrumphed and bustled toward the kitchen. She and I had the talk weeks ago about my refusal to drink Teddy's blood. Though she understood my stance, she also thought I was an idiot.

Realization hit me with the force of an ogre-sized gong. Of course she thought I was being stupid. She'd known about this whole mate thing all along and didn't believe Teddy would ever leave me.

More and more I was coming to believe that too, but that didn't mean he couldn't, or wouldn't, come to resent me. I would not be a needy burden, not just to Teddy, but to anyone. I despised being weak. I would find a way around this.

And if I told myself that a few hundred more times, it might actually happen.

Mae settled us on the sofa, and we sank into the plush cushions. She took my hands, guiding me to face her. Her blue eyes were bright with excitement, or maybe that was terror. Same endorphins, so who knew?

"Laney," Mae said, and squeezed my hands.

I needed to stop her, to tell her the awful news anchored to my tongue, but I couldn't spit out the words, any words, because once one came out, the rest would follow.

"Laney," Mae repeated, which told me she was anxious. "Iola brought me to the stones."

Well, shit. I'd all but forgotten about the stones singing for Mae, and the certainty that my sister was slowly slipping away returned. More and more, Mae was becoming a creature of the court, not in attitude, but in power and, apparently, in her blood.

My smile felt as fragile and fleeting as a snowflake. "I'm so happy for you."

"I met Brenyn, who was there gathering the shards." Excitement glowed in Mae's voice. "She was lovely."

"Who?"

Mae gestured to Iola, watching our exchange quietly from across the room. "Iola's sister."

"She has a sister?" *Well, of course she did.* The female was not the first keeper, but she was ancient. Much of the so-called royal blood within the Eodrom court flowed from her and Torneh. I studied Iola. "Her sister gathers shards? That makes so much sense. All those baskets, I'd wondered who collected them."

During my visit to investigate the sun garden after the sun stones were stolen, I'd found hundreds of baskets filled with differing amounts of sun shards—the shards shed from the sun stones that sun fae used to focus and funnel their magic through.

"Brenyn is a keeper?" I tried to look at Iola without being too obvious. "How have I never heard of her?"

"Oh, no, she is shy and rather solitary, from what I understand, and only tends the shards. Iola says the stones sing for her sister, but she isn't linked." Mae adjusted the wide neck of her soft blue tunic dress on her shoulders.

"She must be. During my first meeting with Iola, she said she was lonely in the garden." I gave Mae a soft smile. "She'll be happy for your company."

A glimmer of hope peeked from behind my doom and gloom. The stones sang for me without claiming me as a keeper, and apparently, they sang for Iola's sister, too. It was possible this wasn't as sudden as I'd thought, and Mae just never ventured near the garden before. Wrong conclusion was my middle name, and I might have jumped to it once again.

"It's sad, don't you think?" Mae asked, twisting her hands in her lap. "Sisters not getting along."

"Hmm, maybe. Being sister to the female the fae consider queen can't be easy." I'd never stop thanking my lucky stars for Mae and Y'sindra.

"You're probably right." Her slender fingers crumpled the delicate folds of her skirt.

I slid my hand to cover Mae's and squeezed. *I love you.*

Mae paused, released a breath, and smiled. She rested her head on my shoulder. "I love you, too."

"What? I just wanted to stop you from fidgeting."

Her head snapped up. She stared at me and then laughed.

"Love you, sis." I winked and moved on to a lighter subject. "You finally saw the famous sun garden today?"

"Yes. I understand now what you meant by the stones are dying. I felt it here." Mae pressed a fist to her chest. "And their song is painful—broken."

Well, that wasn't the happier subject I'd been hoping for.

The discordant keys of the song still rang in my head, but had I felt anything? I couldn't remember. Though I'd visited the garden only months ago, it seemed a lifetime. In a way, it was. I'd changed so much since then—my life had shifted in a seismic fashion.

I nodded as if I understood, as if I might feel the same. "We got one. We'll find the others. That's part of what I need to talk to you about."

"Late to the party as usual." Y'sindra's snark preceded her and Lo as he flew them in through a window with a view to the garden. "Unlike some of us who will remain unnamed"—she pointed at me—"I had my crystal with me. I explained we were on recon in Shadwe, that we'd located the stones."

Anger simmering for days finally popped its lid right off that pot and boiled over. I leaped to my feet. "Well, excuse me for being knocked the fuck out."

"Lane!" Mae made a strangled squeak and came to her feet alongside me. "Why did you let me run on about the stones? What happened?"

"I was getting to it, but your experience with the stones is important."

Y'sindra appeared at my side, a rare expression of concern etched on her face. Guilt climbed aboard the roller coaster of emotions ebbing and flowing through me.

"I'm sorry," she said, and the weight of my guilt gained a few more pounds.

"No, I'm sorry." Despite my screaming joints, I knelt so I was eye level with my sister. "That wasn't a fair reaction. It's been a rough day."

"Yeah, well, I'll let it slide this time." Y'sindra sniffed and pulled herself onto the couch, brushing past her brief—very brief—moment of solemnity. Lo settled next to her, the extra weight sinking them deeper into the cushion.

Mom appeared from her work room, an extra large thermos in one hand and an opaque-green glass jar and a roll of jewel-bedecked bandages in the other—bandages that looked suspiciously like those always wrapped around the stump of Y'sindra's wing.

I stood and backed up, giving Mom room to work, my gaze locked on the familiar green jar. Thanks to the goopy stuff inside, I had two pointy ears instead of one. I'd learned my lesson and now checked Y'sindra's breath for the telltale boozy scent before letting her cut my hair.

"You're trying to grow her wing back," I whispered, the false flag of possibility raising in my heart. "Will it work?"

Bent over my sister's wing, threads of silver caught the light on the crown of my mom's head. "I don't know. I hope."

"You and me both," I mumbled.

Y'sindra gave me the thumbs-up over my mom's shoulder and waved her stump as my mom finished removing the bandages. Was I imagining it, or was that fresh feather down near the severed end?

"Stop moving your wing, dear. I need to apply the salve." Fingers covered in pale-blue goop, Mom glanced up at me and gave the thermos in my hand a pointed look. "And you, drink up."

Muttering, I popped the spout, tossed it back, and immediately gagged. "Gross. This is ice cold."

My mom shrugged, her focus firmly on Y'sindra's stump. "You want it warm, you know where to find it."

I could feel the frayed strands of the leash tied to my temper popping one at a time. Frustration kept kicking me in the teeth today, what with everyone wanting to have a hand in my decisions. So I did what I did best and diverted attention from me.

"Hey, so big news." I gave attention to my talons, picking at a cracked edge. They were truly a mess.

"I have bigger news," Y'sindra said, back to her adorably, annoyingly smug self.

"Not a chance."

"Wanna bet?"

I pursed my lips, considering. Y'sindra grinned.

"Fine." I was ninety-nine point nine percent certain Y'sindra could not top my news. This was perfect. "Loser does the ring job."

Y'sindra visibly shuddered.

Jason Olson, an old friend of dear ol' Great-Grandaddy and an Earth mage, ran an animal sanctuary on the outskirts of Las Vegas. He came to the penthouse looking for Blackthorne, found me, and hired YML Investigations to find his mother's wedding ring that had mysteriously vanished the night before he could propose to his girlfriend. We'd figured out where it went, but none of us wanted to retrieve the heirloom ring.

I'd picked up a scent that didn't belong to anyone residing on the ranch. It did, however, belong to Olson's former live-in girlfriend. The angry ex had been so proud of what she'd done, no intimidation had been required for her to spill the truth—she'd mixed the ring in with a bucket of meat for one of the animals. I didn't know what kind of animal, but based on it being a carnivore in a desert sanctuary, my money was on mountain lion. Now, one of us needed to go dung diving and retrieve the blue diamond.

"Deal?" I asked.

"You're on." Wing slathered and rewrapped, she stood on the sofa cushion, putting us once again at eye level. "Better get some shoulder-length industrial gloves, buttercup."

"News on three?" I held up a closed fist.

Y'sindra hiked her chin and nodded.

"One." I popped out my thumb.

Snow fell from Y'sindra's shivering wing from her anticipation—a by-product of her winter magic—dusting our folk's furniture.

"Two." I raised my index finger.

Y'sindra bounced on her toes.

"Three." I unfolded my middle finger and blurted, "I know who Mae's birth mother is."

"I saw Dacian in Shadwe," Y'sindra said, a fraction slower.

We stared at each other while chaos erupted around us.

Eyes wide, Y'sindra scooted to the edge of the sofa. "You win."

I turned my raised fingers into a finger gun and pointed it my sister. "And you're on ring duty."

16

DIRTY MOON FAE

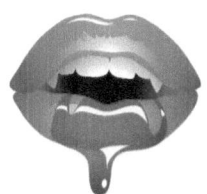

EVERYONE HAD GATHERED AROUND THE EXTRA LARGE TRESTLE TABLE. A wary hush blanketed the room, pulsing with tension visible in the rigid lines and tight jaws of those seated opposite me. A plate of Mom's cookies sat untouched, except by me, and ten sets of eyes watched me chew.

"Malaney, how can you eat?" The exquisitely carved old wood of my mom's chair creaked as she leaned forward in her seat to pull the plate out of my reach.

"What?" I frowned at the retreating platter of cookies. "I'm hungry, and you put them on the table."

My mom shook her head and muttered, "When are you not hungry?"

"I keep asking that same question, Meghan." Chuckling, Teddy scooted his chair back a couple of inches, stretched his long legs out in front of him, and slung an arm across the back of my seat.

After carelessly lobbing the news about Mae's mother into the room with the finesse of a live grenade, I'd so far managed to avoid divulging further details. Everyone present—save Teddy, since he'd known it was coming—had fallen into differing states of shock. Now they were regaining their senses. Jerky movements and sharp glances alerted me that patience with my continued silence on the subject was slipping.

I brushed my hands together, sending a cascade of crumbs onto the table.

Eyes tight, my mom watched. Sighing, I guided the mess toward the linen napkin held in my lap.

"Oh, for sun's sake, Malaney. Leave the crumbs be and explain yourself," Mom snapped.

Bristling, I looked at my mom. "I'm sorry I don't have the words to tell Mae her own family betrayed her."

My mother slapped her palms on the table. Glasses jumped, silverware clanged, and she pushed to her feet. Though not even five feet tall, she still towered over the room. My mom leaned onto the table, bending toward me, and I paled. "I know you guard your emotions, but I never thought you such a selfish girl."

I shoved to my feet and matched my mom's stance. "Selfish? How am I selfish for telling the sister I love that our own parents have been hiding the fact that they knew the identity of her birth mother?"

The answer was already there. I could have been gentler with my words. Instead, I'd pulled the pin and thrown the words into the room to win an argument with Y'sindra. Chaos be damned. The wall of my aching chest threatened to cave in, but I focused on keeping my shoulders back.

Without the ugly secret weighing me down, I should feel weightless with relief. Yet I'd made it even uglier.

When I finally dredged up the courage to face Mae, who'd seated herself to my left, her eyes were soft and luminous. Her expression was not the stricken map of cracked porcelain I'd expected.

"It's okay. I knew that one day this news would come. Blood does not change my true family." Mae looked across the table to our parents and let loose one of her beatific smiles, and then turned to Y'sindra. "I think the more important news is about Dacian. Why don't you tell us what happened?"

"He did this to me." I answered before Y'sindra, making a generic circular gesture toward my face.

"How? Lo and I just saw him in Shadwe."

"We saw a wyvern," Lo amended. "It was very far away, though. I could not identify if it was Dacian or Ted-D's sister."

Teddy laid his elbows and forearms on the table, gripping his hands together. "But Lavinia hasn't been seen since before I left."

"Oh no!" Lo said, shaking his head so quickly, the tiny round ears atop his head bent with the movement. "The princess returned."

To my right, Teddy visibly jerked. "She went home?"

The fine fur covering Lo's compact form shivered with his exuberance. That guy loved talking about all things Barbout. "When you left Outerlands, she saw it as you won. Lavinia no longer had a reason to fight your parents."

All I heard from that was Teddy had a sister. He'd never mentioned her before—no one had mentioned her before. Would she like me, or would she also try to bang my head against walls? What was I thinking? I'd probably never meet her.

"That's good." Teddy nodded, sounding distracted and distant. Another reminder that there were much more dysfunctional families than mine out there. "You think it was my brother?"

"I do! You and the princess are too similar. She would never travel with those dirty moon fae."

I winced at Lo's unintentional slur, and my gaze shot toward Duskmere. His thin lips had pulled into a bloodless line and pinched at the corners, plucking a chord of sympathy somewhere inside me.

"Corrupted, Lo, not dirty," I corrected him. "They tried to combine their magic with an opposing magic and ended up corrupting the moon magic in their blood."

"Oh, I am so very sorry, Mr. Duskmere. I did not mean—"

"I know you didn't," Duskmere said with a touch of unexpected gentleness. His mouth softened, and he even produced a small smile for the infectiously cheery Lo.

"Magic is not meant to be blended." I gestured to myself.

My father made a tsking noise. "Magic works with its mirror force. This is why I have been able to create a hybrid version of sun and moon magic. I wish there were more moon fae with the magical power of Duskmere to work spells with."

"I thought we were talking about wyverns. You know, big teeth, bigger wings?" Y'sindra asked.

"Right, that." I mimicked Teddy's position, placing my elbows and forearms on the table, folded my hands together and leaned forward. "I had a chat with the grounders when they picked up the house keys."

I told everyone about the tunnels Nyle and Etta'wy hired the grounders to dig into Eodrom, and where they led. The tunnel Teddy had explored led to a forest. I wasn't sure where since I hadn't seen it myself, but the other tunnel was the one that mattered, since it led to the dungeon.

"My sorry luck, I stumbled into Dacian as he was making his escape. I... uh..." I'd forgotten about this part, sucked in a breath, and spilled. "I might have borrowed Pru's jacket and let myself into the dungeon earlier. He was still there, but someone else was down there."

Duskmere's loud laughter was not the reaction I'd expected. "I understand now."

I gave him a questioning look.

"Her questions about a job and the soffleberry pie." He laughed again and wiped beneath his eyes. "She really wanted that pie, you know?"

A conspiratorial smile twitched on my lips, and I shrugged. "Of course she did. Mom is a goddess in the kitchen."

Mom harrumphed, trying to sound annoyed, but failing miserably. Nothing pleased her more than compliments on her confectionaries.

"Why don't you keep the jacket?" Iola spoke for the first time, her voice much calmer and more melodic than I'd imagined it being under the circumstances. "We will replace Prunettia's. I do not believe there is any harm in you having your own. It is a good idea should you need to conduct any other interviews."

I sat a little straighter. At last, my own insignia. It didn't really matter, but it was cool. And there might be a tiny bit of validation involved.

"We do not have to worry about Lane making the trip down the stairs often." Duskmere gave me a bland look.

Whatever this was, I didn't like it. Mr. Stick-up-his-ass had learned to joke, and at my expense. I bared my fangs at Duskmere.

"Malaney Callaghan." Gentle as Iola's voice remained, I sobered, remembering I had an audience. She asked, "Someone else was in the dungeon when you first paid a visit to Dacian Barbout?"

"Right, sorry," I mumbled, and cleared my throat. "I didn't see them, but I heard them coming. I escaped through the unwarded cell using one of Duskmere's portal stones."

"You heard nothing? Smelled nothing?" The hard lines and angles of Duskmere's sharp face had replaced his moment of congeniality. He was back in work mode, which, frankly, I appreciated. This was the Duskmere I knew.

I shook my head.

"Did they see you? Did they know you were there?"

"Yes. But they only saw me from behind." I wrinkled my nose. "I think they pushed me through the portal, but I'm not sure why."

"Convenience," Cirron suggested.

The sudden intrusion of his voice in the conversation sent my irrational meter pinging. Teddy splayed a palm on my back and rubbed in slow, soothing circles. It worked. I didn't leap across the table to slap Cirron all the way to the forsaken gods. My nostrils flared with a deep, calming breath. "Explain."

Cirron watched me as if I was a curious specimen. Teddy's hand stilled in the center of my back, and I welcomed his heat melting into me.

"If they did not see you, they did not know who you were. They would not know the outcome of a confrontation, but if you wore an RFG jacket, they would have viewed you as a significant problem." Cirron's shoulders rose and fell, his sheet of coppery hair shifting with the motion. "You presented them with the simple solution of a portal in which to be rid of you."

"You know this because it's what you'd do?" I couldn't help it. At least I didn't physically attack him. I should have gotten points for that.

"Yes." Cirron's simple answer blew the wind right out of my sails.

"I agree with my partner," Duskmere said. "It would have been the simplest solution."

"Perhaps it is time we request a consultation with the Iomas." Torneh's quiet suggestion landed like an avalanche. Iomas, the exalted seers. Not the crowd anyone wanted to keep.

"The Iomas?" My father, the most unruffled of ruffles, was visibly ruffled. "They have not been called upon since the Great Divide. It will cause much disquiet."

My brows pinched together as I watched the exchange. What did he care? Most avoided the seers for obvious reason. No one wanted to hang out with someone who could see all their dirty secrets. My gaze slid to Teddy—and thoughts.

"It must be done," Torneh said. "It is the only way we can remove this malignancy once and for all."

"Very well, I understand." My father brushed at his sleeve. "I presume they will need use of the circle in my lab. I would ask they are monitored at all times, and no items removed."

A bubble of laughter swelled in my throat, but I swallowed it, fighting the accompanying grin. My father—the mighty chief royal wizard—didn't want anyone touching his shit.

I wondered if my once-friend Fate still owned that copy of "Fomorian

Mating and Reproductive Practices" she just had to have and then blamed on me when my father noticed its absence? I'd never seen him so angry, and all because he thought I'd touched his stuff.

"Of course," Torneh agreed. He pursed his lips and turned his eyes to me. "You will give us the location of these tunnels."

This guy. Always with the orders. Never mind he could probably send me to stardust with a snap. It was rude.

"I accompanied Lane. We will get those locations to you before we leave," Teddy answered for me, doing a remarkable job of intercepting before my irrational temper got me killed.

"Good. Duskmere Blademoon, you will take two dozen Royal Fae Guard and scour these tunnels." Torneh looked to Duskmere, who nodded. "When you are finished, I want them sealed."

"Should you though?" I clicked my talons against the tabletop.

"Are you suggesting an alternative?" Torneh's golden brows rose in a sharp peak.

"I am. Now you know about the tunnels. You can just keep an eye on them. If anyone tries to use them to get in or out, you'll catch them." I shrugged. "Simple but effective."

Torneh opened his mouth, but Iola slipped her hand over his. He turned to meet her gaze. I had no proof they could communicate without words, but somehow, they always did.

"We agree with you, Malaney Callaghan," Iola said, though she still held Torneh's gaze. At the rate his chin dipped in response, I could almost hear the vertebrae in his neck creak. "It is settled. Duskmere, you will consult with Aventheo Barbout and take a small contingent to explore these tunnels during the moon hours."

"There is no need to consult with them." Cirron's face was a brittle mask of misery.

Of course that guy would know. He'd had a hand in who knew how many escapes. How had I not wondered if he knew the location of the tunnels?

All eyes swung toward Cirron. They all had to be having the same realization. Especially Duskmere, who'd only recently thawed toward the traitor. Naked misery etched lines at the corners of Duskmere's tight eyes. Poor guy had wanted to believe.

"I know where the tunnel is." Cirron held himself so straight in his seat, he wouldn't crack an egg placed behind his back.

Tunnel, singular. He must only know about the tunnel leading from the prison. It was also possible the second tunnel wasn't important. A path to a forest, big deal. Ta'Vale was a forest-heavy continent.

"Nyle Rathmore forced me to release prisoners and lead them to the tunnel. I gave them a phone number and directed them to Interlands. From there, they were someone else's burden. No cog in the corrupted wheel knew every moving part."

"A phone number?" I asked through numb lips. Ice sloshed through my veins. All the prisoners I'd had a hand in locking up had been so close to the Interlands house, and we'd never known. Anyone could have ambushed us while we slept, but Duskmere and his RFG had always decided it was information we didn't need to know.

"Yes. Always a different number slipped under my door with the name of a prisoner to be released. I was not responsible for the release of every prisoner, either."

"Why are we just hearing about this?" Despite the quiet of Torneh's question, lightning cut through his tone—sharp, angry, electric rage.

"I have no excuse." Braver than I would have given him credit for, Cirron held the keeper's furious glare. "We apprehended the traitors I knew of."

A storm gathered behind the keeper's eyes. Where Iola's gaze was a sunset-painted lake, Torneh was the eye of a cyclone moving over deep, dark waters.

"I did not assist in this prisoner's escape, but I accept responsibility." Cirron lowered his head, his low voice a rumble of self-loathing. "I did not think to seal the tunnel. My focus was elsewhere."

On Duskmere. His focus had been on Duskmere, who had potentially lain on his deathbed because of Cirron's actions. I wanted to slap the stupid sun fae silly, but it was clear from his expression he hated himself enough for both of us.

"Since that's settled," I said and twisted toward Mae, but she held up a hand.

"It's been enough. There's no rush to tell me anything, because it won't change anything." Mae reached for a cookie and handed it to me with a mischievous wink. "Let's go home."

"Good idea," Y'sindra said, and bounced out of her seat. "Let's get back and get some dinner, discuss what Lo and I found, and make plans. And Lane, you have to see about a ring, don't you?"

I scowled. My sister had zero shame. She planned to take advantage of my guilt. It'd probably work.

Pushing my seat back, I rose. The ache in my legs had diminished, my medicine having done a mediocre job. Teddy stood and stepped behind me, his hand resting on my hip. I leaned into his warmth, dimly acknowledging I was becoming all too comfortable with my automatic reaction to his nearness. A different worry for a different day.

Thank the gods neither my parents, the keepers, nor Duskmere or Cirron objected to our departure. The mental and physical trauma of the last few days weighed me down. I was exhausted. Nothing a hot shower, a good meal, and my new, supremely soft mattress wouldn't fix.

Without being asked, my father led us from the house and out to the garden.

My mother rushed up behind me and pressed another thermos into my hand. "You need to drink this."

Falling behind the others, I stopped to kiss her on the cheek. "I will."

"You also need to get over this fear of drinking from Teddy." Her lips pinched, and she shook her head. "I can see you aren't healing as well as you once were. You need his blood, Lane, and not this diluted mixture."

"I'll think about it," I lied and made my way to the garden and onto the portal stone where Teddy waited, the others already gone.

"Your mom is a wise woman. You should listen to her sound advice." Teddy squeezed me to his side.

"Don't," I warned, scowling up at him from beneath his muscular arm slung over my shoulders.

"Let's get out of here before you bite my head off," he said and guided me toward the activated portal. "On second thought, you're welcome to bite me anytime you like."

I gasped in outrage.

Laughing, Teddy danced out of reach of my swat and through the portal to the penthouse.

17

THAT VEGETABLE QUACKS

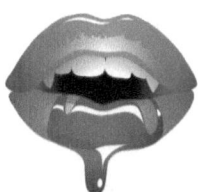

I set the last plate, napkin, and utensils on Blackthorne's table—our table, damn it. This had been a harder adjustment than I'd expected. We'd moved right in and adopted the druid's belongings.

"How much longer?" Y'sindra asked. Seated on the far side of the table on seats with extra cushions, wings folded tight to their backs, my sister and Lo waited for everyone to join us.

"Teddy should be back soon with the food." I pulled my seat out and dropped into it, glancing over my shoulder at an upstairs hallway leading to the bedrooms—all master suites. "Do you think she fell asleep in there?"

Mae had disappeared into the bathroom when we got back, almost an hour and a half ago.

Y'sindra played with her cutlery, trying to get her fork and knife to balance together atop her plate in an inverted "v" shape. "She's going to use all the hot water."

"It's a big resort."

She shrugged. "It's a long shower."

I leaned back in the seat to get a look at the clock. Almost 4:23 p.m. "She can't hide forever," I said, mostly to myself.

Utensils clattered on ceramic. "You think she's avoiding talking about her mother?"

"Yes." I rested my elbow on the table and chin in my hand. "I think she meant it when she said she didn't want to know."

"Why would she? If my clan came for me, I'd invite them in and turn up the heat."

She meant that in the literal sense. For a snow fairy, there could be no bigger insult. Her clan kicked her out and expected her to die, so I wouldn't expect any tender feelings from my sis. Of course, with Y'sindra's pilgrimage to death came the fact she'd been sent down the mountain with the infant sun fae delivered to their village—Mae.

I rubbed my lips together in thought and nodded. "You're right. You were both abandoned, so why should it matter? Is it wrong if I say I'm glad it happened? I wouldn't have two amazing sisters if life hadn't taken the path it had."

"Nah." Y'sindra waved a hand. "We both have way better lives than we would have otherwise. I don't know who Mae's mother is, but she abandoned her, so she can't be very good."

"Understatement," I scoffed.

Y'sindra sat up straight and pegged me with a serious look.

Oh, shit. Did I say that out loud?

"Something you want to tell me?" Y'sindra narrowed her eyes.

Saving me from deciding if I should spill the truth all over Y'sindra before Mae arrived, the topic of conversation padded into the room on plush pink slippers and draped in pink silk pajamas.

A wary mask etched onto her face, Mae gave us a sideways look as she turned around and went to the kitchen. She disappeared around the corner, only to reappear through the pass-through next to the dining table. She went straight for the liquor cabinet and put a bottle of Macallan and Crystal Head on the counter, followed by five tumblers. Fancy ice globes our new refrigerator made, one each, went into each tumbler, along with a lone blueberry in one glass.

I sighed at the appearance of the berry, but a single blueberry wouldn't even bring on mild snow fairy inebriation. Oddly enough, Y'sindra had no snarky comments to add. My gaze found Lo, who watched Mae with fascinated attention. It was adorable how enraptured he was with his new world. He was also a tempering influence on Y'sindra, for which I was forever grateful.

Mae slid all the glasses, save one, across the pass-through to the dining room side. She opened the Macallan and gave the bottle a generous pour. The deep-amber liquid cascaded over the fancy ice.

Still, no one spoke.

Ice clinked against the sides of the glasses as I retrieved them two at a time and handed them out. I didn't miss the fact that Mae set out a glass for Teddy without me asking. My cold little hearts warmed, thinking how easily he and Lo had slid into our lives, complementing our sibling trio the way chocolate made peanut butter better. It was hard to remember a time before them.

Sliding the bottle to me across the counter, Mae exited the kitchen and rounded the corner into the dining area as I began pouring drinks for each of us, including Teddy, who was due back with our takeout from the cantina any minute.

I cleared my throat, the discomfort of our continued lack of conversation pulling across my skin like plastic wrap. "We could have ordered sushi. I'm not allergic to seaweed."

"You are," both my sisters answered at the same time, and the uncomfortable atmosphere abated.

Pleased with my tactic, the corners of my mouth twitched with a small smile, even if I disagreed with their response. I made a face and splashed vodka into my glass and then poured slightly less for Y'sindra and Lo. Unlike Mae, when it came to liquor, I was cheap. The glass skull bottle had been a gift from Teddy.

Mae took a sip of her scotch and leaned back in her seat, deceptively casual. "All right, I still don't think it's important for me to know, but let's hear it. Who's my mother?"

Taken aback by the sudden, blunt question, I curled my hands around the chilly glass and stared into its shallow depths.

"Black wolf got your tongue?" Y'sindra prodded, and then slurped from the tumbler she needed both hands to grip.

I heaved a sigh, heavy with the awful truth. There was no point dancing around the facts. I'd delayed long enough. "I overheard a conversation between our folks, Duskmere, and the keepers yesterday."

While I recounted what I'd heard, what I knew, and what I'd extrapolated, Teddy returned and quietly set out a mouthwatering spread of Mexican food before taking his seat next to me.

"Well, now we know," Mae said when I finished. She pointed down the table to a foil container in front of Teddy. "Pass the enchiladas. I've been dying to try them since I saw them on the menu."

I gaped at her. "Seriously, Mae? After everything, all you have to say is 'pass the enchiladas?'"

"What? You know how I feel about a good mole sauce, and these are stuffed with duck and plantains." Mae held out her plate for Teddy, who spooned on two enchiladas. "They are going to be amazing."

"You know who Hielmal is, right?" I sat rigid in my seat, watching her continue to pile food onto her plate. I used food to avoid tough conversations. Y'sindra used food. Mae did not. Mind scrambling as it was, her nonchalant reaction had to be authentic.

"Of course I know," she answered, her tone scolding, as if offended I might suggest there be a piece of history not already locked away in her memory bank of knowledge. Placing her heaping plate in front of her, she folded back into her seat. "What would you have me say? I'm grateful she gave me up?"

"Well, I don't know—" I began.

"Because I am," she said. "I know who Hielmal is. I've not only read the accounts but also practiced the magic Dad used to counter the assassination attempt she almost succeeded with. She did a kindness giving me up, even if it's not how she intended it. Look where I am now, look who I am now. I am glad."

A splash of warmth hit my system. It unwound the knots of tension I hadn't realized I'd been carrying. Hearing Mae say the words was everything I needed to hear, and in that moment I knew my staying silent had been more for myself than my sister. She was a badass bitch who didn't need to be coddled, didn't need to be protected. I'd remember that.

"Someone want to fill me in?" Y'sindra sat at the edge of her cushion, looking between Mae and me.

Right, she'd have no reason to know sun fae history. I gave Y'sindra the abbreviated version.

"So she's the corrupted sun fae who had Mae locked in a cage?" Y'sindra snorted. "Some mother. She ever say anything to you when they had you?"

"Nope." Mae shrugged and glanced at me. I could almost hear the *told you so* in her expression.

"Yeah, that was her. She...she..." My brain screeched to a halt. My blood froze over and hearts thumped hard inside my chest. "Fuck."

Mae put down her fork, seeing something in my expression that finally gave her pause.

"I knew I saw her before." I ran my tongue over the seam of my suddenly dry lips. "In the dungeon, the first time I went there."

The emaciated sun fae had been a dehydrated version of the female we'd first confronted in Outerlands. Her complexion dull, the bones almost cutting against her skin, but her eyes... Those rich, azure eyes had been captivating and impossible to forget.

"She couldn't have been there." Standing in her seat, Y'sindra held a pair of food tongs, waving the utensil as she spoke. "We know she's responsible for the stolen sun stones, and they'd already gone missing by the time Duskmere shoved you into the dungeon."

"It doesn't make sense, but I saw her. I'd remember those eyes anywhere."

"They are a distinct color, even among the sun fae," Mae admitted. "But how could you have seen her?"

I shook my head. "I don't know, but something tells me the RFG and their cagey antics are behind this mystery."

Y'sindra plopped four taquitos onto her plate and pointed the tongs in my direction, flinging sauce onto the table and onto me. "No argument here."

Warm chili sauce slid down my cheek. I scowled, wiped it away, and then licked my fingers. "Mmm, that's good."

"This is delicious," Mae agreed. "I can't believe this place is just an elevator ride away."

"And I can't believe you didn't pick a vegetarian dish."

She shrugged. "I'm not vegetarian. I just prefer vegetables."

"Better watch out, because that vegetable quacks." I pointed at the duck enchilada on her plate.

"They're quacking amazing." Mae winked and licked her fingers.

Y'sindra chortled while I groaned.

Beneath the table, Teddy squeezed my thigh. When I turned to face him, he raised his brows. I smiled, understanding immediately he wanted to know if I was okay.

I laid a kiss on his cheek, nodded, and then pointed to Mae's favorite dish. "Pass the quacking enchiladas, will you?"

18

SUCK IT

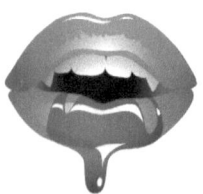

FOUR HOURS, A LONG CONVERSATION, AND A POWER NAP LATER, I SAT ON the marble counter in the bathroom Mae had claimed as her own. I watched in fascination as she applied her makeup with the hand of a genuine artist in a lit, magnified mirror. At last, she dabbed her lips with a glossy reddish-orange lipstick that matched her sequined minidress with a hem so short and neckline so low, it offered the tantalizing promise to meet in the middle if my sister bent just right.

Smacking her lips, Mae turned the light off in the mirror and faced me. "Wish me luck." She nearly sang the words.

I couldn't tell if she was faking this level of cheer or if tonight's news really hadn't bothered her. As far as I could tell, and I was good at reading my sister, she sincerely did not care.

"This is Vaughn we're talking about." I slid from the counter, fuzzy slippers feeling like twin clouds beneath my soles. "That guy has been dying for this date. Oh wait, he's already dead."

Mae gave me a flat look while I snort-laughed at my joke.

"Oh, come on. It was funny."

"You know as well as I do vampires are not dead," Mae said in Vaughn's defense.

How was my learned sister so... Dumb wasn't the right word. Blind to the truth? "When their indefinite existence relies only on keeping their heart inside their chest and the blood in their veins fresh, it sort of classifies them as *dead*."

"Almost dead," Mae insisted with the tenacity of a honey badger.

I was ninety percent certain the grounders' DNA was a twisted strand of hamster and honey badger. Aggressive little beasties.

Bringing myself back to the subject at hand, I said, "Dead," because I could honey badger with the best of 'em.

Mae swung around to face me. She crossed her arms over her chest, her generous and wildly exposed cleavage bulging. Vaughn was going to be a happy vamp tonight. "Says the fae who has literally been staked."

"I staked myself, and I'm alive."

"Lane..."

"Fine, whatever you say, *almost* dead." I rolled my eyes and strode from the bathroom, muttering beneath my breath, "Is there a difference?" I took the stairs to the main floor and headed straight for the dining room table, hoping to nab myself a leftover taquito from our lunch spread. Those had been my favorite, right behind the spicy chorizo queso.

Unfortunately, there wasn't a scrap left on the table, not even a tortilla chip. Y'sindra and Lo lounged on the sofa, the same sofa Teddy and I had enjoyed... Was it really just yesterday? There was a time when my life moved at a nice, leisurely pace, but ever since the sun fae reentered my life, the delineation between days blurred.

Teddy stretched on the recliner adjacent to the sofa. He rolled his head on the back of his chair toward me when I entered the room. As if reading my thoughts, his lips spread in a slow, deliciously wicked smile.

"Later," I mouthed. Although, I was fairly certain it would be days before I'd recovered enough for another round with Teddy. As much as I wished to deny it, Mom hadn't been wrong; the medicine was less and less effective. Life plucked options from me day by day, until soon I'd have none left.

The clack of Mae's stiletto heels on the wooden stairs announced her arrival, and we all watched the landing.

Y'sindra whistled low at our sister's appearance. "You look like a sexy peach."

Depending on the angle, the sequins of Mae's dress changed from yellow to peach to red, just like the fruit.

"Isn't it fabulous?" Mae twisted her hips right to left. The light hit her dress from different angles and shot a fruity prism of color onto the walls. She froze mid hip twist. "You think it's too much for Nuada's?"

"Too much fabric, maybe." Y'sindra stood on her seat and leaned over the back, facing Mae and me standing behind the sofa. "Have you seen the line to get in there? Bare skin for days."

I'd wondered what walnuts Blackthorne possessed naming the resort's flagship nightclub after Nuada the Silver Hand deity, but Vaughn claimed Nuada himself was the chief investor. It could be true. Hundreds of years ago, Nuada Airgetlám wandered Earthside, along with the rest of the Tuatha Dé Danann. Las Vegas was home to an exorbitant amount of supernaturals, so why not deities? Besides, I'd met the Silver Hand, and he was a lush.

Beaming, Mae brushed her hands down her dress—if a slip of shiny fabric and sequins could be considered a dress—and did a full twirl, eliciting a second whistle from Y'sindra. When she faced us again, she put a hand on her chest, her mouth forming a little moue. "I don't think the enchiladas agreed with me."

"Maybe you should take it easy tonight?" I suggested.

"Absolutely not." Mae did a last check in a large, irregularly shaped mirror mounted in a wood frame on the wall—wood that matched the dining table, that matched the staff, that matched the sundial. Blackthorne had surrounded himself with pieces of focus for his power.

"There's some antacid in the druid's medicine cabinet," Y'sindra suggested.

"Excellent idea. I'll take some when I get home if I'm still not feeling well." Mae planted a kiss on my cheek and then Y'sindra's. Fortunately, her smear-proof lip gloss did not transfer.

My gaze remained on the elevator long after the doors had closed, worry for my sister's future winding through my ribs. Or maybe I just had heartburn, too.

Footsteps approached from behind, and then Teddy's forearms, bare and all muscly, wrapped around my middle and pulled me into his heated embrace. I tipped my head back onto his chest and closed my eyes, allowing the comfort inside his arms to leech the trepidation from my bones.

No matter how many times I told myself I would not become dependent on Teddy's fresh blood, I never stopped to consider how much I'd come to depend on *him*. His touch, his presence, his unwavering faith in me. Block by block, it had become the support structure to my soul. I feared I might crumble if I ever lost this male.

"Maerwen is stronger than you think. She'll be fine." Teddy's words ruffled the hair at my ear, sending shivers tumbling down my neck.

I pulled a breath into my lungs and myself from my morose thoughts. "You're right."

With a squeeze, he let me go. "Come hear what Lo and Y'sindra have to say."

"If I have to." I followed him into the sitting area and confiscated the overstuffed toffee-colored chair next to the sofa. It wasn't a recliner, and it wasn't a chaise, but somewhere in-between. I pulled my legs up and curled them beneath me, leaning onto the arm of the chair.

"Comfortable?" Y'sindra drawled.

"Almost." I rose onto my knees and pulled the hem of my "Suck it" T-shirt depicting a fangy mouth sipping a bloody martini under my butt, so my heels held it in place when I sat back down. I shot my sis a bland smile. "I'm good now. Proceed."

Y'sindra gave me a narrow-eyed look before bouncing to the edge of her seat. She picked up a small light-blue box and delivered it to me. "Remember I tested your phone in Shadwe last week, same results as Ta'Vale?"

I nodded, turning the plastic box over in my hands. It was some sort of camera I'd never seen before. "I remember. I assume any alternate realm will have the same results."

"Right, well, I have a hunch something without wires and microchips might work, so I picked this camera up from a shop downstairs. It's an updated version of an old Polaroid camera."

"Polaroid. Instant camera, right?"

"Yep." She pulled herself onto the extended end of my seat and pointed to the slide lever on the front of the camera. "You load a film cartridge here, take a picture, and voilà, a physical picture pops out here."

I eyed the slit in the front. It was a smart little gadget. "Pretty clever of you to come up with the idea."

"Hold the praise until I know if it works or not." Y'sindra slid from the chair, grabbed a bag from the coffee table, and slung it crosswise across her body. When she held out her hand for the camera, I handed it over, and she dropped it into the satchel. "Lo has some connections inside Shadwe. They left a note in Lo's old room about information on the Sun Stones. We're going to head there now and hook up with them in Outerlands, see what we can find out."

Excitement and fear writhed in my gut. We might actually have a lead, but this seemed a little too convenient. "What if it's a trap?"

"It's not a trap."

"And you know this because...?" I tossed my legs over the side of the chair and pushed to my feet. My legs still ached. I had one more thermos of blood-medicine in the fridge, and I needed to take it before doing anything else.

"Because," Y'sindra said and dug into her little bag, "Lo was a spy, and he had a network. Tell her, muffin."

Muffin? I choked, but Lo beamed at my sister. I scratched sugar muffin off my mental list of nicknames for Teddy. There could only be one muffin.

A vague recollection of Teddy mentioning Lo had been his family's best spymaster resurfaced in my brain. Considering everything between then and now—including a coma—I could forgive myself for forgetting those details.

Puffing his chest, Lo turned to me. "I have a network. I maintained my Shadwe connections, even after I moved with Ted-D to Outerlands. He and I installed hidden panels for passing messages and bolt holes all over the bar so my associates can get in and out without being seen."

Y'sindra pulled one of our father's portal devices from the same satchel and checked its marking. She dropped it back in the bag, grabbed a second, and turned it over, confirming it was the correct device.

Taking Lo's hand, she led him toward the balcony. The massive, three-pane glass door slid open with only a small tug. It had been sticking. Someone recently greased the track, and I'd put money on that someone being Teddy.

We'd agreed portals were for outside use only, and I was both surprised and pleased to see Y'sindra abiding by the rule and heading for the spot where we'd installed a temporary portal platform.

"Be safe," I shouted as Y'sindra and Lo hopped through the portal and disappeared.

Teddy grabbed his flannel from the back of his chair and shrugged it on over his plain white T-shirt. No jacket for him. Shifters, I was learning, ran hot. He came back toward me, buttoning his shirt as he spoke. "I need to fill in at the bar. Zee texted. Dexter had unexpected guests drop in from out of town."

"Is that what they're calling a hangover these days?" I gripped the hem of

Teddy's flannel and pulled him against me, nuzzling my cheek against his chest. "For a bartender, he can't hold his liquor. I'm sorry you had to take him on because of me."

Dexter, the only moon fae I'd ever met living outside Ta'Vale who wasn't one of the corrupted. Teddy had hired the guy to fill the hole his absence left at the bar when he'd been glued to my side, an IV feeding me his blood during my coma.

"It's not your fault. I needed more help anyhow."

"He has definite sex appeal. I guess you needed to fill the eye candy role since you're off the market." I rolled my chin onto his chest and grinned up at him.

"Dexter is a good bartender, and the customers do enjoy looking at him, but this is the third time this month. I'm going to have a talk with him." Teddy stroked his hand down my hair, from the crown of my head to the hem of my shirt, and dug his hands beneath, branding the small of my back.

I followed him into the hall leading past the kitchen to the elevator. He stomped into his boots. "What do you plan to get up to?"

"There's a broken druid circle calling my name."

"Why?" He knelt to tie the laces, glancing up as he looped them. "You have an easier way in through Ta'Vale. Even if you fix the circle, why would you want to go through the druid's door to Outerlands? You'd lose time on the trip."

The memory of my last trip through the circle was still a sore subject for Teddy. I'd promised to be back in an hour, and instead returned three days later, a brush with a druid spell leaving me covered in blood. Saying he'd been worried was an understatement.

"To prove I can." But that wasn't the whole of it. It wasn't a reason I could easily put into words. Somehow, it didn't feel like I'd fix myself until I fixed the circle.

"Always ready to sink your fangs into a challenge." Teddy pulled me against him, and his mouth was on mine.

Gripping my waist, he brushed his thumbs beneath the hem of my shirt and tickled my ribs. My blood went from simmering to scorching. I slipped my arms up and around his neck. He bent over me and canted his head. Our tongues danced.

Our kiss slowed, grew airy. His breath flowed into me, and my chest stuttered.

Teddy finished with two slow, final kisses and stepped back. "The things you do to me, woman."

Though inside I was a flesh-bag of gelatin, I gave him a look designed to make his pants tight and the ride to the casino floor very uncomfortable.

His forehead puckered. "Did you eat the enchiladas, too?"

"I'm fine." I scowled and shooed him toward the elevator. "Go help Zee."

He planted a final, lightning-quick kiss on me, and then he was gone.

In the great room, I pulled the bag of supplies he had picked up for me from the shelf and headed for the balcony. "I'm coming for you, circle."

19

WHAT AM I

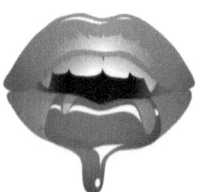

L<small>IGHTS MOUNTED DISCREETLY IN THE TREES BATHED THE ROOFTOP IN A</small> warm yellow glow and revealed the evidence of failure. Bottles of glue, rolls of duct tape, lengths of rope, and even a chain with a useless padlock littered the ground in and out of the druid circle. I sat in the grass, slouched over my legs, and finished my third full-sugar Cherry Coke. I'd be awake for days.

Music trilled into the quiet that came with high-rise living. A shock squirmed over my skin, and I leaped to my feet and spun, looking right and left. In the trees. The mellow, windswept sound of "Margaritaville" crooned.

I strode toward the stairs, but the song faded. The music seemed to come from behind me and to the right. Near a smattering of citrus trees, the song grew louder. My steps slowed as I passed from one tree to the next.

At last, I spotted a small box behind a lime tree. *Wasn't there yesterday*. A rectangular, blue device sat on top. Someone had left a cell phone. It lay facedown. A cover with a beach scene glared up at me.

My jaw clenched as I connected the dots between the song and the phone case. I stabbed the phone with a dark look until the musical ringtone cut off. It began again.

Rather than pick up the phone, I bent to flip it over atop the box, slid my finger on the call accept, and stabbed the speaker. "What do you want, Blackthorne?"

A lazy chuckle drifted into the garden. "So clever, granddaughter."

"You forgot the ten or twenty greats between you and me, old man."

"Blood is blood," Blackthorne said flippantly, and I could hear it in his voice—he was having fun.

"I assume you dropped this little present off, but how did you know I was up here?" Even as the words left my mouth, I turned to stare up at the camera mounted in the trees and already knew the answer. Security, those voyeuristic assholes.

"Vaughn was notified you were on the roof, and as directed, he contacted me."

"He's on a date with my sister. Bad move, old man."

I considered climbing the tree and ripping out the camera, but the small pragmatic voice in my head said not to. Intrusive as it was, it could also come in handy. Instead, I flipped off the camera. Juvenile, but it made me feel better.

"If you didn't destroy your phone, this wouldn't be necessary."

Too tired to argue, I squeezed my eyes shut and pinched the bridge of my nose. "Tell me what you want, Blackthorne."

"Why are you trying to fix the circle?" he asked, his voice muffled by the thunder and whoosh of crashing waves. "You have an easier method of accessing Shadwe. Well done parting the veil, by the way. I have been remiss in not mentioning your accomplishment sooner."

"To make a point." I picked up the phone, headed for the druid circle, and began shoving the empty rolls of tape and bottles into the box I'd used to carry them up here in.

"What point might that be?"

Abruptly, the murmuring roar of wind and surf cut off. A door clicked, indicating Blackthorne had gone inside his hotel.

"Are you renting rooms out over there?" I asked.

"Ah, avoiding the subject."

"It seems weird you would live in a hotel by yourself. Or do you plan to move to Shadwe?"

"Alas, no. The door I created here to Outerlands was more like a keyhole." Blackthorne's voice grew muffled but cleared as he spoke, and he let out a long sigh. "Much better. Nyle was an abysmal decorator. I've had to replace the furnishings. Thank you for dispatching that unpleasant individual."

"It was my pleasure." The act hadn't been enjoyable, or cathartic, but a necessity. Nyle Rathmore had been the catalyst who forced me to sever Y'sindra's wing. He had to die, and I'd been numb delivering the final blow.

"Granddaughter?"

"What?" I paused on the mat set outside the sliding glass doors to scrape off bits of grass gathered in the treads of my soft-soled house shoes.

"You forgot something resembling a chain on the roof."

I stepped inside and stopped short to glare at the phone. "Get to the point, or this conversation is over."

"So impatient. Where was I?" Blackthorne mused. "Oh yes, the portal was a rush job, and rather than passing through a door, this is more like pushing through a spiderweb-covered tunnel, where the spider never stops spinning."

Color me interested. I supposed it wouldn't hurt to hear him out. He was older than most dirt. There had to be a lot of knowledge tucked away in that evil head of his.

"So let me get this straight." I strode for my chair, sat down, and retrieved the phone before tucking the box out of the way. "You're saying you cracked the door but didn't actually open it?"

"Not quite. That is what you accomplished between Ta'Vale and Outerlands, my brilliant girl," Blackthorne said. "I, on the other hand, rubbed the veil thin between realms. Thin enough so one could pass through, but I didn't bring them together. There is still distance involved. Without a protective bubble surrounding the transportation provided, one would be lost to the vacuum of space."

"What does any of this have to do with you visiting Shadwe?" I kicked my legs out in front of me and sank into my seat, head resting on the chair back.

"The name of this establishment needs to change, don't you think?"

"Blackthorne..." I growled. Although, the name *was* the worst. Why Shadwe? Did the corrupted need a literal neon sign?

"You're no fun. Fine, I compared the veil here to a keyhole, because I can lock it, and I have. I know the sun fae are patrolling Outerlands, so I have no intention of visiting, nor do I have any intention of allowing visitors." I heard some sort of crinkling and a crunch.

"Why are you telling me any of this? What do you care?"

"Isn't that the million-dollar quest—" Blackthorne spit on the other end of the line. "This place needs more than a name change. It needs a facelift and new amenities, including a chef. The local fare is lacking."

I sighed.

"Fine, fine, why do I care?" Blackthorne paused. "I don't. My problem is not with the sun fae who employ you. There is only one fae I take issue with, and I no longer believe I need the machinations of the banished to reach them."

"What's changed?" I asked, reasoning boredom and loneliness were driving Blackthorne to talk. I might as well dig for all the answers I could get. "Since the corrupted moon fae are still in possession of two sun stones, it weakened the sun fae enough they would never risk a fight outside Ta'Vale."

"True enough, granddaughter. The answer to what has changed is you."

My jaw clenched at Blackthorne's familiarity, but I breathed through my irritation. "What do I have to do with anything?"

"I believe if you embrace your true nature, you will flush out the fae I desire."

"What do you mean, my 'true' nature?"

"You are not a druid, yet you are," he stated.

I licked my lips and sucked air through my nose. "What am I?"

"You are not a blood fae, yet you are."

As if I didn't already know this. "Who are you? The fucking Sphinx?"

"Why are you still trying to fix the circle?"

Flinging my legs over the side of the chair, I pushed to my feet. "What. Am. I?" I enunciated each word slow and precise.

"It's an honest question," Blackthorne responded, and damn if he didn't sound sincere.

"An answer for an answer." I laid out the bargain. A buzz built in my ears.

"Something new, I suppose." A tsk came from the speaker, and I glared at the timer on the phone's screen—9:11. How had I been on the phone so long? "A blood fae druid, perhaps?"

The world came to a crashing standstill and tilted. I sat down before I could fall over. Such an absurd declaration, but the gong of truth vibrated against my bones.

"My turn. Why are you trying to fix the circle?" He repeated his original question.

Swallowing, I slowed my breathing. Blood fae druid. The symphony of emotions slowly settled, and the definition Blackthorne had tossed out so carelessly sank into all the empty places inside me.

"Granddaughter?"

"What?"

"We agreed. It's your turn to answer."

Right, the circle. "To prove I can."

"This is the answer I expected." The druid's voice was thick with self-satisfaction. He wore the creation of my hybrid nature like a badge. "However, until you accept what is necessary for your nature, you will not accomplish your goal."

This again. "I'll figure it out, and I will figure it out *my way*."

Blackthorne's sigh came through the tiny microphone, hard and heavy. "Duct tape and superglue will not work. I'll see you when you figure it out. I have faith you will."

"I care more about a hairy ogre's ass than your faith in me."

No answer came.

"Blackthorne?"

Still no answer.

"Son of a troll humper hung up on me." I stomped a foot. "Again."

I stalked onto the balcony and launched the phone into the night sky.

20

DEFY THE UNIVERSE

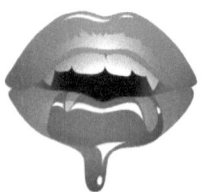

THE ELEVATOR DOORS HISSED OPEN, AND THE CLACK OF STILETTOS MEANT Mae had returned from her date. I glanced at the clock perched directly ahead of me on the bookshelves.

"It's not even midnight. Was the vampire bad company?"

A miraculously unharmed beach-themed phone landed in my lap.

"I think you dropped something." Mae shimmied past my chair and lowered herself onto the sofa. Kicking off her heels, she dragged a fuzzy blanket onto her lap.

"How?" I turned the phone over and over in my hand. Not a scratch.

"Security delivered it to Vaughn as I was about to come upstairs." She fell back into the cushions and closed her eyes. "They installed a net a few stories below the balcony. Blackthorne anticipated your temper and suggested they get ahead of any potential lawsuits resulting from items, like cell phones or teacups, hitting casino clientele in the head."

I pushed deeper into my seat. If I hadn't already known Blackthorne was still sailing this ship, I'd know now. It was likely if I removed the camera, he'd have another one installed. Probably more discreet and harder to find. Related or not, I didn't love that a superpowerful druid had such easy access to my life, but for now I could live with it. YML Investigations already picked up more jobs than we had in Interlands. And our new, rent-free home was a sweet bonus.

"How'd they retrieve it?" I asked.

Lips twisting into a wry smirk, Mae opened her eyes. "The fairies."

"Oh man, don't tell Y'sindra. We'll never hear the..." I choked on my words. How did I continue to forget my sister could no longer fly?

"Hey." Mae sat up, a small squiggly line of concern marring her smooth brow. "Mom's salve will work." The gentle, soft smile and lack of fidgeting told me Mae believed her words. Lying didn't come easy for my sister. She chewed her nails ragged every time she tried.

Unable to show the same faith, I only nodded.

Mae sucked in a sudden breath and bent over her legs until her head almost rested on her knees. I was on my feet, hovering over her in a heartbeat.

"What's wrong? Are you okay?" My sister's shoulders shuddered beneath my palms, and a cavern opened in my chest. I dropped to a squat and tried to see my sister's face. "Talk to me, Mae."

"I'm okay." She unfolded herself one vertebra at a time until she sat upright, though her arms remained tight across her middle. "I just...I don't think this is a bad enchilada."

My sister didn't get sick. Nothing had changed but the stone's acceptance of Mae. This was my nightmare.

"Wait here," I said and jogged into the kitchen. I dumped the basket containing Dad's portal disks, and they clattered onto the counter. One rolled off the edge and bounced on my toe.

Slight tremors shook my arms. I fumbled with the disk I tried to grab. "Come on," I said, flexing my hands.

The first device I turned had a frowny face on the back and would lead to Outerlands, as did the next. A smiley face that should lead to Eodrom but I knew would land me in Interlands followed. I flipped three more—smile, smile, frowny face.

Shit. Had we used all the devices for Eodrom? I checked the next five. Two more frowny faces and three smiley faces. Snatching the disk from the floor, I turned it over and almost collapsed with relief. A heart—Y'sindra's intentionally mislabeled mark for Eodrom.

I ran back to Mae and held out my hand. "We need to get you to Mom. Can you make it to the balcony?"

She nodded, gripped my hand, and I pulled her to her feet.

"Do you have any idea what's wrong?" I asked. With my arm wrapped around Mae's waist, we limped toward the balcony. I shouldered most of her weight.

"No. It came on slowly, but eventually the pain started coming in waves." We crossed over the door track to the balcony. Mae's steps were so heavy, they almost dragged. "I started feeling light-headed and knew I needed to get home. Please extend an apology to Vaughn for me. He said he understood, but I feel awful."

I tsked. "That vampire will be fine. Let's focus on getting you healed, and you can tell him yourself."

An open space, cleared of plants and furniture, marked the location we'd designated for portals. I leaned Mae against a column beneath the short awning outside the glass doors and set the device on the temporary portal pad.

"It'll be okay, Laney." Mae pushed upright. Her golden complexion had dulled, but she looked much better than five minutes ago. Whatever was wrong, she'd said it came in waves. "I'm sure it's just magic exhaustion. I've been training hard with Dad."

Mae let me take her hand and help her toward the device. "Maybe the stress of all this news today hit you harder than you realized."

Smiling, she tucked a strand of hair behind my ear. "Maybe. Mom will know."

I crouched to activate the device, but Mae pulled me up.

"No, you need to stay here and get the latest report from Y'sindra and Lo. They should be back soon." Mae squeezed my hand and let go. "I'll be back in no time."

"Fine," I grumbled and stepped back to give her room. "But if it takes too long, I'm coming to get you."

She laughed and activated the device. "I know you will. Try to get some rest. I'll take care of the report for Duskmere when I get home."

Mae, with her meticulous attention to detail and talent for organization, took care of compiling our weekly reports to the RFG—specifically to Duskmere. Regardless of my feelings, if we were still patrolling, we should still report.

A musical chime filled the air, and an oval opened to my parent's yard. In the distance, bright light flickered from the front window of my old home. It wasn't the low burn used to maintain light and heat. My parents had company. They were probably still talking about the shit storm I'd brewed earlier.

Mae stepped through the portal, turned to wave, and then she was gone.

"SWEET FANGS." MY SUGAR DUMPLING'S VOICE PIERCED THROUGH MY dream of chocolate, cheesy poofs, and kisses.

Quiet moans and wet kisses filtered into my reality. I sat up and blinked stupidly at the TV and the coffee table strewn with empty cellophane wrappers and two empty family-sized bags of cheesy poofs.

"I thought I was dreaming."

Teddy braced himself, an arm on either side of me, and came in for a kiss. There were no words to describe the rancid flavors at war in my mouth, and he was coming in for a taste. Panicked, I turned my head and took it on the cheek.

He leaned away, and I winced an apology. "I have really bad breath."

Still lying down, I wiggled to the back of the seat, making room for Teddy to sit in front of me. He picked up an empty snack cake wrapper coated in powdery orange fingerprints. "This might be why. Did you eat all of this before or after you fell asleep?"

"Ha. Ha. Aren't you funny?" I slid into a sitting position and swung my legs from behind Teddy onto his lap.

"Your poor eating habits are not helping your healing, you know."

"Geez, you sound like Mae. Not eating you isn't helping my healing either," I snapped and then winced. Holy Twinkies, where did that come from? My precaffeinated brain worked apart from my mouth. "Sorry."

Teddy laughed, loud and open. "Sorry you said that to me, or just sorry for what you said?"

I made a face. "Both. I need coffee so I can have a coherent conversation."

"Fair enough." Teddy took my chin in his hand before I could stand. In the gold light of dawn, his gaze glowed with an inner warmth, like looking at the sun through black tea. "I don't care about your breath. I'm going to kiss you now."

And he did, so slow and hot, my tendons let go of my bones. I slumped against the armrest, smiling and dazed when he pulled away and stood.

"Maybe brush your teeth before coffee?"

I gasped and swatted at him.

He dodged and laughed, jogging to the hallway. "I'm beat. Let me grab a shower and a quick nap. I'll join you in an hour?"

"See you then." I blew him a kiss.

With a yawn, I slid my legs over the side of the sofa, my feet into my slippers, and stretched. My back cracked three times. The sofa might be comfortable for sitting, but not for sleeping.

The bright gold and pink of dawn splashed through the glass wall separating the living area from the balcony. Taller than most buildings on the strip, the Blackthorne's height afforded views tourists shelled out big bucks for, including a picturesque horizon.

While I appreciated the view, I'd appreciate a dose of caffeine more. In the kitchen, I poured whole beans into the grinder and the fancy, filtered water from the system Gramps had sprung for into the coffeemaker.

I yawned again and checked my talons, waiting for the machine to do its thing. It occurred to me the sun was up, but neither of my sisters were home. Or if they were, they didn't wake me.

Since the layer of coffee dripping into the pot was still too shallow to pour, I headed upstairs to check Mae's room and then Y'sindra's. Both were empty. I stood in the hall and scratched my arm, looking from room to room. Unease itched across my nerves.

My sisters had no way of reaching me. They wouldn't have the number to the phone Blackthorne left in the garden, and I'd trashed my cell phone. Neither of which mattered since they themselves carried communication crystals not phones. I still hadn't retrieved my crystal from the Interlands house, something I needed to rectify, stat.

I wasn't so worried about Y'sindra and Lo not being home. They had a good deal of travel time involved in their trip. Mae's continued absence was a different story.

The shower cut off in my bathroom, and I headed for the stairs. What Teddy needed was rest, not to find me loitering outside the bedroom. No telling where that would lead, and stars take me, I still needed to brush my teeth.

At the bottom of the stairs, I took a sharp right, taking a detour into the half bath to gargle some mouthwash. That would have to do.

In the kitchen, I grabbed the first oversize mug my hand landed on from the cabinet and filled it to the brim. The hot plate sizzled with a drip of coffee from my premature pull, but this addled brain waited for no machine.

Cupping the mug between both hands, I padded to the stools at the end of the island counter and took the deepest sip my tongue could tolerate. Mouthwash and coffee did not mix, but I kept drinking, and eventually the minty flavor wore off.

Once I'd injected enough neuron-firing caffeine into my body, I hunched over the mug to enjoy the curls of steam wrapping themselves around my face. Like a magnet, my gaze eventually strayed from one digital clock to another. Something buzzed along my nerves. I couldn't be sure if it was the first blast of caffeine hitting my system or my worry for Mae.

From the other room, the glass door glided open on its track. I hopped off the stool and rushed to the kitchen pass-through window. Across the open living space, the subject of my concern walked inside. She spotted me. When her mouth wobbled, every piece of me shattered inside.

My hand dropped to the counter. Hot liquid sloshed from the mug. Coffee dribbled over my knuckles and puddled on the granite. I ran from the kitchen, clipping my hip on the sofa as I passed, and stopped in front of my sister. She didn't say what was wrong, but her despair burrowed into my marrow.

"Oh, Mae." I pulled her to me with the care of fine china, afraid she might splinter into a thousand pieces in my arms. She buried her face in my hair. "What is it?"

"I don't know what to do." Tears clogged her voice.

Gently, I pushed her back and dragged my thumb beneath her eyes. "Whatever it is, we'll figure it out."

She bit her lip and swallowed. The blue of her eyes rippled like a tropical ocean beneath the wash of tears she struggled to hold back. "It's the stones."

My insides went subzero, the cold so instant and intense, pain lanced my chest. Mae was watching me, and I fought to keep the reaction from my face.

I licked my dry lips and forced a smile. "Coffee's fresh. Let's sit down and talk whatever this is through, yeah?"

Predictably, Mae grabbed a dishrag and a damp paper towel to clean up my spill. It was an automatic, soothing action for her.

Once again settled on the stool, I sipped my coffee and waited. One minute ticked by. It surprised me to find the sweep of the rag on granite calming. I could see how Mae found Zen in the whisper and whoosh. Didn't mean I'd be picking up a dust rag anytime soon, but it made waiting for Mae marginally less terrible.

Three full minutes later, her hand stilled. She tossed the coffee-stained paper towel in the garbage and faced me across the large, square island counter. She threaded her fingers together and pulled them against her belly so they resembled a white-knuckled, fleshy knot. "I saw Mom," she said, and I nodded. "The keepers were there, too."

My pulse trotted into action. "I saw the lights were still on. I figured. You look better."

"I am." She peeled her hands apart and pulled three silver chains from beneath her shirt. Sun shards, larger than any I'd ever seen my sister wear, drooped from the end of each chain. "Iola sent me home with several more."

My recently defrosted hearts iced over. Fuck. Of all the things Mae could have said, this was the worst. I knew the implications, but I couldn't stop the question from leaving my mouth. "Why?"

"The stones." She crushed her lips together.

My own lips too numb to form words, I nodded, encouraging her to continue.

"They chose me as a keeper."

Heat tore through my body, chasing away the cold. My head swam, and somewhere deep inside, I imploded. I didn't want to ask. I really, really didn't. "What does that mean?"

Her shoulders rose and fell in a loose, helpless shrug. "I don't know. But..." She shook her head.

"But it hurts to be away from the stones," I said for her.

"Yes." How could a single word sound so desperate? Mae folded at the waist. She dropped her elbows onto the counter and buried her face in her hands.

I surged to my feet. The stool knocked on the wood floor behind me as I ran around the counter to Mae.

"Hey." I pried her hands from her face and ducked to meet her gaze. "It will be okay. I promise. I will find a way to make this work."

She snorted her disbelief. "How do you intend to defy the universe?"

"Teddy says druids are of the universe." I worked my lip between my teeth and glanced at the empty arch to the kitchen, as if Teddy might appear to support my claim. "And I'm part druid, right?"

Mae nodded, waiting to see where I was going with this.

She wasn't the only one.

"Well, then I can defy whoever the fuck I want."

She laughed, and it was the sweetest sound.

"I promise you, I will figure this out." Promises were dangerous, but this one I would keep. I'd be damned if I lost my sister.

21

UNTIL WE COME TO IT

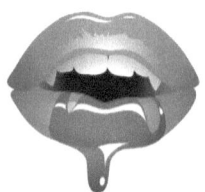

M AE AND I RECLINED ON PATIO LOUNGERS, TWO SHOT GLASSES AND THE now empty bottle of Crystal Head perched on a small round table between us. A blanket draped over each of us, keeping the winter desert cold air at bay. The fancy heat lamps didn't hurt either. Blackthorne spared no expense for his comfort.

Despite wearing the magic-crafted, clear contact lenses that kept my bicolored eyes on full display while protecting my pupils from sunlight, it was still difficult to rest in the full light of the sun. That was where the owl-like shades perched on my nose came in. They added extra protection and extra relaxation.

The sounds of the Strip were barely a murmur at this height. Between the mellowing vodka buzz, the sun toasting my face, and the cool, city-scented air, this was the most relaxed I'd been for days. It was almost like the news Mae brought home hadn't been spoken aloud. Almost.

For now, she was fine. The problem was, all sun fae were better, more powerful, more at ease when they were in the same realm as the sun stones. Which was why I rarely saw them after the day I'd left Ta'Vale.

Until now, Mae had gotten used to her break with the stones. She'd built up a tolerance to their absence. Still, wearing shards only went so far. She'd had to visit regularly to recharge her connection, but this situation was different. For the moment, the extra sun shards helped, but I figured they acted like antibiotics. Her system would get used to their presence and need more and more until only being near the source of the shards—the sun stones—worked.

If it came down to it, I could live in Ta'Vale, just not Eodrom. But would it be enough? I didn't know what it meant to be a keeper, and neither did Mae. From what she told me, Iola and Torneh didn't have a clue what it meant for her either. No keeper had ever *wanted* to be apart from Ta'Vale and the stones.

We'd cross that bridge when we came to it. More accurately, we'd fall in the water and try not to drown.

I turned my head and studied Mae. She looked at peace. My chest felt heavy and thick. I hated to intrude, but I also couldn't lie around wallowing in what-ifs all day. Time to do something.

Sitting up, I rubbed my breastbone while I slid my legs over the side of the lounge and faced her. "Why don't you get some rest?"

A smile pulled across her lips. "I thought that's what we were doing."

"We were, but I made a deal with our tricky sister, and it's time I honor it."

Mae ripped off her sunglasses and sprang upright in her seat, laughter lighting her eyes. "No!"

"Yep," I said, popping the "p" to emphasize what a shit job this literal shit job would be.

Pressing the back of her hand to her mouth, Mae trapped the laugh shaking her shoulders.

I rolled my eyes and stood, reached my arms toward the sky, and twisted side to side. My back released a gratifying one-two crack. "A job's a job. Who knows what news those two are going to come back with? I should get this out of the way and get paid now, in case I end up in another coma."

"Don't joke." Mae pursed her lips in disapproval and stood. She pulled a robe on over her loose-fitting pj's, draped the sun-toasted blanket over her shoulders, and went inside.

The open glass doors created cool, comfortable airflow, but it was the early hours. Winter or not, it was only a matter of time before the scorching desert sun took over. Fortunately, the glass had a magic, reflective film. I slid the three massive glass panels closed behind me.

Through the pass-through, I spotted Mae filling two glasses with water. She stretched across the counter to place one glass in front of me.

"Thanks." I drained half of it, set it down, and picked up my new Margaritaville phone. Temporary solution to my no cell phone problem. After a few minutes of searching, I located the phone number and scribbled it onto a sticky note for Mae. "I'll take this phone with me since I still need to swing by the Interlands house and pick up the crystal. Call me when the tiny terrors return?"

"Will do." Mae washed and dried her glass.

"Do me a favor and let Teddy know when he wakes up?" I hadn't woken him up and instead opted for sister time. He needed the rest, anyhow.

"Of course," she said. "It might be a good idea for you to dress for work."

"Well, I am going out on a job." I drained the rest of my water and slid it to Mae, who promptly delivered it to the sink to wash and set on the drying rack next to hers.

"Yes, but I mean your good work attire. Your leathers, your weapons. Depending on what Y'sindra and Lo find, we might need to head out right away."

I groaned. "You think?" The last thing I wanted to do was wear my good, expensive gear to dig through dung.

She pressed her lips together until they rolled into a thin line as she fought off her laughter. Unable to speak past her amusement, she nodded. It was great seeing Mae happy. I just preferred it not be at my expense.

"Fine," I grumbled and pushed back from the counter. "I've got heavy-duty gloves and waders from the swamp job—which was the worst, by the way. Can you set a few portal disks out before you head up to sleep? One each, including Interlands. I'll swing by and grab my communication crystal after I have the ring."

When I reached the base of the stairs, Mae called, "You should probably take some wet wipes."

Her musical laughter chased me up the stairs, and I couldn't help but smile. But she was right. I needed to bring wet wipes, and plenty of them.

THE DARK-GREEN HUMMER, COURTESY OF THE BLACKTHORNE RESORT and Casino, rumbled down Jason Olson's long drive. Our new residence might give my wannabe grandpa more access to my life than I'd like, but I couldn't deny the perks. I hopped from the large vehicle, slung the backpack I'd dragged with me over my shoulder, and waved the driver away.

My second impression of the sprawling ranch was no less impressive than the first. An hour and a half north of the Strip, nestled on over two hundred acres of swells and valleys of the Spring Mountains, sat what I suspected was more than just an animal sanctuary.

A tall stairway, wide at the bottom and narrowing at the porch, led to the Spanish-style home in terra-cotta tones. This was only my second trip here, and it was no less impressive.

Strapped with a small arsenal, I climbed the stairs. It felt good to be back in my heavy-duty, oiled fighting leathers, weighed down by the comfort of my blades. Two bandoliers of push daggers crisscrossed my chest. A tri-blade dagger and torpedo dagger rested in each thigh sheath. Across my spine, good ol' Pru's sword rested in a hard leather holster I'd commissioned. I'd had to. Dacian's wyvern claws had destroyed the original scabbard when he'd hauled me into the sky all those months ago.

Two large ceramic pots filled with flowers and draping greenery flanked the glass, inset double doors. Carved into both panes, a creature resembling an aloughta—massive, deerlike beasts the sun fae rode to war—faced whoever approached. An interesting choice for a human mage.

Through the frosted glass, I spotted a woman walking past the foyer. Tall, and with enough golden hue to pass for a sun fae, she caught sight of me and pivoted in my direction. I raised my hand in greeting, but when she was close enough for a clearer view, she paused, turned, and hurried into the depths of the house.

Frowning, I glanced down at myself, taking in the array of weapons attached to my body. Fair enough.

I didn't have time to be courteous and wait to see if the woman notified anyone of company. I pressed the doorbell. A deep gong reverberated through the house. I toed the backpack I'd set at my feet out of the way, against the wall to the right of the door.

The trip out here only cost me an hour thanks to my driver and his lead foot, but I still had a job to do, and a communication crystal to pick up from the Interlands house. Provided the new residents hadn't already tried to use or pawn the last of Duskmere's portal stones, I'd grab those too. I'd brought one of each of my father's portal devices, but I had a feeling we would need all the options at our disposal.

Counting off twenty full unanswered seconds, I reached for the doorbell again. A smudge appeared behind the glass. A male silhouette walked briskly toward the door. As the figure neared the frosted panes, I recognized our client.

The right side of the double doors opened. Jason Olson glanced behind him and stepped outside. Taller than me, but shorter than Mae, he had the frame and weathered complexion of a man who spent most of his time outdoors. He looked like he'd just come in from working outside. The cowboy hat he wore might have started out as white, but between sweat stains and dirt had turned beige. Dust clung to his jeans from hem to shin, a shirt emblazoned with the sanctuary's name—Mojave Second Chance Sanctuary—had been untucked, one corner still caught beneath his waistband, as if he'd been getting comfortable when I showed up.

"Ms. Callaghan, I wasn't expecting you." Jason Olson scanned the driveway behind me, no doubt looking for my car. He smiled, but the expression was tight and didn't quite meet his mossy-green eyes. I recognized forced politeness when I saw it.

"It's just Lane. I apologize for not calling ahead." Stupid of me, I should have called, but I'd planned to search for the ring whether or not Mr. Olson was home. Few knew I had a way with animals. Though I'd yet to test the theory with Earth creatures, I was at least ninety-five percent certain I could check the animal enclosures without losing a few pounds of flesh.

"It's no problem, just a surprise." He chuckled, sounding a tad nervous. His attention slid to the sword pommel protruding behind my right shoulder and then down my body from blade to blade.

A tangible fission of energy hummed from Jason Olson. His expression never changed, nor did his posture, but the spill of energy cut sharply across my skin. This simple earth mage was packing some pretty powerful magic.

Right, the weapons, the fighting leathers. I supposed it could intimidate humans. Probably what chased the woman who'd spotted me through the door away. I smiled. Closed lips, no fangs.

"I'm sorry. The outfit is overkill." I held my hands up, palms out. Not because this guy worried me, but because getting into a brawl with a client would probably be bad for business. Mae would kill me if I landed us our first one-star Yelp review. "I'm pressed for time today, and I've got another job after this."

"Of course, sorry." The tension left Jason's shoulders, and he slipped into an easy smile. He took off his hat and ran a hand through his hair. "How can I help you?"

"We know what happened to your ring."

"Wonderful." He waited expectantly.

"Your ex was...creative."

"My..." His brow ran the gamut of emotions. Furrow from confusion, arched in surprise, and finally, his eyes crinkled with the last thing I expected —humor. "She stole the ring? I should have expected that. How do you know?"

"Stole isn't the word I would use. It's still on the property." I tilted my head, my focus finding a corner beneath the porch overhang, and I scratched my neck. "I came across her scent when we were investigating, and it was complete chance we crossed paths in the Blackthorne. She was happy to tell me what she'd done."

"It's no surprise you ran into her. She works at the Blackthorne." He slid his hands into the front pockets of his jeans, relaxing into the conversation. "I forgot blood fae can track scents."

"If I've smelled blood." I glanced toward the path at the side of the house leading to the animal enclosures. With so much acreage, there had to be far more animals than I'd seen on my previous visit. "There is a tangle of scents around here, but I imagine it comes with the territory. I've got yours."

It wasn't exactly a threat, but it wasn't innocent, either. I'd learned long ago to make sure I had a client's scent. So far, no one had successfully skipped out on paying us. A few tried, but it was hard to outrun your scent trail if you remained in the area. Of course, we were based in a big city now. That trick might not work.

"Injuries are a hazard of working with wild animals." He rubbed his jaw, drawing my attention to the faded yellow bruise. Only a slight hint of purple remained. The scent I'd picked up on previously, peppery with floral notes, rose from an old bloodstain on his collar and sleeve.

Despite the urgency to get on with the job and get to Interlands for my stuff, I couldn't squash my curiosity. "I thought you minimized physical contact with animals while they rehabilitate. So they don't get comfortable with humans, you said."

"True for most animals here, but some injuries are too great to return to the wild. Those get some extra TLC. We also have a breeding program for some domesticated beasts." He shook his head. "Shame about my ex. I'd hoped we could stay friends. She's good with the animal. That's what she does at the Blackthorne—she's a trainer for the animal show."

And there went my curiosity. I had no idea what ended their relationship, but I'd wager it had something to do with the blonde I'd seen.

"Mr. Olson—"

"Jason."

"Sorry, Jason. Let's talk about the ring." Preparing to investigate the animal enclosure, I picked up my backpack and slid the strap over my right shoulder. The action drew Jason's attention to the sword pommel rising behind my back.

"Well," he said, his deep-green eyes peeling away from the sword to meet my gaze. "I was going to invite you in for some of my famous green chili, but you said you're in a hurry. Let's get you on the road."

"Rain check on the chili." I meant it. Green chili ranked close to cheesy poofs and Ho Hos.

"You got it. Just come prepared for spice."

"No other way to appreciate green chili, if you ask me." I winked and pulled my backpack around, opening it and tugging the waders and gloves out far enough for Jason to see. "The weapons aren't for your job, but these are."

"Son of a bitch. Did she throw the ring in the lake?"

"Worse." I made a face. "Can you point me to your big cat enclosure?"

"Which one?"

"How many do you have?" I zipped the backpack and slid it over my shoulder. This was looking a lot more complicated and a lot filthier than I'd planned. "Exactly how many carnivores do you have on the property?"

"Quite a few. What's this about?"

I recounted the conversation I'd had with his ex.

"Clever minx." Jason laughed.

"You aren't angry?"

"I'm mad as hell, but I can appreciate the woman's creativity. Frankly, the lake would have been worse."

I disagreed, and he must have read it on my face.

Stupid face. I couldn't keep any thoughts to myself.

"The lake might be man-made—or mage-made." He grinned at his joke. "But it's ten acres, deep, and fed by an underwater spring. If she'd thrown it in there, it would have forced me to hire water fairies or selkies to search.

Neither option is cheap, and even then, chances are slim they would have found the ring."

"But you realize it's in an animal's digestive track right now or, you know." I shuddered. "And she didn't clarify which animal got the special surprise. My mistake not considering there would be options."

"I know exactly who she would have fed the ring to. Your job is done. I'll have the payment wired to YML Investigation." He smiled and held out his hand.

Confused, I shook it and asked, "Don't you want me to collect the ring?"

"Ha! Absolutely not. Thank you, but I won't have Angus Blackthorne's granddaughter sorting manure." He glanced around the obviously empty loop and down the long stretch of driveway. "You need a ride somewhere."

"No, I have—" The words evaporated on my tongue. Nerves tingled beneath my skin, and I licked my suddenly dry lips. "How do you know that name?"

To everyone who knew Gramps outside Ta'Vale, he was Andrew Black. I'd only recently learned the very generic first name he'd chosen for himself on the Blackthorne Resort and Casino paperwork. Yet this simple human earth mage knew his true identity.

I flexed my hands, fighting the urge to grab a few blades. Blackthorne had that effect on me. If I thought brawling with a client would be bad for business, stabbing them would probably be worse.

"How do you know that name?" I asked again.

Confusion pulled at his features. "All druids know who the great Angus Blackthorne is."

I could be slow, but I caught the implication immediately. "You're a mage."

Jason crossed his arms over his chest and tilted his head, revealing the side of his neck. What appeared to be the tattoo of a large bright-blue Celtic rune trailed beneath his collar. "What exactly do you think mages are?"

"Not druids," I snapped.

Rather than being insulted, he laughed.

My fangs tingled, and my lip peeled up. I was getting really sick of these Mr. Nice Guy reactions.

Wastin' away again in Margaritaville
Searchin' for my lost shaker of salt

I fumbled for my zipper pocket. That ringtone had to go. Punching and sliding the talk button, I growled, "What?"

"We're headed to Outerlands," Mae said. No greeting, no questions about the job. No comment on my terse greeting. "Y'sindra and Lo found the location of the sun stones. They aren't rooted yet."

Holding up a finger for Jason to wait, I turned and strode across the drive to the rock garden in the center of the driveway loop. "You're worried they might still be on the move."

"Yes."

"I'd planned to swing by the Interlands house and pick up my communication crystal and Duskmere's portal crystals. I think there's four left."

"There are. I put them in a box on the top shelf of your closet after your accident. If the new tenants haven't destroyed the place, or dug it into some sinkhole, they should be there." Mae had the memory of a steel trap. Correction, a *selective* memory of a steel trap. She conveniently forgot things like the milkshake with my order. Last week she forgot to supersize my fries. What a disaster.

"I'll be quick," I promised.

"You have time. Y'sindra and Lo are catching a quick nap, and then we're going to eat. I'll bring a couple granola bars for you."

I wrinkled my nose. "How about Ho Hos?"

"A granola bar. You need healthy energy."

"Fine," I mumbled, kicking a rock. It skipped onto the asphalt.

"Laney." Mae took an audible breath, and I went still.

"What is it?"

"The stones are in Shadwe, where we're headed. Make sure you have everything you think you'll need before you join us."

My hand tightened on the phone.

"We've got this. Love you, sis." Mae hung up.

A chill slipped over my body, and I shivered. Shadwe was an unknown, chock-full of enemies, including Dacian, back on his home turf. What about Teddy? What would returning to the home he left behind, to avoid becoming what he was born to be, do to his black wolf?

Fuck.

Resting my forehead in my palms, I threaded my fingers into my hair, tugging strands from my braid. I stared unseeing at the open desert in front of me. *Until we come to it*. My new motto I planned to apply to every potential disaster.

I rolled the tension from my shoulders and slipped my phone into my pocket. Forcing a smile, I returned to where I'd left Jason. He'd pulled out his own phone and was tapping away.

He looked up at my approach and slid his phone into the front pocket of his jeans. "Is everything okay?"

"Fine. You know where to send the payment?" I asked.

"I do."

"Okay, good doing business with you." I pulled my father's portal devices from the backpack and sorted through them until I found the Interlands disk. I set it on the ground, shielding it from view as I drew the activation run on its surface. A musical chime preceded the oval leading to the empty front yard in Interlands that opened above the driveway.

"We should probably talk." Giving the portal a wide berth, Jason stepped into my field of vision. "Why don't you come for dinner this weekend?"

The word "no" leaped into my mouth, but I pressed my lips together and studied him. There was a lot I didn't know about druids, and this guy seemed to have some answers.

"I'll call when I get this job wrapped up." I crossed through the portal to the Interlands yard and turned. "Just tell me one thing. Are we related?"

Please don't say yes. I couldn't take any more realm-shattering news.

"What? Of course not."

"Oh, thank goodness." Dinner wouldn't kill me, and maybe he'd make green chili.

"I'm related to Nuada."

I slow-blinked.

"You're what now?" His connection to Blackthorne made a lot more sense. For an infinite universe, it felt pretty small.

With a musical note, the portal closed.

22

I STILL HAVE A JOB

No one was home at the Interlands house, but Mae would be pleased I'd found the place clean. I didn't look too closely, but for creatures who spent so much time in the dirt, I saw no trace of it inside.

The hole large enough to drive my Bronco inside between the driveway and the forest was a different story. An urge to grab a dagger and start relieving a few grounders of their fuzzy blue pelts rose, but I'd agreed to it. I'd have to live with it, even if it was much larger than the tunnel the grounders had dug in Ta'Vale.

It took no time to locate the box Mae mentioned, still here and undisturbed. Of course, I'd needed a stepladder to reach the closet's upper shelves. Those oversize rodents hadn't stood a chance.

I dug the crystal and portal stones from the box, secured them in different jacket pockets, and climbed off the ladder. Apparently, I didn't stand a chance with these shelves either. No wonder I forgot about the box. Who put vaulted ceilings in a closet?

Forgotten box epiphany in mind, I dragged the stepladder with me to the kitchen and rescued an unopened box of Y'sindra's precious Sno Balls where I'd hidden them in the tippy top of the pantry. My memory wasn't the best, and they'd been there for years. Good thing these sugary wonder-treats could outlast an apocalypse.

As I made my way from the kitchen back to the great room, I unwrapped a Sno Ball and tossed the cellophane wrapper over my shoulder. And froze.

Next to the fireplace, the grounders had tucked an old-fashioned steamer trunk. Upon arrival, I'd been so focused on getting the crystal and portal stones, I'd rushed through the room and missed the hulking trunk.

Palms itching with curiosity, I curled my fingers until I felt the prick of my talons. When Rip first sent me after the grounders to collect the debt they owed, I'd seen the pile of ill-gotten gains on the table where I'd caught the furry little deviants gambling. Anything could be in there—rare coins, sun shards, gemstones, a mechanical hand, a hook. Had I ever seen them with artificial body parts? No, but those tiny degenerates would take anything shiny and valuable.

Mae, ever the voice of reason, would kill me if she found out I went through our tenants' things. Y'sindra, though, wouldn't just encourage my snooping—she'd freeze the lock and break it for me. If Y'sindra supported it, I knew it was a bad idea.

With more aggression than necessary, I sank my teeth into the spongy cake, tearing off a huge bite. I left pink coconut shavings in my wake on my way to the porch. It left a mess for the grounders to clean, but I also left half a box of Sno Balls on the counter. I'd call us even.

I flopped onto the porch swing, sending it swiveling in a side-to-side corkscrew motion. Planting my feet on the ground to bring this ride to a standstill, I placed the portal disk to Outerlands on the seat beside me, and the communication crystal in front of my feet. I pressed a finger to the crystal and said, "Duskmere."

Nothing happened. I licked my fingers free of coconut and tried again. "Duskmere."

He didn't answer. Unlike me, the uptight, by-the-book captain of the Royal Fae Guard wouldn't be caught without his crystal. He was ignoring my call.

I pressed my finger onto the crystal until either my flesh or the crystal threatened to give, "Duskmere, answer, you asshole."

Despite the light chill, the air above the crystal shimmered like a hot asphalt mirage. Duskmere appeared, arms folded across his chest, glaring at me. Even with the faded holographic image, his silver eyes sparked with ire. "What?" he snapped.

"Excuse you," I said, affronted by his poor—but typical—lousy attitude.

He had a lot of nerve coming at me like that after everything I'd done for the sun fae, and he'd not done for me. "How do those enormous balls of yours fit in those tight pants you wear? I think I've finally solved the mystery of why you're always such a grumpy bitch."

Duskmere's nostrils flared, and his chest expanded. "We have a situation I must return to. What may I assist you with, Malaney Callaghan?"

Instantly alert, I scanned the scene behind Duskmere. He held the crystal, rather than put it on the ground, which didn't afford me much of a view. The closer it was to the user, the less you saw on either end. Since I had placed my crystal in front of me, Duskmere would see a small image of me sitting on the cotton candy–pink bench and much of my surroundings. I had a view of Duskmere from chest up, with only bits and pieces of his surroundings visible over his shoulder.

He stood in a hallway I recognized as being outside the official RFG office. Through a small crack in a door behind him, I caught glimpses of RFG members, including Cirron and Pru. I waved when she passed the door and looked out. She bared her fangs and kept going.

Obviously, I was too far away for my new bestie to recognize me.

"What's going on in there?" I asked.

A thunderstorm gathered on Duskmere's brow, and he turned to pull the door shut behind him. "Nothing that involves you."

"You could fill the ocean with what you think I don't need to know about." I dragged a talon along the bench armrest. "This was one secret too many. Moving forward, I don't know how we'll navigate a working relationship, or if we can. For now, I still have a job."

Duskmere gave a curt nod. "We thank you for honoring your agreement."

I rolled my eyes. "Don't thank me. I'm a professional. You know as well as I do I want those stones back for more than a job."

"The news about Maerwen, I heard."

"She needs those stones," I said. "I will get them for her."

"Malaney Callaghan, what is it you need?" Duskmere rubbed a hand over his face, an ever so slight slump breaking the rigid line of his usually straight back.

"Tell me what's going on in there, Duskmere, and I'll fill you in on some news you're going to want to hear." I pounced on my chance for information. The moon fae was clearly exhausted, and where some might feel pity, I saw opportunity. Whatever it took to get the truth.

Duskmere turned his head to the side. His jaw flexed, and a muscle feathered in profile. "Fine." He shifted his back to me. His intense, steely gaze drove through the crystal projection. "It is regarding the sun fae whose rooms you investigated. We have discovered the route she might have taken leaving the grounds."

Boring. Not the juicy intel I'd been hoping for. "You found her?"

He shook his head. "This is a trail we will follow."

Curiosity itched my frontal lobe, stronger than the urge I'd had to break into the grounder's trunk, begging me to ask more about this trail I'd missed. In another life, I must have been born a cat.

Get it together, Lane.

With a mental slap, I tamped down the urge and leaned close to the crystal, intentionally filling Duskmere's side of the projection with a smartass grin. "Thank you for sharing. See how easy that was?"

"Your information, Malaney Callaghan."

My upper lip lifted on its own accord. I snatched the crystal from the ground and stood. "We think we've located the sun stones. They aren't in the ground yet, so I suspect they plan to move them again."

I could almost feel Duskmere's energy come alive through the projection. His eyes widened and then narrowed. That impeccable charcoal-shaded complexion pulled tight across the sharp angles of his face.

"This is good news."

"It is," I agreed. "I'm on my way now to check it out, but there's a problem."

Quickly, Duskmere said, "No RFG sun fae can assist."

"Did I ask for help? No," I answered for him. Irritation rubbed against me. I knew my reaction wasn't fair, but the RFG, Duskmere in particular, had burned me enough I doubted I'd ever treat him or his precious Royal Fae Guard fairly again.

"You misunderstand." Duskmere looked over his shoulder and stepped away. After he walked for a moment, he stopped and faced the door he'd walked away from, no doubt to ensure no one could eavesdrop. "This is sensitive information. Is there anyone near?"

"I'm at the Interlands house. You've been here." I fluttered my hands at the yard and the trees in every direction. "It's in the middle of the woods, and the tenants are out."

Tongue darting out to wet his lips, Duskmere scanned the area around him once again. I'd never seen him so uncomfortable, so nervous.

"We discovered the unrooted stones have an ill effect on the sun fae." As Duskmere pointed out the obvious, I fought to stop my eyes from rolling and kept my mouth shut. "The moment members of the RFG who are sun fae entered Outerlands, following your altercation with Dacian Barbout, they felt ill."

I snorted. Altercation was putting it mildly. I pressed a hand to the hard ridge resting beneath my shirt and jacket.

"Sorry, but don't worry, I am not asking for your help," I reminded him. "At least not yet. That's why I'm touching base now. The stones are in Shadwe. If we can grab them, we'll have to act fast."

Someone called his name in the distance. Duskmere glanced toward the door and held up a finger. "What do you need from me?"

"Nothing yet." I patted a chest pocket. "I have your portal stones, and my sisters each have extra of my father's devices. Just be ready to respond, no matter how I contact you. Don't make me call you five times on the crystal before you answer."

Duskmere nodded. "Understood, and Lane?"

His rare use of my simplified name stopped me short of curling my fingers over the crystal and ending the call. Duskmere had fallen back into his annoying formal habit of using my full name since we both woke up. This was the first time he'd used the name I'd asked him to.

"Yes?"

"You have what appears to be pink sponge on your fangs." The crystal projection ended.

23

IRON, STEEL, AND A STINKY BOOT

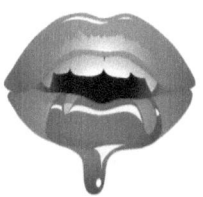

I STEPPED THROUGH THE PORTAL AND INTO A LITERAL PILE OF SHIT. "Seriously?"

Curses that would make foul-mouthed Y'sindra proud flew from my mouth as I yanked the portal chain with more aggression than necessary. The portal snapped shut, and I bent to retrieve used disks, but stumbled back when the smell bulldozed into my nostrils. I gagged into the elbow I threw across my face and quickly grabbed the device.

Somewhere, Fate was laughing her pretty, blue-haired head off about this situation.

Only a foot away sat a fresh pile of manure. The unique chicken egg shape and size of each "pellet" laid the blame at the hooves of an aloughta. Correction. At the feet of whichever RFG sun fae asshat let their mount do its business on top of the portal location.

I hurried away, dragging the offended foot through the grass as I went. This had to be karma balancing the scales for Jason letting me close out the job without physically returning his gods damned ring.

While I finished scraping my boot clean, I scanned the area for any signs of life. Despite the evidence of a recent visitor on my shoe, everything appeared quiet and still. Trees with fat trunks hugged the clearing where the portal landing was situated while thick, interlocking branches of large, spade-shaped leaves blotted out the full moon rising overhead.

When I'd walked through my father's portal, the late afternoon sun still shone in Interlands, but time mirrored the east coast of the United States. Before Blackthorne supposedly closed the door to Earth, Outerlands opened to the west coast, which explained the soft darkness of early evening.

"Ow," I complained and dug a finger beneath the twisted harnesses digging into the side of my neck. Somewhere during my stumble away from the portal, my push dagger holster shifted and pulled my jacket along for the ride. I'd left the straps too loose when I dressed. I was out of practice wearing my weapons, and it showed.

While I looked around to get my bearings, I straightened the harness until it crossed directly over the center of my chest and tightened the straps. Sometimes, I learned from my mistakes. Finally, I tugged the hem of my jacket smooth beneath the harness rigs and set off in what I hoped was the right direction.

My patrol with Teddy the other day had been my first visit to this portal site, and I'd followed him to town. On my best day, I could barely navigate the casino.

Remembering directions might not be my superpower, but I remembered the long walk. Once I reached the path, it would speed up my travel, but I was probably still about four miles from my destination. My father linked his devices to coordinates, and whoever gave these coordinates to him sucked. Sure, this was closer to the Ta'Vale border and therefore safer, but still... walking. Not a fan, especially when weighed down by close to thirty pounds of iron and steel and a stinky boot.

I released all the noise in my brain and focused on navigating between trees and through the thick underbrush. Time passed quickly, and before I knew it, unobstructed moonlight kissed my face. Pale-blue light bathed the ankle-tall grass. At least a hundred feet wide, the natural clearing led away from the Ta'Vale border to the defunct border to Earth, with a forest on each side.

Open ground wasn't the smartest place to stroll around solo, especially when I wasn't at my best, but I was more into being direct than smart. The path was the fastest, most direct route to where Teddy, my sisters, and Lo waited for me.

On the far side of the path, something was coming toward me through the trees. The muscles between my shoulders pulled taut. I slowed my footsteps, rested my right hand on the sword hilt rising behind my shoulder, my left on the leather-wrapped grip of a tri-blade dagger, and faced whomever, or whatever, deemed it unnecessary to hide their approach.

Bright-copper eyes preceded a silver-plated shield draped over the chest of the largest aloughta I'd ever seen. My hand tightened on the sword, joints went loose, and I sank my weight into my knees. The closer the aloughta came, the clearer I could make out the Royal Fae Guard insignia embossed on the front of the shield and the sun fae whose throat I still very much wanted to remove.

"Cirron," I spat, releasing my grip on both weapons to plant my hands on my hips. In a power move I'd been practicing, I let my fangs lengthen slowly. Neither my lip nor my tongue suffered a puncture.

"Duskmere asked I escort you and yours to the Shadwe border."

"Of all the rotten RFG, why are you in charge of anything? You should be in a cell." I crossed my arms and cocked a hip. "You know, the ones you repeatedly freed prisoners from?"

It hurt my neck to stare up at the sun fae. The aloughta was tall enough Cirron could play tic-tac-toe on the top of the seven-foot ogre Rip's bald head.

I took several steps back until my neck was no longer in danger of breaking so I could make eye contact. It had nothing to do with the fact those sharp, massive chompers could take off more than half my face in one bite. I took two more steps back. The freakish beast wasn't natural.

"Cirron Brightstone is not in charge." A familiar, scarred-face fae led more RFG from the trees, all seated on similar mutant mounts. He and his furry tank plodded past Cirron to stop in front of me. "I am."

The muscles across my neck tightened, pulling my shoulders closer to my ears as I stared down a new set of teeth. I looked past its muzzle to the wood fae seated on the aloughta's back. "Odo."

His war-weathered face, with its thick scar running from his hairline, across his milky left eye, and over the cheekbone, had been the last face I saw before falling into a coma. Technically, his decision to disregard keeper Torneh's orders to remain on the Ta'Vale side of the veil had probably saved me that night.

Thank the gods he swung off his mount and dropped to the ground. "Malaney."

He'd used the semi-simplified version of my name since we met as an insult. But it didn't land the way he'd intended. It wasn't Lane, but it was better than Malaney Callaghan.

Odollam, aka Odo, aka the wood fae I'd once referred to as Scar for my personal amusement, patted the umber-shaded beast on its bulky neck. The besotted aloughta nuzzled his shoulder. Odo smiled affectionately, the expression crinkling the corners of his eyes and pulling the hard ridge of his scar taut.

"How about you tell me what you're doing here?" I asked, watching the display with open astonishment. In my first experience with Odo, we'd nearly come to blows. In my second, I stole his belt for Teddy, after I popped the buttons off my love muffin's jeans. At Teddy's insistence, we made peace over drinks the third time we met. A lot of drinks.

"Cirron Brightstone already told you." He pushed his unusually fair hair, which reminded me of birch bark, behind his shoulder to drape unbound down his back.

I scanned the rest of the RFG quickly. Unlike my thick fighting leathers, they each wore thin, pliable, everyday work gear, some leather, some cloth. Few weapons were visible, and their hair wasn't bound, meaning they weren't here expecting a fight. Unsecured hair was a liability, which was why I'd twisted mine into a tight braid from the crown of my head all the way to my waist and tucked it beneath my jacket.

Though shorter, the wood fae had a stockier build than his sun fae brethren. When he crossed his arms over his chest, his biceps and forearms bulged, becoming obvious. I couldn't be sure if this flex was a power move, but oddly, I didn't think so.

"Is there anything else, or shall we escort you to your party?" Odo arched a brow, and I could almost see humor in his good green eye. It was probably a piece of dirt.

"Fine." I made a face and glanced at the hulking beast hovering over Odo's shoulder like a lapdog.

The creature's large, weirdly green gaze lowered to my boot and back.

Caught by surprise, I froze and openly gawked at the creature. Surely that wasn't intentional?

With a loud, wet snort, the aloughta turned its head.

That oversize cow dismissed me! I stroked a push dagger hilt and glared at the beast's backside.

"Why are looking at Grace like you plan to stab her?" Odo drawled.

"Grace?" I scoffed. Major misnomer. "She's unnatural."

Odo laughed. "You are a hybrid."

Anger leaped to the surface. My fangs tingled. I shifted my glare from Grace to Odo and blew a hot breath through my nostrils. I had no reason to be mad. He'd only stated a fact.

"Touché." I shrugged and started walking.

VEGETATION ON AND AROUND THE PATH LEADING TO TOWN HAD THINNED, the grass shorter from the constant wear of patrols. We were close to town. Once buildings came into view, I heard Odo's deep, gravelly voice call my name, but I kept walking. I needed to get to the bar. I needed to see my sisters. I needed Teddy.

"Did you not hear me, Malaney?" Odo jogged to my side, his mount following, hoof to heel. "I have been calling you."

It surprised me he hadn't climbed onto his asshole aloughta and spent the entire trip looking down on me. I'd mentally filed Odo under asshole the moment we met, but it seemed like our bender had softened the guy. Life was confusing enough. Everyone should stay in the category where I put them.

"Nope, didn't hear you." I fingered the hilts of my tri-blade daggers as we walked. "Big night. Got things on my mind."

"I understand." Odo looked thoughtful.

"Well, what did you say?" I prompted. He didn't answer immediately, and seeing no reason for conversation, I said nothing else.

"You are traveling into Shadwe."

"That's the plan." My brows pinched together, and I studied his profile.

He nodded, and his jaw worked as if chewing on his thoughts.

With Odo, it had been hate at first sight, and it had been mutual. Yet the spot the hate had filled felt empty—or empty-ish. I couldn't even think of him as Scar. How disappointing. Watching the way he moved, it struck me he was the type of warrior I'd want at my back. He didn't have the tight, rigid manner of the sun fae, or Duskmere. He prowled like a big cat.

It helped he wasn't spitting accusations and curses in my face like our first meeting. He'd blamed me for Duskmere taking two daggers to the chest, and I couldn't hold it against him. I'd blamed myself a little, too.

"I chose RFG who were not sun fae for a reason," Odo said at last.

"Um, last I checked"—I looked at the group following us and hooked a thumb in Cirron's direction—"sun fae."

Odo scoffed. "He is Duskmere's doing."

A laugh burst out of me. I immediately frowned and busied myself adjusting the hilts of my push daggers. "What's your point?"

"Dacian is free."

There he went, pointing out the obvious again. "Yep."

We were close enough to the bar I could see faint smudges through the windows, moving inside the building. Maybe Mae decided to be nice and brought something besides a granola bar.

"Wait, Malaney." Odo stopped walking. "I want to speak with you before we accompany you to the border."

"I don't need an escort." I came to a halt and crossed my arms over my chest as I turned to face him. "Why are you really here?"

Odo's mouth flattened into a thin line, but he nodded. "Very well. I am aware of your sister Maerwen's new status."

I realized two things. First, he said Maerwen, not Maerwen Callaghan, and there was no way he'd insult my sister. It forced me to rethink his use of Malaney. Perhaps he hadn't been trying to insult me after all.

Again, everyone should stay in the box I fucking put them in. Or I should stop getting drunk and making frenemies, because in my experience, if a fae was nice to my face, they were about to literally stab me in the back.

Second, he knew Mae had been chosen as a keeper. News had already spread through Eodrom. This train wasn't coming off the tracks. If I didn't figure something out fast, my sister was going to get locked behind the walls of that beautiful, rotten palace.

My mouth had gone dry. "So?"

"He is telling you she is a sun fae—" Cirron said, but Odo sliced a look his way, instantly silencing him.

Well, this was interesting. My father once told me Odo was Duskmere's second, but Odo was Cirron's superior. Cirron was Duskmere's partner, so what did that make Odo?

"Your sister has a deeper link to the sun stones than any sun fae." Green gaze so intense even his milky eye appeared sharp. He waited, watching me.

Unsure what he wanted, I nodded.

"Each time she leaves Ta'Vale, leaves the sun stones, she will not just have diminished magic. Your sister will feel as if she has lost a vital organ."

"She's wearing extra sun shards. She's fine." I said it, but I didn't believe it.

"For now. The bond is early. Eventually, no amount of shards will replace the living stone."

I looked away, unwilling to share the pain I knew he'd see in my eyes. Pain was vulnerability.

"You are going into a realm with unrooted stones."

A hard knot hunkered in my gut. I had a feeling where this was going.

"When we entered Outerlands to bring you and the stone you found back, the unrooted stones struck the sun fae with us down with an illness." Odo dragged a hand over his mouth, looking past me to the bar for a moment. "It wasn't immediate. But the closer those sun fae were and the longer they were near the unrooted stone, the worse it became."

"Yeah, I've been told." I dragged a talon over the pad of my thumb. Would this conversation never end?

"Two of those guards have yet to regain their full connection to the stones."

Ice injected into my veins. My arms fell to my sides. "Are you telling me Mae could lose her magic?"

He gave a fast, jerky nod. "There is potential. I see two options: she will be hit harder, lose her magic, and potentially her life."

I almost threw up. Right there.

"Or," Odo continued, as if I wasn't about to lose my Sno Balls all over his boots, "because she has a stronger connection, she will withstand it longer."

"How?" I demanded.

"Think of the bond as a shield. It might insulate your sister."

"This is all your opinion?"

"Yes and no," he said and glanced over my shoulder.

I followed his gaze and found the subject of our conversation on the front deck to the bar. "Be there in a minute," I yelled.

Odo raised his hand in greeting to Mae. To me, he said, "It has been discussed. Ultimately, we do not know. Duskmere proposed Maerwen return to Ta'Vale with us as a precaution."

"Ha!" I laughed and shook my head. "There's a better chance of your fancy aloughta shitting sun stones than Mae admitting defeat."

A ghost of a smile twitched his lips. "I told Duskmere not to count on it."

I grinned, and for a moment, I remembered why I might like this guy. "Anything else?"

"Yes."

Of course, there would be more. As if dropping a "hey, your sister might die" bomb wasn't enough. I waved my hand for him to get on with it.

"You are entering a realm where a very dangerous enemy resides. I, a wood fae, am a general for the sun fae army. Do you know what it takes to achieve that rank?"

"A lot of stabbing?"

"A lot of skilled stabbing. And more, much more. Yet the fae who gave me this." Odo pointed to the scar bisecting his eye. "He is in there. Prince Miro, the only moon fae noble left alive. He's still alive because he's the most dangerous of them all."

"I know who he is. I know where he is. Why are you telling me all of this?"

"And then there is Dacian Barbout," Odo continued. "The wyvern shifter you already had one very bad experience with. Hielmal, the—"

"I know who she is," I snapped. "I don't need a dossier from you."

His lips flattened. A muscle twitched in his square jaw. "We cannot accompany you into Shadwe, but we will remain in Outerlands until you return."

"I... Well..." Closing my eyes, I bowed my head, not enjoying the tickle of shame. I met his gaze and nodded. "Thank you."

"Do not thank me," Odo said grimly. "Return alive."

24

EMOTIONAL GRENADE

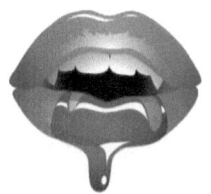

"HEY," MAE SAID, STARING DOWN AT ME FROM THE BAR'S PORCH.

Only one step separated the porch from the ground, but as the humid chill of an Outerlands night curled around me, she felt a million miles away. A hard knot twisted in my chest. It was time to admit the conversation with Odo had terrified me.

I rubbed my arm while I considered my words. "How are you feeling?"

"A little out of sorts, but nothing I can't handle." Mae crossed her arms over her middle and leaned a shoulder against a support post. She'd dressed appropriately in black leggings with thick but pliable leather panels sewn over vulnerable areas. A formfitting, long-sleeve black shirt with similar panels covered her torso while soft black boots reinforced with spider silk protected her feet.

My sis was sleek, fierce, and dangerous. She was also in more danger than she realized. Mae leaned a shoulder heavier than necessary against the porch post, as if not for comfort, but because she needed the support. I had to figure out a way to get her to go home. Telling her not to come was a surefire way to ensure she crossed the border to Shadwe first.

"Mae, I think..." I thought what? She should stay the hell away? Wrong thing to say. "Maybe..." *Maybe you should stay away* was no improvement. "I mean—"

"What's wrong with you?" Mae asked, but she wasn't watching me and didn't wait for an answer. She thrust her chin toward Odo's form, retreating to the waiting RFG. "What was that about?"

Thank the gods. This tactful stuff was harder than Mae made it look. I set my fisted hands on my hips and turned to watch Odo. Funny how an opinion could change so swiftly. I still didn't like him, but I no longer wanted to drive my talons into his eyeballs. Baby steps.

"Duskmere sent them along to wait here for us."

"In case we need to be rescued again?"

I turned on her with a scowl. "They didn't rescue us."

"If you say so." A smile ghosted over her lips.

"They didn't." But they did. I might have won the fight, but I would probably have died in the street if Odo and his team hadn't brought us home. The reason Teddy insisted I make peace. I groaned. "Fine, they helped."

Mae nodded, her smile an open grin now. "All right, they helped."

While she did seem off, she was clearly in a good mood. That gave me hope the extra sun shards she wore might work as a shield, like Duskmere theorized.

I climbed the stair and leaned against the porch post opposite Mae. "Listen, I talked to Duskmere."

"Oh no. Laney, you need to let his part in not telling me about Hielmal go. It wouldn't have been his call to make."

"What? No, nothing like that. I have a long list of grievances I hold against Duskmere, but she isn't what we talked about."

"No?" Her brows rose in a subtle arch.

"No. He...he had things to say about what happened to the RFG sun fae who entered Outerlands with Odo to *help* us." My gaze disengaged from hers and dropped to study my toes. "And what he thinks could happen to you."

Mae jerked from the post as if I'd physically assaulted her with my words. "What does he think will happen to me? I am not fine fucking china to be locked in a cupboard, collecting dust."

"Whoa." I blinked at my well-mannered sister's blistering reply. Slowly, my lips pulled and bent, growing into a grin. "Down, girl."

Behind Mae, Y'sindra came outside. Through the open door, I saw Teddy waiting. With a crooked, sexy smile and a nod, he acknowledged seeing me. He was giving me the space my sisters and I needed. More and more I realized I'd somehow landed the best of partners.

Mae tossed her hair and huffed. She crossed her arms over her chest and tapped her foot. It was too comical not to laugh. A snicker forced its way past my teeth, and she turned a top-notch death glare on me. It was almost as good as mine.

I laughed harder.

"This isn't funny."

Palm pressed to my mouth, my eyes watered, partly from the situation, partly from the gold glow leaking from her skin. "It is."

Y'sindra stopped next to Mae and looked up. "What's up, sunshine? Who stuck a beehive up your butt? Language, tsk."

"Oh, stop. Both of you." Mae rolled her eyes, but her aggressive posture softened and light faded. She had like one angry bone in her body, and it had run out of juice. "I don't know what any of this means, but I have also made up my mind I am not leaving you two. I am going to figure out how to beat this connection the stones have formed with me."

I watched Y'sindra's reaction, but she showed no surprise or confusion. Mae must have filled her in before I arrived. Y'sindra reached up and took our sister's hand.

"We will figure it out," I said. "You aren't in this alone."

"Yeah, stop going emo and turning into a night-light. It's not a flattering look," Y'sindra snarked, but I didn't miss the squeeze she gave Mae's hand before letting go. "Come on, you two. We need to get our game plan straight. And Lane, you need stronger soap. Didn't you clean up after you got the ring? You smell like literal shit."

———

TEDDY LEANED AGAINST THE BAR NEXT TO ME AND PLACED A BLUISH-white ring on the bar top. Except for the spikes pointing inward, it resembled a dog collar.

With wet hands, I gripped the edge of the sink where I'd been washing my boots and bent closer forward for a better look. "You asking me to take you for a walk?"

He snorted. "It's for Dacian."

"Your brother is into some weird kink." I eyed the sharp points on the inside of the collar. "Aren't those spikes on the wrong side?"

"This cuff is infused with a rare metal that interferes with shifter abilities when introduced to the bloodstream."

"What metal?"

The corner of his mouth dimpled. "You think you'll know it?"

"I might." I would not, but rude of him to assume.

"It's called osmium and found in many realms, but in extremely small quantities. The metal is difficult to harvest and extremely rare. So rare, there's only a trace amount in there." Teddy tapped a finger on the hoop and slid it from the counter. Along with spikes, there were four hinged sections folded together in a jigsaw fashion. Two sections of spikes interlocked with spikes, back-to-back, creating a bar the length of my index finger and width of my hand. He put it back on the bar in front of me. "I want you to carry this with you."

"All right, I'll bite. Why?"

"If we have a run in with Dacian, get this on him." He tapped a finger on the brilliant hunk of metal. "You'll have to do it while he's in his prime form. Just be sure it punctures the flesh. If he's in wyvern form, it won't fit."

And if he was in that weird half form, it wouldn't pierce his scales. I bit my lip and studied the folded loop. "Will it prevent him from shifting?"

"Any other shifter, perhaps, but my family has a higher resistance." He brushed a strand of hair from my face, his thumb lingering on my cheek. "Shifters are limited to one or two full shifts a day. Barbouts are not. That's the reason for the harness. So long as the metal remains in contact with his bloodstream, it'll buy us time before Dacian's system works past the osmium."

"Shouldn't you keep it? He's more likely to go after you."

"Precisely why you should have it. You'll have a greater chance to get it on him while he's distracted with me."

"Good point. All right, zip it in here." I lifted my right elbow, giving Teddy access to my jacket pocket.

After securing the collapsed loop in my pocket, Teddy leaned against the bar and waited while I returned to scrubbing my boot in the sink. I'd worry about how unsanitary this was, except the bar hadn't been open for years.

My jacket shifted with my movement, and the folded loop was a noticeable ridge against my ribs. I wasn't a fan of being forced to adjust to new weapons on the fly, but I'd make it work. How hard could it be to slap a collar on someone?

Water splashed my cheek. I flinched and lifted my shoulder to rub my cheek on the leather. This joint might still have running water, but it was so cold, my fingers were going numb.

"How is the well still functioning and not filled with sludge?" I asked Teddy. "And why are there clean bar towels? I thought you haven't lived here for what, a hundred years?"

"Something like that." Teddy nodded to the side, to where Lo and my sisters sat around a large table. "Lo takes pride in keeping everything in top condition and tidy."

I snorted. "Better keep my room locked. I don't need him folding my undies."

"Can I?" Teddy's voice was rich and smooth, like the dark rum he favored.

A smile curled my lips as I put my boot on a towel and scoured my hands with soap and water. "I hoped you were the rip and tear, not sort and fold type."

He gripped my hip with his large, warm hand and spun me toward the wall of muscle that was my honey cake's chest.

"My hands are wet," I protested with a sound dangerously close to a giggle.

Teddy bent and put his lips against the shell of my ear. Shivers rocketed down my body. "I plan to make much more than that wet when this is over."

A shock of lust arrowed straight to my core.

"Hey!" Y'sindra shouted.

Instinctively, I jumped away from Teddy, but lasered a look promising retribution on my sister. Teddy chuckled and smacked my butt as he passed, making his way out from behind the bar to the others.

I jabbed a still-wet finger at my mouthy little but older sister. "Mind your own business."

"Your business is my business when you make out in front of my eyeballs."

"Making out? Maybe we need to resubscribe to that porn channel and educate you."

"It's still there. There are seven different channels, I recommend 192. It's tasteful and very artistic," Mae said, frowning at her nails. "Anyone have a file?"

Y'sindra and I gawked at Mae and then each other. I shrugged.

"Almost done here." I flipped the boot over and began rubbing down the rough treads with the towel. While I dried, I turned the news my sisters had shared over in my head.

It had been too long since either Teddy or Lo had spent time in Shadwe. The news had been worse than I'd hoped to hear, but there wasn't much we could plan for. The stones were close to the Barbout family estate. Close enough to see it, but not close enough to be seen, or so Y'sindra claimed.

I'd made my doubts clear, but Lo insisted the family would not be in residence, and Teddy had agreed. While he and Dacian had split their time between the royal residence and family estate as boys, Dacian had made the palace his permanent address even before Teddy left Shadwe.

Y'sindra and Lo had spotted only a few guards near the stones. There had been no sign of Hielmal, Dacian, or Prince Miro. The lack of eyes on their prize spoke to their confidence no one would follow them over the Shadwe border. It wasn't an unreasonable assumption for them to make.

Even if the corrupted moon fae weren't aware of the unrooted stones impact on the sun fae—and I doubted they were—they would still know no sun fae would want a fight away from their precious sun stones. In my mind, the sun fae had become too dependent on the extra power. It was a crutch destined to crumble. And soon, if we didn't get the last two stones.

After I'd settled in at the sink, Y'sindra had filled me in on how she and Lo spent the past day and evening checking for traps on the path they'd laid out for us to take. As with the lack of guards, there were also no traps, save for along the border, which Lo had taken care of shortly after they'd been placed.

Lo was scary good at what he did. Teddy's claim his family had been loath to let Lo go felt like an understatement. I could only hope Lo's skills weren't indicative of the rest of his family's abilities.

There really was nothing else for us to do but go get those stones. It was a strange feeling not being the one in charge of these high-stress missions.

At the table, Y'sindra fist bumped Lo, who'd learned to add the exploding fist to the action. These were the pieces of my heart, free of my chest, gathered around the table, talking and laughing. With a smile, I set aside the towel and hummed in astonishment at the pristine state of my boot. Using a narrow, rough bristled brush I'd found beneath the bar, I'd scrubbed the boot cleaner than it had been in years. A cleaning utensil Mae would covet if she knew how well it worked.

Teddy saw me heading for the table and pushed the chair next to him out with his foot. I flipped it around and straddled the seat, folding my arms over the back. It was that or remove my sword. Two feet of steel across the spine did not make for comfortable sitting. Weird Y'sindra and Lo had no problem with their folded wings, yet I couldn't find a way to manage a sword.

I looked at each face around the table. "Let's go over this one last time. What's the plan?"

"Get in, get the stones, go home," Y'sindra answered, slumped low in her seat so she could prop her heels on the table. I could barely see the top of her head.

I swatted her feet from the surface. "You look ridiculous."

"So." She glowered.

"So I can't see your face when I'm talking to you."

"I didn't realize seeing was a requirement for hearing."

"Teddy." Mae spoke above Y'sindra and me, cutting our bickering short. "What do we do if we come across your brother?"

"Stab him in the face," I answered first, pushing up on my toes, letting my chair tilt forward on two legs.

"Don't engage alone," Teddy said. "But if you see the opportunity for a kill shot, take it."

"Really?" Y'sindra appraised Teddy. Next to her, Lo's puckered expression screamed remorse.

"Yes, really." Teddy' slid his fingers beneath my braid on the back of my neck. "It's something I should have done years ago."

"Why didn't you?" Mae asked frankly.

Teddy shrugged. "We were close once. It's hard to kill the things you love."

A heavy silence unfolded over the room.

I cleared my throat and looked at Teddy's best bud. "Are you okay with this?"

Shadows gathered close around that side of the table. His small chest heaved, scattering the hazy darkness, and he nodded. "I am okay. My family is loyal to the Barbouts. My eldest brother, Enode, was in the employ of Dacian when I left with Ted-D. If he still is, I hope we can avoid harming him."

"We'll make sure he isn't hurt, bud," Teddy promised.

Inwardly, I winced. Those kinds of promises were like emotional landmines. Lo had quickly become family, and I'd do everything in my power to make sure this promise-bomb never went off.

My chair legs came down with a heavy thump. I stood, stretched, and looked down at Mae. Casual as I could manage—which was about as casual as the sword on my back—I asked, "And Hiemal?"

Mae's blueberry-blue gaze rose. "Capture her if we can. Kill her if we can't."

The anchor of fear chained to my hearts released. Mae didn't care who her birth mother had been. She was devoted to this family. I'd known, but still I'd feared.

I nodded and knocked the side of my fist on the back of the chair. "Like Y'sindra said, get in. Get the stones. Go home."

With purpose, everyone rose. One by one, two by two, they passed me, and went out the door.

Around the table, some chairs had been left pulled out, some tucked. The absence of life felt weirdly permanent. An unexpected chill twisted down my spine.

"Let's do this." I cracked my knuckles, cracked my neck, and strode for the door, ready to crack some heads.

25

RELOCATE THE SUN

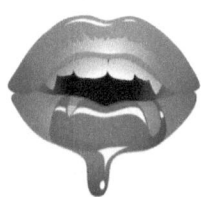

Shadwe was not what I expected. Not because it felt foreign, but because it felt familiar. I said as much to Teddy.

"I've visited as many realms as you have at this point. Though magic changes, small details change, they all feel the same." Even as he spoke, Teddy's sharp gaze never stopped searching the shadowy pockets surrounding us. "You should ask Blackthorne."

I stumbled, but quickly caught myself. "Are you seriously suggesting I talk to that guy?"

Teddy put out a hand to steady me. "If he's going to hang around in your life, you might as well get everything you can out of the relationship."

"He has seen a lot," I mused.

"More than you know, I reckon."

It went back to something Teddy once told me. Druids were among the first of the fae, and they were "of the universe"—whatever that meant. Were they even fae? He'd compared them to dragons, which were elemental creatures quite literally of the universe that lived in whatever realm they wanted to nest.

He'd also said his family, the ruling family of Shadwe and the only wyvern shifters, were also of the universe. It was all a little too metaphysical for me and hurt my brain to think too hard on.

At least fifteen minutes passed while we wove through a tidy forest. I smelled citrus and flowers, trees and decay. Teddy was right. The sights, the smells, and the landscape were the same as anywhere else. Even Ta'Vale was a wild version of Earth and probably resembled what would have been without skyscrapers and industry. Or maybe it was the other way around, and Ta'Vale was what Earth would be, if Earth had magic.

With Lo flying above, keeping a lookout, Teddy dropped back, and we fell into a single file line. I'd always been the one out front, the shield for my sisters, but now I wasn't strong enough to be reliable.

Teddy reasoned most attacks would not come head on, which was why, as the strongest among us, he'd dropped back to protect our rear. Mae and her shields were out front, which twisted me into all kinds of knots. Walking behind my sister forced me to witness her crumbling before my eyes.

She began our journey sure, steady, and determined, but as soon as we crossed from Outerlands to Shadwe, a switch flipped. Mae struggled, and she was trying to hide it. As minutes passed, her naturally elegant posture bent, and each step grew heavier.

I called out, "Mae, maybe you should—"

"No," she bit off.

My brows shot up. On a scale of sunshine to grumpy, Mae's suffering had to have reached serial killer level for that sort of reaction.

Y'sindra, who'd been walking quietly—for once—between us, dropped back to walk alongside me. She looked up to where Lo would be skimming the treetops and then behind to where Teddy brought up the rear.

Jaw tight, I glanced back too, irritation sliding over my raw nerves. I wasn't fit to bring up the front, nor the rear. All because my body refused to do its job and heal.

All because you refuse to drink Teddy's blood, a small voice inside me said.

"We need to get her home," Y'sindra whispered as not to rile Mae.

"I know." I pressed a fang into my lip, watching our sister limp along ahead of us. Even from this angle, I could see she hugged one arm over her middle while the other held tight to the sun shards anchored around her neck. She periodically released her grip to wipe her brow. "Mae is more stubborn than both of us put together when she digs in her heels. She won't leave voluntarily."

"Twist an ankle," Y'sindra said.

"What?"

"Fake it." She wobbled around, demonstrating what she meant. "Pretend to twist an ankle. We all know you aren't healing. We'd have to go back."

"Ouch." I unsheathed a push dagger, took the wide tip between two fingers, and held the handle toward Y'sindra. "No need to use words, just use this."

She looked up at me and rolled her eyes so hard, for a moment, they went completely white. "Don't be so dramatic. You aren't healing. I don't have a wing. We move on."

My feet stopped moving. "Never mind, I'll do it myself." I flipped the blade. The black rubber handle rested against the meat of my palm and the notched blade extended between my middle fingers, pointing toward my chest.

I was only half kidding. Her words hurt.

Y'sindra stomped back toward me and blasted me with a glare. "This isn't about you or me, Lane. This is about our sister. She's hurting, or worse. Put away your delicate feelings and figure out how to get Mae to leave before her stubborn streak gets her killed."

With a dramatic twirl, Y'sindra flounced away, resuming her position between Mae and me.

She'd never spoken to me like that before. I didn't like it, but I'd needed to hear it.

"I can carry Mae out of here and be back before you reach the stones," Teddy offered, taking the spot next to me Y'sindra vacated after putting me in my place.

"You might have to." I shifted my attention to him as we walked. "I don't know how to fix this."

He nodded slowly. "I know, but you will."

"How can you be so certain?"

A smile kicked up the corner of his mouth. "Because I know you, and you'd relocate the sun to save those you love."

His words doing weird, warm, fuzzy things to my insides, I returned his smile. The question of whether he considered himself among that group weighed down my tongue, but wasn't that a question I should ask myself? And what was the answer?

"Mae will go ballistic." I eased closer to him, letting his warmth filter into the cold, scared places in my hearts. "But it's probably best if you take her."

A half scream, half screech sliced through the quiet of night. The hairs on my neck rose in response. Above, meaty thuds sounded again and again. Branches rustled and cracked. Something pounded the ground with a solid thump. It didn't bounce. It didn't move.

"Lo!" Y'sindra's shriek nearly brought me to my knees.

In the distance, she hunched over the deathly still, crooked outline of Lo's body.

Oh gods, he wasn't moving. Red-hot fury came up against a wall of blistering cold in my chest. The icy fear speared my hearts.

The treetops shook. In the span of a breath, shadows melted from a hovering form. The fine fur covering what could only be Lo's brother shivered over his body. He was paler than Lo's hodgepodge of light to dark taupe. His eyes were a darker, deeper orange, but just as bright.

"I warned you what would happen if you came back." He spat the words at Lo's still form and hovered closer. His quadruple, dragonfly-like wings fluttered with an eerie quiet, faster than I could track.

Y'sindra only had eyes for Lo. Her fingers danced over his body as she plucked not one or two, but three darts out of him and tossed them aside. She screamed, a brittle, keening sound, and bent to press her face to his chest.

The Lo look-alike's mouth twisted. He pulled what appeared to be a wooden tube from his pocket.

"Enode!" Teddy thundered.

Seeming to notice Teddy for the first time, the perfectly round eyes of Lo's attacker widened. The tube tumbled from his fingers, and he clutched his hands to his chest. "Master said you were dead."

"No, but Dacian will be soon." Teddy's voice had dropped an octave and grated over itself.

I slid a look over my shoulder at Teddy. "What the...?" I took an involuntary step away. My hearts leaped into a gallop.

Predator! Instinct pushed me to run or attack, but no, this was Teddy. I stood my ground.

An absolute black consumed the usually warm, brown-black of his eyes. The red rings circling those onyx irises were thicker than the first time I'd seen them. The combination of Shadwe and emotion must be pushing his black wolf to the surface.

"I am letting you live, only because your brother begged me to do so. If he dies, you die, Enode. Now, go back to your *master*." Teddy spit the word.

"Tell him I'm coming for him."

Get in. Get the stones. Go home. Sending a warning shot across Dacian's snout wasn't in the plan.

Enode wasted no time pulling shadows to himself.

No! He couldn't leave. What was Teddy thinking? I looked at him, could almost see the black wolf prowling beneath the surface, and cursed.

He *wasn't* thinking, and that was the problem.

Well, I always said I could take the wings off a fly from twenty paces. How much harder could a flying shadow be? I pinned my focus on Lo's brother and followed his movements. Unless I wanted to break Teddy's promise to Lo, this had to be exact.

I found the cold steel of the two thin, cylindrical weapons strapped to my thighs behind the tri-blade daggers. I popped the clasps holding them in place and pulled the torpedo daggers from their sheaths. Tips gripped between my fingers, I raised them, bent my arms, and let the daggers flip back to rest on my shoulders.

A single breath in through my mouth cleared the white noise. My focus was diamond sharp. I arced my arms forward on the exhale and let knives fly.

They cartwheeled through the air. End over end, point over point. My pulse thrummed in time with their rotations.

Enode rose and retreated in the direction I'd predicted. He could still change course.

I forced myself to breathe.

It felt like minutes, but only a fraction of a second passed before the daggers did what they were named for and torpedoed Enode's wings. Holes opened in the nearly translucent membranes. A spray of red arced through the air like a bloody rainbow. The scent of basil, berries, and ginger hit my nostrils, and I suddenly, inappropriately, craved a mojito.

There was no dramatic pause. Unable to push against the air with his Swiss-cheesed wings, Enode dropped. Mae was on him before he could bounce with strips of fabric torn from her hem, trussing him like a holiday pig. My sister knew her knots.

Satisfaction vibrated through my blood until I heard Teddy's labored breathing.

I spun. He stood in the same spot, his breathing harsh, head bent, fists clenched.

Holding out my hand, I took slow, deliberate steps so as not to startle him.

He heard me coming and held up a hand, signaling me to stop.

I wasn't sure if I was relieved or hurt he didn't want me near him while he was in this state. I might be stubborn, but I wasn't stupid. Whatever lived inside Teddy might have chosen me, but I wasn't fully his.

You aren't mated. You are weak. You are not worthy.

The horrible litany of truths tumbled to the forefront of my brain. My chest constricted until each beat of my hearts threatened to crack ribs. I was so convinced drinking Teddy's blood, depending on him for my strength, made me weak. Maybe the simple truth was being weak when I didn't have to was weak.

"I'm okay," Teddy panted, not sounding fine at all. Yet he grinned like a lunatic.

"Are you...are you happy?" I gaped at him.

He nodded, and his shoulders shook. Was he laughing?

This was it. Whatever Teddy just did, he broke his brain.

"Okay, we don't have time for whatever this is." Palms forward, I waved my hands in a big circle in front of Teddy. "We have to get Lo out of here."

"Don't worry, sweet fangs. I'm just relieved. It was a risk, but I let the black wolf rise to the surface so Enode could report what he saw to Dacian, and I was able to push the wolf back when it was over." He turned to a trussed-up Enode. Lo's evil twin appeared to be attempting to flay the skin from my bones with his glare over the strip of torn fabric Mae had gagged him with. "I suppose he won't be reporting anything now. Your idea was better."

"It's not like I knew you had a plan. You were all...beastly. Not very communicative." I kicked a loose rock. It nearly hit Enode, who spewed what I could only assume were curses behind his gag.

"It was good practice," Teddy said, and nodded toward Lonwie. "If we get Lo to a healer fast enough, he'll be fine."

"Do the darts use a sleep spell?" I glanced behind me to a still unmoving Lo, and an eerily calm Y'sindra, now listening to our conversation.

"No," Teddy said and retrieved a dart lying a few feet away, half hidden in the grass. He spun the plain-looking thing between his fingers. "It's poison. A special blend made and used solely by Lo's family."

"Poison?" Mae blurted the question.

"I told you his family is the best at what they do." Teddy pressed his thumb against the side of the silver needle until it snapped off, leaving the dart harmless. "They make the poison, so they have an innate tolerance, but we need to hurry. It can kill him if we take too long."

"Then what are we waiting for?" Y'sindra snapped.

"Me, perhaps." A deep voice, thick and warm like caramel, preceded a tall figure who strolled through the trees. A puddle of sparkling black magic dripped from his fingers.

Before my sluggish brain had time to catch up to what was happening, his arm arced back, and he aimed not at me, but at Y'sindra, an easy target still crouched by Lo.

Like a stretched rubber band snapping back to its form, the reality of what was happening blasted into me. I leaped for Y'sindra, but the magic would beat me. My equilibrium jerked as a horrible sense of déjà vu hit me. "No!"

Even as the word burned my throat, Teddy sprinted past me, but he wasn't fast enough either. Fighting his shift must have taken too much out of him.

A gold dome exploded over Lo, Y'sindra, and Mae, who had thrown her body over both.

Oh, gods no. Her shield couldn't possibly be strong enough to stop that power.

The black magic had eaten an entire banshee in seconds. It had almost taken Y'sindra after it ate through her wing and forced me to cut off what remained before it devoured her, too.

The abominable power smashed against Mae's shield.

Black swirled into gold. I skidded to a stop and stared, transfixed, as sparks flew. The two magics wrestled for dominance. Mae's shield held, but it quivered. Some sections went opaque, some completely clear. All the while, thin strands of black snaked its way over the dome, seeking a way inside.

Abruptly, the gold edges of Mae's magic slammed together, crushing the trapped black magic. Her shield dissolved in an instant. Mae lay sprawled on the ground, unconscious and vulnerable.

Miro clapped his hands together and formed a ball of magic between his palms.

"Fuck you!" Y'sindra screamed.

I registered the dull thunk and brittle crack of ice a millisecond before

Miro's magic evaporated as he flew backward and collided with a tree. He bounced off the trunk and fell forward, sliding face-first down Y'sindra's spear of ice protruding from his chest. His head lolled toward the ground and arms hung loose.

The most feared moon fae to walk any realm taken down by an enraged, three-foot fairy. He was probably dead.

I ran toward the fallen prince and kicked him in the face, just to make sure. His head bounced like a tetherball. Satisfied, I bared my fangs, only then realizing they'd extended, and I hadn't bitten myself. Life was about small victories.

"'Ane," Y'sindra slurred, snapping my attention to her.

"What did you do?" I demanded. She must have burned through a hell of a lot of magic recently to go down this hard so soon. I raced to Teddy and my sisters, pulling out Duskmere's communication crystal. "Just hang on. I'm getting you all to the healers."

My hand trembled. I traced my thumb over its surface and whispered, "Duskmere."

This time, there was no wait. His image rose above my hand. He paced back and forth in front of the crystal. "Report."

"Listen close and don't interrupt," I snarled, and Duskmere stopped pacing to face me. "I'm about to open a portal, and you need to come through."

"I cannot—"

"What did I just say? Listen to me. Do not interrupt." I leaned close to the crystal. "Gather three RFG to assist you and make sure one is not a sun fae. I'm going to open a portal with one of your stones. You'll come through with the non–sun fae RFG. Bring two of my father's portal devices."

Since my father's hybrid portals remained active longer than moon fae portals, one device would probably do it, but it was better to be prepared.

Duskmere picked up the crystal and began moving as I spoke. I could see him gesturing to others but couldn't see to who. He was doing something, but not fast enough.

"We're running out of time. We have injured who need healers immediately. Prince Miro is down. We captured one of their spies." I quickly aimed the crystal at my sisters and Lo, the prince's body, and finally a furious Enode. "When I trigger a portal, you will come through with the RFG I've requested and open a second portal to send Miro to the dungeon. Try to keep this one locked up."

Duskmere's lip quivered at the barb.

I continued. "Meanwhile, send one RFG to ready the healers while the other notifies my parents to prepare for you and the injured. We'll use my father's portal to send all of you to my parent's home. I'll give you five minutes to get to the dungeon. Understood?"

He nodded and unleashed a feral smile I'd never seen on his angular face. "I only need four minutes."

The 3D image vanished, leaving me staring at the crystal in my palm, and below that, the bloody toe of my boot where I'd kicked Miro in the face.

26

A REAL KICK IN THE SUN FAE NUTS

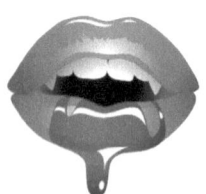

CONVENIENTLY, TEDDY WAS A FAN OF SOLAR-POWERED WATCHES. SURE enough, precisely four minutes later, Duskmere and my best gal pal, Pru, crossed the portal from the Eodrom dungeon to Shadwe.

I pasted on my brightest smile and waved at Pru. The carved-in-granite scowl I was fairly certain she reserved for me etched deeper into the severe lines bracketing her mouth. If I wasn't careful, my orchestrated jovial attitude, designed to piss her off, was going to become the real deal, and we might end up friends.

By all the forsaken gods, do not let that happen. It was bad enough Odo and I sort of got along.

"New coat?" I smoothed the lapel of Pru's replacement jacket, smiled, and stepped back. "It looks nice."

Her upper lip twitched, and she swiped at her lapel where I'd touched it. Nope, no danger of becoming gal pals anytime soon.

The first thing Duskmere keyed in on was not our injured, but Prince Miro and the pissed-off Enode propped against the unconscious fae. I wasn't surprised by where Duskmere had placed his attention, nor was I offended. He had his priorities, but I had mine.

I strode toward Duskmere and snapped my fingers in his face. "Did you send someone to my parent's house like I asked?"

"You did not ask. You demanded, but yes." Duskmere's gaze finally unlatched from the face of the fae prince, who probably prowled his nightmares.

Well, not the face. The heat of Miro's insides had melted Y'sindra's ice spear, and he now lay nose-first on the ground, sporting a significant hole in his back. Against the prince's hip, Enode glared over his gag. I wondered if he'd get a smaller cell for pint-sized prisoners.

"The spy?" Duskmere stood over Enode, studying him.

"Yep. Did you bring my father's devices?"

"Yes."

"What are you waiting for?" I thrust a finger toward my sisters and Lo. "Get them to my parents."

Duskmere crouched next to the prince. "We should first send Miro to the dungeon."

With her hands clasped behind her back, Pru cleared her throat and stepped forward. "Sir, I believe Malaney Callaghan is right. Miro is currently incapacitated. The injured should be our priority."

Had Pru just agreed with me? Did all the Twinkies of the world just expire? Had the unfreezable underworlds just developed a chill? I shook my head free of my shock and focused on what mattered. "He's dead."

"Not dead." Duskmere stood and nudged Miro with his toe. "However, Prunettia is correct. He is incapacitated. I must set my emotions aside."

There had to be some mind-altering toxin in the air for not only Pru to agree with me, but also for Duskmere to give in so easily.

"What are the odds backup will arrive soon?" Duskmere surprised me further by addressing not me, but his not-so-long-ago nemesis, Teddy.

Sure, they put up with each other, but when did he value Teddy's opinion over mine? I couldn't help but take it personally. Y'sindra would say not everything was about me. But she once challenged Thor on the size of his "hammer" so what did she know?

"We have a little time." Teddy joined Duskmere by the two captives. Staring down at Enode, he took his time formulating an answer. "They were coming from somewhere, maybe the border, or they were on a routine patrol. If they'd planned to intercept us, there would have been more than just these two."

"This is also my assessment. Thank you, Aven...Teddy." Duskmere corrected himself and pivoted away from Miro. With Pru tight on his heels, he strode for the pile of unconscious Callaghans and Lo. "King Torneh and

Queen Iola would be displeased if we did not attend to Maerwen Callaghan."

And there it was. The crux of his pliability. My sister, Mae, chosen by the sun stones. What remained of my sugar-bomb dinner disintegrated to acid in my gut. I took a deep breath to calm my riled emotions and followed Duskmere and Pru.

It would be a real kick in the sun fae nuts when I figured out how to separate my sister from the stones, or at the very least, from Ta'Vale. I smoothed a hand over the flyaway hairs on the crown of my braided head and smiled. Knowing she wanted her autonomy as much as I wanted it for her, I would do anything to make it happen. Even, as Teddy put it, relocate the sun.

Duskmere was placing my father's portal device as I caught up. Pru reached down to take hold of Mae.

"Wait," I said and pointed to Lo. "What about him? He was poisoned."

"Be at ease, Malaney Callaghan. We are able to carry all." Duskmere approached the group and carefully picked up first Y'sindra and then Lo. "This is as you asked. Finnlay and Meghan Callaghan are waiting, as are the healers."

"Right. You're right." I twisted my hands together in front of me. This whole situation had me so out of sorts, I couldn't stay still.

"I am leaving one portal device I ask you to activate in five minutes," Duskmere said. "I need time to ensure your sisters and Lo receive the care they require and speak with your father before I return."

"Why so long? We're in a hurry here, and you lot have made it very clear you have no intention of helping."

His lips curled in a wry smile. The expression looked foreign on the severe moon fae's face. "Besides the fact I must return to send Prince Miro and your captured spy to the dungeon? As you say, you are in a hurry. Shall I take the time to explain my intentions?"

"Fine, I'll wait. Get my sisters and Lo to safety." He made a good point, but I didn't have to like it.

Conceding, he inclined his head. "Remember, five minutes."

Five minutes was a long talk with my father. I planned to find out what was so important Duskmere would risk the delay in getting Miro under lock and key.

With nothing left to say on the matter, I reached for the device and ran my thumb over the trigger runes. A musical note trilled, and an oval of space cracked open to reveal my parent's garden and my mom, waiting with a cluster of sun fae. Unlike the typical palace fae, their hair was bound, and while the robes were soft and a lovely pale blue, there was nothing showy about them. The healers had come.

Duskmere led the way through the portal and was quickly relieved of his burden.

Pru followed, murmuring as she passed me, "We will ensure your sisters and the little one are cared for."

I gawked at her backside as she stepped through the portal and went directly to where my mom and the healers waited with Y'sindra and Lo. The portal closed on another musical note.

"She was nice to me," I said to no one, and made a gagging noise. "Ew!"

Teddy slid his arm across my shoulders and spun me toward him, pulling me against his broad chest, rumbling with quiet laughter. "With all the waving and compliments, it looked to me like you were already friends when she showed up, sweet fangs."

I muttered into his jacket.

"Sorry, I couldn't hear you," Teddy prodded, laughter barely contained in his voice.

I heaved a sigh and tipped my face toward his. "I was doing it to make her mad, not to make a friend."

"Mission failed." He tilted my chin with the crook of his forefinger and stroked the calloused pad of his thumb over my lips. "It might be nice for you to know another blood fae."

"Uh, my mom is a blood fae."

"It's not the same." Teddy came in for a kiss. He lingered long enough to make me weak in the knees.

Had it not been for the knife of fear for my sisters' and Lo's well-being continuing to shank me over and over, I might have dropped to my knees right there and used him like a lollipop.

As if sensing the moment my mind wandered, Teddy orchestrated a gentle end to our kiss. He pulled me against him, cocooning me in his embrace, and rested his chin on my head. "We have an audience."

I rolled my head toward Lo's brother, who was busy trying to burn a hole in our heads with his glare. A trick I'd been attempting and failing for years. So good luck.

"Don't care."

Teddy stroked a path down my back, his warm hands leaving a familiar trail of heat. "I hear we already put on a show for the casino security."

Heat erupted on my cheeks, and I groaned into Teddy's chest. I didn't really care. I just hoped to all the forsaken gods it didn't end up on one of Mae's favorite channels.

"Should we go back, too?" I asked, already knowing the answer. After seeing the debilitating impact of the broken stones on Mae, I had to return the unrooted pieces to the sun garden.

"You'd regret it."

"I know." I froze, a thought planting itself with poisonous roots. A breathy gasp stuttered into my lungs. "Do you think the effect the broken stones have on the sun fae only happens outside Ta'Vale, or do you think..."

The words wouldn't cross my lips.

"Don't go there, Lane."

Too late. I was sliding down that slippery slope. What if the corrupted moon fae marched on Eodrom, unrooted stones in tow? They could cripple the majority of the sun fae defenses before even reaching Grian Valley. Who knew the scope? It could happen the moment they crossed the border.

If I, someone whose education in war came from movies—and I preferred comedies—realized this, then it was definitely in the minds of the exiled moon fae. They'd lived through a war. A war that they lost but were obviously attempting to orchestrate a different ending.

"The door between Ta'Vale and Outerlands needs to be closed." I stepped back and searched Teddy's gaze. "I opened the way to the sun fae's downfall."

Once I would have believed me being the evil supervillain responsible for the sun fae's demise would make me drunk on satisfaction. The reality did not follow through on those feelings.

"I don't believe that." Teddy's statement was resolute.

All at once, my clothes felt stiff. I crossed my arms over my chest and itched at each bicep through the heavy-duty leather of my sleeves. "How can you say that? They have..." I licked my lips and looked around, all at once hyperaware of the fact I was talking strategy in the middle of a foreign forest where spies could lurk anywhere. Exactly how big was Lo's family? Sneaky little suckers.

"I know what you're thinking." Teddy picked up my dropped thought. "The door you created barely allows for you and me to walk through side by side. It's difficult to launch an invasion two by two when the other side is heavily guarded, which it is."

"You're right." While out loud, I might agree, I could still conjure too many Doomsday scenarios to be comfortable leaving the door as it was. I'd have to figure out a way to implement some sort of fail-safe to prevent a full-scale attack by the corrupted.

One more thing to add to my list of impossible things to do, right after severing the hold the sun stones had on my sister.

Fuck. What happened to the days when all I had to do was flash a little fang and punch a few faces, collecting debts owed, or dragging wayward spouses home? I'd take shaving grumpy grounders over all of this.

I rubbed my hands over my face. "Why is everything so hard?" I whined.

"Because you take on the world, and I love you for your brave heart."

27

WHO WERE YOU PROTECTING

Everything stilled. My gaze snapped to Teddy's. Love was an unsaid word between us. My tongue felt heavy with the weight of my reply, too heavy to push the words from my mouth.

Teddy smiled, crinkling the outer corners of his eyes. "Breathe, sweet fangs. I'm confident enough in us to say what I feel. When you want to voice your emotions, you will."

Gratitude for his understanding wrapped itself around my hearts like my favorite fuzzy blanket. Voicing emotions gave me hives, and right now my world balanced on shaky bedrock.

Later, I promised myself. Later I'd admit to Teddy, to myself, everything I felt.

"Five minutes are up." Teddy's words rescued me from the introspective mire I'd sunk into.

Thank the stars. I preferred to examine myself in the mirror, not from the inside out.

"Let's get this over with." I threw my shoulders back and strode to the disk Duskmere left behind. My fingers flew over the trigger runes in rapid succession, following the particular sequence my father designed.

Nothing happened.

"Crap." I balanced on the balls of my feet, braced my elbows on my thighs, and shook out my hands.

Things were getting to me more than I cared to admit. I'd incorrectly entered a code I'd known since childhood. My father used the same pattern to unlock the runes on the house. Not the pattern he used for his precious labs, of course.

"I need to go on a meditation retreat after this." I'd never meditated, but Mae swore by it.

Behind me, Teddy chuckled. "That can be arranged."

"Something to look forward to." I smiled over my shoulder.

He raised a brow, and those sexy lips of his curled up at one corner. "Only one thing?"

All at once it felt like a heating pad gave me a full-body hug. I rubbed a hand over the butterflies caged beneath my breastbone and laughed. "Stop it with the smoldering. We've got business to handle."

Teddy rolled his hand in my direction and bowed his head dramatically. "By all means, proceed."

Still smiling, I shook my head. Silly male. I placed my thumb on the first rune but stopped before sketching the pattern. I looked over my shoulder and mouthed, "Thank you." He'd calmed me, made me forget the worries pounding for attention in my brain.

Teddy winked. The light flutter of butterflies beneath my ribs unfurled their wings and took flight. It left me with a euphoric weightlessness and a dopey smile I couldn't scrub off my face if I tried. Yep, I'd be revisiting this whole "L-word" conversation very soon.

With a sense of tranquility and renewed confidence, I once again ran my thumb over the runes. Instantly, the familiar bright musical note struck the air and an oval eye poked through the universe to reveal the crowd gathered in my parent's garden.

Duskmere wasted no time crossing and strode directly for Miro. Pru followed Duskmere and knelt by the felled prince. All business, she held up his bound wrists and slipped a transparent bag over his hands. What looked like clear, chunky jelly and bits of green material coated the inside of the bag. As soon as she had it in place, the bag and its contents sealed to his skin.

"Magic dampener?" I asked.

Pru's attention remained on Prince Miro, but she nodded.

I'd never seen anything like that before, but it had my father's fingerprints all over it. He wasn't the chief royal wizard for nothing. The presence of what I strongly suspected was organic matter in the form of some sort of plant indicated my mom had a part in this creation.

Four more non sun fae RFG hurried across the threshold. Two joined Duskmere and Pru while two moved to stand on either side of the portal. My breathing grew shallow when I spotted the figure bringing up the rear of the procession. A sun fae. My father.

I rushed toward him and demanded, "What are you doing here?"

Despite a robe woven with sun shards hanging heavy on his body, and a thick layer of chains around his neck sporting even more shards, the impact of the broken stones on him was instantaneous. His proud posture bent, his complexion grew waxy, and he stumbled.

Ignoring all of us, my father paused and withdrew into himself to draw on the power of his sun shards. I'd seen him do it a hundred times, but always to perform intricate magic workings, not to protect himself. Placing one hand over the other atop the lump of sun shards hanging around his neck, he bowed his head.

Motes of gold magic rose from the shards he wore. Sparkling light swirled around his tall, lanky form like glitter caught in a sandstorm. His pale-blond hair, bound by a strip of leather at his nape, lifted in the magic-fueled currents surrounding him.

I knew better than to maintain such close proximity to the magical vortex, and I stepped back. The fae standing guard nearby also kept a distance, but neither appeared alarmed. They must have seen this sort of high magic worked before.

One by one, the sun shards my father wore dimmed as he pulled on their power, strengthening his resistance to the toxic effects of the broken, unrooted stones. Their light didn't extinguish, but he was here on borrowed time.

"Whatever you're here for, you need to hurry," I told him.

My father took a deep breath and rolled his shoulders. "I am aware, Malaney. Everyone remain at a distance. I need room to work this binding."

"What binding?"

"Shh."

Rude. I crossed my arms and glared like a petulant child. I huffed and forced my arms to hang loose at my sides.

What sounded like Velcro being ripped apart came from behind me. I swiveled to find Duskmere getting to work. Moon fae portals were quick and violent without the elegance of my father's hybrid invention.

Pru and a wood fae carried a limp Miro and writhing Enode into the Eodrom dungeon through Duskmere's portal. The remaining fae, a stone fae with the stocky stature of the element where his kind drew their power, crossed the clearing and joined the pair of fae guarding my father. It was an orchestrated dance this group seemed familiar with.

Unlike my father's hybrid portals, which could remain open for a full minute, the moon fae portal snapped shut with the precision of a guillotine and a loud clap mere moments after Pru and the wood fae passed into the dungeon.

Duskmere approached me. He watched my father work as he spoke. "Finnlay Callaghan is forging a link between that device and this location."

"I've never seen him actually do it." My eyes could barely follow the acrobatics his fingers performed, weaving complicated runes on and around the device. This sort of magic was far beyond my understanding, but Mae would get it.

At the thought of my sister, my stomach twisted with a sharp cramp fueled by the worry I'd tried but obviously failed to ignore.

"I have seen it many times, but my fascination does not diminish," Duskmere said.

I shifted my weight and watched my father push what looked to be motes of essence from the air and earth into the device. "I thought he only needed the coordinates."

His weaving complete, my father picked up the device he'd just finished shoving magic inside and stood, depositing it into a satchel slung across his chest. "Coordinates are unreliable. Sometimes, one ends up in a dragon's cave."

"Is that a joke?" I asked, incredulous. "Did you, Finnlay Callaghan, chief wizard of the sun fae, just make a funny?"

Teddy snorted, but turned the sound into a cough to hide his amusement. *Coward.*

My father made a face, his nose wrinkled like he'd smelled something terrible. "I can use provided coordinates, but it takes time and does not guarantee accuracy. This method is precise and instantaneous."

Silly of me to think my father had a sense of humor. He'd only been stating fact. A fact that happened to me. I'd been the one to end up in a dragon cave while the dragon was in residence.

"I return now," my father said, smoothing his long-fingered hands over the satchel containing the new portal disk. "These coordinates must be bound to more devices."

"That disk looked different. It serves as a 'mother' device?" Teddy asked, sounding legitimately interested.

How had Teddy noticed a difference? I hadn't, though now that he brought it up, I realized the disk he'd imprinted was an octagon shape, not a circle.

"It does, indeed." My father beamed with pleasure.

Teddy just catapulted himself up the ladder of my father's assessment of him.

"Interesting." Teddy rubbed his chin. "I assume it's used to forge copies, like the ones Lane and her sisters have?"

"Precisely." My father smiled—actually smiled. I could count on two hands the number of times I'd seen that expression on his face. Not because he didn't have affection for me, but because we didn't share a talent for magic.

Mae probably saw that smile.

I sobered and cleared my throat. "What about Mae and Y'sindra? Are they okay? What about Lo?"

"Y'sindra will recover with rest. Lonwie is still undergoing care." My father's eyes tightened, and his nostrils pinched on a long draw of air. "We do not know the full impact of the unrooted stones on Maerwen. Every shard she wore was not only drained but also broken. Your sister must have expended a tremendous amount of energy."

"She did." I flexed my hands at my thighs and shifted my focus to somewhere over my father's shoulder. "Protecting Y'sindra from Miro's magic."

Who were you protecting? The insidious voice could have been my father's, could have been mine, could have been anyone's.

I bowed my head at the answer. No one. I could protect no one. Not unless something changed.

Not unless *I* changed something.

"Miro's magic. Indeed, that would do it," my father said absently as he dug a second portal device from his satchel. The sun shards around its perimeter shone brightly, indicating the disk was charged. He shifted his attention to Duskmere. "I presume you will attend to the prisoners?"

"I will." Duskmere pulled his own portal stone from a pocket inside his jacket and rolled it between his thumb and forefinger. "And I will try to bring your daughter around to reason."

I bristled, but Teddy's warm hand landed on my back, between my shoulders. He squeezed my neck, kneading the knot of tension Duskmere's mere presence could manifest.

Teddy leaned in until his lips brushed the sensitive shell of my ear as he spoke. "Holster those things before you hurt yourself."

His words and soft laughter puffed the small hairs loose from my braid and sent an electric tingle down my neck. The sensation pierced the knot his talented fingers continued to massage.

Wait, holster what things? I traced my tongue over the sharp points of my teeth. Damn it, my fangs were out. I hadn't even noticed they'd elongated, but I also hadn't stabbed myself with the unintentional action.

It only took twenty-three years to learn how to control my fangs.

I was busy rolling my eyes at my own sarcasm when the musical note of my father's portal sang. Looking over, I found he'd joined the waiting crowd in his garden. He did not look back. The three fae who had silently stood guard followed him.

Another musical note struck the air, and the portal closed. I immediately turned on Duskmere. "Want to tell me what that was all about? What was my father doing here?"

"You cannot bring the stones back alone."

"True," I drawled.

"Your party has taken losses today."

I flinched. "Ouch, did you bring your own salt to rub in that?"

He ignored me and continued. "You captured Miro and were seen by a spy, albeit one you took into custody."

"Your point?" I asked, though I was fairly certain I already knew his point. We were fucked. I wondered if he'd use those exact words.

"Shadwe's spy network is legendary. If Dacian and Hielmal do not yet know of your presence, they soon will."

"Unless Miro and Enode got a message out before they engaged, no one has any reason to suspect we're here. Let's hope we can get to the stones before they notice they're short one prince."

I spotted one of the torpedo daggers I'd used to bring down Enode. A spicy, sweet, and bright scent twisted into my nostrils as my feet crunched across the blood-dappled grass to retrieve the weapon.

Duskmere followed me and held out a flat, amber-colored disk, nearly the size of my palm.

I bent to drag my dagger through the grass for a quick clean and then straightened, sliding it through its holster loop, all the while keeping my gaze locked on whatever Duskmere held. "What's that?"

"It is a way to track you once you have located the stones."

I brushed off bits of debris transferred from the dagger to my palms and took the small circle from Duskmere. It was smooth and warm, with a series of runes etched on both sides. By the color and its unnatural warmth, this had to be a sliver of stone shard. Though I'd never seen this before, I once again detected my father's handiwork.

"Do not lose it, or we lose you," Duskmere said, all ominous-like.

"You couldn't wait until, I don't know, I was at the stones to bind here? I have no idea how much farther they are." I unzipped my jacket and slid the holster aside just enough to slip the runed disk in an inner-chest pocket. "In fact, without Y'sindra and Lo, I don't even know where we're headed."

"I have a rough idea," Teddy said. He stood stoically at my side, staring at Duskmere. "You were wise to bring Finnlay here now. I assume it's what you proposed when you returned with Lane's sisters and Lo?"

"It is," Duskmere confirmed. "I did not want to wait until you were at the stones and put our royal wizard in danger's path."

Teddy nodded. "Understandable."

A few feet away, I spotted my second torpedo. *Sweet!* Those babies were custom-made and easily in my top five blades. I jogged to the dagger, dragged it through the grass, and slid it into its sheath as I stood.

Duskmere followed and handed me two more portal stones and another of my father's devices. "Your sisters are being taken care of. Focus on the mission."

I bit back a snide response. Duskmere's bossiness was akin to the human male's rendition of mansplaining. Both were equally annoying. "Just be ready when I call."

"Of course."

"Of course," I mocked under my breath in an ugly, nasally voice.

He either didn't hear me or decided he wanted to keep his teeth and didn't respond. I might have diminished strength, but I could still deliver a helluva left hook.

A rip opened through space and the Eodrom dungeon appeared. No guards or dungeon guests waited, indicating someone had done their job and moved the prisoners.

Duskmere stepped through and turned to face me through the portal. "Be safe, Mala—"

The portal snapped shut.

I burst out laughing. "Thank you, universe."

28

THE TRUTH HURTS

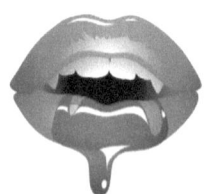

THE FARTHER WE FORGED INTO SHADWE, THE DEEPER TEDDY WITHDREW into himself. I wanted to believe he was being careful not to draw attention to our presence, but he wasn't. Not at all. He pushed on relentlessly, Godzilla-stomping through the forest. Rather than quietly navigating around obstacles, he snapped tree limbs and kicked debris that dared to be in his path.

I worked my hands into my jacket pockets, conveniently placed on the outer edge of the straps crossing my chest. My worried gaze darted between Teddy and our surroundings.

Potential stalkers in the shadowy pockets beneath the trees should be my concern, yet instead I obsessed over my sugar stud. Sugar stud? Nope. I mentally tossed the nickname in the garbage, and my thoughts circled back to Dacian. A by-product of this obsession.

Fucking Dacian.

Instinctively, my gaze rolled to the sky, gray now, as night tilted toward dawn. Nothing flying overhead, no ominous silhouettes. How long would that last? For the first time since Teddy had slipped it into my pocket, I patted the pocket situated against my ribs, feeling the bulge of the cuff—a small reassurance if I needed to use it.

We'd been walking for hours since we left Duskmere, and we'd walked for hours before that. If Enode and Miro notified anyone we were here before they tried to spring their trap, we would have seen them by now.

Several steps ahead of me, Teddy continued with his stomping and shoving. Not for the first time, a tree limb that refused to snap under Teddy's rough treatment sprang backward, toward my face. I ducked fast. The branch swept close enough to catch a few hairs and pull as it whipped overhead.

He hadn't noticed, which bothered me more than the potential stick to the face. I studied the rigid line of his broad back, the tension around his collarbone, the way his muscles bulged and pulled his shoulders toward his ears. Frenetic energy radiated from him, the hair on my neck rising in response.

"Teddy?" I hissed, glancing every which way, his anxiety fueling my paranoia. He didn't answer, didn't seem to hear me.

Irritation rolled over my skin, crested, and fell beneath a tsunami of apprehension. Ludicrous as Dacian claiming the black wolf wanted to keep me for itself but would eventually kill me might have been, I couldn't shake the irrational fear. Especially with Teddy at war with his black wolf.

Oh, he'd claimed to have let it rise to the surface to scare Enode and then reclaimed dominance, but I wasn't so sure. At first, Teddy had seemed like himself, but the deeper we traveled into his home realm, the longer and heavier the silence between us felt. And the harder it was for me to deny something was wrong.

I ran a hand over my head and smoothed my braid along my neck until it disappeared beneath my collar. Next, I gripped the hilt of my sword, testing its position. Finally, one by one, I pressed a finger to each blade strapped across my body, ensuring myself they were all still present and secure.

It was a prebattle routine to calm my live-wire nerves, and it worked. I added one last thing to my checklist and rested my palm over the folded collar inside my pocket.

You're being an idiot. I puffed a breath, anxiety releasing my shoulders. I'd seen Teddy push down his black wolf. He had control. This discomfort was something else. I jogged to catch up with him and took hold of his hand, threading my fingers through his.

He pushed out a long breath and slowed his steps until he turned to face me. A deep V pulled his brows together. "It's not safe to stop, Lane. We need to keep moving."

"Hey." I searched his gaze. The cresting sun brought forth the brown tones in his eyes, warming them. But the skin around his eyes pulled tight... With what? Frustration? Anger? Worry? He let me hold his hand, but if I relaxed my fingers, our hands would fall apart. I gave his arm a playful shake. "What's going on in that fuzzy head of yours?"

Surprise rippled through him. He stared at me and then laughed. "Fuzzy?"

"You're right. Scruffy is more accurate. When did you shower?"

"You said you liked my sexy bedhead." He released my hand to flamboyantly flip the ends of his hair. "Your words."

"I do," I admitted, smiling. This was better. This was my Teddy.

Mine. A mysterious ache pulsed in my chest. I could admit it to myself, so why not him?

"Listen, I'm all about focusing on the mission, but I'm worried about you." I reached up and brushed a wayward strand of hair from his cheek. "This place has an influence on your black wolf. I can see you're struggling."

"It's under control." His expression went stony.

I shook my head. "Don't insult either of us with that lie. We both know it isn't, not completely. I saw what this place did to Mae, and I don't want to risk losing you, too."

"The stones got to your sister, not Shadwe."

"I don't care if it was a unicorn fart. I won't risk it."

A low growl rumbled his chest. He dragged his hands down his face and paced away. When he turned to face me, his eyes were hard. His expression, uncompromising. "Do you want to know what's wrong?"

"Of course." My answer was immediate, but I wasn't so sure. This flip-flop of emotion from my easygoing honey bunches confused me. His unusual behavior, the frustration in his eyes, was unmistakably directed toward me. I actively tried to get a reaction out of him on a regular basis, but not like this, and certainly not today.

Teddy came toward me, not stopping until I had to tilt my head back to meet his gaze. "You. You're what's wrong."

Each word landed like a physical blow. Something rotten sank in the pit of my stomach.

He cupped the side of my head with his large hand, palm against my cheek, fingers applying pressure to the back of my skull, the touch firm yet gentle. "I don't take back what I said. I do love you, but you are too stubborn for your own good. It doesn't just hurt you—it hurts everyone around you."

Stubborn—*gods damn it*.

This was about me refusing to drink his blood. I bit back my instinctual reaction to brow beat him into dropping the subject. A small piece of me understood where this was headed, and maybe agreed.

"Yes, the black wolf is fighting me for control, but not for the reasons you think." Teddy stroked his thumb along my jawline, leaving a trail of tingling heat in its wake. "Not because we're here."

A dark cloud gathered inside me, putting my emotional equilibrium on shaky ground. I rolled my lips together for moisture and forced myself to ask, "Then why?"

"The black wolf can sense how vulnerable you are and is on high alert." Teddy traced the calloused pad of his thumb along the corner of my lips. "You have the means to protect yourself, but you refuse."

I'd seen it coming, and there it was. "I don't want—"

"You're strong and you're smart, Lane, but right now, your refusal to see the truth is making you stupid."

"You ass." Whiplash from kind and comforting to...whatever this was, had me reeling. Teddy never spoke to me like this, even when I deserved it.

I tried to step back, but he tightened his fingers. I could easily break his one-handed hold, but my struggle was half-hearted. My pillowy-soft honey muffin had turned hard and sharp. His words hurt.

The truth hurts, a voice inside me mocked.

"Healers will stabilize Lo," Teddy continued. "But to flush the toxins from his bloodstream completely, he'll need my blood—the blood of a Barbout. That's how his family design their poisons. A safety measure to ensure whoever the shadow shifters mean to put down stay down, unless we, or they, say otherwise."

"We have to go back." All at once, Teddy's observation on my state of mind didn't matter. I pushed away to slide my chest harnesses aside, unzipped the inner jacket pocket, and slipped my fingers inside, searching for the portal stone.

"He'll be fine until we return." Teddy put his hand on my arm to still my searching fingers. "Since I told you what it will take to purge his system, do you think it's wrong for Lo to take my blood?"

I narrowed my eyes. "I see what you're doing."

He shrugged and gave me a smirk that made my hearts say giddyup.

He wasn't wrong, but damn it, what if—

A dull thud, like the punch to a pillow, sounded. Teddy grunted. He let go of me and tried to look over his shoulder.

It took a few seconds to register the knife sticking out of his back, still vibrating near his shoulder blade.

Wide-eyed, I spun in the direction the knife had come from. The thunder of footsteps hit my ears just in time to twist and avoid a different knife plunging toward my neck. Not fast enough to evade the big body that followed the weapon, though. It collided with mine and took me to the ground.

The uncompromising line of the sword strapped to my back pressed mercilessly against my vertebrae and shoved my shoulder blade to the side. Bright-white flares burst in the there-and-gone darkness that rolled across my vision.

"Lane!"

Teddy's roar pulled me from my daze. I bucked and twisted beneath the heavy body straddling my thighs. The moon fae bent toward me. His face was heavy with the corruption. The black web of lines beneath his charcoal complexion wiggled like worms as he snarled. I tore a fistful of dirt and grass from the ground and threw it into his face.

While the moon fae bellowed and flailed, I risked a glance at Teddy. Five attackers came at him in a relentless onslaught. Stiff leather hauberks protected three corrupt moon fae and two, I assumed, shifters. One on the ground, struggling to rise. Though they moved with the practiced fluidity and precision of soldiers, Teddy was holding his own—for now.

I focused on the moon fae crouched over me. His legs blocked my thigh holsters, not my arms, not the ten blades strapped across my chest. As he spit grass and dirt, I slid two push daggers from their holster. The crossbar cradled against my palm, the crook of the blade between my middle fingers, I punched.

A shout burned from my lungs with the force of my punch. I stabbed my right hand into the moon fae's throat and drove my left into his side. The jacket he wore made of thick, rigid leather protected him from the side punch. Nothing shielded his throat. The knuckles of my right fist met flesh. The cartilage around his larynx crunched and buckled beneath the impact. Warm blood gushed over my fingers and down my forearm.

The noxious amalgam of overripe, too-sweet oranges, onions, and an acrid chaser of burned rubber exploded in my nostrils. With an audible gag, I pressed my face into my left biceps, trying to cut off the olfactory assault.

With the potency I smelled blood, particularly fresh blood, I should be prepared for this by now. In my defense, I rarely came across scents so vile. It ranked worse than the aloughta shit I'd scraped from my boot.

Focused on breathing through my mouth, I looked up into the blank stare of the moon fae slumped against my fist. My arm shook beneath his literal dead weight. I bucked my hips and pushed the body off me.

The dead fae slid to my left. I withdrew my daggers and rolled right—or tried to roll to my right. I shouted in surprise and pain as the dumb sword slung over my back brought me to an abrupt halt. This was at least the third time I'd done that.

Though I practiced with swords frequently, a minimum of two days a week at peak health, I rarely wore them on the job. When knocked down, I'd yet learned how to do much more than wobble on the ground like an overturned turtle. I needed a new scabbard.

Pissed as hell, I rocked forward onto my knees and pushed to my feet. I kept the momentum going and rushed toward Teddy. One moon fae lay twisted and still at his feet, but he was losing ground fast. His back against a tree, the three remaining attackers came at him from the front and both sides.

A shout of pure fury scorched my throat as I launched myself at whoever's back had the misfortune to be in my path.

We'd tangled with these soldiers in the past. Normally, the hauberk-like jackets they wore barely gave under pressure from my short push daggers, but the hard leather couldn't protect against the full-force, free-fall weight of my body coming down behind my blades.

Beneath me, the moon fae I landed on staggered forward and face-planted on the ground, dazed but not dead. I yanked the weapons from the shallow cuts they'd made in the soldier's back and punched the wide, arrowhead-like blades into the sides of his neck. He writhed and gurgled, choking on his own blood. The struggle came to a rapid conclusion. His toes scraped against the grass one last time, and his bowels loosened.

I'd remembered to breathe through my mouth. The too-sweet, too-sharp, fetid stench I was coming to associate with all corrupt moon fae blood wasn't as bad, tolerable, if barely, along with the other unpleasant scents of death.

Someone landed a blow to my ribs with the subtly of a sledgehammer, lifting me up and off the dying soldier. A scream tore out of me. My vision wavered. Blood fae bones were tough to break, but that could have done it.

I rose onto my knees, but my attacker didn't slow down. He grabbed me by the shoulders and wrenched me to my feet until I faced him. Tanned complexion, sandy-colored hair, bright-turquoise gaze, it was a shifter, not the remaining moon fae.

Throwing his support behind the corrupted must have addled his brain to handle me like this. Sure, he had my arms trapped beneath his viselike grip, but I didn't need hands for all my weapons. He should have left me on the ground. *Idiot.*

I lunged forward and sank my fangs into his throat. Hot blood sprayed against my face. I squeezed my eyes shut against the salty spurts pulsing from his torn jugular. Sweet, creamy blood filled my mouth.

The shifter's fingers sprang open. He gurgled through the hole I'd made in his throat. Slapping a hand over the gaping wound, he stumbled backward into the remaining moon fae soldier.

Never taking my eyes from either of them, I spit the shifter blood pooled in my mouth. It felt like I had bits of flesh between my fangs. Even for me, gross.

The moon fae's bloodshot gaze tracked from the dying soldier to me. He shoved his not-quite comrade-in-arms aside and stalked in my direction.

Fangs fully extended—yay me—I flashed a bloody grin and palmed two more push daggers. "You think you can handle this?"

The moon fae pointed a short sword at me.

"That all you got?" I taunted.

As the moon fae stalked in my direction, I tensed and checked his hands. No dark magic dripped from his fingers. In fact, all these moon fae had used weapon, not magic. My breath hitched as realization clanged like a gong in my brain. Only the most powerful corrupted used deadly black magic. Good news for us.

I stepped back, crossing my feet to step to the side, making him follow me, to hopefully make a mistake. Another step, and my breath left me as the flash of pain punched my ribs. I stumbled, nearly going down before I steadied myself. I was broken, tired, and not sure I'd win another fight.

Where was Teddy? I didn't dare look.

Letting out a slow breath, I let my muscles go loose and relaxed into a crouch as—

Two large hands came around the moon fae's head, one under the chin, one over the crown of his skull, gripping in opposite directions. The hands twisted, and a brittle, gut-churning snap echoed through the trees.

The moon fae crumpled like a marionette whose strings had been severed, revealing Teddy, who stood panting behind the body.

Teddy stepped over the corpse and strode toward me. He held me at arm's length, his gaze scouring me from head to toe. "That's a lot of blood. Are you okay?"

"It's not mine." I smiled, but yelped at a sudden flash of pain and pressed a hand to my ribs. "I took a good kick. Might have cracked a rib, but I'll live. You?"

It was my turn to look him over. Shallow cuts covered his torso, but it was mostly split leather, not flesh. His shoulder where he'd taken the initial dagger still leaked blood, but it had slowed to a drip. My gaze drifted past him to the bodies—and body parts—in the grass. Two more soldiers who hadn't been with the first wave of attackers lay dead. One impaled on his own sword. That explained what took Teddy so long.

"They came out of the trees," he said, following my gaze to the bodies. "No telling if any of this was an ambush, a patrol, or a search party hunting for Miro."

I nodded. "But whatever it was, we need to hurry. With these guys missing on top of Miro, they'll know something is up soon, if they don't already."

"Yes." Teddy rubbed dried blood from my lips and then brushed his hands together and grinned. "Anyone ever tell you you're a messy eater?"

29

MY FIERCE LITTLE MONSTER

As we continued our inexorable push toward where we hoped the sun stones remained, I brushed my fingers over my lips and cheeks for what had to be the twentieth time. They still came away with dried blood. Teddy was right. I was a messy eater.

More troubling than the blood on my face, I could still taste the divine flavor on the back of my tongue. Yet I hadn't fallen into a blood-drunk haze, my typical allergic reaction to blood that was not Teddy's.

"Well, you were right," I said at last. "I definitely swallowed blood, and I haven't tried to tear out your throat."

Teddy, walking at a slower pace to allow me to keep up, he glanced toward me. His gaze traveled from my fingers to my face. I caught the tightening of his eyes and downward tilt of his lips before he turned away.

"Shifter blood." His voice rode the thin edge of a growl. "We've been over this."

"Drinking is believing." I went for humor. Judging by his deep scowl, it did not land. The effects of the random shifter's blood weren't mind-blowing, but my steps came quicker, and my limbs felt lighter. I still felt like a battering ram had hit me, but a smaller battering ram.

In profile, his jaw flexed, and a muscle ticked. I had a feeling I'd stepped in it, but I wasn't sure what *it* was.

"This isn't great, but it feels okay." I rolled my shoulders. I wasn't healed, but a new spurt of energy coursed through me, tamping down the associated pain. The blood triggered at least one part of my faulty blood fae abilities. It didn't replace my medicine, and it definitely didn't replace Teddy, but I could work with this.

Teddy stopped so abruptly, I walked several steps before I realized he was no longer next to me.

Annoyed, I turned to face him. The anger radiating from him rocked me back on my heels and evaporated my irritation. His strong jawline clenched and flexed. His biceps and forearms bulged from the barely leashed emotion that curled his hands into fists against his thighs.

I'd never seen him so angry, not at me. I had the distinct impression I'd messed up, but I didn't know how.

He crossed his arms over his chest and stared me down. "So it's okay to drink any other shifter's blood, so long as it isn't mine?"

"That's not what I meant! I...uh..." Sometimes, I was a real idiot. The prospect of not depending on Teddy's blood—on Teddy—had excited me so much, I hadn't thought about how offensive my enthusiasm might be. I repeated, softly, "That's not what I meant."

"That's exactly what you meant." His voice was flat, eyes hard, but the hurt was clear.

Damn it, maybe—

"Get down!" he snarled and threw himself at me.

We went down in a tangle of limbs. The glint of a blade whipped over Teddy's head as we hit the ground. All at once I understood what it felt like to play chicken with a rhinoceros and lose. Teddy's chest, an unyielding wall of muscle, pushed against me with his harsh breaths. My sword pressed painfully against each vertebra it crossed.

With the ounce of oxygen I could pull into my lungs, I wheezed, "Move."

Probably not the politest thing to say if he just saved my life, but for star's sake, I couldn't breathe.

"More soldiers." On his hands and knees, Teddy crouched above me, my body caged beneath his. "Keep to the trees."

In an enviable show of strength, Teddy pushed upright in one fluid motion, took hold of my forearm, and pulled me to my feet.

I still wobbled for balance as three soldiers broke from the tree line. Teddy met them in an audible collision of flesh hitting flesh, taking all three to the ground at once.

Slower than Teddy, but as quick as I could manage, I twisted and located a dense cover of trees.

No! What was I doing? I wasn't the damsel who needed rescuing while someone else fought her battles. I did the fucking rescuing around here.

I turned toward the fight. In the few heartbeats it took me to look for and dismiss safety, Teddy had liberated a soldier of his sword and put it to use. A glistening pool of liquid outlined one soldier, who lay twisted and still in the stained grass. The second soldier fumbled to cover a dark, ragged hole in his throat, but his hands kept sliding away, as if too heavy to hold up.

Teddy faced down the last soldier, circling to the right while his opponent mirrored the action, sidestepping to the left. My Teddy was big, but the other guy was bigger—taller and broader—and blond. Moon fae were lean, thin whips of pure muscle, and they were never blond. He had to be a shifter.

"Screw this." My feet were already propelling me toward the soldier's back as I pulled both tri-blade daggers from their holsters.

Adrenaline fired too fast and too hard to feel the aches and pains I knew I'd regret the moment this was over.

My pulse pounded against my eardrums, drowning out the sound of my feet hammering over the space between me and the soldier.

As I ran, my thigh muscles tensed. I dipped into a crouch but used my momentum and bunched muscles to launch myself across the last few feet, bringing my body weight down behind my blades.

The moment of impact hit like a freeze frame. For a microsecond, the soldier's hard leather armor resisted the needle-point dagger tips. The material gave with a dull pop. The deadly daggers sank to their hilts in the big man's upper back. He grunted, a half-stunned, half-pained sound.

My knees rose, thighs bumped my chest, body continuing its forward trajectory until my boots slammed into my target's back. The collision tipped the already stumbling shifter forward, toward the ground. Despite my clenched jaw, my teeth rattled, and the tips of my fangs scraped the inside of my lip. The salty-sweet metallic tang of my essence filled my mouth.

Perched atop the fallen soldier's back, I rose to my knees and twisted the blades. The move elicited a harsh scream from the male beneath me. Muscle and tendon fought against the spiral blades of the deadly daggers and lost. They popped, tore, and shredded. His arms went dead at his sides.

The daggers slid free from the large holes with a wet slurp. I glanced up and found Teddy watching me with narrowed eyes.

"What?" I scowled. "You didn't actually think I'd go hide in the shadows and let you have all the fun, did you?"

He arched a brow. His mouth moved, but I couldn't hear a thing above the mix tape of cursing, whimpering, and wailing going on beneath me.

"I can't hear you. Hold that thought," I shouted and drove a dagger through the soldier's thick neck—back to front and twisted—severing the spine. The moment the blade sliced between the vertebrae, his body slumped into the ground, doing an excellent beanbag impersonation. The shifter had already lost too much blood to survive before the neck skewering, and after a prolonged gurgle through the large hole I'd punched through his neck, he was gone.

Thank the gods, because my ears were still ringing.

Dragging both daggers through the grass to scour away blood and gooey bits of shifter, I glanced back at Teddy. "What'd you say?"

He shook his head. "Should I be worried about you?"

"I don't think so?" My answer came out more like a question. "Why?"

"Because, sweet fangs," he drawled. "You have a weird idea of fun."

"It is fun. Better than feeling helpless." This small zip of energy from the shifter blood felt like magic. Even so, it was nothing compared to my reaction to Teddy's blood.

"You make a valid point." His mouth tilted into a smile I'd never get enough of, and he sauntered toward me. He hooked a finger under my chin, tipping my face toward his, and used his thumb to wipe away what I assumed was blood. "You noticed Dacian wasn't with this group?"

"Yes." I closed my eyes and sank into the calming feel of his fingers brushing over my cheeks. My arms hung loose at my sides, the tri-blades lying against my thighs.

"And you know we should have kept the last soldier alive?"

I blew out a breath and tried not to enjoy the gentle slide of his fingers wiping the now cool blood from my face. "Yes."

"My fierce little monster." He chuckled, laid a kiss on my forehead, and stepped back. "Let's work on that temper, hmm?"

Dragging a toe through the grass, I scowled and holstered my daggers. "He wouldn't shut up."

"You're so stabby." He grinned and gestured toward the recently sheathed daggers. "Those things have hilts, don't they?"

I fidgeted, scratched my neck. Dried blood was itchy.

"You know as well as I do, a solid hit to the base of the skull would have done the job. We could have removed him for questioning."

"Ugh, I get it," I said and threw my hands wide. "I messed up."

"Never say that. I know you've been having a rough adjustment. I get it, and I understand." He glanced into the shadowy nooks of the surrounding trees, to the sky, and back to me. "Let's just call it a learning experience."

I made a semi-agreeable grunt. It wasn't like he was telling me something I hadn't already known. My elbow brushed the bulge in the side of my jacket. "Could I have used the collar on these shifters and again on Dacian?"

"It's not a one and done, but each use draws the osmium from the cuff. To contain a Barbout, the cuff should be at its most potent."

"Good to know."

Teddy surveyed our surroundings and looked into the distance. "We're close enough and it's early. Those soldiers might have been hunting for dinner."

"Makes sense. They would have sent more if they suspected we were here."

"Exactly." Teddy nodded and brushed hair from his face. "We might have been lucky so far, but it's unlikely a second encounter will go undetected."

I tugged at my lip. "Be honest. Do we have a shot?"

"Let's change our approach." Instead of continuing the same path we'd been following, Teddy turned to the right and started walking.

Not an answer, but I let it go and followed.

"Will this really help?" I asked in a stage whisper—as if being quiet made a difference at this point—and hurried to catch up. Every tree I passed appeared ominous, with the threat of who knew what lurked behind.

"I don't know." Teddy glanced at me. "The grounds are directly ahead, but based on the photos your sister and Lo took, going around and coming in from the east will put us closer to the stones."

My brain snagged on one word. "What grounds?"

Teddy glanced at me, his expression flat. "The house I was raised in."

I cliché stumbled. Teddy slowed momentarily while I steadied myself. "As in your family's house?"

"Yes, and no."

"That was a very yes or no question," I said, my tone dry as the Mojave.

"It belongs to the Barbouts. I was raised there with my siblings, but my parent's permanent residence is the palace. Dacian and my sister eventually joined my parents, while I chose to live alone at the house. When I left Shadwe, all my kin still lived at the palace."

"Your sister?" He never spoke of her, and I wouldn't have known she existed if Lo hadn't once made an offhand comment. I had so many questions.

"Not the best time for a family history, but I'll tell you all about Lavinia. She was—is—the sweetest soul." There was no disguising the smile in Teddy's voice.

I brushed my fingers against his hand. "I look forward to it."

Teddy returned my touch. "We're skirting along the edge of the grounds and need to be on high alert."

Thank the stars he knew where we were, because it all looked the same to me. Same trees, same grass, same meadows and hills. I had the vague sense we'd changed direction, but I would never find my way here alone.

Eventually, we moved from another strip of forest into a wide, rolling meadow with thigh-high grass and dotted with wildflowers. Now and then, I glimpsed some small creature running through the weeds or birds in the trees.

Though he showed no reaction to the creatures, I eyed every one of them with suspicion. How did one know what was a shifter and what was just an animal? I added that to my long list of questions I had for my sugar buns.

My stomach rumbled, and I pressed a hand against my belly. Great, I had to think about food. I should have taken Mae up on her gross granola bar. Too bad those things weren't the good kind. All oats and nuts, with only enough honey to hold them together.

Teddy chuckled and shook his head. "Your stomach is going to lead them right to us."

I made a face at his profile.

"Never fear, I brought your favorite Fruity Pebbles *granola* bar." He patted the side pocket of his jacket.

"Your tone implies you don't believe it's a granola bar."

"I am fairly certain Rice Krispies Treat is not synonymous with granola."

"Pfft. It's an edible rectangular bar form."

"And you may have your rectangular sugar bar once we reach that tree line over there." Teddy pointed across the field. "We will be close enough for you to contact Duskmere and have him send the backup we'll need to get the stones through the portal."

I followed Teddy toward the tree line. The morning sun had begun to burn off, revealing mountains rising in the distance. Between there and here, what looked like a roofline sloped beyond the trees. It was far enough I couldn't be sure I didn't just want to see something other than trees.

Whether or not it was real, Teddy had given me the okay to bring in the RFG. Thank the gods this sun stone bullshit was almost over once and for all. Time to move on to the next problem: separating Mae from the stones. Or at least figuring out how to give her space.

My gaze remained on my feet as I mulled over potential solutions. Would placing large shards, maybe even chunks of the stones, in our home be enough? They would have to periodically be charged at the source.

"More soldiers," Teddy growled.

I whipped my head up. "Don't tell me to stay behind you."

He flashed me a bloodthirsty grin. "I won't."

I turned to the tree line Teddy watched and counted two soldiers—no, three—all shifters.

A sudden gale-force wind whipped up behind me, tearing hair loose from my braid. I spun. My eyes were instantly assaulted by wind. It scoured my face with dirt and debris blown up from the ground.

Teddy began shouting. It was a muffled, panicked sound, directed at me. He glared up. His muscles bunched, body seemed to swell, but I couldn't see anything clearly. I threw an arm across my eyes to protect them from the dirt tornado.

The ground shook. I stumbled and lowered my arm in time to see the pointed tip of a large, sinewy, scaled tail coming right for me.

I tensed but had no time to react. I was so screwed.

The spear-like tip nailed me in the dead center of my breastbone, impact lifting me off my feet. My ribs compressed my lungs, and the air whooshed out of me. My vision flared, grayed at the edges.

The lights went out.

30

I HAVE A SHARP SWORD AND I KNOW HOW TO USE IT

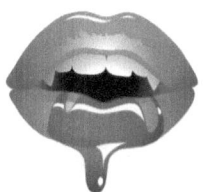

MY EYES FLEW OPEN. I GASPED FOR AIR THAT WOULDN'T COME. SOMEONE had parked a car on my chest. And then that car got rear-ended by a bus. Beyond the excruciating ache, something stabbed me from the inside out with each breath. A broken rib? Two? All of them?

Oh gods, it hurt. I couldn't breathe. My gasps were razor blades scraping inside my sternum.

Muffled grunts, thuds, and shouts pushed their way through the cotton-filled sensation in my ears.

I rolled to my stomach and slid my hands beneath my shoulders, preparing to lift myself up, but the ground tilted. Who put a fun house in the middle of Shadwe? Despite lying prone on my belly, I swayed, and the ground rolled in the other direction.

Bile rocketed up my throat, and I couldn't choke it back. I pushed my weight onto my palms, raising my upper torso with no time to spare, and retched. The first time I heaved because of the awful, unsteady ground. The second, from the new wave of agony twisting through me.

I didn't know which forsaken god I'd pissed off enough to try to kill me. Neither the fall from the sun bridge nor the plummet from the sky after my fight with Dacian hurt like this.

Of course, I'd been in a coma afterward both times and possibly paralyzed, unable to feel a thing. Still, holy moldy Twinkies, this was pain.

A final dry retch proved the last of my Sno Ball meal had evacuated my volatile stomach. I dragged my knees forward and rolled onto my toes. Still on all fours, I struggled to lock my loose joints. The ground continued to do a slow, exaggerated side-to-side roll. I fought the sway and looked for the source of the fight sounds—for Teddy.

In the distance to my right, he wrestled a wyvern.

No way.

I shook my head. Yep, he was manhandling his brother, who was still in wyvern form. If Y'sindra got into a fight with a Humvee, this was what it would look like. I wasn't sure if I should laugh or have a breakdown.

My left elbow, the one supporting most of my weight, gave out suddenly. I almost performed another face-plant but caught myself before I ate grass.

Forget laughing or losing it, I might take door number three and pass out again.

No. Not an option. *Get your shit together, Lane*.

A well-timed distraction, the guards had stepped out of the forest when Dacian nailed me. I'd been out long enough that they'd joined the fight, though they kept their distance. I suspected to avoid being flattened by Dacian's large, flailing body. Yet they still landed physical blows on Teddy.

I heaved to my feet and swayed. Squeezing my eyes shut, I took slow breaths.

The aftereffects of this injury were as bad as a blood-haze hangover, and those sucked big, hairy ogre balls. Were ogre balls hairy? Every ogre I'd ever met was as bald as a spit-shined bowling ball. Made one wonder.

Dacian's wyvern screech, sounding part fury, part pain, shook me. My eyes snapped open.

Shit. *Focus, Lane*.

My first few steps led me in the wrong direction. Another few steps, and I was back on track. My legs overcame their rubbery wobble, and I increased my speed until I executed a pathetic limp-sprint across the open distance between us.

Using his grip on Dacian's wing, Teddy flipped his brother's bulk onto his side and hammered a blow against the wyvern's ribs. I wanted to howl in victory. A malicious smile on my lips, I charged toward the guards who continued to hound Teddy.

Before I reached the fight, Dacian's tail rose behind Teddy. The spear-like tip usually resting flat along the tail hinged forward—sharp, straight, and deadly.

Ice and adrenaline dumped into my bloodstream. My face went numb.

"Teddy! Behind you!" I screamed past the death grip terror had on my throat. Agony flared in my chest, reminding me of the power in that tail.

At the last second, Teddy twisted and bent, and instead of taking the strike through his chest or gut, it opened a wide gash along his left side. At first it was only torn clothing. Then came the blood. His dark jacket disguised the flow, but even from a distance I could see the deep-red stain growing along his denim.

He swayed, stunned.

"Teddy!" I screamed again.

The wyvern whipped his head toward me. Dacian bared his teeth in a hideous expression I could only describe as a predatory smile.

Teddy took an awkward step, as if trying to catch his balance, and fell to a knee. Behind him, a flash of brilliant light burst outward from the wyvern's form, haloing Teddy.

My world went whitewashed. I threw an arm across my eyes, burying my face in my elbow. Sheltered behind my arm, the swell of my harsh breath filled my ears.

When the light at my feet receded, I looked to where Dacian and Teddy had been. I blinked and squinted. A black hole burned in the center of my vision. I'd been too slow protecting my light-sensitive pupils, and I might as well have stared directly into the sun. All I could see were indistinct impressions.

The scene crept into focus. Where Dacian had returned to primary form, the soldiers who accompanied him had shifted to their animal forms. They watched the pair from a distance, their eyes burning brighter than my Bronco's high beams.

Beneath my jacket, warm dampness saturated my shirt. A burning pain radiated out from the center of my chest. I curled my arm protectively across my midsection. Something hard pressed into my side under my palm.

The cuff.

It was nice of Dacian to shift so I could fit him with this fancy osmium cuff. He could have stayed in his big scaly skin, or even his half form, but he'd shifted into his weakest form to taunt Teddy.

Quietly, as not to draw attention, I unzipped my jacket pocket and withdrew the thick metal bar. Despite being tucked against my side, the cuff was cool inside my palm. I crept toward Dacian in an almost-straight line. A small clink accompanied each section of the loop I unfolded and locked into place, sending an electric bolt of anxiety sizzling over my skin.

In my peripheral, a big cat turned toward me. A shifter soldier spotted me. I set my jaw against the oncoming pain and sprinted the remaining distance toward Dacian. The cat shifter charged. Its chest dipped toward the ground, preparing to leap. I dove toward Dacian.

Not anticipating that move, the cat sailed over me. I collided with Dacian's legs, knocking him up and over my back.

Pain seized my chest. It stole my breath, and I almost blacked out again. Sheer stubbornness kept me this side of conscious.

I spun on my knees toward Dacian, who had already gained his feet. Stretching to catch his leg before he could pull it out of my reach, I grabbed his shin and closed the cuff over his ankle. His pants bunched. The rough material was thicker than it appeared. I didn't hear the snick of a latch, but blood bloomed on his khaki-colored pant leg.

Dacian let out a half shout, half roar. He shook his leg. His attempts to free himself from the cuff grew more frantic. He spun and kicked and kicked, kicking me in the face.

My head jerked. Stars cartwheeled across my vision. The blow laid me flat on my back, but I smiled as I rolled away. The salty-sweet taste of my blood ran hot into my mouth. He'd split my lip, maybe knocked out a tooth, but I'd done it. I got the cuff onto him.

"Got you, motherfucker." I laughed, spit blood, and awaited a mauling from the shifters.

It didn't come. I ran my tongue over my teeth—all thankfully accounted for—and looked down the length of me. The shifters gathered protectively around a still ranting, stomping Dacian.

If they were going to just let me get up and stab them, who was I to not oblige?

After a few false starts, I made it to my feet. It was only a matter of time before Dacian and the shifters remembered Teddy and finished him. Not a chance I'd let that happen.

I cracked my neck and gingerly rolled my shoulders. Ignoring the sensation of tearing flesh and searing pain grinding a fist into my chest, I pulled my sword from its sheath and pointed the blade at Dacian.

"Round three is mine." I shouted the challenge. My arm shook, ruining the effect. I lowered the sword to my side before Dacian or the shifters realized how much effort it took to hold it up.

Dacian faced me with a snarl. Fortunately, or unfortunately, I also got the attention of all three soldiers in their creature form. I couldn't take them all down. I wasn't even sure I could bring one down when I could barely stay on my feet. But by all the forsaken gods, if it drew them away from Teddy, I would stay upright.

"I do not think the odds are in your favor," Dacian called. Cuff forgotten, he made a sweeping gesture, indicating his shifter companions.

Though he tried to hide it, his movements were stiff. Red stains blossomed beneath his clothes, testament to the damage Teddy had wrought. The sweet burn of satisfaction heated my blood.

"You're a fool if you think you have the upper hand. Especially with your new jewelry." I didn't have Y'sindra's flair for getting under someone's skin, but I managed all right. "Don't forget I brought you down from the sky and took a souvenir."

Intending to show him his scale, I laid a hand to where it should have rested against my chest and almost screamed. A fresh burst of white-hot agony exploded. I breathed through my nose.

All at once, I realized why I was alive and wanted to laugh. Dacian saved me from himself, or a piece of him did. The scale took the blow meant to skewer my hearts. Unfortunately, it had also been driven into my flesh.

A flicker of something behind the group grabbed my focus, and I went still. Teddy moved, if only slightly. My stomach clenched. I still had Dacian and his soldier's attention, and I needed to keep it that way.

Maybe I could put enough distance between us to use Duskmere's portal stone. Though I hadn't contacted him. It wasn't like he'd be in the dungeon waiting for me to use the stone. If I used it and he wasn't precisely where he needed to be to open the portal, I would waste the stone.

I had no endgame here, no solution. I growled my frustration and rolled my wrist, giving the sword a slow spin, and began backing away. Heads lowered, teeth bared, the shifters followed my movement at a slow, menacing stalk.

All at once, Teddy was there, barreling into Dacian, moving faster than I could have imagined possible. He had to have been faking the severity of his injury. No. He couldn't fake the amount of blood he'd lost.

They both staggered forward, but Teddy got his arms around his brother's waist and body-slammed him to the ground. A large, scaled wolf collided with Teddy, knocking him off Dacian's prone form.

Dacian rolled to his feet and staggered away from Teddy, backing toward me. After several steps, I noticed his pant leg was looser. The silver cuff was slightly askew, not as tight.

The closer Dacian came to me, the clearer I could see the clasp hadn't caught. Panic rode my nerves like a zip line.

Teddy followed Dacian, exhaustion and pain easy to read on his bruised face. He limped. The entire waistband of his jeans was red, the stain dipping lower on his right hip. How was he even on his feet?

And he still had the attention of all three guards.

"Hey!" I shouted to no one in particular and made of show of spinning my sword in a large circle, all fancy-like, stretching and flexing my wrist. Enough adrenaline powered through me that I could manage the pain from my new chest accessory.

One guard angled toward me.

Gotcha. Pasting on a feral smile designed to enrage and taunt, I turned to face it and blinked. "That's...different."

Almost as thick as a regular bear, its shoulders, the highest point of its body, only rose to my hip. It had a wide, square head on a short, thick neck. A coat of bristly, dark-brown fur with patches of paler brown covered a stocky body bizarrely elongated, like a weasel's, with an equally elongated, fluffy tail. Were it not for the exaggerated length of sharp teeth lining its jaws, I'd say it was cute.

And I always said cute things fucking sucked.

It loped into motion.

Gripping my sword with both hands, I surged forward to meet it.

From my right, a set of glowing turquoise eyes turned on me. I'd caught the big cat's attention. One less thing for Teddy to worry about.

When the weasel-bear and I were almost close enough for me to reach out and touch it with my sword, it rose onto its stumpy hind legs. The beast towered over me by double my height. Caught off guard, I stumbled back.

"What in the Flaming Cheetos are you?" I shouted, getting the attention of the final shifter.

"Your death," it chuffed in a gravely male voice.

"Not very original, are you?" I rolled my eyes and cast a surreptitious glance around the battlefield. While Teddy and Dacian still faced off, I'd pulled the others to me. It would really piss Teddy off if I died now. I'd try not to do that.

The other two shifters came at me, slow and methodical. These were no amateurs willing to do me a favor and sprint onto my sword. Needing to take this bear-weasel down before his buddies joined the fight, I circled to the left, away from the big cat and scaled wolf.

"I have a sharp sword, and I know how to use it," I taunted with a grin.

Usually, I was anti-smack talk. It was stupid, and I'd look really dumb if it got me dead. But I had no idea how to take down a ten-foot weasel-bear, and I needed to buy time. He had a short reach, like a T-Rex, but he could also bend in half to crush me or eat me before I was within striking distance.

"Waving it around won't hurt me." The bear-weasel's lip rose and rippled above overly large, cone-shaped teeth. I wasn't sure if that was a sneer or it needed to sneeze.

"Why don't you come and try me?" I had a much better chance if I could provoke him into attacking while on all fours.

Too bad for me, these weren't just dumb beasts. Apparently, this guy knew the same thing I did because he settled onto his short hind legs, leaning most of his weight onto his thick, furry tail.

An idea took root, and before I could think better of it, I ran as fast as I could manage in a wide arc, still to the left, still away from the other two shifters and out of the weasel-bear's reach.

Creepy weasel-bear tried to keep me in his line of sight but couldn't. Unless he wanted to lower himself to all fours—which he apparently didn't— he had to shuffle his stumpy little legs slowly, corkscrewing his body at the waist to keep track of me.

When I was just behind him, I executed a lightning-fast turn. Pain was a distant hum in my body beneath a new dump of adrenaline. Sword raised, I ran straight for the creature.

Thinking I was going for a gut stab, he hunched to protect his stomach, bringing his blocky head and big teeth into my path. Just like I'd hoped he'd do.

I veered at the last moment, running past his open jaws, and brought the sword down, severing his tail.

Hot blood arced, sprayed across my face, my neck.

He screamed. The terrible keen of an injured animal blended with a male's bellow ripped through the meadow. Without the balance his tail provided, the weasel-bear flopped onto all fours, writhing in distress.

Would he heal if he shifted? I had no idea, but I wasn't about to take that chance. I stepped closer and drove the sword, point down, into the weasel-bear's skull.

Pulling my sword free, I looked for Teddy. He and Dacian were in hand-to-hand combat near the trees. The cuff still glinted on Dacian's leg. Despite the pain he had to be suffering from the osmium in the cuff, Teddy was slower than his brother, his hits clumsy.

Damn Dacian to the deepest, darkest hole in the universe. Teddy had fought off too many to maintain the same stamina as his brother without shifting. And he wouldn't shift.

I adjusted my grip on the sword and moved toward them. This time I wouldn't just take a scale, I'd take his head.

A snarl on my right alerted me just in time to avoid the wolf's snapping jaws coming for my throat. I spun out of the way. Continuing the spin, I brought my sword up in front of me.

The wolf executed a tight turn and threw himself back at me...right onto my sword. Who said these guys were too smart for that? He *was* smart enough to register his mistake before he hit the pointy end face-first but had too much momentum to avoid it completely.

The blade bit into his side and split open his shoulder, stopping when it met bone. My teeth rattled from the contact. A high-pitched whine tore across the meadow. The wolf's body weight and speed pulled him off the sword, and he kept going.

Light shimmered around the wolf. I shielded my eyes, and when I looked, a man knelt in the grass several yards away. His arm hung limp at his side, and blood ran freely. With his other arm, he fumbled awkwardly with a weapon sheathed at his waist.

Well, I had an answer to one of my many questions. Shifters didn't heal when they changed forms. At least not completely. Goody. This should be easy.

I'd been holding the sword for a long time, and the damage to my chest was only getting worse. With a hiss, I holstered the sword.

After a breath to steady myself, I drew a push dagger with my left hand

and a torpedo with my right. The torpedo was a throwing weapon, and I was a righty.

"Night, night," I mumbled under my breath. Grip solid on the end of the throwing dagger, I bent my elbow and let the torpedo flip backward until it rested on my shoulder, took aim at the male turned wolf turned man...and my muscles locked.

Beyond the shifter who had noticed me about to put out his lights, Teddy took Dacian to the ground. Dacian shouted, ripped out of Teddy's choke hold, and rolled away. He gained his feet, staggered a few steps, and the loose cuff finally dropped off his leg.

Dacian looked down. His laugh carried to my ears.

A rustling noise built and swelled in the trees behind Dacian and Teddy.

Beneath the sun, the torn side of Teddy's jacket glistened with blood. Hand pressed to his side, he looked from the cuff, to Dacian, to the tree line. At last he turned to me, unable to hide the raw pain and exhaustion on his battered face.

Something was very wrong.

"I love you," he mouthed.

"No! No, no, no!" I screamed.

The shifter took advantage of my distraction and charged. He came at me with a fat-bladed machete-like knife.

He was almost on top of me. I didn't stop to think, just dropped to my knees. The shifter stabbed into the empty air and stumbled from his misplaced momentum. As he tripped over me, I bent backward and drove the palmed push daggers into his torso. My left hand sank into his squishy center, my right punched into his sternum.

"Oof." He came down on his side and let out an airy grunt. The blade in his chest hit a lung.

Withdrawing the daggers from his flesh, I bounced to my feet, spun toward Teddy and Dacian, and went still. Soldiers, a dozen, maybe two dozen, emerged from the tree line.

As I tried to reconcile this new situation, a blur warned me of an incoming collision. I had a shred of sense to bring up my right elbow to block and aim with the push dagger in my left before the big cat I'd somehow forgotten rammed into it at full speed.

Claws sank into my collarbone. I screamed before pain turned my vision white, red, and then nothing.

31

HINDSIGHT REALLY WAS THE MOTHER OF ALL BITCHES

I SLOW-BLINKED MY HEAVY EYELIDS OPEN. BLADES OF GRASS TICKLED MY nose. I sneezed to expel them. Agony ricocheted across every inch of me. Bright light chased by darkness rolled across my vision. Teeth gritted, I played tag with consciousness for several minutes. I might have lost a few rounds.

How many times could I pass out today?

At last, I rose onto an elbow, or at least I tried. My right arm was a tangle of unimaginable pain. I bit back a sob, part frustration, part agony.

How did I end up down here in the first place?

Flashes of the big cat. Big claws, big fangs. Right, that.

I closed my eyes, pulling air in and out of my nose. Pain throbbed with each breath, and I focused on wrestling it into submission.

Beneath the torn jacket, sticky blood added an uncomfortable weight to my clothes. They stuck to my body, would dry inside the torn flesh. More coated my hands. A lot of blood. Too much to be only mine.

I sat up slowly, spitting more grass.

A heavy wash of warm spiced blood rolled over my senses, teasing my super sniffer.

The final shifter—the source of the delicious scent—lay dead several feet away. He'd lived long enough to shift, which sucked for him.

I'd opened him from gut to gullet, like a macabre zipper. His glistening pink innards peeked from the wound. My push daggers still hung in his throat. No doubt about it. He was dead.

That was the thing about weapon training and more than once being forced to put practice into real-time action—eventually, it became automatic.

After several false starts, I made it to my feet. My ankle throbbed. Great, on top of everything else, I'd twisted an ankle, the left one. I'd braced myself against the cat, but must have gone down at a bad angle.

Unable to put my full weight on my foot, I hobbled a drunken diagonal line toward the shifter and bent to retrieve my dagger. What blood remained in my body rushed to my head and then drained to my toes.

"Ah!" I cried out and collapsed. My vision refused to focus. It spun and spun and spun.

A host of injuries competed for my attention. Chest, head, shoulder, and now my ankle. I knew pain, but I didn't know it without healing.

I lay perfectly still, waiting for the world to stabilize.

The moments before the cat shifter's attack ripped into my brain with sudden clarity.

Dacian, free of his cuff. Teddy bleeding and bleeding. The fresh group of soldiers entering the field.

Dread laid a clammy hand on the back of my neck. Only corpses, carrion birds, and me in the field now.

Where was Teddy?

The question had yet to really dig into my brain when I was upright and moving across the tilt-o-whirl terrain. My feet tangled together, but unadulterated stubbornness kept me up and whatever remained in my stomach down as I limped toward the last place I'd seen Teddy.

Silvery-blue metal winked in the grass. The osmium cuff marked the spot.

Bodies littered the ground in a large radius near the cuff. The sheer amount of blood caused my senses to go haywire.

I flexed my hands and squeezed them into fists against my thigh as I turned in a circle, studying each corpse that littered the field. Turning, turning, a hot jolt seized my muscles, and I came to a sudden stop.

Everything went numb. White noise buzzed in my ears.

A large male with whiskey-brown hair, wearing denim and a leather jacket, lay face down. Strands of grass twined perversely with his hair like a lover's caress.

One second I was staring in horror, the next I knelt by the body and flipped it.

"Thank the stars." I studied the stranger's battered face, not sure if I could believe my eyes. Bones bulged against the side of the shifter's throat. His head flopped at a weird angle. This had to be Teddy's handiwork.

Talons digging into my palms, I wrestled my emotions into submission. I focused on one body, taking in all the gory details of death by hand-to-hand supernatural combat. Just a few feet away lay another body, and another.

Livor mortis had set in. I'd been out a lot longer than I'd thought. I scratched my head and winced at the squishy goose egg. Of course, on top of everything else, but a concussion explained why I kept passing out.

At last, I focused on the immediate scene. My mouth went dry. The fight here had been intense. A multitude of feet had flattened the grass. In the center of the loose ring of corpses, the earth had been churned into a messy pile of dark soil and clumps of grass.

That was where they'd subdued Teddy. Subdued, not killed. No body. Why?

A sucking, hollow sensation opened in my chest. I wanted to be relieved his body wasn't here, but why wasn't it? Dacian hated his brother. He'd tried to kill Teddy with a bullet to the chest just a few months ago. Tried to stab him with his tail, too.

I took a step toward the tree line. "Holy mother of Ho Hos!" Pain shot up my leg, and I quickly shifted my weight from left to right.

My ironclad grip on my emotions wavered just enough for the helplessness to creep in. Even if I wanted to track Teddy, they had a massive head start. I could barely stand up, let alone track through the brush.

What would I do if the universe felt benevolent, and I did catch up? I scrubbed my hands over my face. Blood flaked into the wind. I had some sort of hole in my chest, a twisted ankle, a bum arm, and probably a concussion.

I squeezed my eyes shut. *Mistake!* The image of Dacian's spear-tipped tail ripping through Teddy's side played behind my eyelids. The blood, the bruises. His final *I love you* when he saw the cuff on the ground. Lastly, the soldiers coming from the trees.

All this because I couldn't swallow my pride—and Teddy's blood. I laughed without humor.

Teddy had been giving my mother his blood since before I knew it was his. He had been happy to do it. How could I have ever believed it would change if I took it directly from the vein? Something he'd been begging me to do.

I swallowed and licked my dry lips. My tongue tingled, and blood-tainted saliva burned a pleasurable path down my throat. Euphoria lit up some primal part of my brain.

Shifter blood.

Turbo mode kicked in on my hearts. The spicy-sweet taste coating my mouth felt like a betrayal. I'd refused Teddy's blood and then hurt him, considering I might drink from a shifter—any shifter—so long as it wasn't him.

I held my breath and eyed the dark blotches where the blood had concentrated in the corpses. I'd eaten worse. Kale was pretty bad, and Mae force fed that crap to me once a week. But this wouldn't be worth it. It wasn't my mate's blood.

Surprised, my muscles executed a full-body pinch. I'd called Teddy my mate. Pain that had nothing to do with my injuries turned in my chest. It twisted tighter and tighter until I gulped for air.

He wasn't my mate yet, but he would be.

"I'm such an idiot." Too late I understood what refusing to be at my best wrought. What Teddy warned. The danger I'd put everyone I loved in. How much I might have lost.

Hindsight really was the mother of all bitches.

If I didn't find him, if I didn't tell him how wrong I'd been, it would be how he remembered me. Simple answer—I had to find Teddy.

All right, chasing them down on my own in this condition wasn't possible, but there had to be something. I traced a talon over my lip in thought.

On my own.

My hand stilled and then dropped to my side. A deep, painful breath ballooned my lungs. With agonizing clarity, I accepted what needed to be done. I had to ask for help, even if I'd prefer to eat glass.

Gingerly, I shifted my weapon harnesses and pulled down my jacket zipper until I could reach my inner chest pocket. My fingertips grazed the smooth sides of the crystal, and I wiggled them until I'd worked it into my palm.

Holding my hand in front of me, I eyed the crystal. This was for Teddy, I reminded myself. And I was out of options.

I traced a finger over the communication crystal's surface. "Duskmere," I said and cleared my throat. It sounded like I'd been on a week-long bender of booze, or blood, or both.

Duskmere's image rose before I finished setting the crystal at my feet and stepping back.

His sharp silver eyes quickly scanned the area, cataloging the situation. "You are alone."

"I am, and you promised backup. Time to deliver."

"You are at the stones?" His gaze dropped pointedly to the body I hadn't bothered to move away from. "There were no other guards?"

"I'm not at the stones. We were ambushed." I swept my hand up and down my body, just in case he missed what an absolute disaster I was. "Dacian attacked with these soldiers. I was knocked out. When I woke up, these bodies were here. Teddy was not. They took him. You need to send help so I can track them before it's too late."

Duskmere shook his head. "It is not that easy, Malaney Callaghan."

If I didn't know the guy better, I'd say he sounded regretful. But I did know him. He didn't give a monkey-flung shit.

I paced, stopped, and jabbed a finger at holographic Duskmere. "You better make it that easy. You need me to get those stones. I need you to help me get Teddy. Simple."

"Malaney Callaghan." Duskmere turned to put his face in profile and sighed. "It is not—"

"If you finish that sentence, I swear I will mount you on this sword and use you as a scarecrow to keep those birds away from my balcony. They keep pooping on my patio furniture."

His teeth clacked together, and he scowled.

I flashed a humorless smile and leaned down toward the crystal. "About that backup. And medicine. I need a lot of medicine."

Duskmere opened his mouth, but my father pushed into the frame. Though his pale, wheat-blond hair was tied in a queue at his nape, a long strand fell forward across his face. He brushed it aside and fixed his deep-sapphire gaze on me.

A scream of frustration filled my throat. I knew my father and his loquacious lectures. "I don't have time for this," I snapped before he could build any momentum. "I am sorry to be short, but Teddy's life is on the line. It might not matter to you, but right now, it's all I care about."

"Let me speak, Malaney."

My eyes tightened. I felt the wrinkles and cracks forming in the dried blood on my face. I'd think my macabre visage alone would project the magnitude of this situation. Then again, he'd put the sun fae and the sun stones over his own daughter's lives when both were taken, so why was I surprised?

He'd been talking, but I hadn't been listening. I was so tired. Tired of being a tool for those who made my life a waking nightmare and, until less than a year ago, wished me dead. Most probably still did, but they hid it since I'd saved them, and open hate was no longer en vogue.

I dragged my hands down my face, scraping away at least some of the dried blood. "I won't budge on this."

Whatever he'd been droning on about cut short, and he brought his hands together in front of himself. "You are selfish."

"Yes," I said simply. "Let's be honest, I think you—the sun fae—owe me."

My father pursed his lips. "Perhaps."

Shocked he'd agreed, I pushed on. "I love you, but you will listen to me. You are not getting those stones unless I get Teddy. He's hurt, badly. So is Dacian, but if Dacian shifts..."

I couldn't say the words. *Teddy could be dead*. I squeezed my eyes shut and breathed through my mouth, forcing myself to remain calm.

"They will not kill Aventheo," Duskmere said, moving back into the frame at my father's side. "I will not promise he will not suffer, because he will. But he will not die."

"You don't know that," I snapped.

"In fact, he does." My father absently shook his robe, as if it needed rearranging. "This is what he has been trying to tell you."

I ran my tongue over my teeth. "All right, I'm listening. Explain."

"We have gathered knowledge from the spy you captured," Duskmere said.

"You got that information pretty fast." Intrigued, I perked up. Until I realized how they must have coerced that knowledge. Regret rose but quickly flitted away. Teddy made the promise to Lo, not me.

"We used no extraneous extraction," Duskmere said, reading the thoughts my face never failed to project. "The spy has been forthcoming with enough information to be deemed cooperative, though none of it has been helpful in ascertaining plans for the stones."

I snorted. "It's pretty obvious. They plan to use the stones for power."

"But for what?" my father asked.

"For. Power." I enunciated each word and leaned down to tap the crystal. "Do we have a bad connection?"

"This is not a joke." It had been a very long time since I heard genuine anger in my father's voice.

"Do I look like I'm joking?" My own ire rose to meet his head on.

Duskmere's gaze scraped over every gore-covered inch of me. His lips thinned.

Fine wrinkles draped my father's eyes.

"Right," I said. "Now, tell me why you think Teddy is safe."

My father opened his mouth, but Duskmere placed a hand on his shoulder. They looked at one another, and some sort of understanding passed between the pair. My father gave me a long look, dipped his chin, and stepped out of the frame.

Duskmere picked up his crystal, and I did the same. It wasn't necessary, but otherwise he'd be staring up my nostrils. His projection from chest up rose over my palm. He would see the same of me on his end.

"The spy reports Dacian requires Aventheo to become the black wolf."

"He won't shift," I blurted.

Duskmere nodded. "I know this. While Aventheo—"

"Teddy."

He gave me a hard stare. While I wanted to return his look with a harder stare, one of my infamous death glares, I didn't have the energy. Instead, I raised in eyebrow. "It's his name."

"It is not," Duskmere snapped. "For the sake of expediency, I will humor you."

"Not that expedient, you just wasted..." I counted on my fingers. "Ten, wait no, twelve words."

Duskmere's charcoal complexion deepened with a ruddy red undertone. I'd made the big bad RFG captain angry.

I waved a hand. "Go on. While Teddy what?"

"He is very difficult to kill." Duskmere opted for the third option of not using a name.

Sly or stubborn. I could respect that.

"But he can be killed." Feeling the sudden weight of exhaustion, I crossed an arm over my chest, beneath the arm holding up the crystal.

"Yes. However, in black wolf form, he is nearly indestructible. It takes a monumental effort and many lives to bring down the black wolf." Duskmere tilted his head and watched me. "Or his mate can do it."

I hissed a breath. It wasn't the first time I'd heard that, but it would never happen. Nothing could make me hurt Teddy.

"So you see, for whatever purpose they have captured him, it is not to end his life," Duskmere said. "We will help you, but we need time."

If I had time, if I returned to Vegas, there were things I could do to tilt the odds in our favor. We needed all the favors we could get.

"All right, I'll come back, but first is my father still there?"

"I am here," my father spoke from off screen.

"Here's what I need you two to do."

32

HEART'S BLOOD

DUSKMERE AND MY FATHER JOINED ME IN THE SHADWE FIELD TO CREATE new bindings—which they argued were unnecessary. I informed them the matter was non-negotiable. We were close to the Barbout family home and the stones. They wanted the stones. I wanted Teddy. I had no evidence I'd find Teddy and Dacian there, but I'd bet a lifetime supply of Ho Hos that was where they'd be.

The great Finnlay Callaghan got right to business. He headed to an area free of corpses to begin the process of linking a new portal device to this location. Duskmere handed me a thermos of my medicine before leaving to do the same.

I drank down the concoction, barely registering its foul taste.

The blood moved sluggishly through my system, but at last superficial wounds knitted together. The flesh itched. Thin scabs covered shallow wounds. One wrong move and they'd bleed again. My chest and collarbone grew warm, taking the lion's share of blood. Distantly, I wondered what my chest would look like when this was done.

I was far from healed, far from fighting condition. I would need much more than this before we went after Teddy. Unfortunately, the medicine worked no better than a bandage. I wasn't sure it would ever be enough.

Duskmere finished bleeding on his stone, or whatever he did to bind to the location, about the same time the medicine in my system ran its course. He returned and stood next to me while we waited for my father to finish.

"My sisters and Lo?" I asked.

"Still unconscious. Your mother bid I inform you they appear stable. She is certain Y'sindra will wake soon, but it is unclear when or if Maerwen and Lonwie will recover."

When. If.

I pressed a hand to the bitter lump in my abdomen and focused on the word stable. "Thank you."

Duskmere nodded his acknowledgment.

Together, we watched my father work on his device. He'd blamed me for "wasting" the first device and its unspent shards he'd used to bind to Shadwe. I'd pointed out if we got the sun stones, he'd never have to ration shards again.

That was the end of that argument. I loved being right.

"It will take time to gather a fighting force," Duskmere said at last.

I'd worried about this. I braced myself for the answer and asked, "How long?"

"At least two days."

"You have one." I drilled a look into the side of his skull. Duskmere continued to watch my father, but his shoulder twitched toward his cheek, like he could feel the intensity of my glare.

"As you know, most of the Royal Fae Guard are sun fae. We must comb our ranks for—"

"One day," I repeated. "And we aren't talking a full twenty-four hours here. When I finish at the penthouse, we leave."

Duskmere swiveled in my direction, a thunderstorm brewing on his brow. "It is not enough time."

"Look, get Odo and his crew from Outerlands. Kick that loser Cirron to the curb since he's a sun fae, or don't because he sucks and who cares if he gets sick? You'll have almost a dozen right there. I have confidence you can gather another dozen capable RFG, or army, or whatever class of fighting fae groups you have milling around Ta'Vale."

"That should be possible," Duskmere capitulated, surprising the hell out of me.

"Good," I said and scratched the itchy new skin at my collar. Fresh blood sprang free. Fan-fucking-tastic.

"Please stop injuring yourself. Your mother also sent this." He slid a canvas bag from his shoulder, removed a smaller satchel from inside, and shoved it into my hand.

"Why couldn't you just give me both when you got here?" I withdrew a container from the bag. A ceramic jar, its lid sealed with wax. This wasn't a typical thermos. Mysterious stuff.

"Your mother asked I ensure you drink your regular medicine first. She bids you wait until it has fully infused your system before you drink the second," Duskmere said. "You must be seated and drink slowly."

Way too many things to remember. I shook the smaller thermos. Shrugging, I hooked a talon beneath the edge of the seal.

"Don't," Duskmere said.

"Why?" I tore through the seal and discarded it in the grass. Wax was biodegradable, right? "I've been drinking this for years. I don't need to sit down."

"Because those were your mother's instructions." Duskmere watched me pop the lid from the jar and take a whiff.

The smell that erupted from the thermos-jar was the same twisted scent of awful and awesome, but thousandfold

"Holy Hot Tamales! What is this?" I held the container at arm's length and, after two false starts, awkwardly screwed the cap in place without taking a single sip and slipped it back into the satchel.

"Aventheo's—"

"Teddy's." The correction fell automatically from my lips.

"Teddy's heart's blood."

I gaped. "His what now?"

"Heart's blood."

"What?"

Duskmere's jaw flexed. "Blood drawn directly from the heart."

"You're telling me my mom stuck a needle into Teddy's heart?"

"You must ask your mother for details," he said, exasperation apparent. "I only know what she told me."

"Right. Well, this is…" I held up the bag containing the ceramic container and gave it the stink eye. "Special."

"It is. The heart pumps magic into the blood where it resides. It is the source and, therefore, the most potent. Second only to mating bond blood."

Duskmere's gaze drifted from my face to my feet. "Which, based on your continued lack of recovery, you have yet to experience."

"Judge much?" I sneered and then glanced at my father, still muttering over his devices. "Listen, I've got places to go, and you've got troops to wrangle. Do you have the disks?"

"This is to your Earth home." He placed a device that would take me to my penthouse in my palm and handed over two more. "These will lead to Eodrom."

Tucking the Eodrom disks into thigh pockets, I saluted him with the third and then set it on the ground. "Expect me at my parents' around sunset."

I activated the portal and stepped through to my Vegas balcony. Without collecting the spent device, I pulled my phone from its usual inner chest pocket. I flipped it over once, twice, relieved it had miraculously avoided breaking.

There were two numbers under the contact list I pulled up: Vaughn and Grandpa.

Both options gave me heartburn. I pressed Blackthorne's name.

"Pick up." My foot tapped an anxious beat. After seven rings with no answer and no voice mail—not that I had time for voice mail—I hung up and dialed option number two.

"Yes?" His clipped, cultured voice came at me before the first ring finished.

"I need you to get hold of Blackthorne."

A deep sigh filtered through the earpiece. "Mr. Black left instructions. Should you wish to speak with him, you may travel to his hotel in Treasure Island, Florida."

Did I hear him right? Surely not. "This is a fucking emergency. Call him."

"Lane, I have worked many years for Mr. Black. If he says this is the only way he will speak with you, then it is your only option."

This couldn't be happening. I pulled the phone away from my ear and stared in disbelief. I'd finally squashed my ego and tried to contact Blackthorne for the training he'd promised, and he wouldn't take my call?

I pressed the phone to my ear. "Is this a joke? I'm supposed to catch a plane to Florida when there are lives on the line?"

"He did not say fly, only that you visit him at his hotel."

My arm arched back to throw the phone, but I stopped myself, screamed, hung up on Vaughn and dialed Blackthorne again. This was some bullshit.

I jogged directly for the spiral stairs leading to the garden.

Setting a foot on the bottom step, I gave the area a quick scan and every muscle in my body clenched. My eye twitched. The sliding glass doors were open.

"Son of an ogre fart." I squeezed the handrail.

Since I knew it wasn't my sisters or Lo, that left two choices for the B&E culprit. Blackthorne or the guy working for Blackthorne.

Growling, I hit Vaughn's name on the screen.

"Yes?" he asked again.

"Were you up here today?"

"No. I—"

I hung up, dialing Blackthorne again as I mounted the spiral stairs to the garden. The satchel containing Teddy's heart's blood—*his heart's blood*—bounced against my hip. Very aware how valuable and precious the contents were, I put a hand on the leather pouch to stabilize it.

It took only moments more to cross the garden and plant myself directly in front of the camera. "Pick up, *Grandpa*," I yelled at the blank, glassy eye.

Of course he didn't.

Fuck it. I didn't need whatever mystical mumbo jumbo he planned to spew. Duskmere was bringing troops. Though the effects of my medicine had notably diminished, I could still get the pointy end of my dagger where it belonged.

I pulled out my communication crystal, brushed a thumb across the surface, and spoke Duskmere's name.

"Yes?" he answered almost immediately, his face the picture of impatience when it rose over my palm.

I wrinkled my nose. "You related to a vampire named Vaughn?"

"What?"

"Never mind. How long before you're ready?"

"You only just left," he said. "We will need several more hours to pull together enough fae capable of traveling into Shadwe."

"Ugh, fine." I closed my fist over the crystal, hanging up. If I didn't do something, I'd go out of my mind.

I squinted at the broken pillar of the druid circle and blew out a breath. A few druid lessons wouldn't kill me.

Fixing what felt like a reasonably potent glare on the camera, I punched the phone's screen without looking.

Vaughn's irate voice answered immediately. "Yes?"

Seriously? I had a fifty-fifty shot of pulling that off.

"Wrong number." I hung up and dialed Blackthorne.

Leaving the phone on speaker, I let it ring and stared at the object of my ultimate frustration. I could make that druid circle work. I *would* make it work. If Blackthorne came and went at will with a broken stone, I could too. Hadn't I ripped open a door in the universe and bound two realms? This should be nothing by comparison.

I hadn't been paying attention, so it surprised me when the ringing cut off abruptly and a voice said, "Leave it," followed by a beep.

"That's that then." I slid the phone back into its pocket.

I sent a final black look at the camera, because even if Blackthorne wasn't watching, Vaughn was. I spun on my heel and marched to the heart of the circle. Turning slowly, I took my time studying each pillar around the perimeter. They ran from knee high to nearly ten feet. Each pillar had at least one rune carved into the rough gray stone. Inside the deepest carvings, glittery bits of crystal sediment flashed.

I'd only managed circle hopping twice before, accidents both. My sisters swore it happened when I said the word "Go." Blackthorne implied it was my intent behind the word, not the word itself, that flung us from west coast to east.

Fine, I'd try. I closed my eyes and rolled my head side to side, bouncing on my toes. This was it. I licked my lips and projected the word. "Go!"

I stilled, waiting for the world to spin away.

Opening one eye, I squinted at my surroundings—the familiar penthouse roof. I hadn't traveled an inch.

Defeat pressed down on me. I'd been irrationally confident that would work. Blackthorne's first crash course had been something like "trust your instincts and will it to happen." Sure, it worked once, but since then, my blood fae abilities had taken a nosedive. Silly of me to expect druid powers I hadn't known I possessed until a few months ago to function.

Eyes down, I paced along the inner perimeter of the circle. I stopped when I reached the pillar's broken capstone nestled in the grass. I nudged it with my toe. That shouldn't be here. I'd thrown it into the bushes after my last colossal failure trying to repair the pillar.

Anger flickered inside me. Finding further evidence Blackthorne had recently passed through the circle stoked the flames.

No matter what lie I fed myself, I knew I needed any advantage at my disposal to have a shot at bringing Teddy home.

Choking on my pride, I swung toward the camera. "You win, Blackthorne. I want your help. I...." My stomach revolted. This sucked. "I need your help."

Still nothing.

I bit my lip and looked at my phone. *Ring, damn you, ring.*

"Come on, isn't that what you wanted to hear? I need you."

No call, no text came. The capstone didn't leap onto the pillar.

With no idea what to do, I sat down. The satchel tied to my belt rested awkwardly in the grass. Its weight tugged my belt. I withdrew the jar and held it in front of me, as if I might see through the thick ceramic to Teddy's heart's blood.

Blood from his heart.

His heart.

My own hearts seemed to skitter into the crevices and shadows of my rib cage at the thought. The idea Teddy allowed my mom to insert a needle into the most vulnerable and vital organ would have brought me to my knees if I wasn't already on my butt.

Well, Mom said I should sit to drink this. *Bottom's up, I guess?*

Hands shaking, I carefully unscrewed the cap, steeling myself for the noxious scent I knew was about to punch me in the face. It wasn't the blood component that stank—Teddy's blood was the ultimate scratch-and-sniff for my senses. It was the concoction of preservatives and enchanted herbs my mother stirred into the mixture.

I tossed back the contents of the entire thermos in four long swallows.

The universe took a breath. It expanded to infinity and constricted to a single molecule.

Fireworks burst across my vision. Cold fire blazed a trail through my veins, over my nerves. My muscles pinched and went liquid all at once. The dichotomy of sensations tore me apart, pieced me together.

Pain, pleasure, strength, all flooded me. Oh, the astonishing power knitting my flesh, warming my joints. My spine arched, and I threw my head back, panting at the sky.

It was orgasmic. I might have, in fact, orgasmed.

I was an idiot.

This was what I'd been denying myself. Holy cheesy nachos with extra cheese. It felt like sparks bled from my pores.

Somehow, I was on my feet. I didn't remember standing, but here I was. I reached over my shoulder and drew my sword. How well would I heal while hopped up on this turbo-charged blood?

"Let's find out," I said to absolutely no one and swiped my thumb along the cutting edge of the blade. The edges of my skin came together before the bite of pain flared and faded.

I laughed, only slightly hysterical. This was amazing. I hadn't felt this... I searched for the word and then landed on it—*whole*. I hadn't felt this whole in a very long time.

Yet I wasn't, was I? Teddy was still out there and needed saving, whether he liked it or not. He wouldn't like it, wouldn't want me to put myself in danger for him. Too bad.

"Go," I said again. But I didn't. Since I hadn't really expected that to work, the lack of transportation didn't hit me too hard.

Still riding my heart's blood high, I wrapped my hand around the blade and pulled. The sharp edge cleaved deeper into my palm, and I hissed at the burn. No instantaneous healing this time.

Would direct contact with Teddy's blood speed the healing? Time to find out. I swiped my sliced palm around the inside of the thermos through the thick layer of heart's blood medicine.

I kept my focus on the injury while I meandered around the circle, ending where I started, next to the broken stone.

The deeper cut slowly knit together, but barely. Contact with the medicine hadn't made a difference. Frustration, a simmering, soupy thing, filled the emptiness of my stomach. I slapped my hand against the broken pillar. The cut reopened. An angry spike of pain stabbed my palm and burned up my arm. I dragged my hand down the stone, leaving a long red streak.

I turned to face the camera tucked in the trees. Raising the sword, I pointed it at the lens. "I swear, Blackthorne, when I fix this circle, I'm coming over there—"

33

TECHNICALLY, THIS WAS TRAINING

THE WORLD TILTED.

In the span of a breath, I wobbled like a flagpole in the wind, not on a Las Vegas rooftop, but on a beach across the country. A thick carpet of sand hugged my boots, toasting my feet through the thick leather. The sticky, damp air clung to my skin. This state seemed to operate on one season, one climate—hot and humid.

I'd made it. And I wasn't on my knees, tossing my cookies—or Teddy's blood. The first time I'd made this journey, I'd thought it might be the end of me. I'd used my hidden druid power since then, ripped open a hole in the universe, and bound two realms. No biggie.

Instinctively, I knew the speed with which I was adjusting to this new power was also what was changing me from the blood fae hybrid I'd always known. Even with Teddy's heart's blood pounding through me, healing me, pushing power into every cell, I didn't have the same strength. I was weaker, less than, yet more.

Realizing I still stood inside the perimeter of the circle, I hurried out before I accidentally thought myself back to the bright and bawdy lights of Las Vegas.

Miles of water licked at the white shoreline where I'd landed. The Gulf of Mexico, according to Google Maps. I'd done my due diligence after our last trip here—or Mae had done hers and I'd watched over her shoulder. Tourists sprawled on colorful beach towels dotted the shore. More humans swam in the water.

A natural salt-based sauna. I'd prefer to do the same. But I had a stubborn male with one hell of an ass to rescue.

I turned to put the froth-tipped waves at my back and faced the small powder-blue hotel. The plans I'd found in Blackthorne's office at the penthouse called this a motel, but somewhere in its development, it grew to at least ten floors.

My brows winged toward the sky when I spotted guests gathered on the large back patio. There weren't many, but more than one was more than just Blackthorne. When I'd last seen him, he implied he had intentions to renovate before opening to the public.

Whoever they were, his guests would take those margaritas to go. Great-Gramps and I needed privacy.

As I made my way up the wood plank walkway laid almost flush with the sand, I narrowed my eyes on one person in particular. A blue Hawaiian shirt with bright-yellow flowers had replaced his sanctuary shirt. A clean cowboy hat sat next to his elbow on the bar. Otherwise, same tanned complexion, same sun-streaked brown hair, and same deep-green eyes.

My attention shifted to the smiling blonde at his side. She sucked her drink through a long, curly straw and then laughed so hard she had to cover her mouth with her hand.

Fate was playing jokester today, because that was the sun fae whose rooms Duskmere took me to investigate. With a smile to rival the great star that lent her kind power, she gripped Jason Olson's chin and pulled his face closer. In a disgusting display of cute, she rubbed her nose with his and laid a sloppy smacker on him before returning to her drink.

"The fiancée," I muttered. She was the female I'd spotted in the hall at Olson's place who ran, but how did she end up there in the first place?

A moon fae, Teddy's wayward bartender, Dexter, pushed through the back door. I managed not to stumble at the hot splash of shock. My eyes pulled wide and then narrowed. Unexpected guests, my ass. This kept getting weirder and weirder.

Seeing these three vacationing with Blackthorne couldn't be a coincidence. Considering the frequency Dexter had recently called into work, it was a safe bet to assume he was the mule moving the Eodrom runaways.

Pieces of the missing sun fae jigsaw inched closer together. My sugar snookums—nope—sugar buns would not be happy about this.

Dexter crossed the deck with an exuberant shout, waving a pitcher of what, based on the ringtone to the phone Blackthorne left on the penthouse roof, I assumed were frozen margaritas.

Popping up from behind the bar, Blackthorne set out four cups.

Beneath my boots, fine grains of sand grated and hissed against the driftwood planks of the walkway as I lengthened my strides.

"Granddaughter!" Blackthorne's voice boomed. He had to shout to be heard above the frolicking tourists and surf behind me and soft beachy music coming from speakers somewhere in front of me.

A nerve at the base of my neck tweaked, and my shoulders tensed. His voice really brought out the worst in me, and based on my violent history, that said something. My palms itched to feel the cold steel of my beloved torpedoes. I flexed my hands, splaying my fingers wide to shake the desire.

"You're just in time," Blackthorne called and once again ducked behind the counter, coming up with a large cup, the hard plastic kind, with a beachy, pastel design.

I jogged up the stairs to the deck, bellied up to the bar, and stood on my toes to scope out the inventory.

My sisters and I had once hidden behind this bar, but the place had been vacant. Used only as a front for an interdimensional portal, the one Blackthorne claimed to have closed.

The shelves behind the bar had been empty then. Now ice filled the drink well, beer and soda nestled in the ice, and a decent assortment of liquor bottles lined at least one shelf. Not the cheap stuff, either.

As if those wouldn't be stolen as soon as the lights went out. Not my problem. Plus, Blackthorne was super rich. He could afford it if a bottle or ten walked away.

Built for a party—a really big party—the bar was one large square with an open corner diagonal from me, near the front wall of the hotel.

I slid onto a stool at the counter, opposite Jason and his sun fae fiancée. The wall behind the pair was floor to ceiling glass. In the reflection, I watched the female's hand twist in Jason's shirt.

Smiling with a little more fang than necessary, I waggled my fingers at Jason and his missus. At that moment, if the sun fae could self-combust, she would have immolated.

It would probably be nice if I put her at ease, but I never claimed to be nice. "Boo!"

She jerked and pulled Jason's shirt so tight it creased his throat. The top button fought the good fight to hold on, but it wouldn't last if she didn't let go soon. His eyes bulged, and he coughed.

"Relax. I'm not here for you." I laughed and dragged a bowl of nuts in front of me. Why did every bar have nuts? I eyed the contents. Were those macadamias? *Fancy nuts, score!* "I don't care that you split from the sun fae. Those guys don't like me, which means I might like you."

Probably not. I could count on one hand, maybe two, the number of people, fae, and otherwise I liked. Besides, I knew where to find her if Duskmere was paying.

"You don't care she planned to join those corrupted rascals you're after?" Blackthorne attempted to stir the pot.

I gave him a baleful stare and popped a macadamia in my mouth. His statement confirmed at least some of the missing sun fae had joined the corrupted. Past connections to the corrupted further solidified my suspicion he'd played a role.

Blackthorne slid a Big Gulp-sized frozen margarita in front of me. A whiff of coconut hit my nose. Correction, piña colada. I stirred the slushy goodness. A sip wouldn't kill me.

"Everyone makes mistakes." I was more interested in the how and why of it all. Blackthorne might be an outside facilitator, but someone had to be recruiting from inside Eodrom. It wasn't Cirron. He said he only had a hand in releasing prisoners. I didn't want to believe him, but it made sense. If he'd been caught recruiting, they lost their access to prisoners.

Pondering the issue, I sucked piña colada through the crazy straw until brain freeze hit.

"Argh!" I sat back and clutched my skull.

"It's good?" Dexter asked.

Momentarily unable to form a coherent sentence, I gave him a thumbs-up.

Dexter laughed. "There's more where that came from."

The guy sounded way too jovial, not at all prepared for the deep shit he'd waded into. It was possible he didn't realize I knew he'd fibbed to his boss.

"I didn't know by unexpected guests, you meant unexpected at my super great-grandpop's hotel in Florida." I grinned and waggled a talon at Blackthorne. "By super great, I mean Blackthorne here is really old."

Dexter's grip on the almost-empty pitcher tightened. A pale but pure white light emitted from his palm. The slush coating the inside evaporated. *Interesting.* According to my father, few moon fae had more than a few drops of power. Just enough to sustain Eodrom's fae lighting, which their moon magic powered. He'd lose his mind if he knew what I'd just witnessed.

"Lighten up, all of you." I latched onto the straw a second time, but I paced myself. Due to lack of napkins, I dragged the back of my hand across my mouth and spotted a few flecks of bloody colada.

"You guys can get back to your day drinking." I waved a hand and gave Blackthorne a meaningful look. "I'm here to talk to him."

"Relax, enjoy the sun and sea." Blackthorne leaned over the counter to get a gander at my filthy self. "You could use a dip."

I scowled and smoothed a hand over my hair. With the level of crunch I felt beneath my palm, I'd need an entire bottle of shampoo.

"We need to talk." I slipped off the stool and nodded toward the hotel's rear door. "Inside."

"Why not here?" Blackthorne threw his arms wide. "Nice day, nice breeze. Let's not waste it."

I rolled my lips together, looking at Dexter, Jason, and the sun fae refugee glued to his side.

"That offer you made for training. I'm here for a crash course, and we don't need an audience."

Blackthorne laughed. "Where's your luggage?"

Confused, I frowned. "My what?"

"Luggage. Did you fly here?"

"Of course not."

"Of course not, because...?" He let the question dangle in the salty air.

I'd never taken him for a simpleton. "You know how I got here."

"How?" he pressed.

"Listen, you fairy fart." A true insult. I lived with a fairy, and her berry butt burps rivaled anything an ogre could produce. "I came through your stupid circle."

Unperturbed, or unaware of the depth of my insult, he nodded. "Then you got the training you needed. You're welcome."

I threw my cup at Blackthorne's head. He ducked. The oversize cup hit the glass wall, leaving an ugly piña colada spatter before hitting the ground on the other side of the bar. Jason casually slid from his seat, retrieved the cup, and set it on the counter.

It had cracked from top to bottom. Whatever slush hadn't splattered on the wall oozed from the crack onto the counter.

"Was that necessary?" Blackthorne tsked.

I pulled a push dagger from my chest harness and pointed it at Gramps. "Is this necessary?"

The other bar occupants dropped from their seats. Blackthorne threw up a hand.

"Let's not do this." His tone was an obvious threat, even if his words weren't. He scoured me with a hard look. "In the shape you're in, it wouldn't even be fun to put you in your place."

My dagger-wielding arm fell to my side, and I gaped. No one spoke to me like that. No one. I told him as much.

He chuckled. "There probably aren't many who should. Now, I distinctly recall triggering the break spell after I brought my fine friends here for a visit. Tell me how you got through the circle."

I dropped onto the stool and returned the push dagger to the harness. Sighing, I set my elbows on the bar top and slumped onto my fists. "I don't know."

"You don't know?"

"Let's not do this." I parroted his earlier threat.

"I know what you did." He pointed beneath the counter where my elbows rested.

Because curiosity was my weakness—along with cheesy poofs, Ho Hos, and all the trashy reality TV—I dropped off my stool and walked around until I could see a series of monitors beneath the counter. All but one were different views around this hotel.

I stared at the oddball monitor featuring the stone circle on the other side of the country.

Jason squinted at the screen. "I didn't see what happened."

"You're drunk," Blackthorne replied.

"Right," Jason agreed and got to work getting drunker.

Blackthorne's attention never wavered from my face. "Now, tell me exactly what you think you did to get here."

Frustration went to war with desperation. I laced my fingers behind my neck and tilted my face toward the bright-blue sky. Eyes closed, I breathed deep and slow, trying to remember.

Finally, I shook my head. "Nothing. I did nothing but threaten you through the camera. Are you messing with me? Do you have some druid circle on-off switch hidden around here?"

"Nope. What did you do before you pointed that blade at the camera?"

"I made a damn fool of myself."

"Doing what?" he pressed.

"What is this? Are you asking for a play-by-play?"

Blackthorne smiled. "Tell me what you did, Lane."

He called me Lane, not Malaney. This guy might be eccentric and evil, but he was all right.

"I don't know. I drank some blood, cut my hand, ranted and raved. Screamed. Threw a few things. Made a pretty red streak on the pillar..." My eyes widened and met Blackthorne's smug gaze.

Teddy's blood. Mate's blood. The same way I reopened the door to Shadwe. My hands trembled, and I clutched them together in my lap.

"Exactly!" Blackthorne smacked a hand on the bar and grinned. "I wove a familial link into the spell that triggers the restoration of the broken pillar. We might be related, but we are vastly different. I was unsure what it would take for you to trigger the spell. I left it as it was, knowing you would one day figure it out."

"And if I didn't?"

"Then I'd buy you a plane ticket." He pulled a beer from the ice and plopped the sweaty bottle on the counter in front of me. "But here you are. Let's celebrate."

"So you really didn't know how this would work? What about that promise to train me?"

Blackthorne popped the top on a beer for himself and tipped the bottle toward me. "Technically, this was training."

Technically, he wasn't wrong, which annoyed me worse than a burr in my panties. I had one of those last year after chasing a mark through a field of waste high grass and weeds. Not an experience I wished to repeat, just like this "lesson."

"Interesting you didn't need the staff," Blackthorne mused.

It was interesting, but right now I didn't have the bandwidth to figure out the mysteries of magic.

I snatched the beer and drank it down in a few deep swallows. Some might say I shouldn't get tipsy before a fight, but I'd argue I did my best work a little drunk. It warmed the muscles, lubricated the joints.

"Ahh." Newly hydrated, I put the empty bottle on the sweaty ring it had left on the counter and blinked at the fading blue sky. "What time is it?"

"Clock right there." Blackthorne gestured to a hideous, seashell-encrusted pastel circle mounted on a pole in the center of the deck behind me.

5:20 p.m. Damn. I'd lost a few hours hopping time zones, but it would still be too early to do more than sit on my hands if I went home. Might as well do my job while I was here.

"All right, talk to me about this. I've got an open case. It involves missing sun fae." I reclaimed my stool and planted my focus directly on one of the missing seated across from me. Seeing where my gaze landed, Jason put his arm around... "What's your name?"

She didn't answer.

"I don't bite."

Blackthorne's brows rose in obvious doubt.

"I don't bite *often*." I made a face. "Listen, all I want is to tie this little mystery in a box and shove it in a certain RFG's face."

A tiny smile bent the corners of her mouth. At last, her stunning indigo gaze met mine.

"Elisette," she whispered. "My name is Elisette."

"I have to assume someone recruited you?"

She nodded.

"Specifically to join the corrupted moon fae?"

Another nod, but then she blurted. "I don't have any loyalty to the corrupted. I have never even met any."

"But you voluntarily left everything behind to join them," I said.

"I have minor magic and no connections. I lost my family to a war they told me I was too weak to join." Her chin lifted ever so slightly, and her voice came with more conviction. "It is a lonely existence, living an invisible life."

Jason pulled her tighter against his side. He rubbed his hand up and down her arm. Her hair swished with the motion of his arm on her back.

Elisette looked at Jason, her expression completely besotted. "I just wanted to belong somewhere."

"You do," he replied with equal adoration.

A foreign feeling spread inside me: happiness—for someone else. If I was into self-reflection, I might recognize I saw a little of myself in Elisette. But I'd pull my fangs out before I ever admitted to a kinship with a sun fae other than my sister.

"Who recruited you?" I asked.

She shook her head.

"Come on, I'm trying to play nice here." I fingered a push dagger hilt I had no intention of using, but she didn't need to know.

Jason scowled at me. Blackthorne rolled his eyes.

I shrugged.

"I would tell you if I could, but I can't," Elisette said quickly. "All contact came through my communication crystal. There was never a fae on the other end, just a black void and a voice. Never the same voice."

I scratched my cheek and watched her, more than a little surprised. By all indications, she was telling the truth. "A black void?"

"Yes. As if they were in a dark room or perhaps put something over their crystal."

"Unlikely. They'd need to see you to be certain they were contacting the correct fae. What happened on the first contact?"

"The only fae who reached me through the crystal were those I worked for at the stables. The call came in very late, so I knew it wasn't them. I was...excited. I rushed to answer. That's when it started. They talked to me about how I was unappreciated, and they knew a place where that would change."

She laughed and ducked her head. It wasn't a funny ha-ha sort of laugh. More sad, and damn it, my insides pinched in sympathy.

"I'm so embarrassed." Her quiet words barely carried above the ambient noise.

"You shouldn't be. Whoever this is, or they are, knew who to target." I slid my gaze to the man attached to her hip, then Dexter, and finally Blackthorne. "Anyone else have information they want to share?"

Blackthorne held up his hands. "I had nothing to do with any of this."

"Bullshit."

"I only recently met Angus," Dexter supplied.

Angus—not Andrew or Mr. Black.

"Yet here you magically are. On a first name basis." I drummed my talons on the bar.

"Jason introduced us," Dexter said. "And it's true. A banshee recruited me."

My fingers stilled. It couldn't be. "Was her name Etta'wy?"

His eyes widened slightly. "You know her."

"I did."

His mouth twitched to the side, and he nodded. "I wondered what happened to her. She left packages with me to hand over to the sun fae who showed up and spoke a key phrase. Like a password."

"In umbra luna est," Elisette said, drawing my attention. "The phrase."

"The shadow of the moon," Jason said.

"Or the moon is in shadow." Blackthorne smiled in a not-so-humble sort of way. "My Latin is rusty. You may be more current, Jason."

"Moon. Shadows. Sounds like evil shenanigans to me." I rolled my eyes and motioned for Dexter to continue. "What else?"

"My instructions were simple. Hand over the package, drive the sun fae into the desert, and leave them."

I blinked. "Wow, I'm cold, and even I would think twice before leaving someone in the middle of the Mojave."

Embarrassed or guilty, he shrugged but wouldn't quite meet my eyes. "I needed the money, and Etta'wy gave me a song and dance about these fae needing a fresh start and a means of escape. She swore no harm would come to anyone."

"You were okay working for the corrupted moon fae?" I gave an aggressive wave of my hand in his direction. "Since you clearly aren't one of them."

"I didn't know who I was helping. Etta'wy is—was—a banshee."

And a raging bitch, I thought, but didn't add. No reason to malign the dead if I wasn't the one who killed them.

"You never saw a single corrupted moon fae."

"No way, man. I haven't seen a moon fae in years, let alone a corrupted."

"Why should I believe you?" I dug a talon into the bar and made a nice long scratch. The annoying thing was I believed him.

"Listen, I was just like these sun fae—alone. My family were corrupted. If they didn't die in the war, they were banished, and good riddance. I was young, but old enough to remember they did a lot of nasty deeds." Dexter dragged a hand through his dark, shaggy hair. His dove-gray complexion shone, as if there were strands of silver in his skin. An unusual trait. It was probably just suntan lotion. "I was restless in Eodrom and dead broke in Interlands. So, yeah, when Etta'wy offered me not only an unbelievable amount of money but also a place to live in my name, I took it."

"Long story short," Jason butted in.

I snorted. "Not that short." Reminded I was still here, and Teddy was still missing, I twisted to check the clock and groaned. Less than five minutes had passed.

"Right, well, I was on my way to Interlands to deliver..." Jason's eyes went shifty. "Something."

The mutant mounts. The etching on his sanctuary doors. His breeding program. "Aloughta."

Jason's mouth opened and closed. "How'd you know?"

"I kill on trivia night. Figuratively, not literally," I clarified, since they got really antsy all the sudden—except for Blackthorne. The need to be on my way, to get to Teddy, turned things fuzzy in my head. Moving this conversation along, I prompted, "You were on your way to Interlands?"

"Yes, that's when I came across a dehydrated, sunburned, lost Elisette wandering along the road." Jason smiled at Elisette, who beamed in response. "She showed me a package containing a portal stone she'd been instructed to use. No one answered."

"They wouldn't." My smile was feral. "I'm certain you were supposed to contact Nyle Rathmore, and he's dead."

"Rathmore?" Dexter paled at the notorious spymaster and assassin's name and took a deep pull on his drink.

A genuine reaction, and damn if I didn't believe his story. He hadn't known how close to that devil he'd been dancing.

"I killed him, but he killed the banshee, not me," I said, since Dexter seemed to like the swamp dweller. "So where were we? Elisette alone in the desert?"

Jason cleared his throat and continued. "After she explained everything, I brought Elisette back to Dexter, but he didn't know what was in the package, let alone why the stone hadn't worked. So I offered to let Elisette stay at my ranch while she figured things out. It turns out she has a way with animals. The rest is—"

"History?" I guessed. A stable master's apprentice, of course she had a way with animals. Probably better than his ex.

"I was going to say fate."

"Don't bring her name into this," I mumbled and glanced at the clock. 5:35 p.m.—time was crawling. I pointed at Dexter. "Let me guess what happened next. When another sun fae showed up, being the chivalrous, money-grubber you are, you waited around to see if their portal stone would work. When it didn't, you brought them to Jason."

Dexter nodded. He was turning into a bobblehead. I pointed at Jason next. "And you called your good buddy Blackthorne for advice?"

"Exactly." Jason's sun-bleached brown brows rose, surprised by my astute deductive reasoning, perhaps. I had my moments.

Finally, I swung my pointy finger at Blackthorne. "And you are not involved."

Gramps grinned and saluted me with his almost-empty beer. "Not until Jason called. However, there are now two sun fae in residence here until they decide if they wish to return to Ta'Vale."

"Or if they want to live on my grounds," Jason said.

I jerked in surprise. "You'd do that?"

"Why not? After what Elisette went through, it's the least I can do for these lost souls." He rubbed her back and smiled. "And the sanctuary can always use extra hands."

Recognizing the end of any useful information, I pushed back from the bar. The stool rocked as I hopped off and paced a few feet away. I glared at the clock I would have sworn had not moved. It didn't matter. If Duskmere wasn't ready, I'd go on my own.

"It's been fun, but I got places to be, black wolves to save."

"Granddaughter, if Shadwe is your destination, you should know you might run into many of these missing sun fae you mentioned."

"Not possible." Dread crawled inside. If what he said was true, I'd just wasted a lot of time Teddy couldn't afford. "The stones aren't in the ground. They will make them sick."

"Hmm," he hummed. It was annoying. "Based on our Elisette, the sun fae will have very little to no magical abilities. The stones will not cause any more than an uncomfortable sensation to one with so little magic."

"Noted." That opened a whole new door to shit I would have to deal with, but it closed the door on any chance I'd let the RFG accompany me. The potential of letting them face down their own people in a tense situation had catastrophic potential.

Frustration rippled through me at all the time I'd wasted on frozen drinks and solving an unimportant case. I jerked a disk from a thigh pocket and dropped it on the ground. The device rattled on the concrete deck. My father would be unhappy I used his device in front of witnesses. I also didn't care.

I took a knee, hunching over the disk in a half-hearted attempt to hide the pattern I traced over its surface. An oval opened to my parent's front yard. An audience including Torneh, Iola, my parents, plus a whole lot of weaponed-up RFG stood there.

They looked not at me, but at the wanted criminal serving beers and piña coladas behind me.

Well, shit.

34

RADIO SILENCE

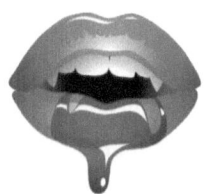

DOING MY BEST INTERPRETATION OF "GIRL ON FIRE," I RUSHED THROUGH the portal, flapping my arms and forcing the sea of fae to part. The last thing I needed was these yahoos losing their minds if they ran into a bunch of sun fae. "False alarm. You can all go home. I don't need you."

I pushed through the crowd and hurried to yank the other half of the disk through before spells flew. It bounced into my parent's front yard, and the proverbial door slammed in the gawker's faces.

The disk I tossed landed at my father's feet. "You finish the new portal device? I'll be needing a lift to Shadwe."

Based on the incredulous expressions of everyone momentarily frozen in place, including my father, who had yet to retrieve the spent device, they were either astounded I planned to go alone, or—

"Was that Angus Blackthorne?" someone in the back asked.

Or that. I glared in the voice's direction. "Yes. About the disk? Is it ready? I'll take one now to get back to the site, and I'll take a few more for here." I started popping fasteners of various small pockets to stow the devices. "Duskmere, I'll let you know when I've handled business, and you can retrieve the stones."

A shadow fell over me, and I straightened, expecting to find my father with the items I asked for. I squinted at Odo. Silly me. When did I ever get what I wanted? "Unless you're about to hand me a candy bar or wish me luck, you might as well just walk away."

"You should not go alone."

"Oh good, I thought you were going to pester me about what you saw." I hooked a thumb toward the empty air where the portal had been.

"You will undoubtedly answer for that, but right now I must stress you do not go alone."

"Thanks for caring, but I know what I'm doing." I was winging it, but I was doing it with confidence. "If you don't hear from me in a few hours, you know where I went."

"I say this in concern for the mission."

"In other words, not for my well-being. Got it." I was more comfortable with that. My distrust for fae outside my family ran too deep, and this nonhostile thing between Odo and me wasn't right.

My father came over and handed Odo the disks, who took them but didn't give them to me. His brow dropped low, doing weird things to his scar. He looked me over. "If you do not come back, this will most likely mean you are dead."

"Probably." I lifted a shoulder. "Listen, I promise I'll come back to haunt you and you can say you told me so. Deal?"

I found it interesting Odo argued while Duskmere hung back. Further proof of the RFG hierarchy.

Odo came at me with the hard stare. I gave him my blankest look in return. At last, he shook his head and slapped the disks into my waiting hands.

"I see the medicine worked, Lane." Mom elbowed Odo out of the way. "The effects won't last forever, so don't dawdle. I also don't have anymore, so please try not to almost die again."

"I never try to die, Mom." I gave her an awkward, one-arm hug, but she squeezed me to her ample bosom—the one I didn't inherit—so tight my lungs fought to expand. Wriggling from her freakishly powerful grip, I folded my lips together, fighting the questions I was afraid to ask.

"We still don't know." Mom patted my cheek. "They are all breathing, and with breath, there is hope."

"Hope, right. You're right." I swallowed and bent my head as I shuffled through the devices. "Which one is Shadwe?"

"In your right hand," my father said.

They were all in my right hand. "Which one?"

"The one with the most shards. An experimental attempt to hold the door open longer."

It surprised me he wasn't putting up more of a fight. I was about to waste his experiment.

My gaze briefly met Iola's sunset eyes—an orange-and-pink ring surrounding her pupils rippled along the interior of her bright-blue irises. Her expression remained neutral, but she returned my nod. Torneh simply raised an imperious golden brow. Relatively certain no one was about to smite me, I slipped the two extra devices into pockets and secured the closures.

I used my free hand to go about my prebattle ritual of patting down my person. Each weapon was in its place and every pocket was secure. My braid was tight and disappeared beneath my jacket.

Satisfied, I placed the disk on the ground. "Hopefully, this won't take long. Be ready to come collect those sun stones when I call."

Right ear to right shoulder. Left ear to left shoulder. Breathe. I ignored the uncharacteristic flutter of nerves. The stakes were high, but I could do this. I knelt and traced the rune on its surface. Nothing happened.

Did I fat thumb it? I frowned and drew the rune again. Nothing.

"The batteries are dead in this thing," I complained and tried again.

Slippered feet I recognized as my father's appeared on the other side of the portal device. "There are no batteries, Malaney."

"Figure of speech."

"This device uses a different rune."

Irritation crawled under my skin, and I surged to my feet. "Seriously? Of all the times to decide you need a new password."

He sniffed. "Considering the sensitivity of the destination, yes, a new rune was required."

I rolled my eyes and waved a hand at the disk. "Well, have at it."

Fortunately, he didn't argue, but knelt and traced a design at lightning speed, ensuring no one would catch the pattern.

An oval into Shadwe yawned. Before committing myself to the crossing, I looked through the portal as far right and left as I could manage. Squinting, I peered into the trees directly ahead. The field was still empty except for the corpses left behind. No one had been by to clean those up. No animals had scavenged.

Odo strode past me, right through the portal.

"Are you kidding me? What did I just say?" I shouted.

Minus Cirron, the fae who'd accompanied Odo in Outerlands followed. Duskmere crossed through next. Four more fae I didn't recognize filed through.

Pru stopped next to me. "Your father only had time to make one device. You should hurry."

I gaped. She shrugged and crossed through.

Torn between anger and gratitude, I stomped my foot and threw a tantrum instead.

The fae Duskmere had gathered finished filing through.

"Malaney?" my father urged.

"I'm going," I snapped and strode across the threshold, muttering expletives that would make Y'sindra proud the entire way.

"Hold the door!" an impossibly familiar voice said.

As if summoned by my thoughts, Y'sindra tottered through the portal.

"You should be in bed!" Mom shouted.

Y'sindra took up the device recovery chain with one hand, waved merrily with her other, and then tugged the disk to her, closing the portal.

"You're in big trouble." I told her. Her curls were frizzy, clothes tattered, and the rosy tint was missing from her cheeks, leaving her complexion dull.

"I know." She grinned up at me. "We need to make it worth it. Let's go take a few heads, freeze a few nards."

"This is serious stuff. There's no way you're recovered enough. You look terrible."

She grew deadly serious, a rare state of being for my sister. "Lane, they don't know if Lo will make it. I need to make someone pay."

Lo...

Her words were a cannonball to my midsection. I understood her need to hurt someone, knew the feeling intimately. Hooking my thumb talons at my waist, I watched the fae gather into a loose formation.

I sighed. "You win. How are your freezing skills? You burned a lot of magic earlier."

Y'sindra visibly relaxed. "I'll be fine. They gave me the good stuff."

"Come on," I said to Y'sindra, and started toward the peeks of the Barbout estate, barely visible above the distant trees. "What exactly is 'the good stuff'?"

"Odin's eye knows, but I woke up with a taste worse than rotten egg in my mouth, a needle in each arm, and feeling like I'd been pounding energy drinks for days." She hurried to keep pace, her shorn wing bobbing above her shoulder.

As usual, guilt pinched at the sight, and I shortened my steps. "Cool, but are you sure you should be here? I can't carry you with all these weapons."

Without the wrap on her wing, it looked longer, and a few feathers had replaced the furry down. Maybe it was actually growing back. Or maybe "the good stuff" was the liquid form of whatever Mom had been slathering on her stub.

"I'm fine," she said and hooked a thumb over her shoulder, gesturing behind us. "And if I'm not, that's what those pack mules are for."

I glanced over my shoulder and pictured Duskmere giving my sister a piggyback ride. "I'd like to see that."

"Now that you mention it, I should conserve my energy." She gave me a wink, turned away, but stopped. "You still have that tracking crystal?"

"The what?"

Y'sindra rolled her eyes. "That crystal Duskmere told you not to lose. You lose it?"

"No." I dug it out of a pocket and handed it over. "Why?"

"You know how I like to wander off." She grinned and shoved the crystal in a pouch at her waist. Toddling toward the fae, she called, "Duskmere, my man."

Left feeling confused and amused, as always, I headed for the trees. A small part of me, like a microscopic-sized part of me, was grateful for backup. Mostly, I worried about the potential catastrophic fuck up if the RFG who'd joined me saw a sun fae face.

Miles passed before Odo decided I needed company and caught up to me. I looked up at him and then over my shoulder and laughed. An aggrieved Duskmere carried my sister on his back. She saw me looking and waved with enough exuberance to flap her hand in front of his face.

Chuckling under my breath, I turned my focus back to Odo and put on my serious face. "I prefer the quiet."

He ignored me. "Do you have a plan?"

"Yup." I stared straight ahead and increased my speed to a brisk jog. The faster I moved, the more difficult conversation would be. Unfortunately, he was in way better shape than me, and I had to slow long before he did.

"Damn it, Odo," I complained, or more accurately, wheezed. Digging a hand into my side, I nodded to my destination directly ahead. "You see those roof peaks? We're getting close. I need to stay sharp. Radio silence until we need to speak, okay?"

"Your plan is to simply march in there?"

Maybe he didn't understand the phrase since fae did not have radios, but I thought the silence part was pretty clear. "Basically, yes."

"This is a stupid plan."

"This is a brilliant plan." I beamed at him. "They won't expect it. I'll have the upper hand."

"They have met you. They will expect it."

I shot him one of my infamous death glares, but it had been months since I'd put it into practice. His dubious expression told me the look wasn't packing much juice. "Whatever. I told you I wanted to do this alone. Follow me or don't."

"Unfortunately, I must."

"Fine. Shoo." I flipped my hand at him. He started to drop back, but I said, "Where's Grace?"

He grinned. "Miss my beauty already?"

I snorted. "Hardly, but it seems like those aloughta would have been helpful."

Odo nodded. "They would have, but we do not know the effect the broken stones might have had on them. We were unwilling to take that chance."

"Fair enough."

Contemplative silence rose. Eventually, he dropped back. That had been the perfect opportunity to warn him about the sun fae, but I couldn't bring myself to do it. It was a terrible thing they might be forced to do, and I had all these weird, soft feelings. It was the worst.

I rolled my shoulders, settling back into my personal bubble of space. My gaze continued to roam, digging into every nook and cranny capable of concealing an ambush.

The kicker came at me as the occasional whiff of vanilla and forest. Kicker, as in a kick in my ass to *move*. I looked for Teddy's blood. Sometimes I spotted it, sometimes I didn't, but always I kept moving. Relief lightened my steps, knowing I was at least headed in the right direction.

The forest gradually thinned. It wouldn't be long before it disappeared completely. In the distance, open field rolled out beyond the trees, gold and green beneath the high sun. Beyond the field was a tall stone wall surrounding an even taller stone building. This was Teddy's definition of a house? It was a massive thing, complete with plenty of turrets and towers poking the sky. It resembled a medieval castle straight from a fairy tale.

Electricity tickled my nerve endings. My arms hung loose at my sides, ready for whatever might come. I flexed my hands and wiggled my fingers, palms itching to feel steel.

I emerged from the trees and stepped onto a wide path of flattened grass eventually giving way to packed dirt. That path led between the large, open double doors of a gate set in the stone wall. Relief and anxiety washed over me at the sight. Teddy was here.

Dirt and bits of rock crunched beneath my feet as I followed the path toward a wide turn leading to the gate. If I stayed the course and there was anyone beyond the open door, they would see me in a matter of minutes.

If they planned to keep Teddy alive, if they wanted to force him to shift, they'd have him locked up or locked down somewhere wide open. They would want the privacy of the gated grounds, but they'd be outside where, if they forced Teddy to shift, they could make a quick escape before he freed himself.

I didn't know any of this for certain, but based on everything I did know, I was betting my life, Teddy's life, everyone's life on my deductions. I had better be fucking right.

Sudden pressure built beneath my sternum. What a time to get indigestion—or have a panic attack. I stopped walking, rolled my shoulders back, and gave my rib cage a good stretch. Breathing through my mouth, I faced the ragtag group of fae following me.

Odo and Duskmere—Y'sindra no longer on his back, but at his side—caught up first. I gave them a quick rundown of my assessment.

Squinting at the gate, a ghost of a smile—there and gone—whispered across Odo's mouth. "Your lack of plan was indeed a plan."

I'd told him my plan was to march right in, and I hadn't lied. It sounded crazy, but the one thing I needed to make this work was Teddy. "It was."

Y'sindra shook out the dirty tunic she still wore from earlier. Her winter-blue gaze traveled from the gate back to me. "What do you need us to do?"

"Whatever happens, I need to get to Teddy. Let me go first. The rest of you spread out. Keep Dacian distr—"

A roar rolled from behind the gate. My bones shook with recognition, and any semblance of a plan crumbled to dust in the wind. "Teddy," I breathed.

"Lane." Odo's voice held a warning tone.

My wide eyes snapped to his face. I took a breath and nodded. "Focus on the soldiers, distract Dacian and Hielmal if they are here. Let me find Teddy."

"I understand the black wolf is important to you," Duskmere argued, though he pulled weapons as he spoke. "But we must gain an advantage if we will win this fight,"

"I am the advantage, and I need Teddy. You need me to find Teddy."

"We've got your back," Y'sindra said. Her rising adrenaline pushed a dusting of snow from her fluttering wings.

I did a double take. From both wings. The stump was definitely longer, and those were feathers, not down. It really was healing.

Another roar erupted behind the wall. Shouts followed.

I'd been right. They had him in the yard, but much closer than I'd expected. My better-than-the-average-fae hearing told me he was somewhere to the right.

Anticipation dumped heat into my veins.

"Change of plans. They have Teddy somewhere to the right. Duskmere, you go first. Divert all the attention you can and go left." I jerked my chin toward his troops. "You need to tell them quickly so we can go."

Duskmere turned to leave, but I grabbed his wrist.

"Wait." I let go and looked between him and Odo. "You should know you might also face the missing sun fae."

"But the sun stones..." Duskmere let the obvious question hang there.

"Won't bother them," I said. "I'll explain later, but you need to trust me. This sort of surprise could get your troops killed if they hesitate. Make sure they understand."

Thankfully, the stubborn jackass didn't press the issue. He jogged to the soldiers. Pru stepped from their ranks to meet him as he approached and gave instructions.

I turned to Odo, who also didn't ask for details. "Pick your best soldiers and lead the way straight down the middle until we find Teddy. I'll follow behind."

"This I can do." Odo pulled a gladius from a sheathe on his hip. Short, heavy, good for battle. Not as maneuverable as the daggers I favored, but it could remove a head. Daggers couldn't. The hilt was the weird part. It was wooden. Dude would have a fistful of splinters in no time.

"No magic?" I asked to keep the impatience of waiting for Duskmere and his troops at bay.

Grinning—which was a weird look for Odo—he lifted his left arm. My gaze immediately went to the thin vine wrapped around his forearm I'd mistaken as a part of his jacket. He made a fist. The vine thickened, went slack, and then snapped taut. A large, round, wooden shield grew in a flat, spiral pattern from the vine. A flicker of green flame danced over the shield's surface.

"Neat trick." I eyed the green magic and wood. "Related to any druids?"

"Cool sparkler," Y'sindra said and leaned in closer than I was comfortable with her being to the green flames.

Odo stared at each of us and shook his head. "Excuse me, I must also relay the news about the sun fae."

I watched him go.

"Decent dude," Y'sindra said and threw a couple shadow punches at the gate. Snow trickled from her fists. She bounced on her toes and angled a look up at me. "I'm sticking with you. Don't even try to get one of these RFG pansies to babysit me."

"Wouldn't dream of it." I shrugged. It would do me no good to argue. Freya herself could come down from the Drifta Mountains, and Y'sindra would not be swayed if her mind was set.

Thankfully, Duskmere returned, the extra two dozen or so fae that came with him from Eodrom at his back. Five of Odo's elite troops fell behind him, the rest lined up in front of the others. Together, they made a formidable force.

My fangs tingled with anticipation of the coming fight. Teddy's heart's blood still hummed through my veins. The fine hairs on my neck rose.

"Remember, get as much attention as you can and draw the enemy to the left," I told them, my gaze going from Odo to Duskmere and then to every face angled in my direction. "You aren't taking down a wyvern, and you might not be able to take down Hielmal. Try not to die, and get out of my way when I come for them."

"How will we know when you are ready?" Duskmere asked.

My smile was one hundred percent apex predator. "You'll know."

"All right. On me." Odo took charge. Duskmere and Pru flanked him. The rest of the fae took their place behind.

Odo looked over the group and then to me. He nodded. I returned the gesture.

"Take us to the fight, Captain," Odo told Duskmere, who bared his teeth in a bloodthirsty response.

"Sun scorch our enemy!" Duskmere shouted and led the charge through the gate.

35

DON'T LOOK BACK

By the time Y'sindra and I burst into the courtyard on the heels of our RFG reinforcements, the fight was on. The aroma of sweet-and-spicy shifter blood mixed with the rancid stench of corrupted moon fae blood. A mélange of other scents saturated the air.

Teddy's unique smell eclipsed them all. He was here, and he'd spilled a lot of blood.

Desperation attempted to take the wheel and drive me headlong into my death. Without clarity, without my battle calm, I'd be another body in the field.

I forced myself to take a beat, breathe, and scan what appeared to be two acres of courtyard. Large, flat, gray stones wound through the yard. One path led directly to enormous front doors, doors to a castle.

Several walkways branched away from the main path to meander through shrub-lined scenic strolls. Enormous blooms of various hues dotted the bushes. Equally large thorns threatened anyone who sniffed too close would regret their decision.

Great, it was a literal maze in this joint, and somewhere in there was my prize.

Sections of shrubs rose in a magnificent sculpture like a great green floral wave. I eyed those sections, certain that was where I'd find Teddy. But the options were numerous.

There were at least two times as many soldiers as RFG. While Odo and five of his elite RFG cut their way down the center, Duskmere and his troops did exactly as I asked and lured the bulk of the opposition to the left. Though I'd never say it out loud, not even under the threat of death, I was grateful Odo and Duskmere hadn't listened to me and came through the portal.

"How are we going to play this?" Y'sindra hovered in front of my face.

I took one step back. "What the fuck?"

Above her stump, the frosty illusion of a wing stroked the air in time with her healthy wing. When did she learn how to do that? *How* was she doing that?

"What the actual fuck?" I pointed the dagger I'd palmed at her. "When we get home, you've got some explaining to do."

She grinned and executed an aerial spin, shedding snow as she showed off.

Through the dusting of snow, a strange blur traveling from one hedge to another caught my attention. Whatever it was, it was moving fast away from us and toward Odo's unguarded rear.

I squinted and made out the outline of two low-flying creatures the size and shape of Lo, but with far poorer camo capability.

"On your six," I warned Y'sindra, holstered my push dagger, and pulled both torpedoes. "Shadow shifters, like Lo."

More snow sprayed from both wings with a burst of adrenaline.

The shifters flew close to the hedges and low along the central path. The fine layer of fur I knew they possessed continually morphed, almost blending with their background. It wasn't a perfect match, but it made them difficult to look at directly. I was good, but I couldn't hit what I couldn't see.

Odo's ranks wouldn't see them before it was too late, either.

My stomach fell to my toes, leaving a fluttery, hollow emptiness behind. If I could just see them. My gaze snapped to the snow drifting from Y'sindra's wings. "Go high, throw snow."

"Can't fly high." She dropped to the ground. "I can glide. Throw me."

"What? No!" I backed up, sending a frantic look between Y'sindra and the shifter nearly in dart range to Odo.

"Quokka maneuver. You owe me."

"Low blow."

She jabbed a finger at the moving shadows. "Hurry."

"Fuck." I grabbed her by the waist and lifted her above my head, then hesitated. "Fuck," I said again and threw her.

She arrowed toward the shifters.

It looked like one might have turned around. *No, no, no!* I gagged on air lodged in my throat.

I ran after her.

Y'sindra tucked her wings and arms, slicing through the air.

The shadows slipped enough to see the tiny dart tube.

Faster. Run faster!

Y'sindra was almost on top of the shifters. She thrust her arms toward the ground. A wide blast of winter erupted from her hands. The cone of snow was anemic, but it covered a large enough area to hit the moving shadows.

Icy slush stuck to the small forms, knocking them to the ground and revealing their exact location.

Holy shit, it worked.

I skidded to a stop, fought to steady myself, and then threw a torpedo. Still off-balance, it wasn't a kill shot. The dagger hit the female shadow shifter in the shoulder. She spun and went down. The second torpedo left my hand. With a meaty thunk, it hit the second shifter's skull hard enough to disappear into a gory hole of blood and bone.

With her cloud of curls churning around her face, Y'sindra glided to the ground. She strode directly for the shifter I hadn't killed and put a spear of ice through the female's chest.

I jogged down the path toward my sister, marveling at how far she'd traveled and how fast. Odo and his troops had pushed on, unaware of the poison death they'd almost met.

Y'sindra held my daggers out to me as I came to a stop in front of her. "Nice shots. You eat your Wheaties today?"

"Ha ha," I said dryly. "You got your special stuff from Mom, and so did I."

She snorted. "It'll wear off eventually, and then we'll both be dead weight. Emphasis on the dead. Let's find your man."

"Agreed."

Together we muscled our way down the central path, tag-teaming several shifters and corrupted who either got by Odo or gave up on Duskmere. Thankfully, we encountered no more shadow shifters.

I'd replaced the torpedoes with the sword. Gritting my teeth, I withdrew the blade from a corrupted who'd basically impaled himself. Those defending the courtyard were less than competent. Was it only this afternoon I'd nearly died? Where were those soldiers?

I kept walking, mostly unmolested, Y'sindra at my side. "We're outnumbered, but not by as much as I'd expected."

"I'm seeing the same thing." Y'sindra's reply was slow, cautious. Her phantom wing was long gone, and she wasn't shedding snow. The energy output probably wore her down. "We should have passed two stones on our way here. We only passed one. It was hidden off the path. I got that tracker on it."

"You're a smart, sneaky thing."

"I know." Y'sindra grinned, but quickly sobered. "They're probably moving the other right now."

"But they left Teddy?"

"When I woke up, Mom told me you looked like the walking dead when you got back. I doubt any of the fools here expected you to return." She waved a hand at the thinning show of force in the courtyard. "They certainly wouldn't expect you to bring friends."

"Maybe." I scanned the area. Bodies and body parts littered the grass. A few RFG were on the ground. I disliked seeing that more than I'd imagined, but by far the casualties were the enemy. Odo, Duskmere, and their troops were holding their own. We might get through this after all.

I tilted my head and tried to listen above the clatter of steel and wails of the dying. Fear tickled the back of my neck. "I don't hear Teddy."

"No one to guard him if they are busy staying alive." Y'sindra peeked behind a hedge as we passed.

"Good point." I rotated my wrist, giving my sword a spin. Already, the weapon felt heavier, and the movement kept the joint loose. Even if these shifters and corrupted we were up against were fewer and easier than I expected, I didn't know how much longer I could keep this up.

And where were Dacian and Hielmal? I couldn't shake the feeling the worst was yet to come.

The wind shifted. Above all the chaos of smells, Teddy's scent hit hard. I didn't want to think about how much of his blood needed to be spill for me to recognize the smell of him through this carnage.

Oh gods, we were too late. The sword hilt ground painfully against bone beneath my grip. My arm trembled, knees threatened to give out.

"Malaney!" A voice came to me over the din of battle.

"It's the wood fae," Y'sindra said and pointed.

Odo and his elite had pushed the enemy to the castle. He stood in the middle of the path. Behind him, his elite faced down the thickest contingent of enemy we'd encountered. Nearly translucent green flames licked along the blade Odo pointed at a towering hedge blocking my view of whatever lay behind. "He's here," Odo said.

I didn't have to ask who he meant. Relief flooded me, turning my insides into a bowl of jelly.

Unfortunately, between me and my butter buns was the biggest cluster of fighters who actually looked like they knew what they were doing. Odo and his group were trying to push through, but it was slow going.

A corrupted moon fae wielding a sword worked his way around Odo's ranks and charged toward me. My eyes shifted focus from Odo to the corrupted fae.

Y'sindra took a few steps forward and hurled a small ice spear at the fae. The spear was more of a dagger, not much bigger than my hand. Her magic was puttering out, and the weak, quivering sensation in my muscles said I wasn't far behind.

The ice hit, but bounced harmlessly off his hauberk, leaving nothing worse than a wet spot.

Fine tremors of fatigue shook my arm. This was bad. Unlike the others we'd faced, this guy knew what he was doing. I could use the reach of the sword, but I wouldn't last long enough to use it.

"Get behind me," I told Y'sindra. She did so without arguing, which confirmed her exhaustion.

Never taking my eyes from the approaching fae, I slid the sword into its sheath and pulled both tri-blade daggers. My push daggers would barely scratch that hard-leather hauberk. I wasn't sure the tri-blades would be much better, but if I managed to stab him, I'd make a big fucking hole.

"Watch our backs. I've got this." I spun the daggers so their blades lay along my forearms.

"Don't you dare die," Y'sindra warned.

"Back atcha," I said as Teddy's scent twined around me and was gone again. Impatience raked over my skin.

This guy had no idea the mistake he made. I might be tired, but I was also ready to rip through anyone between me and my sugar snack.

I stopped walking and grinned. Oh, that one was good. I might have found the winner.

"What are you grinning at?" the idiot coming at me asked.

I'd almost blown it. That was how tired I was. I let my guard down. He should have taken advantage of my distraction. I'd take advantage of his.

Adrenaline dumped into me, and I put on a burst of speed.

He held his sword in his right hand. I angled in that direction.

Sword raised, he followed my path, turning farther to the right. He settled onto bent knees, ready to use his longer reach.

He tensed to strike, and I spun left. He'd moved too far to the right to block me, couldn't follow me. With his sword out of my way, I brought my body next to his. My back nearly brushed his chest as I rolled to the left.

Using my momentum, I let the lethal daggers lead my spin.

Both tri-blades punched into the exposed side of his abdomen. We were so close his sharp intake of breath rustled my hair. His abdomen spasmed against my knuckles. Hot, dark blood gushed from the large hole the double daggers had made.

"That turned out better than I'd hoped." I laughed in the guy's face. Rude, but really, he had been trying to kill me.

He dropped. The spiral blades ripped an even bigger hole as he pulled off them, but he didn't make a sound. The guy was in shock, dying, and wouldn't feel a thing.

"That was fast." Y'sindra pushed the guy with a toe.

Shouts rose behind us. We both looked back.

More corrupted and shifters poured through the front gate. We'd been too slow. The soldiers I'd expected to find hadn't arrived or returned. It only mattered where they'd been if we got out of this alive, the chances of which just grew slimmer.

My hearts seized at the sight. "Oh no," I whispered.

"What do we do?" Y'sindra asked. Fear filled my fearless sister's voice.

I met her gaze. "Make sure I get to Teddy. It's our only shot."

She nodded, her curls bobbing. "Okay, but if you set him free, he's likely to kill everyone. You better know what you're doing."

"Don't I always?" She thought freeing Teddy was my end goal. Boy, was she in for a surprise.

"Absolutely not."

"You're right. There." I pointed at the tall hedge Odo had indicated. "Do I need to carry you?"

"No, we're close. I can get to Odo. If we get split up, don't look back."

I sobered at her words.

Steel clanged as Duskmere's force met the newcomers. Shouts and screams raked my nerves.

"Let's do this, Laney."

My gaze locked onto Y'sindra. *Don't look back.* My hearts punched my sternum. I adjusted my grip on the blades and nodded. "Don't get dead."

"You either," she said and sprinted for Odo. My sister could move when she wasn't feeling lazy. Or maybe it was because our lives hung in the balance.

Probably the latter.

I pushed a burst of speed into my leaden legs and quickly caught up.

We neared the hedge. Odo cut down two more of the enemy. It was easy to see why the seasoned wood fae was a general. He was something to behold in a fight, a hot, honed blade cutting through butter.

All of Odo's elite soldiers still stood, still fought. They'd either killed or pushed back the bulk of the defenders. No one blocked our way.

Moving fast, I almost lost my balance as I made a sharp right around the hedge.

A cage lay before me.

Teddy. In a cage. What was with these guys and their gods damned cages?

An inferno of fury exploded inside me, burning away the initial icy shock that almost froze me in place.

"Mother Freya," Y'sindra breathed.

The door stood wide open, but Teddy lay unmoving. Blood painted the floor, his blood. I could smell it.

My vision went fuzzy at the edges, crisp and bright at the center. The gravity of my rage pushed on my fangs.

A shifter and corrupted broke away from Odo's soldiers and ran at us.

One of the fae who'd come to Shadwe with Odo saw them and pursued, but he was too far away to intercept.

The pair didn't come right at us but aimed to put themselves between me and Teddy.

It would mean their deaths.

A small slab of ice coated the ground in front of the pair. They had no time to stop before they hit the slippery surface at full speed and skated into the thorn-laden hedge.

"Go," Y'sindra shouted.

She didn't have to tell me twice. I sprinted past the flailing, screaming pair impaled on the thorns.

A huge, undulating shadow fell over me. It darkened the cage, and I looked up. Fear, fury, and adrenaline pumped into me. Fire licked my hearts. "Fuck!"

A wyvern with pink, orange, and cobalt-blue scales the color of a sunrise dropped from the sky and hovered along the side of the castle. It was Dacian, with that gods-cursed corrupted sun fae, Hielmal, on his back.

Dacian had yet to land when Hielmal threw a writhing black ball of magic at the soldier who'd broken from the fight to help Y'sindra and me. The magic hit him. It ate through his shoulder and sped up to devour every inch of his body. Within seconds, he was ash.

Something rotten carved a place for itself in my middle.

The fae had been a stranger, but he'd been one of Odo's elite. It meant he'd survived the Great Fae War, only to die because I needed help.

The spell was a monster. I knew from my experience with Nyle she would have burned through too much power for another one of those spells. But once was enough. The shock and awe could be enough to slow Odo and his elite.

My gaze flew to Odo. He'd paused. They all had. True warriors, they shook off their shock and finished dispatching the last of the defenders. They'd hold their grief for later.

As I needed to do.

Swallowing down the barb of emotions, I turned my attention to Hielmal. She dropped to the ground and looked in my direction. Our eyes met. I hoped Mae wouldn't hate me, but that female would be the first to die.

Dacian saw me too. He landed close—too close. He turned his bulky body faster than he should have been capable, his tail whipping in my direction.

I knew his game now, and I easily dodged.

Fists tightening on the hilts of my daggers, I looked between him and Teddy.

"Lane! Do what you plan," Odo shouted.

Quickly scanning the area behind Odo, I couldn't see Hielmal, but Y'sindra and Odo's remaining soldiers had closed ranks around Dacian.

My pulse pounded my eardrums. They couldn't win.

"Osmium!" Odo waved his weapon at me. "We've got this."

Hearing Odo, Dacian roared. Now that his scaly hide was threatened, he forgot about me and retreated, showing caution.

Y'sindra pulled the same move she'd used moments ago and threw ice. Just a small patch, but enough. Dacian backed onto its surface and went down, roaring and flailing.

I took off, sprinting along the hedge for the cage tucked along the wall surrounding the grounds.

As I passed, Dacian rolled, trying to regain his footing, but couldn't on the slippery surface. Y'sindra cackled and threw another layer directly beneath the undulating wyvern body, thickening the ice. His tail rose and fell, pounding the earth.

The tail came down directly in front of me. The ground shook. I leaped, holding my breath as I sailed over his tail.

I ran and ran, the battle cries growing distant at my back. No one guarded the cage. I vaulted inside and immediately dropped to my knees.

"Teddy," I whispered and laid my palm on his cheek. He was conscious, but he couldn't move.

Our gazes tangled. Pain rode his red-rimmed eyes. His mouth opened, but only a ragged breath emerged.

I fought the burn pushing against the back of my eyes. This was so not the time for that.

"I'm sorry it took me so long," I said, and plunged my fangs into his throat.

36

THE TIDES CHANGED

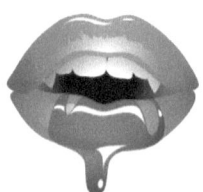

EUPHORIA. BLISS. NIRVANA. THE RIGHTNESS OF THIS *MOMENT* OVERTOOK everything. I tried to hold on to the knowledge Teddy had already lost a lot of blood. I tried to remember we were in a battle for our lives, but those thoughts were thin threads, fraying by the second.

The heart's blood pumped me full of power, but that power high was gone. This was an inferno racing through my body to replace it. Not as powerful, but oh so good. I could feel it soaking into my cells, and it was glorious.

This was mine. He was mine, and bound by blood, I would be his.

One of Teddy's hands slid just enough to touch his fingers to mine, and I snapped the fuck out of it.

Somehow, I maintained a semblance of control. Instead of ripping my fangs loose, I eased away from his throat. Blood immediately welled in the punctures, beading more and more in time with the slow beat of his heart.

"Shit." I cast a quick glance behind to ensure I wasn't about to be run through.

In the distance, the fight raged. Odo, his elite, and my sister were still alive and somehow keeping an enraged Dacian at bay.

Grateful for the distraction, yet terrified by who was doing the distracting, I focused on Teddy. Keeping pressure on the punctures, I scooted even closer until my knees tucked against his ribs. His lids fluttered, and his dark gaze, rimmed with the thinnest line of red, stared unfocused at the cage's metal roof.

My chest squeezed. He was so strong, so powerful, and he'd been brought so low—for me. Because of me. I would not allow it.

Carefully, gently, I brushed matted hair from his brow and cupped his cheek. Teddy ran warm, but the flesh beneath my palm was cool.

An ever-so-slight tilt of his head against my hand was the only acknowledgment he knew I was there. His chest spasmed in a gasp, and those beautiful, dark eyes slid to my face. The red flared briefly. It remained but dimmed, just a whisper of his beast.

"Sweet fangs." The raw words were little more than a breath passing over his cracked lips.

Heat and pressure pushing against my eyes was nearly unbearable. I swallowed and touched my forehead to his. His scent surrounded me, cocooned me. If this were the end, I could happily curl up in this moment and be done.

But it wasn't.

I stole a glance behind us. Y'sindra still fought, but she'd retreated behind Odo and his line. The fight had moved to the side of the castle. Duskmere and his troops were nowhere to be seen, but I could hear them: steel on steel, shouts and screams. We were running out of time.

No one noticed us. Whether it had been intentional or convenience, they did me a favor erecting this cage so far out of the way.

I rested my free hand on Teddy's chest and bent to put my lips to his ear. "Is this what you want?"

His breath stuttered, heart pounding beneath my palm. "What..." He struggled to speak. "Want what?"

Every ounce of love and possession I felt for this male poured out of me in a single word. "Mate."

Teddy went still. His brow creased and chest pumped. His eyes delved deep into mine, as if he didn't quite believe what he'd heard.

My fist turned in his shirt. I leaned close enough for our breath to mingle. "I love you, Teddy Barbout."

The absence of the weight I'd carried from holding those words back was sudden. As if I could float into the sky. It made me giddy.

"I love you," I said again. "You gave me a choice. I will not tie you to me without giving you one, too."

Teddy's tongue darted out to trace the seam of his lips.

"So we doing this?" I asked, half terrified he'd say he changed his mind, half terrified he hadn't.

"About..." His voice was hoarse, strangled. That sexy knob in his throat bobbed. "About damn time."

I snorted a laugh. "You understand what I'm asking, right? You're agreeing to tie yourself to me—*for life*. Have you really thought this through?"

An animalistic growl rumbled Teddy's chest. The red surrounding his irises flared wide and held. His black wolf was so close to the surface.

Entranced, no longer afraid of the beast, I leaned closer.

"Do it." A deep reverberation in his voice sent a delicious chill down my body. My stomach quivered. It had absolutely nothing to do with fear and everything to do with desire.

That wasn't a request, but a command.

I obliged, putting a talon to my wrist, but paused.

This was it. No turning back. I wanted this, but it meant forever. I didn't know how long forever would be for either of us. As far as I knew, we were damn near immortal.

He growled again. A deep, primal part of me responded.

I twisted to look behind us, ensuring one last time we were still safe. We were. I opened my wrist for him and put it to his mouth.

His dry lips sealed against my flesh, tongue hot and rough. But then the blood flowed, coating everything.

My breath hitched at the first pull he took. We were in the middle of a field littered with the dead, yet I became instantly wet. Everything tingled. Damn if what they said about sex and danger wasn't true.

Suddenly, the blood I'd consumed ignited inside me. Electricity raced over and through every molecule. I vibrated, felt my blood in Teddy, filling him, healing him.

He sucked another mouthful from my vein. The silky pressure of coaxing my blood into his mouth undid me. I gasped. My spine arched. Dear gods, it was too much. Each draw of blood was hard, intense, and oh so hot. The pleasure, the pain. I squeezed my legs together, because this was so not the time to turn Teddy into a jungle gym.

He pulled his red-stained lips from my wrist. Our eyes met. "Mine," he said. His guttural voice screamed *fuck me*. I was dangerously close to doing just that. He watched me with hooded eyes, and they didn't waver as he traced his tongue over his lips to rescue errant drops of blood.

Ugh. He knew exactly what he was doing to me.

"Oh, stop," I said, but he continued to *smolder*. A scorching sensation erupted in my cheeks and disconcertingly between my thighs. "Seriously, stop."

"I'm not doing a thing," Teddy said—a blatant lie—and sat up, his movements stiff but strong.

Seeing him up and moving was enough to splash ice water on my libido.

"Are you okay? Have you had enough?" I thrust my wrist at him, my eyes pulling wide at the sight of the pale-pink line. The cut I'd made had sealed. I hadn't dug deep, but deep enough I wouldn't have healed like this since... since before I used my druid power to tear open the veil between Ta'Vale and Outerlands.

"I'm good, sweet fangs." He craned his neck to show me the healed punctures of his throat.

In the distance, the battle raged on. Some of the elite were down, but my sister, Odo, and his remaining troops continued to run interference.

I pulled my arm back and rubbed my fingers over the narrow slit on my wrist. The heart's blood had done a good job of putting me back in the game, but Teddy's fresh blood was the nightcap that put everything to bed. "This feels amazing. I've been an idiot."

"No argument." Teddy stood and stretched.

I scowled, but a sudden surge of panic clawed its way to the surface. "Did it work? I think it worked. I... Your blood felt different. Like I traded in wine coolers for moonshine."

"First mate's blood." Teddy chuckled, that delicious hot chocolate sound for my senses. "Our blood won't always have such a powerful impact, but it will still be stronger than anything else." He held out a hand to help me up.

I didn't need the help but craved his touch. Putting my hand in his, I let him pull me to my feet.

"That power will help us now." Teddy's white teeth flashed. "You picked a good time for the mate bond, even if it was unintentional."

He was right. My muscles felt warm and loose, joints lubricated, movement smooth. For the first time in a long time, nothing pinched, pulled, or stabbed. I raised my arms above my head, curved my spine into a C, and then reversed the stretch, marveling at the lack of pain anywhere in my body.

Not even my sternum.

"Oh, no." I slapped a hand to my chest. Something smooth and hard and definitely not flesh made a hollow thump. I laughed, sounding a little short on my marbles even to myself.

Teddy's brows rose.

A roar rolled over us, and we both turned. The ground didn't shake, but I grabbed a bar of the cage and held on anyhow. My focus flew across the field to the fight, to the original owner of said scale.

Dacian twisted, a spear hanging from between two scales. He lashed out with his tail, sweeping it into the fae who'd landed the hit.

The elite soldier launched into the air. He went up, up and back, into the castle wall. He hit the ground in a tangled heap and didn't get up.

"I have a score to settle. But first..." Teddy pulled me against him. He lifted me so we were face-to-face. I wrapped my legs around his waist. He kissed me with all the violence he planned to bring down on his brother's head.

And I liked it.

I moaned into his mouth and moved my tongue with his. Sucking, tasting, biting.

We parted, breathing hard. Or at least I was. I unlocked my legs and dropped to the ground, amazed I remained upright.

His smile was pure sex. "Later," he promised.

"Better not be much later." I tried for sultry, but was pretty sure on the sexy meter, I landed somewhere around *my appendix is about to burst*. I scowled. "Let's finish this."

Teddy laughed and erupted from the cage at an impossible speed. I'd barely taken a step when he collided with the wyvern. Dacian toppled to his side.

Vicious satisfaction tore into me. I wanted a piece of that fight.

One step out of the cage, and magic hit the bar next to me. I ducked like a dumbass, because no matter what, if it wasn't for the cage's doorframe, I would have been toast. The metal bar blistered and flaked. Or I would have melted.

Beyond the bars, I met Hielmal's bloodshot eyes.

This bitch was going down.

Dacian forgotten, I pulled two push daggers and let loose a banshee scream. I tore out of the cage and pounded across the ground toward her.

Eyes widening, she threw another spell. A lightning-quick spear of magic. It hit like a physical punch against my chest.

My breath whooshed from me. I stumbled backward but didn't go down. The magic had smashed into the fancy new armor embedded in my chest.

Stupid wyvern saved my life twice today.

I shook off the shock of Hielmal's fast spell action and sprang for her. She threw another spell. It missed. A shard hanging around her throat went black and cracked.

Screaming, she pulled a sword from a sheath on her hip.

"That's what I'm talking about." I bared my fangs, eager for the fight.

She pulled another shard tethered around her throat away from her chest and touched it to the blade. Black flame erupted. Tongues of black fire licking the steel.

That was *not* what I was talking about. I put on the brakes and backed away warily, searching for an opening.

Too late, too distracted with the sword, I saw the spell she'd built in her free hand. She thrust her palm toward me.

A fist of cold air punched me. My feet left the ground, and I flew backward.

I hit the hedge. Branches cracked, bent, stabbed. Adrenaline surged through me, insulating me from the impact, from the thorns embedded deep into my flesh. I couldn't move. A bug pinned to a wall.

Warm blood swelled, a fresh wetness beneath my already saturated clothes, my blood, Teddy's blood, leaking out of me. I could feel the wounds trying to heal, but the thorns were too deep.

Hielmal, lips pulled in an ugly smile, took her time creeping closer.

I flailed, tugged against the thorns hooked deep into my flesh, shouted my frustration, whipping my head side to side. A thorn dug into my temple. Blood ran along my eye. I blinked and went still.

I'd smeared Teddy's blood on the staff Blackthorne had given me—aka I took—to part the veil between worlds. I'd smeared it on the broken pillar before passing through the circle. Blackthorne remarked I hadn't needed the staff.

Blood—I'd only needed Teddy's blood, the blood flowing in my veins—from my veins, coating the thorns.

My lids slid shut. I pushed and pulled my breaths, calming my body, my mind, focusing. I sought some elusive place deep inside.

Green and gold and red swirled in my center. I reached into that power and grabbed hold. It was almost too much to touch, to hold on to. My jaw clenched painfully. I trembled and turned my inner focus to the thorns embedded in my flesh.

I didn't understand what I was doing or how, but the thorns sank deeper. They detached from their branches, dissolved inside me, somehow became a part of my body. With nothing left to hold me up, I dropped to the ground in a crouch.

Hielmal stood frozen, a look of disbelief on her face.

I didn't really believe it either, but I wasn't about to waste time figuring it out.

Fists clenched, muscles coiling, I rose and stalked toward Hielmal. Shouts and bloodcurdling screams reached me before I reached her. We both turned toward the sound.

At the end of the hedge wall, more and more RFG backed into my line of sight. Swords flashed, a few tepid spells fizzled, red stained their leathers.

Duskmere and Pru, each going steel to steel with the corrupt, came into view. There were far fewer RFG than we'd arrived with. The magnitude of the loss twisted beneath my sternum.

I looked frantically to Teddy, occupied with his hands full of wyvern. Odo, my sister, and the two soldiers who must have regained their feet wouldn't be enough to stop the oncoming wave of reinforcements.

The enemy on one side, Dacian on the other. They would be crushed.

"No," I whispered.

The crackle of magic hit my ears. I turned in time to see a ball of magic coming for my head.

The magic splatted against an invisible wall and dissolved less than a foot from my face.

My limbs turned to noodles. I laughed a little too loud.

Somehow, the thorns I'd absorbed had formed a sort of shield. I felt the absence of a piece of the barrier after it took that hit of magic, like a tear in my pants I didn't know was there until a breeze nipped cheeks.

Okay, this druid thing was cool.

Hielmal showed visible fatigue. She'd deleted the pile of crystal shards around her throat. No more magic from her.

A renewed call of battle shouts pulled my head around. At least a hundred sun fae poured from the castle, the sun fae who'd shrugged off their loyalty to Eodrom.

I stumbled, dazed, in that direction. Oh, gods. It was too many. With those numbers, it didn't matter if those sun fae were weak. Even Teddy couldn't handle them all, especially not with a wyvern chomping at his throat. Not when he still refused to shift.

Y'sindra! My chest hurt too much to breathe.

"You were so close, hybrid." Hielmal threw the word at me.

"Fuck you," I shouted and sprinted for the fight. I had to help. I had to do something.

Something hit me on the shoulder. I'd been wrong. Apparently not all the crystals were dead. I stumbled and flew forward as the spell took another chunk of the barrier. My forehead bounced on the ground. The impact peeled away most of the rest.

This was it. I pushed to my knees as the undulating wave of golden heads pouring from the castle closed in on the battle.

The corrupted and their cohorts had paused their forward advance to cheer the sun fae closing in on Duskmere and his remaining troops.

Behind me, the crush of grass warned me of Hielmal's approach.

By every forsaken god, I would not return to the stars on my knees. I'd take as many of these assholes with me as I could.

I surged to my feet. My tri-blades slid free from their holsters with a satisfying whisper of steel on leather.

The traitor sun fae bore down on the first line of RFG. My stomach clenched, thighs burning as I burst into motion.

Swords raised, the sun fae met the RFG...and charged past to engage the enemy.

My run slowed to a stunned stop. The tides changed.

"Holy shit," I breathed. My body had that weird, empty, quivering feeling. Too much adrenaline.

More footsteps pounded behind me, fast steps.

"Oh, no, you don't." I rounded on Hielmal. She ran, but not toward me. I flew into motion, trying to intercept her. She headed along the wall, away from me, away from everyone except...

Dacian. He stood on the outskirts of the battle, bloody, but not dead. Engaged with soldiers stupid enough to try their luck, Teddy didn't notice.

Hielmal couldn't be allowed to reach Dacian and escape.

I made a split-second decision, dropped a tri-blade, grabbed a torpedo, and let it fly.

The dagger tumbled end over end toward Hielmal's fleeing back. Time seemed to pause. Every muscle in my body pulled painfully tight. My vision narrowed. The black carbon disappeared against the backdrop of her black coat.

Hielmal's back arched. Her feet lifted off the ground, and she flew forward to land on her face.

Relief tore down a floodgate, and unspent adrenaline coursed through me.

Hielmal struggled to rise.

"Oh, hell no." I snatched the tri-blade I'd dropped and took off on shaky legs. This ended now.

"Lane!" Teddy shouted.

It was all the warning I had before a shadow fell over me.

I tried to stop, but I was going too fast and had to veer right as a wyvern landed between me and my intended target.

"Come on, then." I stalked forward. "Show me your belly so I can scratch it with my daggers."

His tail whipped toward me. I dove beneath, lunged for Hielmal, and plunged the dagger into her back.

Dacian spun, and his tail came at my head. I dropped, rolled, and scrambled on my hands and knees to get out of stomping range. I pushed to my feet and staggered as a gust of wind rocked me back several steps before I could brace myself. I threw an arm in front of my face, shielding my eyes from the grass and debris he'd churned up with his fast launch into the air.

For a moment, Dacian cast a cold shadow across the gruesome courtyard. From behind the crook of my elbow, I watched, helpless to do anything as he pumped his wings and rose higher. Hielmal's limp body flopped in his grip. With an angry roar, he veered right, his bulk growing smaller with distance, until he vanished into the blue horizon.

"No!" I raged, kicking, stomping, screaming. "No, no, no!"

Footsteps pounded the ground.

I turned right into Teddy's arms. He squeezed me against him, but immediately pushed me to arm's length, looking me over. I returned the gesture, drinking in every gore-covered detail.

"When I saw Dacian flying toward you…" Teddy left his fears unsaid.

"I know." I pressed my forehead to his chest.

Odo, Duskmere, and Y'sindra finally caught up. My gaze went to my sister. Blood splatter stained her white hair, painted red freckles on her face, but she wasn't missing a limb—or another wing. She was okay, physically at least.

The two RFG came to a stop behind Y'sindra. Odo had been decorated with several cuts, most still weeping, but he too looked uninjured. Duskmere was otherwise in the same battle-worn state. He had a deep gash in his left leg that forced a limp, but was otherwise upright and whole.

I didn't ask if they were okay. They weren't. So many lives had been lost. I nodded, acknowledging all they'd given. They did the same. I was a warrior, but I did not know war. Odo and Duskmere did. That might force me to look at them a little differently.

"We won," Y'sindra said.

"So we did." My gaze fell over the carnage. We'd won, but was it over?

I shook my head. When did I get so dramatic? Of course it was over. Their numbers were decimated. I got Hielmal. I hoped. More importantly, I got Teddy—*my mate*—back.

The man of the hour brushed his knuckles against my cheek. I smiled up at him and then the others.

"Let's find those stones and go home."

HUGGING AND UGLY CRYING

"ONE LOUSY MONTH OFF PATROL DUTY." Y'SINDRA GRIPPED HER PIÑA colada with both hands and sucked on the crazy straw.

After my visit with Blackthorne, I'd had pineapple on the brain. I gave myself a full day to sleep, but since my sisters and Lo had returned from Eodrom, it had been piña colada o'clock, round the clock. We had cause for celebration today, and I'd used the good rum.

"It's only been a week, and you say the same thing every day." I shoved the straw in my mouth and sucked just enough to avoid brain freeze. That shit hurt. "How about you enjoy three more weeks of patrol freedom?"

"Here, here." Mae toasted the statement with her glass and drank.

"Well, it's dumb." Y'sindra sulked. "It's over. We won. The Iomas told the keepers to look close to home. Eodrom's homegrown cray-cray criminal is dead."

"We don't know for sure." I drummed my talons against my glass.

"Pah-lease. You stabbed her. Twice. Once with your twisty knife. Ding-dong, Hiemal is done."

Flinching, I shot a look toward Mae. She met my gaze, shrugged, and kept sucking on her crazy straw. She really didn't seem to care, but I still worried.

"Won is a stretch. They banished a lot more corrupted than what we faced. Enode has stopped talking. Who knows how many shifters have joined the corrupted?" I drummed my talons on my glass. "And let's not forget Dacian and maybe Hielmal are out there. No body, no proof."

"Fine, live in fear, but I'm gonna listen to the Iomas, same as everyone else. So why are we patrolling?" Y'sindra said, refusing to let it go. Her snit was strong today. "We did what they hired us to do. Thanks to the tracker you put on the sun stone, the RFG knew exactly where to find it. Another stone was recovered. The last one is long gone. No one is bringing that back."

"Because they're paying us, and right now, they're the ones keeping you in berries and funding your slot machine habit." I exaggerated. Things weren't that dire. We had other jobs, but until business picked up enough to support the lifestyle that came with our change of address, we had to take our earnings wherever they came. "It's not like you have anything better to do."

"How would you know?"

"I don't," I answered honestly.

Y'sindra stared at me for a long moment, as if there were more to say. But she didn't. She shrugged and mumbled, "This would be better with berries."

Next to me, Mae shifted and stretched, soaking up the sun. She'd found being directly in the sun eased some of her discomfort of being apart from the stones.

The blanket beneath her embedded with a fortune in sun shards also helped.

After today, I hoped she'd no longer need that thing. Secrets were my Pandora's Box—I couldn't keep them inside. This one was a doozy, and it was *killing me*. I grabbed my cell and checked the time. 1:25 p.m. Ten minutes since I'd checked last. Ugh, what was taking Teddy so long? I glanced at the spiral stairs to the sun garden.

Mae retrieved her glass from the side table between us and sipped. "This tastes different. They're always good, but this batch is a little better."

"Yeah, what'd you do?" Y'sindra asked, her spirits bouncing back faster than a basketball. She tipped her glass and drained the bottom two inches of icy slush. No surprise, snow fairies didn't get brain freeze.

"I used the Bacardi."

"Which one?" Mae asked warily.

I slurped. "The fancy one. Funky Paradise, or whatever."

Y'sindra cackled.

"The Facundo Paraiso?" Mae choked and sputtered. "It's our most expensive bottle."

"Of rum. Most expensive bottle of rum," I corrected, because we had stuff that cost more. A bonus to having a boo with a bar.

"It doesn't matter what it was!" Mae looked like she might faint. "It wasn't for frozen drinks."

Lo padded onto the patio, lacking the usual bounce he had in his step since before his brother had shot him full of poison. Physically, he'd fully recovered. Teddy's blood acted as an antidote, just like he'd said it would. Emotionally, Lo wasn't the same.

It broke my heart a little.

Y'sindra said he grieved for his brother's betrayal. I'd offered to get him in to see Enode using my new RFG jacket, but he'd declined.

I really wanted a reason to flaunt my all-access jacket.

We'd arranged the reclining lounge chairs with their bright-orange cushions in a star shape, facing inward. Mae occupied the chaise to my right. Y'sindra claimed the lounge opposite us, sunglasses perched on her petite nose, taking up half her face. Two loungers had slats strategically removed from the back to allow for wings. Any chair accommodated my sister and Lo. They could both fold their wings against their back, but sometimes, Y'sindra said, it was nice to let them hang loose.

Lo pulled himself into Y'sindra's seat, and my sister scooted a few inches to make room. My heart might be a little broken over Lo's emotional damage, but seeing those two together healed the cracks.

"Ted-D asked me to tell you it is done, and he will be home soon."

"How did he tell you?" I patted down my nearly naked chest, as if I might find a communication crystal tucked in my skimpy bikini top. Swimsuits were handy, but I hadn't kept a crystal there since I scratched the hell out of my nipple. Fortunately, Teddy had kissed it and made it all better. He licked it, too. I flushed at the memory.

"You might be getting too much sun, Lane. Are you using enough sunscreen?" Mae asked.

"Yep, I'm fine." I used the icy sweat from my glass to chill the raging blush on my cheeks.

"Still, you should put on more, just in case." Mae adjusted the wide brim of a sun hat I wouldn't be caught dead in. It looked great on my sister. "Maybe wear the hat I got you."

Never. "Sure, maybe."

I plunked the glass down and spotted my communication crystal on the table next to my cell phone. "Thanks, Lo. You're a peach."

"Oh, did I change colors to match the chair? These pineapple drinks make me a little light-headed."

I laughed. "No, it's a saying. It means you're helpful. It's a compliment."

"Oh. You are also a peach."

Mae's lips closed around her straw to hide a laugh. Y'sindra pulled the corner of the towel over her face. I rolled my eyes.

I glanced at the empty wood platform we'd finally installed where our father's device opened a portal. There were muddy paw prints I'd failed to clean in the dark. Fortunately, my sisters hadn't noticed.

That mouthy grounder wasn't kidding. They dug holes good. I'd gotten them in and out in under four hours. Mae and Y'sindra slept through the entire profanity-laced episode.

The communication crystal buzzed on the table. I jumped.

"What's wrong with you?" Mae's brow furrowed.

"Nothing, I just...fell asleep." I snatched the crystal.

Y'sindra lowered her shades and squinted at me. "With your eyes open?"

I made a face and swiped a finger over the crystal to answer. Mom appeared from the shoulders up. Like me, she held it in her palm.

"Hi, Mom. What's up?" I asked, more than a little surprised to see her. She'd be here in the flesh soon. Worried she might give something away, I added, "Mae, Y'sindra, and Lo are keeping me company, getting our daily dose of sun."

"Our complexion is not made for the sunbathing." She leaned so close to the crystal, I saw her eye. Just one eye. "Do I need to send you more sunscreen?"

"She never wears it!" The peanut gallery, aka Y'sindra, shouted.

"Do too. I smell like a gods damned pickle." The stuff my mom made kept me from turning crispy, but it didn't have the pleasant coconut scent of normal sunscreen. No, it had the briny, nose-puckering sharp scent of a pickle.

"Malaney! Language," my foul-mouthed mom admonished. Seriously, where did she think Y'sindra got it from? "I admit the smell is not the most pleasant, but I made that batch in a hurry. The new batch has a lovely fruity fragrance."

"Did you call to discuss tanning practices?"

"Of course not," she snapped.

I was still number one at trying her patience. Not even Y'sindra could take my title.

"Iola, *who is here*," Mom stressed and angled the crystal to reveal the keeper's impossibly beautiful face, "bid I pass along a message."

"You started it," I mumbled.

She stared hard.

"Sorry, what does Iola need me to know?"

Mom smiled and tucked a strand of blood fae–black hair free of her messy bun behind her ear. "The court ruled the sun fae who helped in the battle may return with no retribution."

"Everyone makes mistakes." I smiled blandly. Armed with makeshift weapons and next to no magic, those sun fae had put their lives on the line to save us. I had empathy for outcasts. Go figure.

"Just so. The sun fae you found may also return."

I sighed. "Her name is Elisette."

Mom wasn't malicious. She probably hadn't been told Elisette's name. Eodrom would never change.

"Elisette, thank you." Mom smiled. "Please let her know she may return."

"Sure thing."

No way in the great hall of cheesy poofs would Elisette want to return, but it would thrill Jason to come home to his sanctuary without the worry of a crack-shot magical sniper coming after the female he intended to marry.

"Okay, see you soon." She waved, and the image blinked off.

Mom had all the subterfuge of a neon sign. My gaze flew to my sisters, who blissfully sipped and sunned. Thank the stars they hadn't read into her comment.

"Lane," Teddy called down from the roof.

"Holy mother Freya!" Y'sindra jumped up on her lounger. "How'd he get up there?"

Mae sat up suddenly. She pressed a hand to her heaving chest. If she wasn't careful, she'd heave herself right out of that bikini top. I thought mine was bad, but dental floss would provide more coverage than hers.

I grinned up at Teddy, who leaned against the railing above us in all his sexy glory, looking like a present I wanted to unwrap in a white tee T-shirt clinging to his broad chest and denim hanging low on his hips. "Ready?"

"Ready." He winked and disappeared back into the garden.

I swung my legs off the lounger and slid my feet into a pair of flip-flops. They made climbing stairs a chore, but it was better than blistering my soles on hot concrete.

Mae's wide, gold gaze flew to me. "What did you do, Lane?"

"Hmm?" I stood and belted on a gauzy beach robe, which covered nothing. Fingers crossed Teddy noticed. "I'm going to see what's happening. You coming?"

When I reached the top of the stairs, hope bubbled in my chest. I'd known what to expect, but seeing it was different.

I ran to Teddy. He wrapped me in his arms, leaning down to bury his face in my pickle-scented hair. Seriously, that stuff was on everything. It was awful.

"Thank you," I said, looking into his smiling eyes.

"You don't have to thank me." He nodded toward the stairs. "Here she comes."

Mae's golden head peeked above the landing, and she froze. Her blue eyes blurred, and then tears poured over her sun-kissed cheeks. She sobbed and covered her mouth, barely getting herself off the stairs and onto the grass before she fell to her knees.

I was about to run to her when Y'sindra popped over the railing. "Hel's horny horns!"

Her flight was wobbly on her one good wing and one made from snow, but she zoomed past me and buzzed a lap around the new sun stone planted in our sky garden, Lo right behind.

At the rate her stump was growing, I wondered how long it would be before she had the real thing.

Her wing finally sputtered out, and she did a second lap on foot. "Is this what I think it is?"

"Depends. If you think it's a giant Twinkie, I'm afraid not." The struggle was real, to maintain a straight face beneath the weight of her glare. "If you think it's a sun stone, you are correct."

"How did you get this here?" she demanded. "We've been on the patio this entire flipping time."

"Long story short, I petitioned to have the stone planted here." I had a theory. Because the seemingly sentient stones were bound to Mae and she was in this realm, and to Iola in Eodrom, the stones halves might heal. It was a long shot, but to my surprise, Iola had agreed.

Getting her and Torneh to temporarily turn a blind eye to Blackthorne's existence had been more difficult.

"They brought it from Outerlands to Treasure Island." I gestured to the cluster of muscled RFG fae. Blackthorne, Jason, and his fiancée were here too, along with Dexter. They'd all helped. "I sent Teddy through the portal this morning to help bring home the stone."

Mae was on me in an instant, hugging and ugly-crying into my hair, pickle scented and now snot crusted. I definitely needed a shower before Teddy and I left for our vacation.

"The stone sings. It's a whisper, but she's coming to life." Mae pulled back. She took a deep breath and walked to the stone twice her size pointing toward the sky and placed a hand on the amber surface. The flare beneath her hand was faint. "Thank you."

I wasn't sure if she was speaking to me or the stone, so I didn't say a thing.

"That's a mighty big hole," Y'sindra said, leaning against my hip.

"Yep. The grounders have free rent for six months."

Y'sindra laughed so hard, snow shook from her wings.

I rolled my eyes. "Happy to be a source of amusement for you."

Mae's palm slid from the stone, and she turned to me with a smile to outshine the sun.

"One last thing." I bit my lip. "Sun fae will be traveling through the portal for a while."

"Hold the hush puppies," Y'sindra exclaimed. She did hate those bready balls. "You, Lane Callaghan, are letting sun fae traipse through our place?"

"Technically, my place." Blackthorne waved a hand.

"You left. Finders keepers," Y'sindra shouted back. She looked at me and hooked a thumb toward the old druid. "That guy, am I right?"

"Anyhow." I dragged the word. "Part of my agreement with the keepers is to allow any sun fae uncomfortable returning to Ta'Vale to remain here."

Mae blinked. "Here?"

Y'sindra's jaw dropped. She clacked it shut. "This place is big, but not that big. I saw how many fae we're talking about."

"They'll be staying on my ranch." Jason Olson, hands linked with Elisette, approached us. "I have the property, and I could use the extra help. Eli will be grateful for the company."

"It will be nice to have more sun fae around." Mae squeezed Elisette's free hand and then turned to meet the fae who helped escort the stone.

"We'll be on our way now. But we're still on for a chili lunch next weekend?" Jason asked.

"You kidding? Lane would never say no to food," Y'sindra said. She and Lo fell in step with Jason and Elisette, escorting them from the garden and to the penthouse below. "Girl, did Jason here tell you about your ring?"

I took his hand and led him to the druid stones.

Blackthorne veered away from the group and approached. "I had the section of the beach around the hotel closed. It's yours for the week. Enjoy your stay."

"You can do that? Thank you." It felt weird saying those words to this guy. Sort of like when I tried to put melted cheese on cheesy poofs.

"You're welcome, granddaughter. I don't need to rack up citations before I even open the doors." Still wearing his flip-flops, cutoff denim shorts, and a different Hawaiian shirt, Blackthorne hurried to catch up to Jason.

Of course, he hadn't done it out of the goodness of his heart, but who cared? We scored a private beach.

"Ready?" I took both of Teddy's hands in mine and walked backward into the stone circle.

"I've been ready."

To eat me alive, if that look he gave me was any indication. I couldn't wait to let him.

"I've got blood to drink and a beach to christen. Let's go—"

***

Thank you for reading! Did you enjoy? Please add your review because nothing helps an author more and encourages readers to take a chance on a book than a review.

And don't miss book three in the *Blood Fae Druid* series, BAD GIRLS BREAK BRIDGES, available now. Turn the page for a sneak peek!

Also be sure to sign up for the City Owl Press newsletter to receive notice of all book releases!

SNEAK PEEK OF BAD GIRLS BREAK BRIDGES

Music pulsed from a multitude of speakers hidden around the amphitheater. It slipped through my body, pulling excitement to the surface and teasing all my tingly girly parts.

It had the same effect on my sisters. Eyes bright, Mae looked at me over her shoulder as she skipped down the front row. "This is such a great idea. I'm surprised you thought of it."

"Thanks," I said in a flat voice.

Her eyes rounded, and her glossed lips formed a horrified O. "I didn't mean it like that, Laney!"

Y'sindra snorted. "I mean it. This isn't exactly your style. The only half naked man you ogle is your boy toy."

I shot a glare at Y'sindra bouncing along behind me. Diminutive my sister might be, but her opinions were not. "First, you could show a little respect and stop referring to Teddy as a boy toy." Though he totally was. I climbed that prime piece of man meat like a jungle gym on the regular. "Second, I can appreciate a good-looking male—or female." I winked at Mae. "This is a mixed revue, ya know?"

Blue eyes shining like polished sapphires, she turned in a circle, taking in the large space. "Where are the girls? I thought you invited them?"

"I did. Zee messaged this morning to say she, Eli, and Pru are driving here together." I dropped onto my seat, sinking into the plump memory form cushion. I didn't do well with crowds, and the closer we got to the big night out I'd purchased tickets for on a crazy whim, the more I had come to regret my decision. "Tickets are at will call. There's still plenty of time before the show."

"All together?" Mae stopped turning long enough to ask. "Dangerous. Who's driving?"

She wasn't wrong about the danger. Elisette was a sun fae who'd recently run away—I'd call it escaped—from Eodrom. The snooty seat of sun fae power in Ta'Vale. Pru still lived in Ta'Vale, and I doubted she'd ever even been in a car. Zee was just a terrible driver.

"Jason is dropping all three of them off here. They'll take resort cars back." Eli's fiancé was a gem. He'd get them here and home safely. In Pru's case, she'd use one of our father's portals to get home. I bounced in my seat. The thing was cushy and comfortable. It had to be expensive.

"Probably a good idea," Mae said. "I'm glad Eli stayed. She's been a big help to me in the garden, and Jason is a gem."

"I'm blown away you invited the blood fae." Y'sindra climbed onto the chair and stood on her cushion to watch the doors at the rear of the large, rapidly-filling space. "It was a good idea. She's cool."

I grunted. It hadn't been my idea. After my attempt to infuriate Prunettia with an obnoxious level of kindness went awry, Teddy low-key pressured me into getting to know the female I'd accidentally befriended. She might be a member of the Royal Fae Guard, he'd argued, but she was also the only blood fae aside from my mother I'd ever met.

I'd agreed, mostly because I hadn't expected her to accept. But she had.

"I'm glad Zee's coming. She seems stressed lately." Mae finally stopped staring and took her seat. "Do you think it's about *Blood and Wine?*"

When my ancient great many times over grandfather and the namesake of the resort and casino the Blackthorne, suggested Teddy open a high-end bar in the establishment we—my sisters, Teddy, and Lo—had taken up residence in, I'd wanted to refuse. Then I woke the fuck up and realized my man would be working a mere elevator ride away.

"No, at least I don't think so. I noticed she was a bit wound up too and thought maybe she was worried about the move. But Teddy said she was the first member of his staff who signed on."

I rubbed my bare, goosebump-covered arm as I glanced at the crowd flowing into the theater. It was cold as the undead in this place, which seemed at odds with the lack of clothes the performers would be wearing. Shrinkage and all.

"Are they really only serving blood and wine? They better carry berries." Y'sindra spun and dropped into her seat. Alcohol alone could not compete with a snow fairy's metabolism. Berries combined with alcohol delivered inebriation.

"Or you can just bring berries down from the penthouse," I said and touched my tingling lips. "Are my lips blue?"

I'd been a sucker and let Mae dress me. I had on so few clothes, there was a strong probability of frostbite in my near future if this place didn't warm up fast.

"Pretty powder blue. They match your fancy breastplate." Y'sindra chortled and tapped the wyvern scale embedded in my chest, on full display thanks to the scandalously low-cut tank top.

"Still, I'm confused as to why Dexter is taking over The bar in Interlands instead of Zee. She's the senior bartender." Mae didn't want to let the topic go. We'd been friends with Zee for years, and Mae was protective. It was cute.

"She'll be here soon. You can ask her." I shrugged. Teddy's choice had surprised me too. Dexter, the only moon fae without the corruption who lived outside of Ta'Vale was the next logical choice to run the bar in Teddy's absence.

"There's the blood fae." Y'sindra waved her hands wildly to catch Prunettia's attention.

Pru and I were similar, yet worlds apart. Teddy might believe it was a good idea for me to get to know another blood fae, but I wasn't so sure how much blood fae was left in me.

"Wow," Mae breathed the word. "I've never seen her out of uniform. She's stunning."

I looked again. Though only five-feet-tall like me, she seemed to tower above those she passed in the aisle. The female exuded confidence and power. She wore black, mesh leggings paired with a long-sleeved, silvery tunic. The slinky material was baggy on her lean torso but bundled tight across her hips. As opposed to my deeply auburn hair twisted into a tight braid and laying heavy along my spine, her silky, onyx tresses flowed and fluttered like a curtain down her back. Her only nod to makeup was her deep red painted lips. With high cheekbones set in an oval face, she didn't need anything else.

Resentment for her blood fae perfection bubbled up inside me but popped and faded just as quickly. Not so long ago it would have gnawed and festered my insides, but now I understood my hybrid nature didn't make me less than blood fae. It made me more.

"She is," I agreed at last, and meant it.

Pru reached the front row and gave us a shy wave. With her other arm, she held a flat, rectangular box against her side.

"What's she carrying?" Y'sindra asked.

I didn't answer because I didn't know.

"Oh good, there's Zee and Eli." Mae waved at the other two females coming toward us. A petite, but powerfully built woman with a broad smile and curly, blonde hair led the way. A tall, willowy, golden-haired sun fae with an equally bright smile followed behind her.

"Zee must have shifted recently," I said. "She had pink hair when I saw her the other day." Werewolves returned to their "natural state" with each shift.

The short, loose slip of shiny, multi-hued fabric came to a stop well above Eli's knees. It looked remarkably familiar. I poked Mae in the shoulder. "You loaning out your closet?"

Mae beamed. "Doesn't she look amazing?"

It was a rhetorical question. Anyone with eyeballs would see the stunning sun fae hurrying toward us, oblivious of the stares following her.

Y'sindra hopped off her seat and fluttered around me, toward the aisle Zee and Elisette made their way down. Though not yet strong enough for extended flight, her wing had grown to almost full extension in only the last few months. Mom's medicine and salves might be stinky, but with them she could turn impossibility into reality.

Pru shimmied past my sisters to the seat Y'sindra had vacated next to me. She looked at me as if asking permission.

"Go ahead," I told her and gestured to my other side. "We have those four seats."

"Thank you." She looked toward the stage and then around the large space.

This was the first show I'd attended inside the Blackthorne, and the theater was impressive. If this was Pru's introduction to the world outside of Ta'Vale, I had to show her the elevators before she left. I knew a certain dungeon in Eodrom that could really use one. Electricity might not work there, but I was convinced someone could magic up a solution.

"Oh, I brought this for you." She held the box she carried.

My brows climbed in question, and I carefully accepted the box. As if it were a snake. Pru had given me no reason to mistrust her, but she had a multitude of reasons to hate me at best, stab me at worst.

I'd raided her closet. Took and then ruined some sweet, red leathers—which I deeply regretted. Borrowed several weapons still residing in my collection, where they would remain. I also broke into her home and stole her official Royal Fae Guard jacket.

Her shy smile slipped into a full-fledged grin which showed off her fangs. She chuckled, a unexpectedly sweet sound. "It's not a trick, I promise. I wanted to show my appreciation for the invite." She nodded toward the box. "Go ahead, open it."

I hesitated, pulling the corner of my lip beneath a fang and then ran a talon along the seam of the box, slicing through the tape. The lid opened to a neatly folded, red leather jacket. I gasped. "For me?"

She shrugged and ducked her head in an adorably bashful manner. "We're the same size, so I put in an order for a second set with my tailor. You can't get the same quality Earthside."

I traced my fingers over the butter-soft lapels. My chest grew tight. "Why would you do this?" Suspicion and hope wrestled inside of me. Hope for what, I wasn't sure. A friend? I had my sisters. I had Teddy. I hated people, I hated fae, especially sun fae...didn't I?

Or had I only believed they hated me? Elisette had only ever been kind, and I liked her.

"It's cold as the Driftas in here. The jacket might come in handy." Pru fanned her hands on her arms, the silver material of her sleeves catching and reflecting illumination from the bright lights from far above.

"It's freezing." I laughed and met her pitch-black eyes. Blood fae eyes. The obvious distinction to my one black, one violet iris didn't hit as hard as it used to. "Thank you."

I peeled the jacket from the box, revealing the folded pants beneath. "You didn't!"

She shrugged. "What's a jacket without matching pants? Don't worry, I used the Royal Fae Guard bank account. Call it payment for all the work you've done. Odo agrees Duskmere hasn't done enough to thank you."

"You got that right." I snorted and slipped into the jacket. It fit as if tailor-made for me, and well, it was. "Send Odo my thanks."

While Duskmere was the Royal Fae Guard captain, I'd recently learned gruff, scarred, Odollom was the RFG general. There was a time I'd have preferred to punch the guy than say hello, but now he was my best drinking buddy. Another fae I liked. What was wrong with me?

"Oh, snazzy." Y'sindra fluttered by my side, caressing the sleeve of my new jacket.

"Pru brought it for me. Isn't that nice?" I gave Y'sindra a crazy-eyed "help me" look, because all this *nice* felt really uncomfortable and confusing.

"Sure is. What were you thinking, girl?" she asked Pru, settling onto my seat cushion. "Have you seen what my sister does to her clothes? Holes. I'm not sure she owns anything without one."

I rolled my eyes, squeezed past Mae, beamed at Elisette, and gave Zee a quick hug. I wasn't a hugger, but Zee was, and I'd long ago learned you don't refuse a werewolf. At least not one you liked.

"Glad you made it." I waved the box at the group. "I'm going to have this delivered to the penthouse. I'll forget it if I don't."

I'd be damned if I lost another pair of those sweet red leathers. They made my ass look great.

Mae's gaze traveled from the box to my sleek new jacket to Pru. "Good idea," she agreed.

I made my way up the aisle, weaving through the crush of bodies still flowing into the theater. The lights flickered before I reached the doors, signaling the show was about to start.

By the time I located someone to run the box to the front desk and have it delivered to the penthouse, the lobby had cleared out. The doors were closed, and an amplified voice replaced the music.

Crap, the show started. I'd be the idiot running solo through the aisle. Holding my breath, I cracked the door and slipped inside. A gush of cold air and hormone-heated anticipation hit me in the face.

The lights were down. No one noticed my entrance. All eyes were focused on the bare-chested, dark-skinned man in a long black cape dancing around a woman seated on a throne center stage. She'd been fitted with what looked like the skimpiest wedding gown I'd ever seen. Poor girl had to be freezing.

The valet inside the door put a hand on my arm. "The Dark Prince is almost done. You can go during the transition," she whispered.

My brows shot up at the name, but I nodded and backed against the wall to wait.

"I will make you my dark queen." The man's voice boomed from the stage with a British accent even I could tell was fake. He slunk behind the woman, trailing his hands over her shoulders. His fingers grazed dangerously close to her breasts, and she thrust her barely constrained chest forward, as if straining for his touch.

"She knows there's people watching, right?" I mumbled and looked above the stage at the large screen showing up-close action. How mortifying!

He stopped in front of the lust-drunk woman and faced her. The cape draped from his broad shoulders facing the audience. His long braids were bound in a queue at his nape and trailed over the cape, down his back.

"It is time," he said, and then gave something hidden from the audience a violent tug.

The woman saw it. Her eyes bulged, and she licked her lips.

With a dramatic twirl, the man spun to the side. The cape flared across his torso and then revealed not just his broad, bare chest, but also thick, muscled legs.

Women screamed, as did several men. I sure hoped this place employed bouncers as well as valets, because this crowd was going to rush the stage any minute.

A true showman, the Dark Prince tossed his pants to the side. His black thong didn't hide a thing. My gaze shot to the big screen for an up-close and very personal view. I couldn't blink. My eyeballs burned. My hearts pounded. Heat raced beneath my skin. No wonder they kept it so cold in here.

Dear gods, what was happening to me? I needed to find Teddy, right now.

"I must prepare you." The Dark Prince's molten voice melted over the audience.

"Prepare me!" someone shouted. Someone from the front row, who sounded a lot like Mae.

The moment the man straddled the woman's lap, my laugh turned to sawdust in my throat. He flipped his cape to the side, revealing rock-hard butt cheeks to the crowd. The tight indents flexed and worked as he ground himself against her.

"Holy stars." I swallowed and pressed a hand to my thundering hearts.

Noting my flustered state, the valet whispered, "And I get to watch this for free every night."

"Are you ready?" The man on the stage asked.

"Yes!" The woman's shout melded with the audience's chorus of agreement.

I snorted, but who was I kidding? With his smooth, obsidian skin, all those muscles, and the not insignificant package inside his thong, I'd be tempted if I didn't already have perfection in Teddy.

All sinew and coiled power, the man spun once again with unnatural grace, stopping behind the woman.

Anticipation swelled. The enormous space, alive and buzzing with palpable energy, suddenly felt cramped.

"Wait for it," the valet whispered.

I looked from her to the stage.

"You are mine." The man's deep voice rumbled his claim. He threw his head back and when his pitch-dark gaze returned to the audience, fangs showed. Even from this distance, I didn't need the screen. I could see them.

Holy hot cakes, he was a vampire! I knew what made this revue special were the paranormal entertainers. But holy hot Cheetos!

Incoherent shouts and voices rose. The amphitheater pulsed with desire.

He was going to bite her. Right there.

"No..." I breathed.

"Oh, yes," the valet answered.

I shot her a stunned look.

She winked. "Wait until you see the next act."

On the stage, the Dark Prince sank low behind the woman. His hands came around to cover her ribs, fingers grazing beneath her breasts. He bent forward until his mouth hovered over her pulse.

This was an extremely intimate act I performed with Teddy. I didn't want to watch, but I couldn't look away. No wonder this show raked in so much cash. It also explained the revue's name: *Taboo*.

The spotlight trained on centerstage revealed every movement, every detail.

With his vamped out, ebony eyes on the audience, the vampire licked the woman's neck, numbing it. She writhed. Her legs fell open beneath the full skirt of the wedding dress. For her sake, I hoped her friends weren't recording this.

Slow and deliberate, like foreplay designed to tease, the Dark Prince slid his fangs into the woman's exposed throat. She jerked and then virtually melted beneath his hold. He drank, slow, shallow pulls. When he withdrew his fangs, he didn't immediately lick her throat. Instead letting a few beads of crimson escape the punctures to trace erotic evidence of the act on her creamy flesh.

At last, he ran his tongue over the punctures, using the natural numbing and healing components in his saliva to seal the wounds. "My queen," he declared, and drew the woman up from the seat.

"Isn't he a prince?" I muttered as the shaky-legged woman was led off the stage, followed by the nearly naked, but satiated and clearly aroused vampire. He certainly didn't suffer from the cold theater.

Bright lights burst to life and bathed the audience, replacing the moody reds and golds. Thunderous applause and screams bombarded the stage.

"I don't think anyone here cares about the storyline." The valet laughed and gestured down the aisle. "They're between sets. You can go now."

I hustled toward the front row, hoping to escape unwanted attention. If I wound up on the stage with a vampire at my throat, it would not end well. I'd bite back.

A woman in a slinky, diaphanous gold dress sauntered from behind the curtains. She praised the Dark Prince and his new queen while all around her things were wheeled off stage and replaced with new set pieces.

When I reached the first row, I made myself as small as I could manage and hurried to my seat.

"Took you long enough," Y'sindra hissed as I passed.

"You missed a good one," Mae said.

"I saw it." I made a vague gesture toward the back of the theater. "They made me wait until the performance was over."

"This was a great idea." Her eyes crinkled with her smile.

"Glad you're having fun."

Pru began to rise from her seat next to Mae, but I waved her back and began to shimmy past. "Stay, I'll take the other seat."

"It looks like we have our sacrifice for the Beast." The woman said from the stage.

Suddenly, a net of floodlights captured me. They came at me from every angle, blinding me.

Oh no. *No, no, no!*

Despite not being able to see a thing, I recognized Y'sindra's cackle. Mae squealed and grabbed my hand, tugging me away from my seat.

A hulking form eclipsed the floodlight coming from the stage. I blinked right, left, and then to the hooded man coming at me.

"I'll pass, thanks." I backed up until my legs bumped the seat.

"No, you don't." Mae grabbed my arms again and propelled me toward the man.

Dumbstruck, I went rigid when he swept me up and over his shoulder. Thank the gods I'd won the skirt versus leggings argument with Mae. I pushed up from his back and glared down at her as he mounted the stairs to the stage.

"You're dead," I mouthed.

Mae blew me a kiss while Y'sindra gave me two thumbs up.

Elisette and Pru appeared dumbstruck, while Zee put two fingers in her mouth and let loose an earsplitting catcall I had no problem hearing over the roar of the excited, hormonal crowd.

The man crossed the stage and climbed more steps. I twisted for a glimpse around his thick, muscled torso, but couldn't see a thing. Where was he going?

At last, he set me on what turned out to be a raised platform and spun me to face the audience.

"What? I don't get a throne?" I joked and looked toward the audience, hidden now by the lights of the stage. "Seriously, though. What do you expect me to do?"

Still saying nothing, the hooded man moved behind me. He took something from a pole mounted on the side of the small platform. It elicited a rattling sound and clanked. He reached for my arm.

Sluggishly, I caught on to what he was doing and backed away. "Nope. No thank you. I unvolunteer."

I didn't make it more than a step. His ironclad grip reminded me all the performers, not just the ones who shed their clothes, were some sort of paranormal. I could probably break his hold, but I wasn't certain. Despite regular nips of Teddy's blood, my blood fae abilities didn't hit the way they used to. Only my family knew, and I wasn't willing to out myself to escape five minutes of embarrassment.

"Come on, lady. You paid to be here." The anonymous man finally spoke, pulling harder.

Yep, he'd definitely win if I put up a fight.

"Fine." I closed my eyes, prepared for the mortification, and let my arm go loose. "Let's get this over with."

"Time to get some panties wet and get paid." His gruff voice was muffled by the hood.

"Helluva motto."

He grunted, slapped the shackle around my left wrist, and then moved around to my right. "Don't worry, you'll enjoy it. They all go wild for Beast."

For the audience's sake, he made a show of tugging on the chains. I rolled my eyes. Whistling beneath the hood, he hopped off the platform and positioned himself to the side of the stage, arms crossed over his barrel chest.

The lights in the theater cut out. Everything went dark. A collective gasp left the audience, followed by excited murmurs. Anticipation rose, palpable, like the zing of electricity.

With a pop, the floodlights came on again, all of them aimed at me. I blinked, my eyes watering against the wash of bright white light.

A deep primal drum beat swelled. My blood spurt through my veins in time with the rhythm. Whoever created this soundtrack knew what they were doing. Could I get a copy for my personal collection? The things I could do to Teddy with this music...

A tall, shadowy figure moved across the stage. It was barely a smudge in my blurry vision—a hulking smudge. Whatever, or whoever it was, had the audience shrieking.

I swear, if a vampire tries to bite me, I'm biting them first.

A howl rippled through the air. The fine hairs on my neck rose. My muscles clenched, and I froze.

Beast was not a vampire.

Don't stop now. Keep reading with your copy of BAD GIRLS BREAK BRIDGES.

And sign up to S.L. Choi's newsletter for news, giveaways, and a FREE novella set in the *Blood Fae Druid* world!

Don't miss more of *Blood Fae Druid* series with book three, BAD GIRLS BREAK BRIDGES, available now.

And follow along with real time writing updates, excerpts, and ARC opportunities, in S.L. Choi's Facebook reader group.

Some bridges are meant to be broken.

Lane Callaghan finally has something to celebrate. Not only did she land a mate who looks stellar in denim, she fulfilled her contract with the sun fae and locked a deadly, dark prince behind bars in the process. To toast her freedom from the realm of Eodrom, Lane, her sisters, and their best gal pals head out for a night on the town.

As expected, the music is loud, the drinks flow, and the snack bowls are bottomless. What they don't expect was the moonbit werewolf stripper who turns the party into a bloodbath, but maybe they should have. While Lane and her sisters have been focused on fae drama, human paranormals, werewolves in particular, have been succumbing to a rare infection, and their good friend Zee fears she's next.

At last, Lane has a case closer to home. Or so she thinks, until Fate arrives to dispense a dire warning that the subterfuge in the fae realm of Ta'Vale isn't over, and it's closer to Lane than she thinks. In fact, it might have everything to do with the reason she ran from home all those years ago.

Escape Your World. Get Lost in Ours! City Owl Press at www.cityowlpress.com.

ACKNOWLEDGMENTS

Had I heard the second book was the hardest to write? A time or two. Was I warned? Yep. Did I believe it. Of course not! Let me tell you, I was not prepared for the mental hurdles and hoops I would have to navigate to dump this story out of my head and onto paper. Without those mentioned here and countless more unnamed supporters that did not go unseen, it would not have happened. "Thank you" is a woefully inadequate expression of my gratitude.

First and always, thank you to my husband, Bryan, whose stubborn belief I can achieve my dreams helps (forces) me to never stop reaching.

To my agent, Julie Gwinn, for keeping me sane and grounded, and standing strong in my corner.

To the City Owl Press team. Tina and Yelena for steering the ship. Heather, for seeing something in my crazy book and bringing it to life. Michele, for dealing with my runaway commas (and so much more).

To the miblart for delivering an amazing cover and making my girl Lane look so cool.

To my fellow Owls for...everything. The owl's nest is the safest space to be.

To my Quokkas who throw support not babies.

Gabrielle Ash, my critique partner, friend, and staunch supporter. Everyone should know how fortunate I am to lay eyes on this woman's pages before the rest of the world.

Charissa, for being there for all my questions when I first reached out and not hitting "block" when I flood your texts and DMs.

Dawn, for supporting my book and truly making one of my author dreams a reality.

Lauri and Kelly, for weathering my moods and always there when I blow up your texts.

The Bad Girls Club. Each and every one of you rock!

Jennifer Estep, for supporting a little newbie author during my debut and your continued kindness.

Kim Harrison and Faith Hunter, for proving the old adage "*Never meet your hero*" wrong.

Finally, to you, reader, for taking a chance on my books.

ABOUT THE AUTHOR

S.L. CHOI is an urban fantasy author with a deep love for humor, fast-paced action, and hit-you-in-the-heart feels . She grew up imagining goblins living in the rocks outside her bedroom window, while fairies flew through the flowers. When not writing, she is either photographing the beautiful New England area, tending to her small furry overlords, or gaming with her equally nerdy husband. To be the first to see news, ARC opportunities, and excerpts from the BLOOD FAE DRUID SERIES, join S.L.' s newsletter or join her on Facebook. Follow S.L. Choi's reader group for the latest news and updates www.facebook.com/groups/slchoisreadersgroup

www.slchoi.com

instagram.com/SLChoi_author

x.com/@SL_Choi

tiktok.com/@slchoi_author

bookbub.com/authors/s-l-choi

ABOUT THE PUBLISHER

City Owl Press is a cutting edge indie publishing company, bringing the world of romance and speculative fiction to discerning readers.

Escape Your World. Get Lost in Ours!

www.cityowlpress.com

facebook.com/CityOwlPress

x.com/cityowlpress

instagram.com/cityowlbooks

pinterest.com/cityowlpress

tiktok.com/@cityowlpress

www.ingramcontent.com/pod-product-compliance
Lightning Source LLC
Chambersburg PA
CBHW032235010726

47494CB00002B/505